Con

Also by Anna Dillon

Consequences

ANNA DILLON

POOLBEG

Published 2006
by Poolbeg Press Ltd
123 Grange Hill, Baldoyle
Dublin 13, Ireland
E-mail: poolbeg@poolbeg.com

© Anna Dillon 2005

The moral right of the author has been asserted.

Typesetting, layout, design © Poolbeg Press Ltd.

1 3 5 7 9 10 8 6 4 2

A catalogue record for this book is available from the British Library.

ISBN 1-84223-231-2
ISBN 978-184223-231-6 (From January 2007)

Typeset by Patricia Hope in Bembo 11/14.5

Printed by Litografia Rosés, Spain

www.poolbeg.com

About the Author

Born and raised in Dublin, Anna Dillon is also the author of the Seasons' Trilogy (*Seasons, Another Season* and *Seasons' End*), *Lies* and the bestselling *The Affair*.

Acknowledgements

Once again I am indebted to everyone in Poolbeg for their remarkable patience and forbearance, especially Paula, Kieran, Gaye and Claire.

And once again, I need to acknowledge the advice of those people – the shy CS, the retiring JC (and MC) and the modest GW – whom I turned to with questions or for advice. I sometimes listened to their answers and occasionally took their advice.

*To Leo Michael, who appeared more or less
as the book appeared, so it seems only appropriate
that it should be his.*

BOOK 1

The Mistress's Story

When did I decide to give him up?

In that instant when I realised that his wife still loved him, and he still loved her?

Or was it earlier, in that single moment when I saw how I would be remembered: as the woman who destroyed a marriage and lured a man away from his wife and children?

Or was it the moment before: when I suddenly glimpsed my future as Robert's wife-lover-mistress-housekeeper . . . and didn't like what I saw?

Yes . . . that was the moment.

But I still loved him.

God help me, but I still loved him. And I didn't think that would ever change.

CHAPTER 1

Tuesday, 24th December

CHRISTMAS EVE

Stephanie Burroughs turned at the Departure Gate, pulled Sally Wilson close and held her tightly. "Thank you," she whispered, her breath warm against her friend's ear. "I don't know what I would have done without you."

Sally hugged Stephanie. "You don't have to go," she said quickly, blinking away sudden tears. "You could stay with me and Dave over the holidays. You wouldn't have to be alone."

Stephanie pushed herself away from the smaller woman and shook her head. "What! And ruin *your* Christmas too? No, I've got to go. Besides, I thought that boyfriend of yours was going to propose to you at midnight tonight?"

"Ssssh!" Sally pressed her fingers to Stephanie's lips and glanced over her shoulder to where Dave, looking miserable and irritated, stood in the bookshop leafing through a magazine. He glanced up, spotted the two women looking at him and smiled his gap-toothed grin before he returned to the magazine. But not before he had sneaked an obvious glance at his watch. "He doesn't think I know about tonight," Sally added, "though he's done everything except take out an ad in the newspaper."

"But a Christmas Eve proposal is very romantic," Stephanie reminded her.

"Stay with us," Sally begged. "Please! I just hate the thought of you leaving."

"I'll be fine," Stephanie protested. "Thank you for the offer. But no, I have to go. You know that. I want to go. I don't want to spend another Christmas alone. I swore after last year that I'd never go through that again."

"When will you be back?" Sally watched Stephanie gather up her outsized vanity case and place it on the small-wheeled Samsonite carry-on.

"I don't know. I could only get a one-way ticket into New York. I'm not sure when I'll be back. Certainly sometime before the New Year, but I'll phone you." She kissed her friend quickly on the cheek, then joined the looping line that led to the Departure Gates.

Sally moved down the line to stand outside the airport bookshop and waved again as Stephanie showed her boarding pass and passport to the uniformed guard at the entrance. Stephanie paused briefly to wave, then she turned and became a vague shape behind the glass panels. Feeling a vague sense of loss, Sally turned to join her boyfriend, linked her arm through his and manoeuvred them though the milling Christmas Eve crowd in Dublin airport towards the exit.

"It'll take us hours to get home," Dave grumbled. "She could have taken a taxi."

Although Sally was dwarfed by Dave's size and bulk, she wasn't intimidated by him. Digging her nails painfully into his arm, she snapped, "No, she couldn't. She's my friend and she's just had a very traumatic experience. I cannot imagine what it was like when she opened the door and found Robert's wife standing there!"

"Well, if your friend hadn't been playing around with the wife's husband, she wouldn't have found herself in that situation," Dave suggested, and then tensed for a blow which, surprisingly, did not come. Glancing sidelong at Sally, he guessed that she might actually agree with him. And that, he reckoned, was a first.

This was not how she'd planned to spend her Christmas Eve.

Stephanie Burroughs collected her vanity case and bag from the security belt, dropped the suitcase to the ground and pulled up the handle. Then, tugging it behind her, she turned to the right and headed down towards Duty Free.

She'd been hoping to spend Christmas Eve in the company – and the arms – of her lover. About this time, they should be sitting in front of a crackling coal fire, sharing a very nice bottle of red between them, the house smelling of pine-scented candles, with Christmas carols sounding low and muted on the stereo. When they'd had a glass or two, they would make love and then open their Christmas presents and maybe make love again.

She had started to build the fantasy a couple of weeks ago. She'd even bought the bottle of red – a disgracefully expensive twenty-five-euro Cabernet Sauvignon – and spent ages choosing the right CD and scented candles to help create the mood. But even as she'd been putting the various elements of her perfect Christmas Eve in place, she knew – deep in her heart and soul – that it would never be.

Her lover would never be able to get away from his wife and children on Christmas Eve. He would want to spend the evening with his family. But she'd accepted that, secure in the knowledge that Robert Walker, her lover of eighteen months, had finally agreed to tell his wife that he was going to leave her. He was going to tell her after Christmas, and then he and Stephanie would spend New Year's Eve together. So, if she could not have her Christmas Eve fantasy, then at least she could make a New Year's dream come true. A new start to the new year with the man she loved.

Of course, that was before she'd had her encounter with Kathy Walker, his wife.

Which left her . . .?

Which left her walking through Dublin airport, pulling a small overnight bag and with less than fifty dollars in cash in her wallet, heading to the family she had told on the phone only last night that she was definitely not coming home for Christmas.

Stephanie turned into Duty Free; she would need to bring something back to America, something Irish. She'd already sent out her Christmas presents to her parents, four brothers and two sisters, but she couldn't turn up empty-handed. Most of the shelves were bare and there were lines at the cash registers. At least they still had the two regulars she took with her every time she returned home to the States: Bushmills Whiskey and Butler's Chocolates. You couldn't get more Irish than that. Then, she turned and headed down to Pier B.

Less than six hours ago, it had been a normal Christmas Eve – if that day could ever be called normal. She'd been happy – no, happy was too strong an emotion for what she'd been feeling. She'd been content. Yesterday, she hadn't been sure how she felt about him telling his wife. On the one hand she knew it had to be done. It was the right thing to do, the proper thing to do: Robert had been stringing the two women along, lying to them both, lying to himself. So, he had to tell Kathy. According to him, relations between them had broken down a long time ago and Stephanie got the impression that the announcement would not be a surprise and might even come as a relief to the other woman. She had felt a terrific amount of sympathy for the woman who was about to be told that her husband of eighteen years was going to leave her.

Then, six hours ago, Kathy Walker had appeared at

5

Stephanie's door. Forty-five minutes later, Robert turned up.

And in the interim between Kathy's and Robert's appearances, Stephanie had discovered several things. She had found that Kathy still loved Robert – loved him deeply – and, shockingly, that Robert still loved Kathy. Stephanie also caught a glimpse of her own future as Robert's partner. And it wasn't something she liked. She realised that whereas she was happy to be Robert's mistress when she believed that his relationship with his wife had irrevocably broken down, she was not content to remain so knowing that Robert and Kathy still had feelings for one another. She wanted to be loved exclusively, not sharing with another woman.

And it was only now, a couple of hours later, that the enormity of the decision she'd made was sinking in: she'd told Robert and Kathy that she'd made a mistake, a terrible mistake. *"I love you, Robert, but not as much as Kathy loves you. I don't want you. Go back to your wife."*

And he had. Without an argument. Without a fight. With barely a word of protest.

But she'd been lying: she did love him as much as Kathy did. Maybe more.

Pier B was jammed.

Stephanie Burroughs looked around at the grim-faced men and women impatiently waiting for the last Aer Lingus flight of the day to London, and wondered who they were and why they were travelling. With Christmas falling in the middle of the week, she assumed most were shop or office workers condemned to work right up to the last minute and then race for the plane to be home with their families for Christmas. She never imagined she'd be one of them.

She fished in her pocket and pulled out her mobile phone. She'd better call her mother and let her know she was coming home for the holidays.

When Kathy and Robert Walker had left her home, Stephanie wandered around the house for a few minutes, arms wrapped tightly across her stomach which was suddenly cramping with tension. She felt light-headed and breathless, and there were tiny black spots dancing before her eyes.

She stepped into the tiny sterile kitchen and made herself a cup of camomile tea – she definitely didn't need caffeine at the moment – and she knew that if she had a single alcoholic drink it would go straight to her head and send her to sleep, and right at that moment she needed to be thinking clearly.

Cupping the steaming cup of aromatic tea in both hands, she wandered back into the sitting-room where, only moments before, her lover and his wife had been. She could see the depression in the cushions at each end of the couch where they had sat, separated by two feet of cloth and too many years. Robert's Christmas presents to her lay abandoned on the floor, a bouquet of flowers already drooping in the heat. Above them a single pink balloon bobbed against the ceiling.

So, now what was she going to do? She looked around the room. With the exception of the presents Robert had brought, and the small Christmas tree she could see sitting in the hallway, there was nothing festive about it. She simply hadn't had a chance to hang decorations this year, and the few cards she had received she'd put on top of the fridge in the kitchen. Was she now condemned to sitting at home over the Christmas period? She'd done that last year, and it had been a miserably lonely couple of days.

What was she going to do?

Her last words to Kathy were that she was going to go home to her family. She'd said the words quickly, casually. . . but even as she was saying them, she guessed that it was impossible. She'd left it too late to book tickets. Or had she? How many people wanted to travel on Christmas Eve?

And once the thought had entered her mind, Stephanie suddenly knew that was what she wanted to do: to go home, back to Long Island, and spend Christmas surrounded by light and life, too much food and too many children.

Anything but spend Christmas alone in an empty house in Dublin.

Leaving her tea on the arm of the chair, she hurried out into the hall and dug her mobile phone out of her bag. She quickly scrolled through the menu until she came to the name of the travel agency her company used and hit dial.

"Thank you for calling International Travel Arrangements. This office is now closed for the holiday season. We will reopen on Monday 30th December. We would like to take this opportunity to wish you . . ."

Stephanie raced upstairs and pulled out her laptop. Sitting on the edge of the bed, she powered it up and plugged into the broadband modem. Now that the decision was made, she was determined to get away for Christmas and, by God, she was going home.

It took her only a few moments to log into the Aer Lingus site. Stephanie rarely booked her own flights – whenever she had to travel, the company made all the arrangements, and tickets and an itinerary landed on her desk. She navigated quickly through the site. All she had to do was to choose her starting city, her destination, the dates she wanted to travel on and enter her credit-card details. Simple. Maybe she would make it home in time for Christmas dinner. Her parents would be thrilled.

She quickly discovered that were no flights to New York. The last Aer Lingus flight to the States had departed two hours previously.

Her mobile phone rang and she jumped, almost knocking the laptop to the floor. It was Sally Wilson, her closest friend.

"Happy Christmas, Happy Christmas! Dave and I are going for a drink and we wanted to know –"

"I can't."

The tone of Stephanie's voice instantly alerted Sally. "What's happened?"

"Kathy Walker was just here. She found out about Robert and me."

The phone crackled with Sally's gasp of horror.

"Then Robert turned up."

"Oh, Stephanie!"

Stephanie suddenly found herself smiling. "Talk about a nightmare scenario."

"What . . . what happened?"

"What you always said would happen: he went back to his wife."

"Bastard!" Sally said grimly. "That's what they all do. Bastard!"

"Well, actually, to tell the truth, I sort of pushed him in that direction. I realised I didn't want him, Sally. Not on the terms he was offering anyway. I realised I didn't want to become like Kathy Walker." Stephanie took a deep shuddering breath. "So, he's gone."

"And you. What about you? How are you doing? What are you going to do?"

"I'm sitting here looking at the Aer Lingus site, trying to get home for Christmas, spend Christmas with the family. But there are no flights out of Dublin," she said bitterly, "so I guess I'm stuck."

"Well, don't give up just yet. Can you get into the UK or Europe?"

Stephanie's fingers danced across the keys. "Yes, I can

get into London on Aer Lingus, and there are also British Midland and Ryanair flights available."

"OK, here's what you do: see if you can get a flight into New York out of London or Paris," Sally said decisively. "It'll mean a few extra hours travelling, and it will cost you a bit extra –"

"Sally, I'll pay First Class if I have to."

"Then you'll definitely get a seat. Look, you organise your ticket. Dave and I are on our way over to you now – we'll drive you to the airport."

"Sally, you don't have to do that! It'll ruin your Christmas Eve. I'll get a cab."

"On Christmas Eve!" Sally snapped. "You'd be waiting hours. We're on our way," and she hung up.

By the time Sally, with a sullen Dave in tow, turned up at Stephanie's townhouse, she had managed to book an Aer Lingus ticket to London, then get a connecting BA flight into New York. She'd bought First Class on the transatlantic flight – an outrageous extravagance of nearly three thousand euro – but she reckoned she deserved the treat. Her only concern was that the timing of the two flights was incredibly tight. If the Irish flight was delayed by even an hour, she would miss her connection and then she'd be doomed to spend Christmas Eve and probably Christmas Day in a grim hotel near Heathrow airport.

It took her less than ten minutes to pack, throwing underwear, a couple of pairs of trousers, half a dozen tops, and one of her good and respectable party dresses into her carry-on suitcase. She didn't need to take much more; she had a wardrobe of clothes in Long Island. When she'd first come over to Ireland, she'd been surprisingly, desperately homesick for the first two years and took every opportunity to head home, often twice or even three times a year. It simply didn't make any sense to keep dragging the same clothes back and forth across the Atlantic, so she'd finally left a huge suitcase full of clothes in a closet. Her mother had been delighted and the last time she'd been home, she'd discovered that her mother had hung up the clothes and laid out the rest in the chest of drawers.

She had just finishing dressing in her preferred travelling outfit – black jeans, black polo-neck sweater and three-quarter-length black leather coat, all chosen to show no stains and splashes – when Sally arrived.

When Stephanie opened the hall door, Sally embraced and kissed her.

"Don't take this the wrong way," the petite blonde said softly, "but I'm glad it's over. Look at it this way: you're free of him at least. Now you can move on with your life."

"I'm glad too," Stephanie whispered. And, in that moment, she meant it.

12

CHAPTER 2

Stephanie was settling into her window seat when she felt her phone buzz in her pocket. The plane was still boarding and, glancing around to make sure that the stewardesses couldn't see what she was doing, she pulled out the phone, leaned against the window and hit the receive button. She had set it to silent earlier. It was probably Sally checking to make sure she'd made the flight.

"Yes?" she whispered, cupping her hand over her mouth.

"Stephanie? Stephanie? Is that you?"

The voice stopped her cold. It was Robert. She felt her breath catch and her mouth was suddenly filled with cotton.

"Steph –"

She hit the Off button, abruptly aware that her heart was tripping. A couple of hours ago, he hadn't been able

13

to look her in the face as he'd slunk from the room. And now he had the gall to phone her!

The phone buzzed again.

Stephanie hit the Cancel button and the call finished. What did he want? To apologise? Possibly. To try and get back into her favours? Probably.

The phone buzzed again, but this time she knew it was a message call; when she'd cancelled his call, it had gone straight to her message machine. It could stay there until after Christmas, she decided. In fact, she might just as well delete it without listening to it, because she was finished with him now. Finished with his lies and empty promises.

Abruptly her throat closed and her eyes stung with bitter tears. Were they all lies, were all the promises empty? And yet when they'd met on Friday, only three days ago, and he'd asked her to marry him, he'd sounded genuine. She'd believed him.

She'd also believed him when he said that his wife didn't love him. She'd been wrong then.

Stephanie reached into her pocket for the phone.

One Missed Call.

It would be the easiest thing in the world to turn the phone off and put it away. Already the doors were closing and the stewardess would soon remind passengers to ensure that all mobile phones were turned off. Stephanie knew from experience that reception in Heathrow was terrible, so she wouldn't be able to listen to the call there either. And this phone wasn't tri-band, so it wouldn't work in the States. If she could just hang on for another ten minutes, it would be physically impossible to listen to the call until she returned to Ireland sometime in the New Year.

Ten minutes.

Pressing her head against the fuselage and crouching down, Stephanie hit 171.

You Have One New Message. Message Was Left Today . . .

Then she heard his voice: *"Stephanie? Stephanie, it's Robert. Look, we need to talk. We have to talk. About today. About us. About everything. Please call me back. I'm on the mobile."*

Of course he was on the mobile, Stephanie thought savagely. He wouldn't want her phoning the house, would he? She deleted the message and turned off the phone.

There was nothing to talk about. Their relationship was finished. She should never have got involved with him in the first place. Stephanie settled back into the seat, tilted her head back and popped two pliable earplugs into her ears. Instantly, the world grew muffled and seemed to go away. She closed her eyes and breathed deeply. She could feel someone settle into the seat beside her, jostling her, but she didn't even open her eyes. On the next leg of the journey she had a First Class seat and would have plenty of space.

It was difficult now, looking back over the past eighteen months of their relationship to remember what she'd seen in him – and really it was only in the last six months that things had turned very serious and she'd begun to think that he might indeed be The One. He was handsome, in an ordinary sort of way, seven years older than her, though there were many times that she felt she was the more mature partner in the relationship. He ran his own business, a small TV production company, now making shorts, fillers and ads instead of the ground-breaking documentaries he had once aspired to. But his grand title of MD certainly wasn't an attraction for Stephanie who drew down a bigger salary than he did and with much better benefits.

So what was it? What attracted a thirty-five-year-old woman, single, unattached, attractive, with her own house and car, to a man with the ultimate baggage – the baggage of a wife, two teens and a struggling business?

It wasn't a question she'd chosen to ask herself too often in the past, though Sally had asked it of her often enough, usually phrasing the question slightly differently, reminding her friend just how one-sided the relationship was. Stephanie brought much more to the relationship than Robert: she was a younger, prettier, slimmer version of his wife, who now had the cares and struggles of raising two teens etched into her face and body.

And she was someone able to bring business to his company. Stephanie shook her head slightly. No, it wasn't just that. She refused to believe that it was just that. Certainly that was an additional benefit for Robert, but all that had come later.

Besides, thinking back to those early days, she had

actively pursued him and she had certainly made the first move.

So what had attracted her to him, with all his faults?

When she first met him, over six years ago now, he'd been lonely and alone. She'd been hired as a research assistant for a documentary that R&K Productions were working on. Little by little his story had come out as they had trekked across Ireland scouting locations. Although he shared joint ownership of the company with his wife, he was struggling to grow the company alone because Kathy had stepped away from the business. He was working fourteen- and sixteen-hour days just to make ends meet. Stephanie had no time for him then; she thought he was ignorant and arrogant and completely absorbed in the company. But Robert had given her her first break in the business and for that she would be eternally grateful. That first job had paved the way for the rest of her career.

When she met him again about eighteen months ago, she'd felt again the loneliness that radiated from him. And nothing seemed to have changed. He was still working outrageous hours, scrambling from job to job and, from what she could gather from what was said – and unsaid – the relationship between him and his wife seemed to have broken down irrevocably. He'd also given her to understand – though he never actually stated this – that when the children were grown, he was going to leave Kathy and start afresh.

Once she knew that, Stephanie had felt no

compunction about letting Robert know that there was the possibility of a relationship if he wanted it. And he had. Of course.

But that still didn't answer the question. What had attracted her to him?

Stephanie was vaguely aware that the engines were revving up and that the plane was moving. It looked as if it was taking off on time; that was a good omen. Maybe she would make the Heathrow connection.

What had attracted her to him? That was going to bother her now until she had worked out a satisfactory answer.

She could feel the sensation in her feet and stomach as the plane took off and with the sudden lift came an answer: it was the sense of loss that he carried around him. When she met him after the absence of nearly four years, she'd again sensed the loss, the hurt that clung to him and perhaps the desperation too. That had appealed to her. Here was someone in trouble and she could make it right.

How wrong she'd been!

She hadn't made the situation right; she'd made it worse, so much worse. Because of her – and Robert too, don't forget him! – his family were condemned to a difficult and bitter Christmas. She'd already disrupted her friend's Christmas Eve and she was doing something she really didn't want to be doing: flying across the Atlantic to a family she didn't really know any more. She'd already been censured at work because of her relationship with

Robert's company and she knew she'd have a lot of bridge-building to do to repair that damage.

Everything had a price, she knew that. You just had to be prepared to pay the price.

And she had a feeling that she was only now beginning to pay for her relationship with Robert Walker.

CHAPTER 3

Stephanie made it onto the transatlantic flight with less than ten minutes to spare. Although it had taken off on time, the Aer Lingus flight had circled Heathrow for the best part of thirty minutes before it had finally been permitted to land. Stephanie then had a mad dash to make it to the international terminal. She was grateful that she was only travelling with hand luggage; she guessed that if she'd had check-through luggage, it would not have made the flight.

"You're the last one," the stewardess said, as Stephanie came running onto the plane.

"I thought I was going to miss it," she panted.

"At least you made it." She directed Stephanie to the right, into the First Class cabin. "Thank God you did. If you'd missed this flight you'd have ended up stuck in Heathrow over the Christmas!"

"I can't think of anything worse!"

"Nor can I," the stewardess smiled.

Stephanie heaved her suitcase up into the overhead storage, pushed the duty-free bag in alongside it, slipped into one of the large comfortable seats and only then allowed herself to relax. She sighed deeply. For the first time since Kathy Walker had appeared at her door, she felt a little of the stress slip out of her system, though her stomach was still cramping with tension.

"That was a close call . . ."

Stephanie buckled her seatbelt and glanced sidelong at the over-large balding businessman in the smartly cut suit beside her. He exuded the faintest whiff of whiskey with every movement.

He stretched out his hand. "I'm –"

Stephanie held up her right hand, palm outwards. "Please do not take this the wrong way. But I don't care who you are. I'm really not interested and I'm don't want to talk to you between now and New York."

The businessman blinked, frowning slightly, trying to decide if she was joking or not.

"I'm just trying to be friendly!" he began to bluster.

"Don't be. I'm not interested."

"Well, I never –"

"I'm glad we got that clear," Stephanie continued. She pulled her earplugs out of her pocket and popped them in. She could hear them hiss and crackle as they expanded and the world slowly went away. She opened the novel she'd shoved in her bag in Dublin. It had been sitting on her bedside locker for months and so far she'd only managed to read three chapters. Richard and Judy had recommended it on their TV show and she'd found their previous recommendations excellent, but she was beginning to have serious reservations about this book. Of course, it might not necessarily be the book; maybe it was just her state of mind. Maybe she should have brought something lighter, easier to read. She'd thought about picking up *The Da Vinci Code*; she'd been promising to read it for ages and at this stage she was the only person in the office – possibly the entire country – who hadn't read it. It had slipped her mind in Dublin airport and she'd simply had no chance in London.

Stephanie closed the book, tilted her head back against the seat and closed her eyes. The stewardesses were going through the emergency escape routine. Stephanie made a point of never watching them. If the plane crashed or fell out of the sky, she didn't think she'd have much chance to put the techniques into effect anyway.

She'd got out of the habit of reading during her time with Robert. He rarely read – claimed he never had the time – and he seldom listened to music. That should have been her first clue that their relationship would never work: she loved her books and music.

However, it also made her realise just how much time an affair consumed. Before she met Robert she would have lunch at her desk or in one of the small restaurants close to her office, and read, and in the evenings she'd come home, set up a long hot bath and lose herself in her current book. She could get through two and sometimes three books in a week, more if it was something from one of her favourite authors.

But that was before Robert . . .

Once she began her relationship with Robert, they ended up having lunch together most days, often in his office or in one of the cafés nearby. Driving to his office and finding parking had cut her lunch-time in half and she'd often ended up with a sandwich — even though she'd been determined to give up white bread — rather than the salads she preferred. Then, Robert would come over to her home two or three times a week. When they were together, there was little time left for reading. The last book she'd read right through was . . . actually, she couldn't remember.

Well, all that was about to change.

After dinner, which, in First Class, was very acceptable, she tried to watch the in-flight movie on the folding LCD screen. It was a three-month-old science-fiction special-effect extravaganza, but it had been so cut and edited to make it palatable for an airplane audience that she found it virtually unwatchable. Turning off the small screen, she tried reading again, but the book, a dreary coming-of-age story, was a dead loss — she'd try and remember to leave it behind in the States and pick up something in the airport for the return journey.

Kicking off her shoes, she pulled the airline blanket up to her shoulders, tilted her seat back and closed her eyes.

And when, exactly, was she going to return? Before or after the New Year? It really depended on when she could get a flight, she supposed. If she got back to Dublin before New Year's Eve, there was bound to be a party she could go to – start off the new year on a high note. Then she wanted to go through the house and strip out everything that belonged to Robert – she was determined to keep nothing of his. There wasn't much in any case: some clothes, a toothbrush, a razor, a pair of shoes, a spare tie. She'd stick them in a bag and drop them around – no, post them – to his office. She wasn't petty enough to send them to his home. She wondered briefly about the jewellery he'd given her. Should she return it, or keep it? But if she kept it, she would never wear it because it reminded her of him. She wasn't sure she wanted to return it to him however; she didn't quite like the idea of him passing it on to his wife to wear. Then she smiled, quickly, fleetingly. She'd grabbed her jewellery case when she was packing. She guessed that most of the pieces were in it. She could always give them away as presents to her sisters and mother.

Stephanie dozed off and drifted into a sleep in which the events of the past couple of hours cycled and recycled through her consciousness, twisting and turning into a dream that was not quite a nightmare, in which *she* was the woman going to face her husband's lover. She came awake with a gasp, and for a brief moment didn't know where she was. Realisation came slowly, but the emotion in the dream – that combination of terror and rage –

remained. The more she thought about Kathy Walker, the more respect she had for the woman. What courage must it have taken to drive across the city on Christmas Eve to face her husband's mistress? A lesser woman would have been inclined to leave it until after Christmas, so as not to disturb the status quo. What would *she* have done, she wondered. She liked to think she would have done the same thing – confronted the other woman – but she wasn't entirely sure she would have.

Despite the comfort of the First Class seat, the six-hour flight seemed endless and she was numb with exhaustion by the time the plane finally touched down. As soon as the seat-belt sign went off, she was out of her seat and had pulled her bags out of the overhead locker in two seconds flat. The businessman sitting beside her opened his mouth to say something, but the look on her face silenced him. She was one of the first people off the plane and the blast of chill air that hit her face and that metallic odour peculiar to American airports finally brought it home that she was no longer in Ireland. Marching down towards the Customs Clearance Hall, she felt as if a weight had been lifted from her shoulders.

At least half a dozen flights, the last of Christmas Eve, had landed within the past forty-five minutes and the Arrivals Terminal in JFK was heaving with people. Airport security were desperately attempting to keep the area clear, but it was an impossible task, and the strains of

"White Christmas" were lost beneath a score of languages.

Stephanie wound her way through the crowd, making for the car-hire desk. God, she hoped she'd be able to get something at this late stage, and then she smiled, and remembered: this was America – everything was available all the time. She walked past couples embracing, families locked together, she saw tears, smiles, laughter and felt just the faintest twinge of sadness. She'd flown in and out of airports most of her adult life and had rarely been met by anyone, and it had never bothered her. Now, for the first time, she felt lonely and alone.

"Stephanie . . . Stephanie!"

Right at the very edges of her consciousness, she caught the sound of someone calling out what sounded like her name. But that was impossible: no one knew she was coming in, except her parents, and they'd hardly driven all the way out from Long Island to collect her.

"Stephanie. . . Stephanie!" The voice was coming nearer.

She fixed a smile on her face as she turned. It would be just her luck to bump into someone she didn't want to see only moments after landing.

"Stephanie?"

It took a heartbeat to recognise the rather plain-looking young woman standing before her, head tilted to one side, smiling quizzically.

"You walked right past me," she said.

"Joan? Joan! My God, Joan, I didn't recognise you."

Joan Burroughs was Stephanie's baby sister, six years her junior, and the last person she expected to see waiting for her in JFK. She wrapped her arms around her sister and hugged her.

"Well, it's no wonder I didn't recognise you," she said with a grin. Joan was bundled up in a heavy padded jacket, black combat trousers over thick boots and was wearing a woollen cap pulled low over her forehead and covering the tops of her ears. Her exposed cheeks and the tip of her nose were bright red.

There were seven children – four boys and three girls – in the Burroughs family, and Stephanie had never been especially close to any of them. They had all stayed close to home, married young and started families early, whereas Stephanie had left home and America as soon as she could and now, at thirty-five, was the only one left without a partner. The last Stephanie had heard of her sister, Joan had been working as a graphic artist in a New York design studio

"How did you know?" she asked, then answered her own question: "Mom."

Joan nodded. "Mom phoned me and told me you were on the way." She stepped away from Stephanie to regard her older sister critically. "You've lost weight and you look tired."

"Thanks," she said sarcastically. "I'll take the weight loss as a compliment. The last couple of days have been tough and I had to take two flights to get here. I'm just flattened."

"Well, I was still in the city, so I thought I'd hang around and wait for you."

"I'm thrilled that you did." Stephanie linked her arm

through her sister's and together they moved through the crowd. "I really wasn't looking forward to the drive out to the Island."

"I was speaking to Mom only yesterday," Joan said, "and she didn't think you were coming home. She was a bit upset about it. Then she phoned today with the news that you were on the way in."

"Mom called recently and tried her usual subtle brand of blackmail and encouragement on me. I told her I was tied up over the Christmas period . . . but . . . but, well, things changed."

"Well, she sounded thrilled on the phone. Looks like all the family will be there, and you know how much she likes that."

The two women stepped out into the harsh New York air. It was so bitterly cold that it took Stephanie's breath away: she'd momentarily forgotten just how chill New York could be in December.

"Here. I guessed you wouldn't have anything with you." Joan pulled a woollen hat from an inside pocket and produced a pair of gloves. "I didn't have boots in your size," she added.

Stephanie pulled on the extremely unflattering hat, grateful that no one she knew could see her now, and tugged on the gloves which were one size too small. The two women cut through to the car park, the air sodden with the stench of diesel and bitter with the acrid tang of car exhausts. There were frozen patches of water on the ground and Stephanie could feel the chill seeping up through the too-thin soles of her comfortable shoes.

"We're here," Joan said, stopping in front of a slightly battered VW van. The remains of dozens of stickers were still visible on its rear; in some places they had been removed so forcefully that paint had peeled off, leaving dappled rust-spots in their wake.

Stephanie blinked in surprise. "You and Eddie were driving an SUV if I remember . . ."

"The Cherokee. Yes, Eddie still has that."

"Isn't he coming with us?" Stephanie asked, as Joan wrenched open the door of the van, revealing its dishevelled interior.

A scrap of carpet covered the metal floor, and the back of the van was packed out with cardboard U-Haul boxes, suitcases and black bin bags obviously stuffed with clothes. One had burst and spilled shoes across the floor. Joan snatched her sister's single case off the ground and squeezed it in between two boxes.

"No, Eddie will not be coming with us. Haven't you heard – or did Mother forget to tell you that piece of family news?" Joan indicated the back of the van. "I'm moving back home. I've left him."

CHAPTER 4

They sat in silence while Joan manoeuvred the sluggish VW through the traffic. There was no air-conditioning in the van and the heater laboured unsuccessfully against the chill that radiated up through the thin floor. Every few moments, Joan would pluck a filthy sodden rag from the dashboard and lean forward to clean an arc of window.

Stephanie huddled in the seat, arms wrapped around her body, gloved fingers tucked into her armpits. She was desperately trying to remember what she knew about Joan and her husband, Eddie. They hadn't been married long – twelve months, fourteen maybe. Yes, a little over a year. Stephanie had not been able to come to the wedding because it clashed with a week Robert had taken off. And, given the choice between spending a week away with her lover – their first real holiday together – or attending a Catholic-Italian wedding in the States, she had chosen the holiday. At one point she had suggested to Robert that they might go to the wedding together, but he'd pointed out that it would raise too many difficult questions. She had sent an outrageously expensive set of Waterford Crystal cut-glass goblets as a wedding present and, she realised now, to salve her conscience.

"I'm really sorry," she said eventually. "I'd no idea."

"Didn't you? I'm surprised. Surprised that Mother didn't tell you." This time she was unable to disguise the bitterness in her voice. "She's told just about everyone else I know."

Stephanie frowned, desperately trying to remember. She didn't think that her mother had mentioned anything . . . and yet Joan was right. There was no way that Toni Burroughs would not have shared this tragedy with her other two daughters, discussing and analysing it to death and wondering where she had gone wrong. Somewhere at the back of her mind, Stephanie recalled her mother talking about Joan's difficulties with Eddie. "Now that I think of it, she did mention something, but it was only a very casual remark – something about you and Eddie not getting along too well. I think she might have mentioned something about children too. He wanted them and you wanted to wait." Stephanie shut up; there was more, she was sure of it. She had the vaguest of recollections that her mother had told her a long and complicated story about Joan and Eddie. But she had been too wrapped up in her relationship with Robert Walker to even listen properly.

Also, she knew she had a habit of tuning out when her mother was talking about her siblings.

"Do you want to talk about it?" she asked.

Joan shook her head. "I'm all talked out,"

Stephanie kept quiet, knowing that Joan would not be able to resist the temptation to give her side of the story to a new audience.

Traffic was backed up across the Triboro Bridge and in the distance they could hear sirens. Snow had been forecast but none had fallen. However, the temperatures had plummeted and ice was beginning to creep across the road in broad sparkling sheets. Looking across the East River, the New York night sky sparkled with lights in the crisp winter air. The Empire State Building was lit up with red and green lights and Chrysler Building was also illuminated. The entire skyscape looked like a huge Christmas display. Peering through the window, Stephanie could just about make out the gaping hole in the night sky where the Twin Towers would have stood. She had been home several times since the terrible events of nine-eleven and, like every other New Yorker, she knew she would never get used to that gap in the skyline. It looked like there would be another building in that space soon, and she wasn't entirely sure how she felt about that.

Joan Burroughs kept leaning forward and tapping the dashboard, where the temperature gauge was beginning to edge upwards. "I hope we don't overheat before we hit Grand Central Parkway," she muttered.

"Looks like there's an accident up ahead. We should be OK once we get past that," Stephanie said.

"What do you want to hear?" Joan asked suddenly. "The truth or the version I told Mother?"

Stephanie took a moment to consider. "Which version do you want me to know?" she said eventually. "But I'm sure I'll get Mom's version anyway."

Joan nodded and smiled. "I'm sure you will." Then she hit the brakes hard and leaned on the horn as a truck cut into her lane. The sound was an anaemic whine. Then, unexpectedly, she said, "I've always been a little jealous . . . no, jealous is the wrong word, envious is better. I've always been a little envious of you."

"Why?" Stephanie frowned, unsure at the sudden change of topic.

"Well, you live in Ireland, happy and contented, with a good job, a nice house, great car . . . at least that's what mother keeps telling us all. She keeps hinting that you've got a man, but we all know that's untrue."

"Why?" Stephanie blurted, surprised.

"Because we all know you're a lesbian. She knows too, but she doesn't want to admit that two of her three daughters are gay."

"What! What?" For a moment, Stephanie didn't know if she had heard correctly.

Joan turned awkwardly in her seat to look at her sister. "There's no need to be embarrassed. You're thirty-five, pretty and successful, with your own home. And no man in your life. But mother says you're always talking about this Sally friend of yours. It was CJ who suggested that she must be your partner. And she should know!"

Stephanie started to laugh. It began as a giggle, then grew into a full belly-aching laugh that came remarkably close to hysterics. She could feel the tension of the past hours seep away with the laughter. The thought of her rather strait-laced mother thinking that her daughter was a lesbian simply because she rarely spoke about men was hilariously funny. The only reason she rarely spoke about the man she was dating was because for the past eighteen months she had been seeing a married man. And that was hardly something she could share with her conservative Catholic mother on a transatlantic call. But because of that her mother had assumed . . .

Pressing the heels of both hands against her cheeks she wiped away the tears. "Let me assure you that I am not a lesbian. My friend Sally is just that – my friend – and is, in fact, getting engaged this very evening. I don't talk about men because first of all, it's not something I want shared and discussed with all and sundry, and secondly, I am concentrating on building a career and simply don't have a lot of free time. It's one of the reasons I don't have a pet either. However – and please don't tell Mom – I have been seeing someone, a *man*," she emphasised, "on and off over the past couple of months. But that's finished," she added, not saying just how recently it had finished.

Ignoring the sudden blaring of car horns, Joan floored the accelerator and the VW lurched forward and managed to crawl across two lanes of traffic. There were flashing blue and red lights ahead and a trio of NYPD cruisers were parked at an angle, blocking two lanes. Beyond them, ambulance lights rotated over a traffic accident. Just at the exit off the bridge, a small nondescript Japanese import had run into the side of a white stretch limo. Half a dozen young men in tuxedos and women in evening gowns stood shivering on the sidewalk, while ambulance crews struggled to cut the driver out of the smaller car.

"Their Christmas party is ruined," Joan remarked, nodding to the party-goers.

"Not as much as his," Stephanie said, looking at the bloody driver of the small car, now being laid out on a stretcher. "I wonder if there is a family waiting for him to come home?" She suddenly glanced sidelong at her sister. "Is Eddie waiting for you at home? Does he know what you're doing?"

Joan drove in silence for two blocks, then said suddenly, "No, he doesn't."

Stephanie straightened in the seat. "You mean, he's expecting you to turn up this evening?"

Joan glanced at the clock on the dashboard, not entirely sure if it was accurate or not. "Yes, he's probably home by now. I left him a note."

"Joan, he's probably frantic. Call him now!"

"No," Joan said stubbornly.

"You have to talk to him."

"No, I don't. You can't talk. You don't know what it's like to have a man lie to you for weeks on end."

Stephanie opened her mouth to respond, then closed it again. "Tell me what happened," she said, breaking her own silent promise.

"He lied to me," Joan snapped.

"You said that. All men lie," Stephanie murmured. And women too, she added silently. "But let's be honest, we wouldn't want them to tell us the truth about everything, would we?"

"We were married for a year in October. We were starting to talk about having a family."

Stephanie was freezing. She was beginning to feel a headache – a combination of stress and recycled airplane air combined with jet lag and the bitter New York weather – pulse at the back of her eyes. Her stomach felt queasy. She'd just flown across the Atlantic, running away from her own affair; the last thing she needed to hear was that her brother-in-law was also carrying on.

"We were doing fine: Eddie was working on the Ground Zero clean-up, I had a part-time job in a graphics studio on the Upper East Side. We were even managing to save a little every month. We talked about getting out of the city, finding a home and then trying to start a family."

And Eddie got bored with this little domestic idyll, Stephanie thought, found himself a woman, made her some promises, told her some lies . . .

"And for six weeks afterwards, morning after morning, he went out to work. He even arrived home at the right time."

"Stop, stop, stop! I think I missed something." Stephanie reached out to touch her sister's arm. "And would you mind slowing down a little – you're speeding."

"Oh." Joan eased up off the accelerator. As she'd been telling the story, she'd unconsciously been pushing her foot to the floor.

"I'm sorry, I'm a little jet-lagged. What do you mean he went out to work?"

"After he was fired," Joan snapped. "He pretended to go out to work. I only realised it when the bank statement came in and I discovered that no salary payments had been made."

"I'm sorry . . . I thought . . . when you said he'd lied to you . . . I thought there was another woman involved."

"An affair! Eddie knows what I'd do to him – and her – if I ever caught him with another woman!"

"So you're leaving him because he lost his job?"

"No, I'm leaving him because he lied to me. More than once. He pretended to go to work for six weeks – and every single day I'd ask him how things had gone at work, and every day he'd spin me a tissue of lies. One lie leading to another leading to another . . ."

Stephanie closed her eyes. Her own affair was built upon a tissue of lies, each one tugging her further and further into an intricate web. She hadn't fully realised until today just how deep and twisted that web was, just how limiting her relationship with Robert had been. A smile curled the corners of her lips: it had even made her mother think she was lesbian!

Consequences

"Maybe it was pride which prevented him from telling you that he'd lost his job," she suggested cautiously.

"Maybe. But he told me that he'd been let go because they were cutting numbers. But that was a lie – another one. He was sacked for claiming overtime that he hadn't done. I only found that out today. Once I realised that, I knew I couldn't live with him any more."

"Why?" Stephanie wondered.

"Because I knew I could never trust him again. Once you catch your man out lying to you about one thing, you know he'll lie to you about others. I didn't want to live with that mistrust."

"What will you do?"

"Go home for Christmas. Talk to a lawyer in the new year."

"And all because he lied to you?"

"Once the trust goes, what's left?"

Stephanie nodded. What was left? She suddenly felt bitterly sorry for Kathy Walker. What future was there for her relationship with Robert?

CHAPTER 5

It was close to midnight before the two sisters turned into the driveway that led to their childhood home. Conversation had dried up nearly an hour ago, with Stephanie drifting in and out of troubled sleep and Joan concentrating desperately on holding the old van on the road.

It had started snowing just as they were leaving the city, huge silent flakes that quickly coated everything they settled on in a festive blanket. But both women knew how dangerous the snowfall could be. There was a very real danger that they could get caught on one of the roads and forced to spend Christmas in a sleazy motel or, worse still, become trapped on one of the minor roads and run the risk of freezing to death in the car.

Stephanie wondered what Robert would think of that when he read it in the newspapers. How would he feel? Relief that the problem that was Stephanie Burroughs had gone away? Or would he feel even vaguely guilty that it was his fault she was driving through a snowstorm on Christmas Eve in a gasping van that sounded as if it was about conk out at any moment? However, inasmuch as he rarely read a newspaper and she doubted that the deaths of two women in a snowstorm would make the international press, he'd probably never know.

Maybe she could haunt him.

The heater in the van had suddenly decided to work, and now pumped overhot and vaguely acrid air into the van. The combination of the heat and exhaustion drove Stephanie into a light uncomfortable doze in which vague thoughts of Robert and Kathy were never far away.

The crunch of gravel and grit under the tyres brought her awake. They had turned off the freeway and onto a narrow country blacktop. As she struggled to straighten and sit up, Joan said, "Nearly there."

Stephanie rubbed her sleeve against the side window and peered out into the night. It had snowed here recently and the world had lost all shape and definition. The streets were deserted, but in the majority of the wooden houses, set well back from the road, she could see a Christmas tree winking in the gloom. Some of the houses had been decorated with thousands – tens of thousands – of lights, but most of the lights had been turned off now and the displays of Santas and reindeers, snowmen and Christmas trees seemed rather forlorn.

At the end of the lane, a single house was ablaze with lights. Stephanie craned forward to look. This was the home of her childhood. She'd been back the previous

Thanksgiving, but hadn't been home since and it had been three years – maybe more – since she'd been home for Christmas.

The wan lights of the van washed across the front of the house. An enormous Christmas tree dominated the sitting-room bay window and Stephanie knew it would be decorated with the same balls and trinkets it had always been decorated with. She knew she would find the silver-foil and pipe-cleaner angel she had made in First Grade; she knew that the crown her eldest brother Billy had worn when he'd played a Wise Man in the Christmas pageant in his second year in elementary school would adorn the top of the tree. She'd once found such traditions rather petty and almost embarrassing, especially when there were visitors, but as she got older she'd come to realise that there was something comforting in them, and the trinkets on the tree symbolised simpler times, happier times.

Climbing out of the car, she was surprised to discover that there were tears on her cheeks and she tried, unsuccessfully, to convince herself that it was just the chill wind on her face.

The front door opened wide and the long shadows thrown by the sisters' parents danced across the snow. The two women grabbed their bags and hurried out of the bitter night air.

Toni Burroughs was a tiny woman, standing an inch under five foot.

Stephanie had no idea just how old her mother was –

late sixties maybe, early seventies possibly – but it was impossible to put an age on her. To Stephanie's eyes, Toni looked the same as she did when Stephanie was growing up in this same house. Her features were all planes and angles: a pointed chin, pointed nose, prominent cheekbones and skin that looked almost unnaturally smooth. Stephanie doubted that her mother had Botox and knew that a face-lift was simply out of the question, so she put it down to good genes and hoped that she would look as good as her mother looked when she was her age.

Toni met Stephanie on the step and reached up to wrap her arms around her daughter. "I cannot tell you how happy you've made me," she breathed in Stephanie's ear.

"This is a flying visit," Stephanie said, and then added, "I'm glad to be home." And she meant it.

"What made you change your mind?"

"Maybe I just wanted to be home with my family for Christmas," Stephanie murmured.

"Maybe," Toni said in that tone of voice of which suggested that she didn't believe a word of it.

Matt Burroughs released Joan and gathered his older daughter into his arms. "Now this is the best Christmas present a man could have."

"Dad . . ." Stephanie could feel tears prickling at the back of her eyes and her throat felt unaccountably tight.

"Come inside now, you both must be freezing."

Matt Burroughs looked every inch the college professor he was. Tall, thin and now beginning to stoop a little, he still possessed the thick mane of jet-black hair that, even now in his seventieth year, was showing remarkably little grey. But she noticed the extra lines around his eyes, the creases in his brow, the more pronounced stoop when he walked. He'd aged since she'd last seen him.

Matt ushered his daughters into the hall and closed the door. The small cramped hallway was made even smaller by the addition of the second Christmas tree — the children's tree — which was put up every year for the grandchildren to showcase their handmade decorations. This year the greenery was almost lost beneath a confection of silver and crepe paper, pipe-cleaner stars and papier-mâché balls.

After the chill drive, the house was luxuriously warm, rich with the odours of Christmas cooking, scented fat-bodied Yankee Candles and pine. In the surprisingly deserted sitting-room, a log fire was burning down to embers.

"Where is everyone?" Stephanie wondered. She'd been expecting to find the entire clan still up.

"Gone to bed," her mother announced, with just a hint of disapproval in her voice. "I thought they'd wait up for you."

"They'll be up early in the morning with the children," Matt said softly. He nodded towards the pile of brightly wrapped boxes piled haphazardly around the enormous tree that filled the window. "This is the first time in I don't know how many years when all the family will be home for Christmas," he said with a smile. He reached out and squeezed his daughter's arm. "I'm so glad you could make it."

"So am I, Dad."

Toni caught hold of Joan's arm and pulled her out to the kitchen, leaving Stephanie alone with her father.

"No doubt your mother is pumping Joan for information right now," Matt said with a grin. He opened the antique roll-top drinks cabinet. "I know you're not really a spirits drinker," he said, opening a bottle of Bushmills with its distinctive label, "but I think you might need this." He poured a double and handed it to Stephanie. "You look like you need it."

"Usually I don't, and normally I wouldn't, but tonight . . ." She tilted her head and threw back half the bitter liquor in one gulp. She felt it sear the back of her throat and then explode warm and soothing into the pit of her stomach. "It's been a long day."

Matt poured himself a tiny drop into a cut-glass goblet that was older than he was, swirled it in the bottom of the glass and breathed in the rich aroma. Placing the goblet on top of the mantelpiece, he poked at the crumbling remains of the blackened log with a fire-iron, watching red-black and yellow-white sparks spiral up into the chimney.

"You were lucky to get a flight," he said, without turning around. "It must have been very last-minute."

"It was. I didn't book flights until this afternoon . . . well, afternoon Irish time."

Matt retrieved his glass and turned to face his daughter. Concentrating on the liquor, he asked, "Didn't you have Christmas plans made?"

"I had," Stephanie said softly, but refused to elaborate.

For a moment it looked as if Matt was about to push for an answer, then he simply raised his glass to his daughter. "Welcome home!"

"Thanks, Dad."

"I'll ask you one other question, then I'll not push further: you're not in any sort of trouble, are you?"

"Dad! What sort of trouble?" she asked, curious as to what he was thinking.

"Oh, I don't know. Job trouble."

"No, Dad, I'm not in any sort of job trouble."

"Man trouble?"

"There's no man in my life right now," she said quickly, determined not to lie to her father, and equally determined not to tell him what had happened. Her parents were devout Catholics. She was not sure how they would react if they discovered that their daughter had been having an affair with a married man. "There's no secret, no big mystery, I promise you. I made a last-minute decision to be with my family for Christmas. The alternative was staying at home in Dublin on my own . . . and I'd no wish to do that."

"Well, we're all delighted you did," Toni Burroughs announced from the door, where she was standing with a tray laden down with a tea-cosy-wrapped pot and a huge plate of sandwiches. Joan hovered behind her.

Without the heavy coat and concealing hat, the resemblance to her mother was remarkable. "Now come and eat up – you must be starved after your journey – then you can head up to bed. I've given you your old room; I thought it might bring back memories of childhood Christmases. Joan, you've got the spare room." She stopped, looked up and tilted her head to one side, listening.

The room fell silent.

In the distance, a church-bell had begun to toll midnight, the sound crisp and brittle, lost and lonely on the night air. Stephanie Burroughs blinked away tears; she was home for Christmas. When she'd awakened this Christmas Eve morning, she'd had no idea this was how the day was going to end.

CHAPTER 6

Wednesday, 25th December

CHRISTMAS DAY

It was close to 3.30 when she finally gave in and realised that she was not going to sleep.

Stephanie sat up in bed, pulled the heavy embroidered quilt up to her chin and looked around the room. Here was a surreal piece of déjà vu: this was the room she had slept in right through her childhood. It was more or less identical to the room she had left more than half a lifetime ago and it looked as if her mother had deliberately set out to keep it that way. Facing her on the wall was the deep shelf crammed with costume dolls from every country in the world. She'd never really collected them, but every birthday and most Christmases, her mother or an aunt would give her another blank-faced doll dressed in intricate home-made, hand-stitched costumes. They were always too delicate, too "special" to be played with and Stephanie quickly grew to loathe the dolls. Below them were two shelves of books and, even in the gloom, she knew she would find *Little Women, Anne of Green Gables, The Adventures of Tom Sawyer* and *Dr Seuss,* alongside about three generations of ink-splotched schoolbooks. In the corner, looking as scary as she remembered it, was the rocking horse that her grandfather had hand-carved from a solid piece of elm. He had then lovingly painted the horse and Stephanie knew if she climbed out of bed and examined its belly, she would see her own name and a date – she thought it might be September 1979 – scratched into the wood. The intricate and ornate doll's house was gone, given away to one of her nieces, but that – and the absence of the posters that had once adorned the walls – was the only difference.

Stephanie swung her legs out of bed. The floorboards were warm and smooth beneath her bare feet. Tugging the quilt off the bed, she padded over to the window, and rubbed her hand on the glass to peer out into the night. It was snowing: huge silent flakes that wiped away all hard edges and blanketed the world in silence.

She wondered – fleetingly – what it must be like in Ireland.

Pulling the quilt tighter around her shoulders, she wandered out onto the landing. She needed some water. She'd had a headache and stomach cramps ever since she'd encountered Kathy Walker, and although the cramps had eased, the headache had never quite gone away. She could feel it pulsing now, throbbing dully behind her eyes.

Consequences

The house lights were still on, but turned to dim, in case any of her nephews or nieces needed to go the bathroom in the middle of the night. All her family were home for Christmas: her four brothers, Billy, Little Matt, Jim and Chris, and her two sisters, CJ and Joan. With the exception of herself and Joan, everyone had arrived with partners and Billy, Little Matt and Chris had brought their children.

She reckoned that tomorrow – *no, today, Christmas Day* – was going to be that special nightmare that is a family Christmas.

She wandered downstairs, feeling suddenly, incredibly guilty. In that instant she became the six-year-old girl sneaking downstairs in the middle of the night to see if Santa Claus had come. She remembered being devastated when she discovered that he had not. She paused at the door to the sitting room and looked in. The only light came from the fat wax candle burning in the window and the glowing red and grey ash from the fire, with the occasional spark spiralling upwards. In the gloom, it looked magical. She was glad circumstances had forced her to come home. While her mother was unchanged and unchanging, her father was definitely aging and with that thought came the realisation that time was slipping by and every Christmas could be their last one.

The door to her father's study was partially open and she peered inside. It was a room she'd always loved. As a very young girl, one of her earliest memories was of standing at the doorway, staring into the dark cavern of the room, awed by the books which lined every wall, from floor to ceiling. The room was dominated by a spectacularly ugly slab of a desk, which had also been carved by the same Grandfather Burroughs who had carved the rocking horse. Behind the desk stood her father's high-backed leather armchair. The red leather was cracked in places now, some of the studs were missing and the two arms were polished smooth by years of use. The room remained unchanged. But whereas the desk had once held an old, battered Smith-Corona, now a sleek Sony Vaio computer, complete with a flat screen, sat in its place. The computer was still on – a spectacularly lifelike aquarium screensaver was active, tropical fish swimming lazily through coral reefs.

On impulse, Stephanie slipped into the room and closed the door behind her. She hadn't had a chance to check her email for hours and, although she very much doubted she'd have anything other than Christmas messages, she decided she'd grab the opportunity just in case anything important had come in.

And was that the only reason? Ignoring the thought, she curled up in her father's leather chair, tucked her feet under her body, and settled the quilt around her. Then she tapped the space bar, and the screensaver dissolved.

She quickly logged into her company mail though the mail server. There were half a dozen virtual Christmas cards sent by people too lazy to send the real thing, and a couple of "*see-you-in-the-new-year*" emails from colleagues.

She then logged into her personal mail. There were fifty-two messages.

The spam filters had caught most – but not all – of the special offers, the free money, the Viagra substitutes and the genuine Rolex watches. Stephanie scrolled down the screen, quickly deleting the remaining ones without opening them, then rolled on to the next screen.

New email from robert.walker@RandKProductions.com.

Stephanie was unsurprised.

Sitting in the chair, she stared at the email for a long time. There was no subject, and it had been sent at 8.15 a.m., but that was local time, Irish time. Stephanie glanced at the clock. About fifteen minutes ago.

She could delete it. It would be so easy. Just highlight it. Click delete and it would be gone. She clicked once on the email, and then she rested her hand on the keyboard, index finger brushing the delete key.

There was nothing Robert could say to her, nothing she wanted to hear from him . . .

But she was also curious. What had happened when he and Kathy got home? Had they argued, reconciled . . . how had that terrible Christmas Eve finished?

She hit Enter, and the email opened.

Dear Stephanie,

I don't know what's happened to you. I am desperately worried. I've tried calling you at the house and on your mobile, but there's no response. You've just disappeared.

Please get in touch with me. Let me know you're OK.

I even went over to the house earlier this morning. I let myself in. I'm concerned there's no sign of you and yet I know you haven't gone away. I saw from the wardrobes that all your clothes are still there.

I am really concerned that something has happened or that you've done something.

I am at my wits' end.

I have no idea how to contact your friend Sally, and I realise I don't know any of your other friends. If I don't get in touch with you soon, I might try and contact Charles Flintoff. I'm half thinking I should contact the police and report you as missing.

If you get this, then please, please, please contact me.

I love you.

Robert

"Oh shit!"

Stephanie's first reaction was one of anger – how dare he attempt to contact her, how dare he invade her home in the middle of the night, how dare he rummage through her wardrobes, how dare he even think about contacting Charles Flintoff, her boss! And how dare he say that he loved her!

There was a tightness in her chest, and she could feel her heart pounding hard enough to make her chest shake. Her stomach clenched and boiled and, for a moment, she thought she was going to throw up. She drew in a deep shuddering breath.

Why couldn't he just accept that they were finished? That their affair was over?

When she had stood at her door and watched Robert and Kathy climb into their cars earlier, she had never expected to see either of them again, and certainly never expected Robert to communicate with her again.

Obviously, she'd been wrong.

Somewhere at the back of her mind, an alarm bell was ringing furiously. Barely a few hours after they had split up, Robert had attempted to contact her, and now she'd discovered that he'd been in her home – why had she given him that key?

A sudden smile curled the corners of her lips.

It was brought on by the thought of Robert desperately attempting to get in touch, failing, then visiting the house to find it virtually abandoned. All her clothes, her shoes, even her computer were still there. He'd no idea where she was: and he obviously imagined the worst. Did he think – was he arrogant enough to believe – that she'd been so upset by the course of events that she'd done something stupid like thrown herself into the Liffey? She realised – not for the first time either – that he didn't really know her at all.

She read through the email again and the smile faded. The last thing she needed was for Robert to talk to her boss or to the police.

She'd have to talk to him.

A sudden thought struck her and she checked the time of the message again. He'd sent it just over fifteen minutes ago; maybe he was still online. Stephanie's father subscribed to America OnLine and every AOL member got a program called AIM – an instant messenger program, which allowed people to have real-time online conversations with one another. The last time she'd travelled to Europe on business, she'd ended up in Latvia. Mobile phone reception was patchy at best and landline calls were equally poor quality, but she had kept in touch with Robert using the AIM program.

Stephanie found the distinctive yellow walking-man icon at the bottom of the screen and brought it up. She logged in with her name and password and waited while her personal contacts were loaded into the address book. She knew the chances of finding Robert logged in on Christmas morning were probably slim indeed . . .

Online: robertwalker.

Stephanie moved her mouse over the name, but didn't click on it.

Online for 35 minutes.

Well that, if nothing else, told her something about the state of affairs in the Walker household. She grinned at the unfortunate phrase. What was he doing on his computer so early on Christmas morning?

Stephanie double-clicked on the name and the message box popped up. It was divided into two halves: outgoing messages were written in the bottom half, while the response appeared in the top half of the screen. She hesitated, looking at her name glowing in red on the white screen: *stephanieburroughs*, then her fingers moved lightly across the keyboard, four characters:

Yes?

Almost instantly, she could see a note appear on the bottom of the screen: *robertwalker is writing*. A moment later, Robert's text appeared on her screen.

Thank God. Are you all right? I was worried sick.

I'm fine.

But where are you?

I'm fine.

Are you not going to tell me where you are?

No.

Tell me you're all right?

I'm fine.

Stephanie. Please talk to me. We have a lot to talk about.

We've nothing to talk about. I want my key back. Don't go near the house again. Stay away from my boss. I don't want to see you again.

It doesn't have to be this way.

This is the way it is.

Please. I need to talk to you. I have to talk to you. About today. About the future.

We've no future together. Go back to your wife, Robert Walker.

Stephanie hit the button which signed her out of AIM. She knew that Robert would get a message on the other end, saying that *stephanieburroughs* had signed off. Jesus, the arrogance of him! The sheer breathtaking arrogance.

"Everything OK, love?"

Stephanie jumped. She looked up to find her father

standing in the door. She wondered how long he'd been standing there.

"I'm sorry, Dad. I couldn't sleep. I was just checking my email."

"Anything important?

"Just spam."

CHAPTER 7

"I'm fine. Honestly, I'm fine."

Stephanie Burroughs was sitting up in bed, her hands wrapped around a bowl of steaming soup.

"You don't look fine." Toni Burroughs sat on the edge of the bed and regarded her daughter carefully. "You look worn and the rings beneath your eyes are so black they look like bruises."

"Well, I'm glad you gilded that lily, Mom."

"You know me; I say it like I see it. Keeps life simpler that way." She watched Stephanie take a sip from the bowl of soup.

"I though it would be chicken soup," Stephanie said. Her mother's chicken soup was one of the great abiding memories of her childhood. Every illness from measles to mumps, every cut, graze and toothache received the chicken-soup treatment. It usually worked too.

"I'd no chicken in the house, so I thought I'd make it out of turkey instead. Seasonal chicken soup."

"Tastes great."

"Bit too salty," Toni said dismissively. "How are you feeling?"

"I'm fine."

"Billy told me you fainted, went right out cold."

"I did not. I was sitting down on the porch, having a cup of coffee after breakfast. The kids were going mad opening their presents, so I thought I'd sit outside for a bit of peace. Billy came out to have a cigarette. I think it might have been the smell of the cigarette that made me feel a bit woozy. That, plus all the travel yesterday and the fact that I was up at 3.30 this morning."

"Your father told me you'd had tea with him earlier. He said he'd heard a noise downstairs. He thought it might have been one of the children sneaking down – remember the year you did that! – but instead he found you in his office."

"I was checking my email."

But Stephanie knew she probably had fainted earlier. There was a little slice of time she couldn't account for: one minute, she was sitting on the porch looking at the winter snowscape that was the garden, and the next, she was staring up into her brother's broad, ugly face, a cigarette dangling from his lips, his dark eyes pinched with concern. He had swept her up into his arms, and carried her upstairs into her bedroom. Moments later, her sisters, CJ and Joan, had appeared, and helped her into bed. Toni Burroughs stepped into the room moments after they left, carrying a tray with a deep bowl of soup and some crackers on the side.

"I worked out earlier that I've had about three hours' sleep in the past twenty-four hours," Stephanie said, "and most of that was on the plane. And I'm just a little run down, I guess."

Toni reached out and pressed the flat of her hand on her daughter's forehead. "You're running hot."

"I'm drinking this soup, Mom," Stephanie reminded her.

"Are you pregnant, Stephanie?"

The question took her completely by surprise. Eyes and mouth opened wide and she spilled some of the soup onto the tray. "Mom! What a question!"

Toni raised her eyebrows and tilted her head to one side. "Are you?" she persisted.

"No, I'm not. Besides, how can I be pregnant if I'm a lesbian?" It gave her some pleasure to see a touch of colour appear on her mother's cheeks.

"Well, I hear of les . . . of gay couples having children every week."

Stephanie put the bowl down on the tray, then moved the tray off to one side. She reached over to take her mother's hands in hers. Her hands were tiny, the joints beginning to knot and swell with arthritis, and each finger was bedecked with a ring. Gold rings on her left hand, silver on her right; it was her only eccentricity. Squeezing her mother's fingers gently for emphasis,

Stephanie said, "Mom, I'm not a lesbian, and I'm not pregnant. I'm just exhausted. That's all. Now go and enjoy your Christmas Day with your children and grandchildren. Let me get a little rest and I'll join you shortly."

Toni Burroughs got up and fussed around the bed, smoothing down the coverlet. "I believe you," she said finally.

"Good. I'm glad."

"About not being les . . . gay."

"Mom!" Stephanie said, then smiled when she saw her mother's rare grin.

"Are you sure there's nothing else I can get you?"

"Nothing, Mom," she said and didn't add: except a little peace and quiet.

"I'll close the curtains," Toni said, loosening the curtain ties and pulling the heavy drapes across the window, effectively plunging the room into darkness.

"Maybe that's what I should have done last night," Stephanie said, watching her, suddenly a child again lying in bed, watching her mother close the curtains every night, before wishing her good dreams.

"Probably."

"I think it was the glare of the snow that woke me. We don't get much snow in Ireland." She pushed the tray away. "Thanks Mom, but I'm not going to be able to finish this. I feel a little queasy."

Toni nodded. She took the tray with the barely tasted soup and leaned in to kiss her daughter on the forehead, the movement straight out of Stephanie's childhood. "Get some rest. This is probably the best place for you," she said, then added, "Having all the grandchildren together was probably not a great idea."

The door clicked shut and Stephanie heard her mother's light footsteps move along the hall and then the squeak on the third stair as she went down. She lay in the gloom, staring at the ceiling. As her eyes adjusted, the room began to reveal itself once more, but now the shadows were deeper and what had once been comforting and familiar now seemed strange and just a little off kilter. Jet-lag – that's all she was feeling: that horrible malaise that was a combination of the worst hangover and leaden exhaustion. A few hours' sleep and she'd be fine.

Of course, she wasn't pregnant. The very thought of it was ridiculous.

Or was it?

Stephanie lay back in the bed and stared at the ceiling, trying to visualise a calendar in her head. Her periods had always been irregular, anything from twenty-five to thirty-two days, and some months were heavier than others. She'd had her last period . . . she frowned, trying to remember.

Oh, it was ridiculous to even think about it.

But once the idea had entered her mind, it was impossible to dismiss. When had she had her last period? She'd left her diary at home in Ireland, but it had to have been some time in November, late in November . . . no, it was earlier, because – she remembered now – it had arrived just before the office Christmas party had taken place. And that had been held on Friday, 15th November.

Which meant . . . which meant that she was anywhere between eight and ten days late.

She slowly shook her head from side to side. She couldn't be pregnant. She and Robert were always careful. Except that the truth, the bitter spiteful truth, was that they weren't always careful, she knew that. In the beginning, when they started making love regularly, Robert had suggested that she go on the pill. She refused. Her agency had just finished working on an awareness campaign about the various dangers of the contraceptive pill, and Stephanie had decided that if she was eating right, not smoking and had given up sugar, then there was no way she was introducing the contraceptive pill into her system. Robert argued with her, reminding her just how safe and successful it was for the vast majority of people.

Stephanie advised him that she was not the vast majority of people, and if she had given up beef because of the tiniest percentage chance that the meat was infected with BSE, then she was equally giving up the pill if there was the slightest chance that it could have any adverse effects on her system.

Looking back on it now, she realised that it had probably been their first real argument. It was only later, much later, that she realised he was being selfish.

Reluctantly and with a lot of griping, Robert had

gone out and bought his first box of condoms in nearly twenty years. And in the beginning, she had been very conscientious about his using them. But as time had gone by, he'd started only using them on those occasions when it was "unsafe". Stephanie tried to remember the last time they'd had sex . . . it was last Friday, in his office. They'd used no protection then. And she remembered thinking that it was safe because she knew her period was due. The time before that had been . . . it had been in her apartment, maybe a week previously. Stephanie frowned. It was a Saturday evening. They'd been to the cinema, had some sushi in Yamamori's in George's Street, then came back to her house. She'd run a bath . . . and again they'd made love with no protection. The box of condoms was empty and by that time they were in the throes of passion and the thought of getting dressed and heading out to a pharmacy or supermarket was unthinkable.

Now her heart was pounding so hard her entire body was shaking with the rhythm and she wrapped her arms across her chest, almost as if she were holding herself together. She could feel her heart thumping beneath her right palm and, almost unconsciously, her hand moved down to rest on her almost flat stomach. Her breathing was shallow and her skin felt clammy and she felt a bead of sweat gather in her hairline and trickle around to curl by her ear.

Pregnant.

Maybe.

Possibly.

But unlikely.

She tried to think of anything that might account for her late period. There were any number of factors: there was the pressure of her affair – she'd known for the past couple of weeks that it was coming to a head and that, coupled with the intense pressure at work to get everything finished for Christmas, certainly hadn't helped. She'd been doing a lot of travelling – usually day trips in and out of London, Paris, Berlin and Rome, and she knew that air-flight played havoc with regular periods. Diet maybe? She'd gone on the GI Diet – could that have affected her system and knocked her cycle out of kilter?

She felt queasy again, and was it her imagination or did her breasts feel especially heavy and tender? And wasn't that supposed to be a sign?

Oh, dear God. What if she was pregnant?

She doubted it, deep in her heart and soul she doubted it very much. She was thirty-five years of age; she knew her body, knew its rhythms and cycles. Her breasts often became tender just before her period. She was sure what she was feeling now was the onset of the delayed period coupled with extreme stress and exhaustion.

But what if it was not? What if she were pregnant?

Stephanie was tired, exhausted by jet-lag and travel and emotionally fragile and she suddenly found that there were tears on her face. Tears of confusion and self-pity, mingled with fear. The fantasy spiralled out of control. Say she was pregnant: what about her career, her home, her lifestyle? She'd have to either give up the job, or take maternity leave, probably have to sell the house and her lifestyle would alter irrevocably. What was she going to do?

And what would Robert think?

That was the sudden thought that brought her bolt upright in the bed. Would he have gone back to his wife so willingly if he knew she was pregnant with his child? Would she have allowed him – even pushed him away – if she had even suspected that she was pregnant?

What would Kathy think? There were two children in the Walker marriage, a boy of seventeen and a fifteen-year-old girl. Stephanie wondered if Kathy had ever wanted more. How would she feel if she knew her husband had fathered a child with his mistress?

Would she tell Robert, she wondered, and the answer was immediate and affirmative. Of course, she would: if she was pregnant, then she wasn't going to do it alone. Robert had got her into this situation. He could support her now. If she was pregnant with Robert's child, she was going to make sure he knew about it and took financial care of the baby.

So much for trying to cut all ties with him, she thought ruefully.

But before she made any decisions, she needed some advice. Stephanie glanced at the clock. Just after 10.00 a.m. on the East Coast, which meant it was after 3.00 p.m. in Ireland.

CHAPTER 8

"Happy Christmas!" The phone was answered with a breezy chirpiness that immediately lifted Stephanie's spirits.

"That sounds like the voice of someone who got engaged last night," she said quietly.

"Stephanie! My God, Stephanie! Is that you?" Sally Wilson's voice rose to a high-pitched squeal.

Holding the phone a little away from her ear, Stephanie said, "Of course, it's me. Well, tell me. Did Dave propose?"

"Of course, he did, the big lummox! Got down on one knee and everything." There was a clinking sound on the other end of the phone. "What you are hearing is the sound of a solitaire in surprisingly good taste tapping the handset. Plus, it's a genuine diamond too, not glass or zirconium. We're officially engaged, and we decided not to have a long engagement, so we're talking about a provisional date in September. And you will be my bridesmaid, of course."

Although she was lying flat in bed, Stephanie felt as if everything had lurched. If − and it was still a big, huge, monstrous if − she was pregnant, then the baby would be due in September.

"Sally, I am so happy for you. So thrilled."

"I knew you would be. So tell me, how are things with the family? You got there all right? But God, what a trip! You must be exhausted."

Stephanie had rehearsed her conversation with her friend. They would chat about Sally's engagement, talk about Christmas, talk about presents, and families and how mad and bad they were and then, and only then would Stephanie indicate her fears to Sally. That was the plan.

Instead she blurted out: "Sally, I think I'm pregnant." She was surprised to hear the crack in her voice. She was thirty-five years of age, and yet here she was, sounding as scared as any teenager.

There was a long silence on the other end of the line. In the background, Stephanie could hear the muted explosions and gunfire of a Christmas Day movie and over-loud and slightly drunken laughter. Abruptly the background noise went away as Sally stepped into another room and closed the door.

"Talk to me."

Stephanie cupped her hand over the mouthpiece and dropped her voice to little more than a whisper. "I think I may be pregnant," she repeated.

Consequences

"And I think I'm rich, but I'm not," Sally said immediately.

"I'm maybe ten days late . . ."

"I've often been ten days late."

"I know. Me too. Plus, I'm feeling very queasy."

"That could be the stress of it all," Sally said reasonably.

"I know. I thought of that. Or it could be my mother's cooking. But there's no sign of anything on the way. Nothing. My breasts are heavy and sore and I sort of fainted this morning."

"What! Sort of fainted! What does that mean?"

"Just like I said. I was sitting outside on the porch having a cup of coffee and then next thing I know my brother is carrying me in. My sisters put me to bed. Plus, my mother's just asked me straight out."

Stephanie could hear Sally draw in a deep breath. "She *asked* if you were pregnant?"

"Straight out."

"Mothers always know," Sally said glumly. "My mother could tell when my sister Rosie was pregnant. And that was usually weeks before Rosie herself knew. What do you think? Is there any chance that you could be?"

"I've been thinking about it. Yes, there's a chance."

"Were you not taking precautions?"

"Most of the time, but not all the time and not for the last two times."

"Oh, Stephanie! Remind me just how old you are?"

"I know, but in the throes of passion . . ."

71

"Well, the throes of passion may very well have thrown you a curveball. How do you feel about the prospect of being a mother?"

Stephanie licked suddenly dry lips. A mother. Sally would make a great mother; Joan her youngest sister would make a great mom, but no, not her. Not now. In a couple of years' time maybe, when she'd a little more money saved, a bit of the mortgage paid off and was further up the corporate ladder. The last time she and Robert had talked about children, she'd suggested in about two years' time . . .

"I'm scared," she admitted finally in a whisper. "And there are a lot of other emotions churning around, and I don't know how to face them, let alone deal with them. But I'm scared, Sally. What am I going to do?"

"First you're going to confirm that you are actually pregnant. You need to get a kit. Any good chemist's will have them. But you're probably not going to find one open today, are you, even in 24-hour-shopping America?"

"Probably not. What if I am, what do I do? Do I tell Robert? Or do I leave him out of the picture completely?"

"You absolutely involve him! You tell him. You also tell him that you expect him to pay. Get some legal papers drawn up and, if he resists, slap a paternity suit on him."

"You're right, you're right of course. When should I tell him, do you think?"

Consequences

Stephanie could almost feel Sally smile down the phone. "Well, if it was me, I'd be on the phone to him right now, ruining his Christmas dinner. He's certainly ruined yours."

It was the answer Stephanie had been looking for.

CHAPTER 9

"Hello?" A man's voice, sounding slightly puzzled.

The same explosion and gunfire sound echoed tinnily in the background and Stephanie knew that Robert Walker was watching the same movie as Sally and Dave.

"Hello?" he repeated.

"You may want to move away from the TV and find someplace private where you can talk," Stephanie said softly. She was sitting up in bed, her chin propped on her knees, her right arm wrapped around her legs, while she pressed the old-fashioned chunky portable phone to her ear.

The transatlantic line hissed and popped, but she could clearly hear Robert Walker swallow. She smiled. She could imagine him sitting at home, maybe surrounded by his wife, children and relatives.

"Sure . . . sure," he said with forced joviality. "And a

happy Christmas to you too. Let me just step out of the room away from the TV . . ."

She heard the phone move away from his lips, and his voice, muffled, as he made an excuse to someone in the background. She heard the two words "Christmas . . . dinner," and was unable to resist a grin. Sally had been right; she was about to ruin his appetite.

There was a click and then the ambient sound on the line changed as Robert swapped phones and his slightly fast, almost panicked breathing was now clearly audible.

"Are you OK?" he asked immediately.

"Yes . . . no . . . I don't know," she answered truthfully.

"I've been so concerned, and when I couldn't get hold of you, I didn't know what to think, and then earlier, when we were instant-messaging and you said you didn't want to see me again, I was devastated."

Stephanie took a moment before she responded. *He* was devastated. And yet he'd lost nothing. His affair with her had cost him nothing. Whereas the same affair had cost her so much more and, if she really was pregnant, it had altered her future irrevocably. There were a dozen responses she could have made – sad or sarcastic, bitter or angry, but in the end, she contented herself with the blunt statement, "I'm think I'm pregnant, Robert."

The silence that followed was so long that Stephanie was forced to interrupt it. "Nothing to say? No quick comment, no remark, no congratulations?"

"I . . . I . . . no, I don't know what to say."

"Well, think of something."

"How did this . . . I mean, when did this happen?"

"Who knows? We've made love a couple of times now without using protection."

"I said you should have gone on the pill."

Stephanie bit back the snap of anger and swallowed hard. This was not a time for scoring points. This was a time for decisions.

"Are you sure?" he asked. "Certain?"

"Reasonably," she lied. "I've just realised in the last few hours that my period is ten days late."

"Ten days isn't a lot, is it?" he said desperately.

"It's long enough."

"But you've done a test, haven't you? Confirmed it?"

"It's Christmas Day, Robert, just in case you've forgotten. Where am I going to get a pregnancy-testing kit today?"

She could hear him licking dry lips. "But you really think you could be pregnant?"

"Yes, I do."

There was a sound might have been either a sigh or a moan. "Have you decided what to do about it . . . about the baby?"

"No. But you're the father. I wanted to talk to you first. Make some joint decisions. Real decisions."

"Yes, yes, yes, of course. Look, can we meet?. Not today obviously . . ."

No, not today because he was having a happy Christmas family get-together and would not be able to fabricate an excuse to get out of the house.

"But tomorrow. Can we meet tomorrow? Where are you?"

Stephanie allowed herself a smile. "Tomorrow might be a little difficult for me . . ."

"I really need to see you to talk to you," Robert protested. "I can meet you. Anywhere," he added.

"Anywhere?"

"I'll go anywhere," he insisted.

"Fine then. I'm at my parents' house."

There was a pause. "In Long Island?"

"Yes."

"What are you doing there?"

"Having a family Christmas," she said, unable to keep the touch of bitterness out of her voice. "Robert," she hissed, "what did you expect me to do? Sit around in an empty house on Christmas Day reminding myself just how stupid I'd been?"

"Look, about yesterday –"

"Not now," she snapped. "I don't want to talk about that. I want to talk about our child." Something shifted and twisted inside Stephanie at the phrase "*our child*" and she was forced to take a deep breath. "You know, I had no intention of ever seeing you again, of ever having anything to do with you. But all that's changed now. If I am pregnant, I have to see you."

"Yes, yes, of course, you must." There was another pause, then she heard him draw in a deep shuddering breath. "How sure? I mean how certain are you that you're pregnant?" She could hear the desperation in his voice, the panic bubbling to the surface.

"You've asked me that before and I'll give you the same answer: reasonably sure."

"When will you know for certain?"

"Tomorrow," she said, wondering if the local Target or Wal-Mart would be open tomorrow and guessing that they would.

"When are you coming home?" he asked.

"I don't know. I'd no plans to come back until the New Year, but I think this changes everything. I'll see if I can get back before the weekend. I'll check flights later."

"Let me know what flight you're coming in on. I'll pick you up. We can talk. Make decisions. See what you want to do with the baby."

Stephanie didn't like the way the tone of the conversation had shifted. "Robert, it's not what *I* want to do – this is *our* baby. It is all about what *we* want to do."

"Well, let's talk about options . . ."

Stephanie frowned, feeling something sour at the back of her throat. "What do you mean by options?"

Something in Stephanie's tone must have alerted Robert, because he immediately changed tack. "I mean what's best for you and the baby. That sort of thing." There was a pause, then he said, "Look, I've got to go. It's great to hear from you, and good to know that you're OK." He attempted a laugh, which sounded hollow, "Though how you got to New York on Christmas Eve, I'll never know. What were you thinking?"

"I wasn't. Bit like when I began my affair with you, Robert. I simply wasn't thinking of the consequences."

She hung up, dropped the phone on the bed and flopped back on the pillows. Then she smiled. There was a certain grim satisfaction in ruining his Christmas. She'd dearly love to be a fly on the wall right about now.

Stephanie's practical nature kicked in. Maybe she was pregnant, maybe not: the first priority was to confirm that. If she was, then she needed to get back to Ireland to confront Robert and decide what they were going to do. There was never any question in her mind that she was going to have the baby. An abortion was out of the question. Even if she had not been born and raised in a strictly Catholic household, she had seen the latest 3D prenatal scans and it was obvious to her that life began almost immediately. Nominally she was Catholic, though well lapsed, and she was not going to be responsible for the death of any living being. However, there had been that moment during her conversation with Robert when she thought he was going to suggest it . . .

There was the problem with her job. If she had a first love, it was her career. How would having a child impact on that? It would certainly restrict her free time and opportunities for promotion, that was for sure. Her particular role entailed a lot of travel; she'd have to cut down on that and she'd have to find a good nanny.

She hadn't really thought about children before until Robert had proposed to her on Saturday. My God, was it four days ago? It felt like a lifetime. Some of her female colleagues had chosen to raise a child without the encumbrance of a man, and Stephanie had nothing but admiration for them. But, she knew she would never consider having a child unless she had a partner, someone to share the responsibility . . . and the burden.

Stephanie suddenly took a deep breath, held it for a count of twenty, then slowly exhaled. My God, but she was getting way ahead of herself. Less than half an hour ago, the thought hadn't even crossed her mind, now she was thinking about managing a child and a career.

First things first: she had to find out if she was pregnant.

CHAPTER 10

Christmas dinner in the Burroughs household finished with their peculiar version of grace: it was said after the meal.

"Dear Lord, for all that we have received and eaten at Your table . . ." Matt intoned.

Stephanie, sitting halfway down the long table, had once asked her father why they didn't say grace before a meal like everyone else. Matt had told her that he always thought that giving thanks for something you had not yet received was somehow presumptuous, whereas thanking them afterwards for their gift was perfectly acceptable.

Sitting around the Christmas table, along with her four brothers and two sisters – all of whom, with the exception of Joan and herself were there with partners – was a trial. The children were eating in the kitchen, but they were in and out of the dining-room every five minutes, or one or other of the parents kept hopping up to check on a particularly loud scream or bang from the other room. Stephanie came roughly in the middle of the Burroughs clan, but there was only a twelve-year difference between Billy, the eldest and Joan, the youngest. The family remained remarkably close, with the exception of Stephanie who had left home early and rarely returned. She felt slightly out of place – almost a stranger – sitting here surrounded by her family. But better, infinitely better, than sitting at home in Dublin in an empty lonely house, she reminded herself.

After dinner, Stephanie and Joan found themselves in the kitchen, loading the dishwasher. The four boys and CJ, who'd always been a tomboy, were ferrying the dirty dishes in from the dining-room, while Toni and Matt played with the grandchildren. The kitchen still smelled wonderful – rich and warm with the aromas of meat and spices, herbs and liquors.

"God, I feel I'm about ten again," Stephanie said. She breathed deeply. "These Christmas smells are *the* defining scents of my childhood."

"Mine was always the odour of tree sap," Joan said. "Remember when Dad would top the trees in the back yard and the boys would drag the cut wood across the garden?"

"And the smell of burning leaves," Stephanie supplied.

"The smell of autumn." Joan looked out through the kitchen window. Most of the trees were long gone now.

They'd simply grown too large for Matt to handle. Five years ago, the four boys had come up late in the summer with their chainsaws and cut down the larger ones. They'd then sliced the trunks into fire-sized pieces and the dry shed beside the double garage was still packed out with the circular and semi-circular sections. There was probably enough wood to last for another three years at least.

"I'm thinking I might move back up here permanently," Joan said suddenly.

"Have you spoken to Eddie?"

"I had CJ talk to him for me. Told him where I was."

"Guess he had a lonely Christmas without you," Stephanie suggested, carefully stacking side-plates in the dishwasher.

"I missed him too. But he lied to me, Stef. And once a man starts lying to you – it's over. And when it's over, it's over."

"Maybe. Maybe not. Sometimes circumstances throw you right back at someone you've left," she said grimly. She looked up and caught her sister looking quizzically at her. "Did you ask Eddie why he lied to you in the first place?" she asked quickly, trying to forestall an inevitable question.

"He was ashamed that he'd lost his job and didn't want to worry me."

"That's reasonable."

Joan blinked in surprise. "You're taking his side."

"Not taking any side, just commenting. He was stupid; he lost his job. But he didn't want to worry you, so he got up every morning – when he could have lain in bed – got dressed and went out and spent the day doing what . . .?"

"Walking the streets. Looking for a job, he said."

"So he spent the day walking the street, looking for a job, because he loved you."

"And I forgave him that," Joan protested. "When I eventually discovered the truth, we had a blazing row . . . well, I had a blazing row and he just listened and finally admitted that he'd lost his job because they were laying crew off. But that was another lie. That was the lie I discovered yesterday. He was sacked because he was claiming for overtime he hadn't done."

"And you've never done that?" Stephanie wondered. "You've never padded an invoice, claimed for an extra hour or slipped in a couple of additional expenses?" Before her sister could answer, she continued quickly, "And was he keeping this extra money for himself?"

"No, it went into the joint account with everything else." Joan bent back to the dishwasher and loaded knives and forks into their little container. "I see what you mean. I never thought of it that way. Everyone here's telling me to ditch him."

"I'm not telling you to do anything. I'm just giving you a different perspective."

"You were always so wise," Joan said. "Gosh, I look around this family and wonder how we've turned out. Mom and Dad have been married forever, but look . . . there's Bill now on to his third wife, Little Matt and that strange older woman – she smells, you know that? Jim who looks like he'll never marry but still has two children by two different women, and turns up today with his fiancée, someone we've never met before – Chris with his Thai wife whose name I can't even pronounce – and CJ who can't quite decide whether she likes men or women, though thank God she brought a man with her today. At least I think it's a man," she added, then fell silent as the very feminine-looking male appeared in the doorway at that moment, carrying the last of the plates. He nodded, smiled and left the kitchen without saying a word. "That leaves just you and me," Joan continued. "And I'm married to a man who lies to me . . ."

"Because he loves you and didn't want to upset you."

"And there's you. Well, thank God, at least one of us is not a complete screw-up. The man who gets you is going to be so lucky."

"Oh yeah, I'm a real prize," Stephanie murmured.

Joan looked across the stacks of crockery at her older sister. "Do you think I should give him another chance?"

"Yes," Stephanie said without hesitation. "I think a man who loves you enough to lie to protect you isn't all bad." But what about a man who was having an affair and lying to his wife: was he doing that to protect her too, and did that suggest that he loved her? Stephanie shied away from the thought, unable or unwilling to follow it to its logical conclusion.

Joan leaned over and kissed Stephanie quickly on the cheek. "I'm glad you came home. If you weren't here,

I'd have kicked him out. I'll give him a second chance."

"Just tell him: no more lying."

A heavy woollen blanket settled over Stephanie's shoulders, making her jump. She was sitting on the back step, staring out across the rolling snow-white fields. She looked up to find her father standing beside her. He was tamping tobacco into his battered pipe. Fragments of the brown leaf spiralled down to settle on the white snow, looking like tiny questions marks.

"This was always your favourite place when you were a child," Matt Burroughs said. "Whenever you were in trouble, I always knew where to find you." He lowered himself gently to the step beside his daughter. She lifted the blanket off her shoulders and draped it around his too, sharing it. The two sat in silence while Matt packed the bowl of his pipe, but they both knew he wouldn't light it in her presence. "Are you in trouble now?" he asked softly.

Stephanie allowed her eyes to drift. There was the tree where the old tyre had hung, over there was the tumbledown barn where they'd played when the weather was poor, and if she followed the narrow path through the trees, it would end up at the tiny pool where she'd first learned to swim. This was a place of innocence, a place where she'd always been happy. And with the thought came the realisation that she wasn't happy now, and she wondered if she would ever be happy again.

"I hope you won't be disappointed in me, Dad," she whispered, feeling like a teen again, "but I think I'm pregnant."

Matt put the unlit pipe between his lips and nodded slightly.

"Did Mom tell you?"

"Your mother has many wonderful gifts, but reticence is not one of them," he murmured, "and don't you dare tell her I said so." He glanced sidelong at his daughter. "You're thirty-five now, but to me you will always be that seven-year-old girl running wild through this garden, chasing the skunk just to make it spray, because you were one of the few people in the world who loved the smell. You will be forever ten, coming to me with the injured cardinal cupped in your hand. I will always remember you in your Communion dress, and your prom dress and your graduation gown. I will never be disappointed in you. You've always made me proud, Stephanie. Always."

Stephanie rested her head on her father's shoulder and remained silent, unwilling to trust herself to speak.

"Do you want to tell me about it?"

Stephanie drew in a deep lungful of the icy December air. "I'm not certain that I am pregnant, but there's a very good chance. The father's name is Robert Walker. He's five years older than me, and runs a small production company in Ireland. And he's married. With two children," she added.

"Still married?" Matt asked quietly.

"Still married."

"Ah."

"I know this goes against everything you've taught us and everything you believe in, Dad. But I fell in love with him. I allowed myself to fall in love with him, because he told me – and, in his defence, he genuinely believed it at the time – that his wife was no longer interested in him."

"But he didn't leave his wife?"

"No. No, he didn't," she sighed. "But last weekend I brought things to a head. Told him he had to choose." She shrugged. "He chose me. Told me he would leave his wife after Christmas, and that we would be together. There was about forty-eight hours, Dad, when I was never happier."

"Let me guess," Matt said, not looking at her, squinting out at the snow-capped field, now losing definition as they drifted into night. "The wife shows up?"

"Yes." She turned to look at her father. "How did you know?"

"Must have been something fairly dramatic that drove you out of Ireland on Christmas Eve. I cannot think of anything more dramatic than that."

"You're right, of course. She turned up yesterday. And then Robert turned up a little later."

Matt Burroughs's lips curled in a tight smile. "That must have been awkward."

"You have no idea. But I discovered a few things in the time between Kathy's arrival – that's his wife – and his. I discovered that she still loved him. And talking to her made me realise — really fully understand — what my future with Robert would be like. So I made him go back to his wife."

"And how did he feel about that?"

Stephanie blinked in surprise. "I don't know. I didn't ask him. I suppose I thought that since they both know there is a problem, surely they can work together to sort it out together — get some counselling or something."

"And now?"

"And now I don't know what to do. If I am pregnant, I'll need to keep in touch with Robert."

"Why?" Matt asked seriously.

"Because . . ." Stephanie began and then stopped. She'd no idea why. "It just seems right. For me, for him . . . and for the baby."

Matt nodded. Then he asked the question that Stephanie had been asking herself for months. "Does he love you?"

"I think so," she said eventually.

Matt stood up and fixed the blanket over his daughter's shoulders again. Then he leaned down and kissed the top of her head. "There are some questions which are like math problems. There should be no equivocation: only one answer — in the positive or the negative. So, I'll ask you again: does he love you?"

The twilight cast long shadows on the snow, turning the pristine whiteness to grey. The familiar lines of the back yard were disappearing into the gloom. High and clear in the cold air, she heard a child's voice, raised in delighted laughter, the sound so pure and innocent. When you were a child everything was so simple, so easy. You believed what people told you: Santa Claus and the Easter Bunny and the Tooth Fairy. And they were all lies. That was the ultimate betrayal of childhood. And was it any different for adults? When a man stood on the altar and promised, in front of witnesses, that he would love and honour the woman by his side for the rest of his days, everyone there realised that it was probably a lie.

So, last Saturday, when Robert had stood in the street and said, *"I love you. I want to be with you. To marry you. Will you marry me?"* had he been lying? She didn't think so.

She nodded firmly. "Yes, I believe he loves me."

"Then let me ask you the question another way," her father said. "Do you love him?"

Yesterday, she would have said no. Yesterday, she hated him, despised him. But that was yesterday. But the day before that the answer had been different, and today . . . well, she wasn't entirely sure how she felt about him today. "One of the reasons I let him go was because I loved him," she admitted slowly and deliberately. "I was angry with him because he went back to his wife so easily."

"But you told me you pushed him away."

"Dad, he didn't fight for me."

"Did you fight for him?" Matt asked, surprising her.

"No." Stephanie turned to look at her father. "I expected you to be angry with me. Angry because I'd been stupid enough to get pregnant, angry that I'd had a relationship with a married man."

"I'm not happy, Stephanie. I'll not lie to you. And who knows how I would have felt ten years, or even five years ago? But as you get older, you do come to realise some simple truths: love is the only thing worth fighting for." He turned and walked away, back towards the house. "Don't stay out too long – you'll catch a chill."

CHAPTER 11

Thursday, 26th December

There were four shelves of pregnancy-testing kits, all in neat discreet boxes, most of them with the word "accurate" built into the title, and most promising instant results. The large print said ninety-nine per cent accuracy, while the smaller print suggested that results might vary from person to person and to consult a doctor.

Stephanie walked up and down the shelves, picking up toothpaste and shampoo – which she didn't need – before she eventually grabbed the first box she had looked at, and walked towards the counter. The small convenience store was practically empty and she was bundled up in a heavy coat she'd borrowed from her sister CJ, so she knew she was unrecognisable, but she felt like a teenage girl buying a packet of condoms before the prom. On an abstract level she found her embarrassment almost amusing; where was the gutsy, ballsy businesswoman who ran multi-million-dollar advertising campaigns?

The Hispanic girl behind the register checked the toothpaste and shampoo through the scanner without even looking at her, but stopped when she came to the pregnancy-testing kit and turned it over in her hands. Stephanie noticed that each nail had a tiny glittering stone set into it. "Oh, this one is very good," she said. "I used it myself."

Stephanie felt herself begin to colour. "And is it accurate?" Her tongue felt too big in her mouth.

"I used it a week after I missed my period and it was able to tell me that I was pregnant."

"Oh. Good. Congratulations." Stephanie didn't think the girl could be older than seventeen, maybe younger, but it was hard to tell.

"Thank you. Little boy, called him Chavez after his poppa." The girl bagged the items, took her cash and made change in one smoothly practised movement. "Have a nice day," she said, smiling brightly.

"Thank you," Stephanie said as she walked away. She wondered if the girl was being sarcastic. Starting off the day with a pregnancy test was not her idea of having a nice day.

As soon as she sat into the car, she opened the box and pulled out the single sheet of instructions. They were fairly straightforward and she glanced back towards the shop, wondering if it had a restroom she could use, then shook her head at the absurdity of the thought: she didn't want to discover if she was pregnant in a convenience store's restroom. That wasn't a memory she wanted to take into her future. Turning the key in the ignition, she gently eased her father's Buick out onto the road. The snowplough had been through earlier, and the roads had been gritted, but she was still not entirely comfortable driving on the right-hand side of the road and she crept home, the needle hovering just under thirty. Although home was only a two-mile drive away, she felt that the journey was taking an eternity.

Option one: if she was pregnant, she would need to return to Ireland, meet with Robert, talk about the future. But, try as she might, she couldn't see beyond that step.

Option two: if she was not pregnant, then she would remain here over the New Year, enjoy her family and return to Ireland to start afresh. She would concentrate on her job, rebuild her boss Charles Flintoff's confidence in her. And ensure that she never saw Robert Walker again.

Stephanie Burroughs sat on the edge of the bath, the narrow strip held delicately in her hands, waiting for it to change colour. She was intensely conscious of the moment. She remembered reading somewhere that in one's life there were a very few life-changing moments – usually no more than five or six. She wondered if this qualified as one . . . or should it have been the moment she made love to Robert, which placed her in this position?

The house was quiet. As far as she knew, everyone had

gone out for a walk. She could hear floorboards crackling and settling, the water tank filling softly overhead, the hiss and thump as snow slid off the roof onto the ground outside. The bathroom was warm, smelling faintly of someone's mint shampoo and the edge of the bath felt hard and cold beneath her thighs.

If she was pregnant, she would go downstairs, get on her father's computer and book a flight – no matter how much it cost, no matter what route she had to take – and return to Ireland.

If she was not pregnant, she would borrow the heaviest coat she could find and borrow a pair of boots and run and kick her way through the snow. Then she would lie on her back in the snow, and move her arms and legs to create a snow angel.

The stick changed colour.

Stephanie looked at it for a long time, and abruptly exhaled. She hadn't realised she was holding her breath. Her one overriding emotion surprised her: relief. At least now she knew.

And then she went downstairs, logged onto her father's computer and booked a flight back to Dublin.

CHAPTER 12

FROM: stephanieburroughs@onlinemail.com
TO: robert.walker@RandKProductions.com.
SUBJECT: Returning to Ireland

Robert,

I have just booked some flights home. There are no direct flights into Dublin, so I'm coming in via Air France leaving Friday 27th (tomorrow), arriving Paris Saturday morning, then connecting with an Aer Lingus flight into Dublin, arriving around 1.30.

You offered to pick me up. Does that offer still stand?

If you cannot meet me on Saturday, then make time on Sunday. This is important.

Leave an email at this address. I can check it from the airport.

Stephanie.

CHAPTER 13

Friday, 27th December

Toni and Matt accompanied their daughter to the airport.

The weather had turned unseasonably warm and the pristine snow immediately melted to slush which made everything look dirty and soiled. The picture-postcard house turned shabby and ordinary once again, and the garden wonderland was revealed to be nothing more than a fenced-in square of seared and withered grass. The tree stumps which had looked wonderfully mysterious under their mounds of snow were once again exposed as ugly burned stumps. Stephanie sat in the back of the car and watched the muddy fields, some still with islands of snow surrounded by green earth and brown soil, fly past. She was glad to be leaving this place. Seeing it now – grim and faded, coated in slush, mud, shards of ice and dirty snow – brought back her original reasons for leaving this place. It was ugly and grim. Depressing.

She saw her mother's head turn and, even before the words were out of her mouth, Stephanie knew what she was going to say.

"Are you sure you have to go, Stephanie?"

"Yes, Mom."

"But you've barely got here."

"Well, I did say it was a flying visit. And we did get to spend Christmas Day together."

"Leave her be, Toni," Matt said.

Stephanie caught a glimpse of her father's eyes in the rear-view mirror. He was watching her closely: he alone of all the family knew the real reason she was returning to Ireland.

Her mother turned away to stare out to where the fields were giving way to houses. She surreptitiously – but very obviously – brushed tears from her cheeks. "And how are you feeling?" she asked, slightly emphasising the last word.

"I'm feeling fine, Mom." Stephanie had thought long and hard about telling her mother the truth about the test, but in the end decided to keep it a secret for the moment. No doubt her mother had already told the entire family that she suspected Stephanie might be pregnant. She knew that her sudden reappearance home for Christmas had already been one of the main topics of conversation over the holiday. She needed to get out of this environment, talk to Robert, make some decisions. Only then would she tell her mother, present her with the facts and the decisions.

"I wish you'd stay another couple of days," Toni

grumbled. "I was really looking forward to spending New Year together."

"Well, I've bought tickets, Mom," Stephanie said mildly, unwilling to argue.

"Could you change them?"

"The girl's going home, Toni," Matt said quietly.

"Her home is here."

"She's thirty-five now; she's lived away from us longer than she lived with us. Ireland's her home for the moment. But she knows she can always come back here. Always."

Stephanie saw her father's eyes in the rear-view mirror again, and she nodded. He was speaking to Toni, but talking to her.

"Maybe you'll come over in the summer," Stephanie suggested.

"Oh, where would we get the money?" Toni said instantly.

"I'd pay for the tickets."

"If we go over, we'll pay for them," Matt said firmly. "There are some really good deals into Ireland." His eyes moved to the mirror again. "You should be saving your dollars – euros," he amended. "Who knows what the future holds?"

Stephanie propped her chin on her fist and stared out at the approaching city. She had a very good idea what the future held.

Although she wanted her parents to simply drop her in

JFK, they insisted on parking the car and accompanying her. Security was tight, and the queue for the Air France desk stretched right through the concourse. Luckily, she'd treated herself to First Class tickets and had the guilty pleasure of walking the length of the queue and right up to the desk. She only had carry-on luggage and check-in took only a few minutes.

"We've a couple of hours," Toni said, looking at her watch. "Maybe we could get some coffee."

"I really feel I should go through," Stephanie said, nodding towards the check-in gates. "There's always a huge queue on the other side at the security gates."

"You should go though," Matt said. He turned and handed the car keys to his wife. "You go and sit in the car, and I'll walk Stephanie to the gates."

Toni blinked in surprise, unsure what was happening.

"You know you always get upset at the last minute, so say goodbye now, and then wait in the car for me. You don't want to upset Stephanie, now do you?"

Toni Burroughs gave her husband that look that indicated that a full explanation would be required later, but obediently reached up to hug her daughter. "Be careful and travel safe," she said. Liquid danced in her eyes, making them huge. "And phone often – reverse the charges if you have to. Just keep in touch."

"I will, Mom. I promise," Stephanie whispered, and kissed her mother's cheek. Holding her close now, she suddenly realised how frail she was and she had the sudden, irrational thought that this would be the last time she'd see her. And now there were tears in her eyes too. "I'll phone as soon as I get home."

Stephanie stood with her hand in her father's, while they both watched Toni make her way across the crowded concourse, where she was quickly swallowed up in the crowds. Then Matt turned to his daughter.

"I'm glad you're going back," he said, surprising her.

"I think it's the right thing," she nodded.

"Take your time. There's no need to make any hasty decisions."

"I know." She took a deep breath and looked around the airport. "But you know something, I want — I need — to have everything sorted out by next Wednesday."

"New Year's Day?"

"I want to start the new year with some sort of direction for my life. I just realised I've let things drift over the past couple of years. Even more so since I began my relationship with Robert." She smiled grimly. "This is a conversation I never imagined I'd be having with my dad."

"I've always loved your spirit, Stephanie. You remind me of myself when I was your age. You were brave enough to leave — first home, then New York, then America. You've never allowed anything to hold you back." Matt hugged his daughter close and kissed her forehead. "I've taught in college for more than thirty years now. I've acted as mentor and teacher, father-confessor and agony aunt for my students, both boys and girls, for most of that time. Nothing surprises me, even less shocks me. They may have thought I was helping them, but in truth, they were helping me too: helping me to understand myself. And what I have learned is that you have to face your problems — more is gained from acting than from ignoring the problem and standing still."

Stephanie nodded. "I stood still for the past eighteen months."

"Move on. Go forward. If you are pregnant, then you're moving forward with a baby. Accept that decision. Plan for it." He hugged his daughter again. "Now, you'd better go before your mother returns to see what's keeping me. And Stephanie, I want you to do something for me."

"Of course."

"I want you to be selfish. I want you to think about what's best for you. And for the baby."

Stephanie nodded.

"You've gone nowhere over the past eighteen months because you were thinking of this man, being considerate of his situation and the world he was in. Now, it's time for him to start thinking of your situation and the world you're in."

Stephanie nodded again. She knew there were tears on her face, but made no move to brush them off.

"I love you," Matt Burroughs said.

Then he kissed his daughter on the cheek, turned and walked away.

"Now, go and be selfish!" he called back.

CHAPTER 14

Saturday, 28th December

So how do you greet your ex-lover?

Especially when you are about to bring him life-altering news?

Stephanie Burroughs walked away from the plane, pulling her carry-on suitcase. On the short layover in Paris, she had bought some new make-up, then showered and changed in the First Class lounge at Charles de Gaulle. She had changed from her black polo-neck sweater into a cream silk blouse and accessorised with platinum earrings and a simple twisted-rope necklace, also in platinum. As usual, she wore no rings. When she estimated that the Air Lingus jet was about to enter Irish air space, she took her make-up bag into the toilets and spent fifteen minutes carefully making herself up, removing the dark bruises from beneath her eyes with concealer, adding a layer of the new lipstick which plumped up the lips, and massaging revitalising cream into the tiny lines which had appeared at the corners of her eyes and between her eyebrows. Finally, she dropped in some eye-drops to brighten and refresh her eyes, but the whites were still threaded with tiny broken veins and she could do nothing about those. When she was finished, she stepped back and looked at herself in the mirror: not bad, not too bad at all.

That's how you meet your ex-lover.

Stephanie strode out through the Arrival Gates at Dublin Airport and scanned the crowd. There had been no time to check her email in either New York or Paris, so she wasn't sure if he had responded.

There was no sign of Robert.

Stephanie kept walking, moving away from the throng pushing out from Arrivals. She stopped by a row of seats and fished out her mobile phone and turned it on, all the time scanning the crowd, looking for Robert.

Her mobile blipped, signifying it was active, and she hit 171 to check her messages.

You have eight new messages.

Stephanie cycled though them quickly. Seven of them were from Robert, all sent on Christmas Eve and early Christmas morning, each one more frantic than the last, all of them saying the same thing: wondering where she was, if she was OK and asking her to contact him. She deleted them without listening to them fully. The latest call was from Sally.

"Not sure when you're getting back but just wanted to leave a hello-and-welcome-home message. Hope you had a fab time. Love you."

Stephanie smiled. Sally could always be trusted to do the right thing. She was surprised she had not heard from Robert today. Unless, of course, he hadn't got the email. But that was highly unlikely. Her finger was poised over the speed-dial button on her mobile when she spotted the Vodafone booth directly in front of the Arrival doors. There was a bank of computers set up around the stand, with people coming and going constantly, obviously checking their email. She waited while an exhausted-looking Oriental student checked emails on an exotic-looking site, then she slipped into his seat the moment he vacated it. It took her a couple of moments to log into her online mail account. Maybe the message hadn't reached Robert and had bounced back . . .

There was no bounce back. Nor was there a message from Robert.

Stephanie carefully logged out of her mail account. She hated using public computers and was always vaguely aware that anyone could be capturing her passwords or that there could be a program running in the background, logging every key she pressed. She was always careful to keep nothing personal in her online account and never transacted any business out of it.

Tugging her bag, she headed towards the taxi rank.

Maybe her phone call to him on Wednesday had frightened him. That had certainly been the intention.

Maybe he now wanted nothing further to do with her. Funny, she'd thought he was a better man than that, but she'd been mistaken about him in other ways, no reason why she shouldn't be mistaken about that too.

Stephanie stepped out in the cold early-afternoon air. The December sky was cloudless, the palest of blues, and the watery sunshine shed no heat. There were no taxis standing at the rank, and she had just resigned herself to a long wait when a taxi pulled in. She flung open the back door and slid her single suitcase onto the seat, then climbed in alongside it.

"Perfect timing," she smiled.

"You were lucky, love – according to the radio, just about every other cab in the city is tied up."

She gave him the address and settled back in the seat.

"Someone let me down," she said.

Not for the first time either.

Even though she'd only been gone for a couple of days, Dublin looked different. Fresher, brighter, cleaner. Living here, it was easy to forget how prosperous the city was, and she'd read a report recently which said that Ireland was the best country in Europe to live in and Dublin one of the top cities. The roads were thronged with cars, but the cab moved quickly down the bus lane.

"Been home with the family for a few days?" the driver asked. He was an enormous man, his cheeks a startling confection of broken veins, but with the tiniest hands gripping the steering wheel.

"How can you tell?"

"One bag, which told me that you weren't shopping. Then I heard the slight American accent. But you gave the address like a Dub, so I knew you'd lived here."

"Right on all counts," she said.

"And you'd a good time?"

"Yes, I had," she said, and was surprised to discover that she really meant it. "It was good to see the folks again, and my brothers and sisters."

"Oh, I saw mine on Christmas Day. Once a year is enough for me. We've nothing in common now. As you get older, you tend to create a family around you, not necessarily a biological family."

"That's true." If she really was pregnant – and she needed to have it confirmed – who could she go to? She was surprised, and almost disappointed, when she realised just how few friends she did have in Ireland. Sally Wilson certainly, but beyond that . . .? There were colleagues, of course, but they were not friends. So if Robert had run scared from her, then she was going to have no one to rely on but herself. "Excuse me," she said, and lifted her phone out of the bag. "I've just got to make this call."

"You work away, love."

She hit the speed-dial for Robert's mobile number. The phone rang and rang before it was diverted to his answer service.

Robert Walker, R&K Productions. Leave a message, the time you called and a number and I will call you back. Have a good day.

"It's me. I'm back in Dublin. Maybe you didn't get my email, maybe you did. Call me." Stephanie hung up and then, on impulse, went into the menu settings on her tiny phone and deactivated the "Send Own Number" facility. Then she phoned the same number again.

The phone rang four times before it was picked up and Robert's voice, muffled, very soft, said, "Yes?"

"Why didn't you answer my previous call?" she snapped.

"Sorry," he whispered, "the phone was in my inside jacket pocket and I had to pull my gloves off to unbutton my overcoat. By the time I got it, you'd gone. I was just putting it back in my pocket when you phoned again. Sorry."

Stephanie didn't know whether to believe him or not. It was a plausible excuse, but Robert was a good liar: after all, he had fooled his wife for long enough. "Did you get my email, telling you I was coming home?"

"No, no, I've not been near a machine."

"Now that I simply do not believe," she snapped.

"Honestly," he sighed, "things have been crazy. Look, I cannot talk now. I'll phone back later."

"You'd better!" Stephanie wondered exactly where he was. He was whispering, mumbling, and she could hear some background noise, so she knew there were people around.

"I'll talk to you later. I've got to go. I'm at Jimmy Moran's removal."

Stephanie frowned. "What? I can't hear you. What did you say?"

"I said I'm at Jimmy Moran's removal of remains. Jimmy died on Christmas Day."

CHAPTER 15

She'd been gone less than four days, but the house smelled stale and empty. She was surprised to find that it felt pleasantly warm however, which suggested that she had left the heating on the timer. Dropping the suitcase in the hall, she stepped into the kitchen and filled the kettle. She pulled open the fridge and checked inside: as usual, it was almost empty, a half litre of low-fat milk in the tray in the door, alongside an almost empty carton of pure orange juice and the bottle of champagne she'd planned to open with Robert when they'd something to celebrate. It had sat there for six months now. She lifted out the milk and sniffed cautiously: it smelled fine.

She returned to the hall, deliberately not looking into the sitting-room, knowing what she would find there, and checked the answering machine which sat on the tiny console table. The figure "4" was illuminated in crude LED letters. How many were from Robert, she wondered as she hit the PLAY button.

You have four new messages.

New Message. Message was left on Tuesday 24th December.

"Stephanie . . . Stephanie are you there? It's me. I want to talk to you, I need to talk to you . . . Please call me back. I'm in the car."

Stephanie noted that it was almost identical to the call he had left on her mobile.

New Message. Message was left on Tuesday 24th December.

"Stephanie? It's me. I . . . I just need to talk to you. About today. About us. About the future. I know you're angry, but please call me, let me know you're OK."

New Message. Message was left on Wednesday 25th December.
"Stephanie. I don't know what's happened. I don't know where you are. It's just after 3.00 a.m. and I'm just leaving your house. There's no sign of you. I'm leaving this message in the hope that you return, hear it and answer me. I'm hoping you're with your friend, Sally. I think I remember you saying that she was supposed to be getting engaged tonight . . . no, last night. My God, I've just realised it's Christmas morning."

Message was left today, Saturday 28th December.

"Stef, it's your mother. I just wanted to make sure you got home safely and to see how you were. Give me a call when you get home. It was lovely to see you, even if it was a short visit. The good news is that Joan's husband, Eddie, is coming up for New Year's Eve. She told me you gave her some good advice. So, you see why

116

you should come home more often. Your father sends his love."

End of messages.

The kettle whistled, startling her, and she returned to the kitchen to make tea. Well, in Robert's defence, he had made the effort and he did seemed to be genuinely concerned for her. She rooted through her range of teas looking for something soothing. In the end she chose a caffeine-free Egyptian Liquorice. She wasn't overly fond of the taste, but she loved the smell. Cupping the teacup in both hands, breathing in the spicy aroma, she wandered out of the kitchen and into the sitting-room, which still bore all the evidence of her terrible encounter with Kathy and Robert. The Christmas presents Robert had brought lay in an unopened pile on the ground. The flowers had wilted in the heat, curled petals everywhere, and the helium balloon lay deflated over the back of the chair.

Stephanie sank into her usual chair and sipped the tea. She looked at the unopened presents he'd brought and felt not the slightest twinge of curiosity about their contents. She'd give them back to Robert the first opportunity she got.

She wondered if Kathy Walker had noticed the gold and silver-wrapped presents piled behind the sofa when she'd stepped into the room on Tuesday. They were gifts Stephanie had bought for Robert and now she wondered what she was going to do with them. She certainly wasn't going to give them to him; maybe she could return them.

117

She glanced at her watch, wondering what time the removal of remains would finish. Would Robert come directly to her, or would he have to drop his wife home first? And if the removal was today, did that mean the funeral would be held tomorrow or Monday?

And then a thought struck her: would she have to go?

She simply detested Jimmy Moran, though she'd always moderated her real opinion when Robert was present, because she knew the two men, despite their age differences, were great friends. Jimmy Moran had built a completely undeserved reputation by a combination of extraordinary arrogance tempered with too little talent.

The last conversation she had with Robert about Jimmy had taken place a week before Christmas. Jimmy's wife, Angela, was finally throwing him out because she'd discovered that he'd had a child by his long-term and much younger mistress, Frances. Angela had put up with a lot from Jimmy over the years – his constant drinking, none-too-discreet affairs, financial difficulties – but that had been the final straw. She was divorcing Jimmy and looking for her share. Stephanie recalled that Robert had been outraged by what he saw as Angela's vindictiveness. He'd been unable to understand Stephanie's support for Jimmy's wife. She'd been surprised, and just a little disappointed, with his reaction. Surely he accepted that Jimmy had treated his wife abominably, and that while he had a duty to his girlfriend and her child, he was also morally and legally obliged to provide for his wife?

Stephanie sipped the sweet aromatic tea and she wondered how this boded for her own news.

A sudden thought struck her and she put down her tea and went back out into the hall to pick up the portable phone. She dialled a number from memory as she carried her suitcase upstairs. The phone rang once before it was picked up and a brusque, cultured and very British voice said, "Flintoff."

"Good afternoon, Charles. It's Stephanie . . . Stephanie Burroughs."

"Stephanie, how wonderful to hear from you!" If her boss was surprised, it certainly didn't show in his voice.

"I apologise for phoning you on a Saturday," she began. She tossed the suitcase on the bed and snapped open the locks. She'd hadn't used half of the clothes she'd packed. Except for Christmas Day when she'd dressed up, she'd worn the clothes she'd left in the States on her previous visits. She lifted out the unworn LBD and decided that it would need to be pressed before she could wear it again.

"You can phone me at any time. That's why I entrusted you with my home number." Charles Flintoff was the man who had discovered Stephanie working as a researcher on breakfast time TV in the UK and had offered her a job in his agency. He'd always treated her as a special protégée, but she knew her relationship with him had been damaged when he discovered that not only was she having an affair with Robert – a contractor – but that she had awarded R&K Productions three lucrative contracts. It would take her a long time to rebuild his trust in her.

"Thank you. I'm literally just back in the country – I visited my parents for Christmas," she explained, also letting him know that she had not spent Christmas with Robert, "and I've just discovered that Jimmy Moran died on Christmas Day. I wasn't sure if you knew."

There was a pause. Then Charles Flintoff cleared his throat. "No, I did not know. Thank you for telling me. Jimmy Moran: I got to know him when I first opened the agency in Ireland. We even worked together on a couple of campaigns, and of course I saw him all the time at various events, though I have not used him in a long time. Poor Jimmy. So much talent and good creative energy. Wasted. Have you any idea about the funeral arrangements?"

"I know the removal of the remains happened today, but I've no idea when the funeral will take place."

"Probably not tomorrow." She heard the sound of a page turning and guessed he was checking a calendar. "Monday or Tuesday." He sighed. "I should go, and represent the firm. It will be well attended. Despite his faults, or perhaps because of them, Jimmy had a lot of friends. I would imagine some of his enemies will turn up too – just to make sure the old reprobate is in the ground." He paused. "If you have no other plans, perhaps you would like to represent the firm with me?"

"Yes . . . yes, I would. Thank you." She was surprised with the offer, pleased too.

"Phone me when you have the details. Now, if you have just come in off a transatlantic flight, you need some rest."

"I'm going to do that now. Thank you."

Charles Flintoff hung up and Stephanie sat on the edge of the bed, cradling the phone, wondering what he would say when she told him that she was pregnant.

And that reminded her . . .

She needed to get to her doctor. Would there be surgery over the weekend? Probably not. Maybe the Wellwoman Centre was open? She was just about to go downstairs to check the number in the Golden Pages when the wan afternoon sunlight flashed across the windscreen of a car as it approached across the courtyard and pulled up outside the house.

Stephanie hurried downstairs. Darting into the sitting-room, she scooped up the dead flowers, gathered up the curled and brittle petals, carried them into the kitchen and dumped them in the trash. Then she grinned: now, if that wasn't a symbolic gesture, then she didn't know what was. She wondered if he would use his key or . . .

The doorbell rang.

CHAPTER 16

"Hello, Stephanie."

Robert Walker's appearance shocked her. He looked ghastly, skin pale and lightly sheened with sweat, his hair was greasy, and there were deep bags under his bloodshot eyes. His black suit was rumpled and creased, there was a dark stain around the collar of his pale blue shirt and the knot on his gold silk tie – one she had bought him – was dark where grubby fingers had tugged it. When he stepped past her, she caught the faintest odour of stale perspiration. And that shocked her more than anything else: Robert was, if nothing else, fastidiously clean.

Stephanie closed the door behind him, took a deep breath to calm her suddenly thundering heart and followed him into the sitting-room. She found him standing beside the chair, looking down at the Christmas presents he'd brought last Tuesday.

"It's good to see you again," he said, his voice flat, emotionless.

Stephanie nodded, unsure what to say. She finally fell back on the old reliable. "Would you like some tea?"

"Tea. Yes, that would be wonderful, thank you."

Stephanie disappeared into the kitchen and Robert took up his usual position in the doorway, leaning against the frame, arms folded across his chest. It looked as if he was trying to hold himself upright. As she filled the kettle with water from the filter jug, she was aware that he was watching her.

"You got back this morning?" he said finally.

"A couple of hours ago," she said shortly.

"I'm sorry I wasn't there to meet you . . . I hadn't thought to download my emails."

"That's perfectly understandable given the circumstances."

"Flight was OK?"

"Fine. I came in via Paris, so it was a bit of the trek, but I'd booked First Class, so I could sleep on the transatlantic leg and that helped."

"Good. Good."

Stephanie found a cup for herself and a mug for Robert – he preferred mugs to cups – and hoped she had enough milk for the tea. It was low-fat, which he hated, but he would have to make do with it. Looking into the fridge, watching him out of the corner of her eyes, she asked, "How was the removal? Where there many there?"

"Yes." Robert drew in a deep shuddering sigh. "I was

surprised by how many. Shocked. I think Jimmy would have been too. He made a lot of enemies over the years, but far more friends it seems. They all came out today." His voice broke then and Stephanie saw him fumble in his pockets for a handkerchief.

The kettle started to boil and Stephanie concentrated on making the tea, deliberately not turning around, not wanting to look at him with tears on his face. She had imagined this moment a dozen times since she decided to come back to Ireland; she had rehearsed her speech, first on Long Island, then on the plane to Paris, and then again on the short hop back into Dublin, and knew exactly how she would handle this encounter with Robert. She would be cool, controlled, as unemotional as she could be. There would be no recriminations. They — she and Robert — had a situation to resolve, and all they were talking about was the most practical and logical way to go about it. That was the plan. But from the moment she had seen him standing on the doorstep, looking ill with exhaustion, she'd felt something shift inside herself. And now, listening to him trying to compose himself, to do that stupid thing men did, she felt all her carefully thought-out plans begin to fragment. And she suddenly — unaccountably — felt guilty that she'd been so hard with him earlier.

"Tea's ready."

He'd managed to compose himself by the time she turned and passed him over the steaming mug of tea.

"I've added two sugars."

"Sorry," he mumbled. "Been an intense few days; I've

not got much sleep." He followed her into the sitting-room, taking up his usual position on the couch facing her.

Stephanie had made herself another cup of liquorice tea. She cradled the tiny porcelain cup in the palms of her hands and sipped. "Tell me what happened?" she asked. Although she really wanted to discuss her current situation, she recognised that he needed someone to talk to. She raised her cup to hide her wry smile. That was how their affair started eighteen months ago. Initially, all Robert had wanted – needed – was someone to talk to, to share with. Kathy was no longer interested in him, or what he was doing, he said, because she was raising the children and running the home.

Robert took a moment to answer. "I got a call on Christmas Day. . . not long after yours. Jimmy Moran had been taken to hospital with a suspected heart attack. I immediately went in to see him. Oh, Stephanie, he looked ghastly . . ." He breathed deeply and took a mouthful of tea. "He said that at first he was trying to make light of it, thinking it was nothing more than indigestion. He was cooking his own Christmas dinner and had sampled the turkey. He reckoned it hadn't been cooked through. It was when he felt the pain move into his left arm that he realised it was serious and dialled 999. But it was Christmas Day and it took the ambulance ages to arrive."

Robert sipped a little more of the hot tea. His eyes glazed and Stephanie realised that he was reliving the events of Wednesday.

"They'd put him in a room on his own. He looked old, so old and frail . . . and the moment I looked at him, I knew he wasn't going to make it. It was almost as if he had given up. The spark had gone. Turned out he'd tried phoning Angela but she wasn't taking his calls, nor was Frances. He asked me to contact Angela. She spoke to me, but she wouldn't come in to see him. She was finished with him, she said. He'd broken her heart with his lies and his affairs and she was afraid that this was just another of his tricks."

Robert fell silent. Stephanie could see the muscle twitching along his jaw-line and the sudden welling of tears in his eyes.

"I phoned Frances," he continued, his voice barely above a whisper. "She wouldn't come either. They'd had a fight and she had thrown him out. I think she thought it was a trick too. He was incredibly manipulative, I think."

"So you stayed with him?" Stephanie asked.

"I stayed with him throughout the day and into the night until . . . until he died," he finished simply. "He died." There were tears on his cheeks now, but he seemed unaware of them. "He squeezed my hand and then . . ." He drew in a deep sobbing breath.

"I'm sorry, Robert. So sorry." It took an enormous effort of will to remain seated in the chair. She had the urge to go to him, wrap her arms around his shoulders and comfort him, but she knew that would be a mistake. "I know you and Jimmy were very close."

And Stephanie abruptly realised why Jimmy's death

had affected Robert so strongly. Although he had three brothers, they were all living abroad and there was no communication between them. Robert's parents had separated when he was fourteen and he had gone to stay with his mother. He rarely mentioned his father, who had died fifteen years ago, and when he did, the comments were always tinged with bitterness and regret. Jimmy Moran had been Robert's mentor, friend and, she realised now, father-figure.

"He died alone, Stephanie," Robert said very softly.

"Not alone. You were there."

"But his wife . . . his mis . . . his girlfriend should have been there. Someone more . . . more significant than me. Someone who loved him."

"You loved him, Robert," Stephanie said firmly. "In the same way that he was very significant to you, then you too must have played a significant part in his life. Why else would he contact you when he went into hospital?"

Robert nodded. "Yes, yes, you're right. Thank you for reminding me." He finished his tea in one quick swallow and put the cup on the floor. "I'm sorry, I guess I'm all over the place. Since everything that happened here on Tuesday . . ." he waved his hand around the room, "then frantically looking for you, then your call on Wednesday, and *then* Jimmy's death, it's just been an incredibly emotional time."

"Yes, I can see that. And Christmas is the most stressful time of the year too."

He attempted a smile. "There were times I thought I was having a heart attack myself." He pressed the palm of his right hand against his chest. "I think it was just stress."

"You should get it checked out, just in case," she said immediately. Then she stopped, realising what she was doing: she was assuming responsibility for him.

"I will. I promise. Jimmy was fifty-two – only ten years older than me."

"He lived a completely different lifestyle," she reminded him.

"Not that different," Robert said quickly, unable to disguise the note of bitterness in his voice.

"But he did smoke."

"He did. And he liked rich food," he added.

"And he drank," Stephanie reminded him, "much more than you."

"Yes, he did that too. I'm only sorry now that we didn't get a chance to have that meal in Shanahan's on the Green before Christmas. We had drinks around the corner in the Market Bar instead – you suggested that, remember? That was the last time I saw him until . . . until I saw him in the hospital on Christmas Day."

"At least you had the chance to see him."

Robert nodded. "Yes. I'm glad."

"Would you like some more tea?" Stephanie asked, filling the long silence that followed.

"Yes. Thank you." He picked his cup up off the floor, handed it across, then sank back onto the sofa, resting his head on the back of the chair and closing his eyes.

Stephanie stepped back into the kitchen. She was unsure what to do: to let him talk out his thoughts and feelings for Jimmy or to raise the subject of her pregnancy? But she wanted him clear-headed when she was talking about that, and right now he was simply too emotional. As she filled the kettle again, she called out, "Jimmy's life was also incredibly stressful, and I'm quite sure he didn't take a whole lot of exercise." Other than the horizontal kind, she thought, but didn't say aloud. She thought she heard Robert grunt in assent, and she continued on, "Plus, the whole issue with Angela and Frances must have taken its toll on him, and I'm sure the prospect of the looming divorce just added to the stress level."

There was no reply.

Stephanie turned and looked into the sitting-room. Robert had shifted sideways on the couch, his head tilted onto his shoulder. He had fallen asleep sitting up. She replaced the kettle, but didn't switch it on, and returned to her chair in the sitting-room. She sat down and watched Robert. Even in sleep the exhausted lines around his eyes and mouth didn't relax and she could see his eyes darting madly beneath the closed lids. She wondered what dreams haunted him.

The events of the past few days shifted and twisted in her unconscious, assuming a dream-like quality all of their own. From the moment Kathy Walker had appeared on Christmas Eve and slapped her across the face, everything had just spiralled out of control. Even though she'd only been home a couple of hours, her flying visit to New York was beginning to fade and recede into memory and she was already beginning to feel as if she'd never been away. Stephanie was concerned for Robert too: he looked as if he might keel over at any moment, a combination of the high emotion of the past few days, too little sleep and, she imagined, little or no food.

A shape passed the window, startling her. Then she realised it was Mrs Moore, the nosy neighbour directly across the courtyard. No doubt she had glanced in. Stephanie wondered what the scene looked like from outside: the woman curled up on the chair, the man dozing contentedly on the couch.

The irony of it was, of course, that she'd sometimes imagined a scene very much like this: it was from sometime in the future when Robert had left his wife and they were living together. He'd come home from work, sit in the chair and doze while she prepared food. In her fantasy, the house would be warm and welcoming, smelling of baked bread or roasting meat. Something gentle – David Arkenstone or Yanni maybe – would be murmuring on the CD. The couple would eat and talk and he would tell her about his day and she would fill him in on her activities. Then they would head upstairs and have a bath, and then to bed, to make love and fall asleep comfortably wrapped around one another.

The reality had turned out to be different: while the house was warm, it smelled stale and slightly bitter with the scent of the desiccated flowers and just the hint of Robert's perspiration. There was no music, no sounds even percolating through from the neighbours.

Leaning forward, she propped her elbows on her knees, rested her chin on her fists and looked at his face. He looked old and tired; he looked beaten. If he kept working his current outrageous schedule, he would be dead in ten years' time. Just like Jimmy. And she realised that she did not want that to happen. Last week she had let him go, allowed him to return to his wife. But that didn't mean that she'd stopped loving him.

Stephanie knew that she still loved Robert . . . but Kathy loved him too. And Robert . . .? Well, only Robert knew whom Robert truly loved. He said he loved her; he'd even proposed to her. But in this very room, last Tuesday, when Kathy had asked him if he loved *her*, he'd replied "Yes."

Nothing had changed since then.

Robert twitched and moaned in his uneasy sleep and Stephanie suddenly realised that she had placed the palm of her hand across her stomach.

No: everything had changed.

Last Tuesday, she hadn't known that she might be pregnant. She wasn't the sort of woman who was going to try and use the baby to trap him. He was the father and she expected him to help her support the child. But if he was the man she thought he was, she would hope he would to do more than just provide financial support. She hoped he would want to spend time with her and the child. His two children by Kathy were almost grown; his son was seventeen, his daughter fifteen. Would they need him as much as a newborn? And even if he did leave Kathy and live with her, that didn't mean that he was never going to see his children again.

The thought stopped her cold.

That was the first time since the argument on Tuesday that she had allowed herself to even *consider* the possibility that he would want to leave Kathy for her.

Would she want him? Even after all that had happened?

Before she could work out an answer, Robert's phone rang, the sound shockingly loud in the stillness of the room, and she jumped. Robert mumbled, and slowly, groggily came awake. He blinked, trying to focus, obviously unsure where he was. Then he groped for the overlarge XDA2 mobile phone. "Hello . . ." he began, then licked dry lips and tried again, "Hello . . ."

Even before he spoke the next sentence, Stephanie realised who was calling. She saw the look in his eyes – a combination of guilt and fear – before his entire expression turned shifty.

"Kathy . . . yes, I'm fine. I'm in the office . . ." His eyes found Stephanie's face and darted away. "Yes, I'll be home soon." He rang off.

"Why did you lie?" Stephanie wondered aloud.

Robert straightened in the chair and coughed. "Well, I could hardly tell her where I was, now could I?"

"You could have said we had some unfinished business," she smiled, without humour.

"I promised Kathy I would never see you again."

"And you're breaking that promise already?" she said evenly.

"Well, I made that promise before . . . before I knew about . . . about you and . . . and . . ."

"About me being pregnant?"

"Yes. That."

Stephanie stood. "I'm going to make that tea now. Why don't you go and grab a shower, freshen up? I need you awake and alert when we talk and right now you're about dead on your feet. You've got some clothes upstairs, and there's a toothbrush and a razor of yours in the bathroom cabinet. Shower and change: you'll feel much better."

"Yes, I will, thank you." He stood up and obviously caught a hint of his own stale sweat. "Gosh, I stink."

"Yes, you do," Stephanie said. *And in more ways than one,* she thought as she turned away quickly, before he could see the grin on her face.

CHAPTER 17

She found him lying asleep on her bed, wrapped in a thick bathrobe. She stood and looked at him for a long time, trying to sort out her conflicting emotions. She wanted to make sure that the feelings she'd had for this man – still had – were not now coloured by her thoughts of pregnancy. And yet she knew they must be.

She had nothing but respect for those women who – either by choice or circumstances – brought up their children on their own. If she was pregnant and had the baby in September, then she had no doubts but that she would be a good mother, and that the child would want for nothing. It would be tough, she had no illusions about that. She would have to make changes in just about every area of her life – but she would make them. She might even have to sell the house – she realised now she should never have converted the smaller second bedroom into a luxurious bathroom.

But if she had Robert's support, it would be a lot easier. He was working in a job that gave him great flexibility in his working regime and hours. He could work from home and look after the child while she returned to her job in the agency. It would make financial sense for her to continue working: she earned much more than he did.

Placing the hot tea on the bedside locker, she opened the wardrobe and took out a thick duvet which she gently spread over him. Then, turning off the light, she stepped out of the bedroom and allowed him to sleep.

"Robert. Robert."

Robert Walker opened his eyes and looked around. And, for the first time since he'd appeared on her doorstep, he smiled. "Hi . . ."

"Hi."

Then the smile faded as his eyes moved towards the curtains, which were pulled against the night outside. "My God, how long have I been asleep?"

"A few hours. It's just nine."

He sat bolt upright in the bed. "I've got to go . . ."

"You've got to eat first," Stephanie said firmly. She was sitting on the edge of the bed with a tray in her hands. It held a broad flat pizza flanked by a bottle of red wine and two glasses. "It's only takeout, I'm afraid. I'd no food in and I didn't want to leave you on your own."

Robert looked at the ham and pineapple pizza and

started to shake his head, but she distinctly heard his stomach rumble. "Just a slice then," he said with a grin.

They ate in companionable silence.

Although Stephanie poured herself a glass of wine, she barely touched it: her stomach was aching.

When Robert picked up the last piece of pizza she smiled. "When did you last eat?" she wondered aloud.

He shook his head. "I've grabbed a few bits and pieces on the run. When Jimmy . . . Jimmy died, I was left to make the funeral arrangements and contact his family. Two of his three brothers are coming home. They're spread all over the world: Lloyd is in Australia, Mikey's in Canada, and Teddy is in Boston. I spoke to Mikey, the oldest. He told me to go ahead with the removal, but to delay the funeral until they arrived."

"When will the funeral take place?"

"Monday the thirtieth, in Glasnevin. Teddy and Mikey are coming in tomorrow morning, but Lloyd's not going to be able to make it."

"That's a shame."

"I know. But they've never been close. Jimmy never really told me the full story, but I know he went to live with his mother when the family broke up, while the older brothers chose to live with his father. When his parents separated, it destroyed all their lives and shattered the family. Not unlike like my own experience." He glanced up at Stephanie and smiled that same shy smile that always tugged at her heart. "I'm sorry, I've done nothing but talk about me. Tell me what you did over Christmas. You went home?"

Stephanie nodded. She lifted the tray and moved around the room to put in on the bedside locker. Then she leaned back against the windowsill and folded her arms. "I went home. It was a last-minute rush, and I had to go in via London, but I made it back late on Christmas Eve and I'm glad I went. It was good to see Mom and Dad again. Made me realise that they're getting on a bit, Dad especially. I know people say that time slips by – it doesn't: it races. I'm going to try and get home regularly, maybe every second or third month to keep in touch with them."

"That's a good idea." Robert pushed away the duvet and slid his legs out over the edge of the bed. "I really should be going." He tugged on his underwear, pulled on his socks and stepped into his trousers.

For a few moments, Stephanie was shocked speechless, then she exploded. "Hang on a second! We've talked about everything, but the most important thing: us. *Me*. And the fact that I might be pregnant."

He opened the wardrobe and pulled out one of the shirts he'd left there for emergencies, then turned to her as he buttoned it up. "How sure are you?"

"Sure?"

"Sure that you're pregnant.

"Almost positive. I'm nearly two weeks late now."

"Did you do a test?"

"Yes. It came back positive. That's why I came home."

He nodded as he tucked his shirt into his trousers and Stephanie realised that he was doing everything but look her in the eye. "So, let's say you are: what are you going to do about it?"

Stephanie came off the window ledge to stand directly in front of Robert. "What do you mean by that?"

He blinked in surprise. "I mean, you can't seriously be thinking of having it?"

Stephanie felt the single slice of pizza she'd eaten curdle in her stomach. "Yes, I am," she whispered.

"But you can't. You've got this place . . . and then there's your job. You can't have all that and a baby."

"I could if I had a partner."

Robert concentrated on his cuffs. "If I'm the father of this child . . ."

She cracked him across the face, the force of the blow snapping his head to one side. For an instant something dark and ugly flared in his eyes and she thought he was going to hit her back. "How dare you! You *are* the father. There's been no one else!"

"I'm sorry," he said, drawing in a deep breath, pressing the palm of his hand to his stinging cheek. "Maybe that was an ill choice of phrase. I'm sorry. I didn't mean to imply anything."

Stephanie looked at him, saying nothing.

"I mean, let's be logical about this. I've reared my family, I don't want to start again. And nor do you. You're on the corporate ladder – a child would seriously curtail any chances of advancement. Neither of us can afford to have a screaming child in our lives." There was a pause, and he added grimly. "And what would I tell Kathy and the kids?"

She was seeing the real Robert for the first time, she realised. She was seeing the selfish, self-obsessed, arrogant bastard that he was. She realised now that this was the sort of man who could enter into an affair without any thought as to the consequences. She didn't want to think it, didn't want to believe it, but the bitter conclusion now was that he'd only ever been interested in her for sex and the work she could bring to his ailing firm. She watched him now, mouth moving, words forming and she knew with soul-chilling certainty what he was going to suggest.

"I mean, it has to be what you want, doesn't it? It makes perfect sense. We'll go to London – I'll pay for the abortion, of course – and I'll accompany you to the clinic." He smiled, a mere twisting of his lips. "We'll have a weekend in London and the problem will be solved. We might even get a chance to take in some of the sights. When we return to Dublin, we can go back to our lives again."

When she spoke, her voice was so low it was barely audible. "Get out."

Robert attempted his quizzical smile again. "Well, what do you think?"

And then she screamed, the sound shocking them both. *"Get out! Get out! Get out!"*

Robert backed away from her. Stephanie reached for the nearest item – the pizza plate – and flung it at him. It missed and shattered against the wall, leaving a bloody smear of sauce.

"You bastard!" she gasped, suddenly breathless. "You bastard!"

"Stephanie . . . I'm just suggesting . . ."

"You've got a key to this house. Give it to me," she demanded. She reached into the wardrobe and tore his other shirt off the hanger and flung it at him. She pulled his tie off its hanger, the silk catching and ripping on the metal, then caught his black patent-leather shoes and threw them across the room.

Robert tugged the key off his key-ring and dropped it on the bed. "Stephanie. Let's talk. I know you're upset now, but –"

"We're finished," she said icily. "Don't you ever speak to me again." There were tears in her eyes now, but she was determined not to cry. "I loved you. I loved you with all my heart. Now, I see you for what you are: just another egotistical bastard. This isn't a problem to be solved: this is a life and a future we're talking about. And you think an abortion will sort everything! A quick abortion, then we take in the sights as if nothing has happened? I hate you, Robert Walker. No, more than that. I despise you. Now get out. Don't come back."

It was only when she heard the door slam and the car reverse away, that she allowed herself to lie back on the bed and cry, huge, heaving, racking sobs that took her breath away.

And buried deep amongst the other emotions, amongst the fear and loathing, the disgust and anger was another: relief. She was glad she was finished with him.

She was glad it was over.

Finally.

BOOK 2

The Husband's Story

First there was the shock and yes, I'll admit it, the shame and maybe a little touch of fear too. Then, surprisingly, came the relief. I was glad Kathy knew, glad that the lies could now end, glad that we could both move on.

But then . . .

I'm not sure what happened. The woman I was sure didn't love me claimed that she did, and the woman who claimed to love me seemed to be pushing me away, as if she didn't want me any more.

Walking out of that house, however, I realised that I'd been given a second chance with my wife, a chance to make a new start, a chance to begin again.

But . . .

But I think the problem was that my relationship with Stephanie had opened my eyes to other possibilities, had given me a glimpse of how my life could be different. So different.

CHAPTER 18

Tuesday, 24th December

CHRISTMAS EVE

Traffic was at a complete standstill in Pearse Street.

Up ahead, Robert Walker heard the sudden wail of a siren as the fire brigade attempted to get out of Tara Street Station. The sound went on and on, suggesting that the engine wasn't moving either. Robert tugged on the handbrake, and put the Audi into neutral. He took his hands off the steering wheel and looked down at his fingers. They had stopped shaking.

When he'd stepped into that room and discovered Kathy standing there, it had actually taken him a couple of seconds to process exactly what he was seeing. There was no possible way that Kathy *should* be standing in Stephanie's sitting-room. It was just wrong. And yet there she was: his wife and his mistress standing facing him, with identical expressions on their faces.

The pieces fell together quickly enough though –

especially when Kathy had stepped forward and hit him across the face. He ran his tongue over the raw chipped edge to one of his brand new caps. In the eighteen-odd years that they'd been married, she'd never raised her hand to him. He rubbed the palm of his hand against his jaw: she packed a fairly good punch too!

His affair had been discovered.

Initially, he thought that Stephanie had contacted Kathy. She'd been putting him under increasing pressure of late to make a decision about her. She wanted him to choose – his wife or his lover. He knew that Christmas was a particularly hard time for her . . . but what she seemed to forget was that it was an equally difficult time for him. Stephanie wanted him to spend time with her, while he wanted to take the time to be with the children. They grew up so quickly – Brendan was seventeen already and Theresa was fifteen – who knew how many more Christmases they would want to spend at home? Robert's own parents had separated when he was fourteen and he remembered that first Christmas after the break-up of their marriage, sitting at home with his mother in the house in Finglas, a ragged artificial tree in the corner and the coal fire leaking smoke into the room, a hissing radio stuck on RTE 1 playing back-to-back Christmas carols and religious hymns. When his father and three brothers had left some weeks previously, his father had taken away the television set, and his mother had been too proud to admit any of this to either her sister or her neighbours. It had been a miserable Christmas – the first of several. But the one feeling which remained with him, the single abiding memory he had of that entire week, was the sense of loss. He missed his father. He was determined that his own children would never experience the same emotion. He was not going to leave his wife on Christmas week. But Stephanie had no children and didn't understand that.

The wailing fire brigade siren began to fade as it moved away and then traffic crept forward. Robert eased the car into first gear and released the handbrake.

When he'd stepped into that room and discovered Kathy and Stephanie together, he thought he was going to have a heart attack or throw up. Or both.

But Stephanie hadn't revealed the affair to Kathy; his wife had discovered it for herself. He didn't know how: maybe someone had spotted him out with Stephanie. But he'd always been careful, so careful. When they went out for dinner, they always dined in restaurants on the south side of the city, where there was less chance of meeting any of his northside neighbours. When they went to the cinema, it was always out to the Square, and not to his local cinemas in Santry, Finglas or even Blanchardstown. When they stayed away overnight together, it was always in an anonymous little hotel somewhere in the heart of Ireland, and Stephanie made the reservation in her name, so there would be no record on his credit card.

When he'd begun his affair with Stephanie, he'd justified these precautions as a way not only of protecting both of their reputations, but as a way of protecting

Kathy too. The last thing he wanted to do was to hurt her. Too late now.

That must be it, he decided: someone had seen them together and informed Kathy. He remembered now the traces of suspicion he'd picked up in her voice recently. He was supposed to be having dinner with his old friend and colleague Jimmy Moran last week, but somehow the reservation in Shanahans' had never been made. Kathy had quizzed him about it none too subtly. He remembered now that she'd even come into town that night and promised to drop in on Jimmy and himself at the restaurant.

She'd been checking up on him!

The realisation was even more shocking than discovering her standing in Stephanie's sitting-room.

She'd been spying on him.

For how long? And what had she discovered? Had she seen him with Stephanie? He knew that he acted differently when he was in Stephanie's company; he was more relaxed, more cheerful, he even felt younger. He tried to remember the last time he'd been out with her. It hadn't been recently. December was such a crazy month and they'd both been extremely busy. He'd visited her at her house, but no one knew him there. Maybe someone in the business had spoken to Kathy? Only last week Jimmy Moran had told him that one of his rivals, Simon Farmer – snivelling little bastard that he was – had been spreading rumours that the only reason R&K Productions had got three major contracts from Flintoff's agency was because Robert was involved with their Senior Accounts Manager, who awarded the contracts. The problem was, the rumour was true. And the business Stephanie brought his company had kept it afloat through a very difficult period. Was there any chance that Farmer had contacted Kathy out of spite?

All she would need would be the barest hint to excite her suspicions. Kathy had suspected him of having an affair with Stephanie Burroughs years ago when he had first met her. He had never been so shocked, so startled in his life than when she'd accused him of that one glorious summer's evening. The irony, of course, was that it wasn't true then.

If Kathy's old suspicions had been reignited, then this time she would have found that her suspicions were fully justified. Once her suspicions were roused, then she'd be watching him like a hawk, no doubt checking up on his excuses like any suspicious wife. Also, he had to admit that, of late, he'd been just a little bit too casual with his lies. In the early days of his affair, he'd concocted elaborate intricate fictions, based around potential contracts, meetings with possible clients, business seminars: anything that would take him away from home and allow him to spend time with Stephanie. More recently, however, he'd fallen back on that old reliable – overtime and pressure of work.

Not that it mattered too much any more. With the truth of the affair out in the open, he felt an extraordinary sense of relief. No doubt he would discover how she'd found out later when they finally got some time to themselves to talk. He grimaced with the thought; he was not relishing *that* conversation. He still didn't know how much she knew and was unsure how much to reveal. But he reckoned he had hurt her enough, and he owed her the courtesy of the truth. If they were to start again, then he had to come clean. He'd tell her everything. Well, almost everything.

Robert swung around into Tara Street, eased the Audi into the middle lane and crept across the bridge.

He'd told Kathy he wanted to come back, he'd told her he wanted to start again. He'd told her that he loved her. And he meant it, all of it. He'd never stopped loving her.

The only problem was that he also loved Stephanie Burroughs.

CHAPTER 19

Maureen Ryan was in her mid-fifties, but could easily have passed for forty-plus. She was a tall, masculine-looking woman, and her sharp features were dominated by almost translucent eyes and a shock of iron-grey hair which she wore in a single tight braid that hung to the small of her back. She had manned the front desk of R&K Productions right from the very beginning and in that time she had come to regard Robert as the son she would never have – thank God! – and Kathy as the daughter she wished she'd had. The moment she opened the door and found Robert standing on the doorstep, Maureen knew that something was amiss.

"This is a surprise," she said carefully, standing back to allow him to step into the hall.

"I've been promising to come out and see you for ages," he said, "but it's just been so manic." He kissed her quickly on both cheeks. "Happy Christmas."

"There's no need to apologise. I know what December is like." Maureen had been on sick leave for the past month and although Robert had phoned on several occasions – usually to ask questions about contracts and appointments – he'd never got around to visiting her.

"I'm sorry for dropping in unannounced like this. I should have phoned . . ." Robert said absently.

"You don't have to phone, you know that. I'm delighted to see you," Maureen's tone suggested she was anything *but* delighted. If she'd known he was coming, she would have changed out of the off-white tracksuit that was too misshapen to do her figure any favours and slippers that had seen their best days at least five years ago.

"You'll have some tea . . . or perhaps you'd like something a little stronger?" she asked, leading him out into the circular conservatory that had been built onto the back of the two-up, two-down terrace house on the old Finglas Road.

"Tea only, please. There are a lot of police about and I don't want to risk getting pulled over." He looked around the conservatory. "I like what you've done with this." R&K Productions had been commissioned by RTE to shoot a pilot for a TV makeover show a couple of years ago and they had used Maureen's house for it, adding a conservatory to the back. Although the show had never been commissioned, the conservatory had turned out to be a spectacular success.

"You've put in a new floor, I see," he said.

154

"It got so hot in here that the original wood warped and buckled, so I replaced the floor and added the blinds."

"The indoor water feature is new too," said Robert.

"Yes, isn't it perfect there? This is my favourite part of the house now – one of the reasons I'll probably never sell," she said as she went into the kitchen.

Robert sat down in one of the enormous fan-backed white wicker chairs and breathed in soothing smoke curling from a slender purple candle. He thought it might be lavender. There was a book opened on the circular glass table and he absently spun it around to read the title: it was a Stephen King title called *On Writing*. Robert thought it was an odd title for a horror novel.

Maureen appeared, carrying a wicker tray which held a hand-painted teapot, two matching cups, a tiny milk jug and a small bowl filled with sugar cubes. Robert stood to take the tray and Maureen set out the cups, milk and sugar on the table. She sat down in the wicker chair opposite Robert.

"We'll let the tea brew for a couple of minutes."

Robert sat, facing her, and fixed a smile on his face. He was conscious that it had been four or five weeks since he'd last seen Maureen and only last week he'd talked with Stephanie about the possibility of letting the older woman go. But with Kathy back in the picture now, he knew that would never happen. "I really am sorry I've not been around . . ." he began.

Maureen held up her right hand, palm out. "Don't be. How is the temp – the Russian girl – working out?"

Robert seesawed his left hand in the air. "I ask her to do something, then end up doing it myself. It'll be good to have you back. You are coming back?"

"If you'll have me." Maureen smiled humourlessly.

"Of course – of course, there's no question about that. There would be no R&K Productions without you. You know that."

Maureen had spent twenty-five years with RTE before leaving to work as a freelancer. Her connections in the business were second-to-none and everyone expected her to end up with one of the big independents; instead she had opted for the unknown start-up company. But her presence with R&K Productions lent it credibility in those early days when Robert and Kathy were fighting to establish themselves. "Have you any idea when you might be back?"

"Early in the new year, I'd imagine. Why?"

"No reason. I'll just need to give the temp, Illona, notice."

"I'll be back as soon as the doctor gives me the all-clear." Maureen leaned forward to pour tea. She saw him squinting suspiciously at it. "It's nothing fancy," she promised. "Just plain Barry's."

Robert nodded. Maureen was constantly experimenting in the office with a range of exotic teas and herbal infusions. He reached into his inside jacket pocket and produced a slim white envelope, which he laid on the table and pushed towards her. "A little Christmas bonus," he said, feeling vaguely embarrassed.

156

Maureen blinked in surprise. "I wasn't expecting anything," she said truthfully. "And especially not having been out for so long."

"I'm just delighted I'm in a position to do it. There were a couple of months there in the summer when I really thought we were in trouble."

Maureen nodded. Out of force of habit, she added milk and two sugars to Robert's tea and pushed it back towards him. She knew that this had been a particularly difficult year for R&K; at one stage, she'd even considered sending her CV out. However she knew, if she did that, then word would get around the business and R&K would be finished.

"If Stephanie hadn't managed to get us those jobs . . ." he added.

Something in his voice alerted Maureen, and she looked up quickly. "Is there a problem?"

"No," he began, then nodded. "Yes," he admitted.

"The DaBoyz contract?" she guessed.

"No, that's OK." DaBoyz were a boy-band indistin-ßguishable from any other boy-band, but hoping to stand out with a cutting-edge pop video. Stephanie had managed to steer DaBoyz's manager towards R&K Productions on the basis of a couple of sharp advertise-ments they had shot for her agency. "That contract is fine. I'd a meeting with the band and their manager last week. They really like the new ideas and it looks like we'll shoot early in the new year."

"Well then, what's the problem?" Maureen asked.

157

"Once that's in the can and aired, we're bound to get other pop videos. And that's where the real money is nowadays."

"I know. Plus, I think we might get the new Renault ad, and I've pitched for the forthcoming Guinness campaign. I think we're in with a very good chance."

"So where's the problem?" Maureen wondered.

"I spoke to Stephanie recently. Apparently she won't be able to put any more work our way. Some people have begun to question why our company is getting so many contracts . . . she had a difficult conversation with Flintoff, her boss. I think he told her: no more work for R&K."

Maureen sat back into the wicker chair and sipped her tea. She stared at Robert over the rim of the brightly painted cup. "I know Charles Flintoff," she offered. "I know him well. I could speak to him."

"Ah no. Better not. Not at the moment in any case."

"What are you not telling me, Robert?"

Robert sipped his tea, grimaced and added another sugar cube. "I'm telling you that I've been . . . involved with Stephanie Burroughs for a little while now. Romantically involved. It's one of the reasons we've got so much work. Some people in the trade started to remark upon it, and Charles Flintoff knows about our relationship." He could actually feel some of the knot of tension ease as he confessed to Maureen. Maybe that old saying was true: confession was good for the soul. He looked across the table towards her, unsure how she would take the news. Maureen was no stranger to the gossip pages of the

Sunday newspapers and magazines: she had been romantically linked to several junior politicians and a TV actor turned movie star. When the silence stretched unbearably, he said, "Well, say something."

"Say what? You're not telling me something I didn't know."

"You knew!"

"I've known for about a year."

Robert stared at the woman, mouth opening and closing. He thought he'd been so careful. "And you said nothing?"

Maureen smiled icily. "What did you expect me to say? Robert, you're a big boy. If you were having an affair, then I was sure you knew that some day there would come a reckoning. And I presume you're telling me this now because Kathy knows."

Robert nodded miserably.

"Do you know she called to see me last Saturday?"

"She mentioned it. But I thought it was just a social call?"

"She told me out straight that she suspected that you and Stephanie Burroughs were having an affair."

"And you told her!" Robert said, unable to keep the snap of anger out of his voice.

"She told me," Maureen said firmly. "She came to me straight from the office, where she'd just gone through the phone records."

Robert stared at Maureen in horror. "She was checking the phone bills . . . why?" he whispered.

"I imagine she was looking for proof. She found it. She discovered that your first call of the day and the last call at night were always to the same number. It didn't take a genius to figure out what was going on. I don't know how she connected the number to Stephanie – maybe she phoned it. The phone bills were the final confirmation she needed." Maureen put her cup down and shrugged. "You might like to think that you're clever, Robert Walker, but Kathy is smarter – far smarter – than you. You made the mistake of underestimating her. And you got a little greedy, I think."

"Greedy?" He tried to swallow, but his mouth was dry. He sipped some of the tea. How long had Kathy been checking up on him? It made him feel ill at ease, almost physically queasy, to think that someone was spying on him, checking up on his every move.

"Greedy," Maureen said. "Why didn't you get a pay-as-you-go phone and use that? No bills, no records. But no, you wanted to be able to claim the calls as a business expense."

"I never thought . . ." he muttered.

"So now Kathy knows. I take it she's spoken to you about this."

"I've just met her . . . and Stephanie," he added glumly.

Maureen straightened in the chair. "The two of them? Together?"

"Kathy went to Stephanie's place to tackle her face-to-face."

"Takes guts to do something like that," she murmured.

"I walked in on them. I was bringing Stephanie her Christmas presents," Robert said miserably. "There was . . . some unpleasantness. Then – and I'm still not entirely sure what happened – Stephanie sort of pushed me back to Kathy."

"Why would she do that?"

"Kathy said that she loved me."

"And was that ever in question?" Maureen asked.

Robert found he couldn't look her in the face. "I was sure she didn't. I think that's the only reason I allowed the affair to happen. Kathy had withdrawn from me. She was looking after the children; she had no interest in me or the work. I was . . . I was lonely," he admitted. "That's the real reason I got involved with Stephanie."

In her life Maureen Ryan had had three long-term affairs. In every case she had known, right from the very beginning, that the man was not going to leave his wife for her. Nor did she want him to. And in every case it was not just sexual chemistry that had drawn the men to her – it was the fact that she was prepared to listen, to be interested in them, in their work, in their lives. Although they were married, the men were lonely.

"I never set out to hurt Kathy," Robert continued.

"Well, you have – you know that, don't you?"

"I do."

"Tell me how the conversation between the three of you finished."

"Stephanie rejected me – Kathy said she would take me back," Robert said quickly. "That's it in a nutshell. I left. The last I saw was the two of them standing together in the door of Stephanie's home."

"So you haven't had a chance to talk privately with Kathy yet?"

"Not yet."

"When you do, you will have to be honest with her, Robert. You know that. Totally honest."

"I know."

"Do you *want* to go back to Kathy, Robert?" Before he could answer, she held up a hand. "Think carefully before you answer."

Robert stared at the table and even before he raised his head to look at her, Maureen had an inkling of how he would answer: if he truly, wholeheartedly, wanted to go back to Kathy, he would not have taken so long to formulate his response.

"I would like to get back together with Kathy," he said very carefully, "for the sake of the business and the children. But I love Stephanie."

"Love or lust?"

He shook his head. "Love. I love her."

"You said you wanted to get back with Kathy for the sake of the business and the children. What about for Kathy's sake? For your sake? For the sake of an eighteen-year marriage?"

"Well yes, of course."

"You don't sound as positive," Maureen said softly.

"Oh, Maureen, you don't know what it's like. I love Kathy, I do. And I adore the children, you know that. But

162

Stephanie . . . well, I love her. When I'm with her I feel young and free . . . when I'm with her the world is full of possibilities. I don't get that feeling when I'm with Kathy."

"You're wrong." Maureen's voice had turned cold and distant. "I do know what it's like. But from the other side of the table. I was the mistress. More than once. I had affairs with men like you, men who thought they loved me." She shook her head quickly and her eyes turned bright. "They didn't love me. They loved the freedom of being with me: it made them remember their youth, before they were married, had children, mortgages, commitments. For the few hours or days they were with me, they were free, existing in a little selfish bubble." She stood up and Robert rose with her. "I want you to think about that. If you leave Kathy and go to Stephanie – that's even assuming she will have you now – then how long do you think it will take for the gloss to wear off her?"

"I hear what you're saying."

Maureen came around the table and laid a hand on his arm. "You know, sometimes an affair can be a good thing. It can clear the air, it forces a couple to re-examine their lives and see where things went wrong. I've seen marriages survive affairs, and come out the other end stronger." Maureen looked into Robert's troubled eyes. "Is that what you want, Robert?"

"I . . . I don't know what I want. I love Kathy . . . but I love Stephanie too."

Maureen turned away so he could not see the expression of disgust on her face and began to gather the cups onto the tray. "Time to choose. Though from what you're telling me," she added with a wry smile, "Stephanie may no longer be available to you."

CHAPTER 20

Traffic heading to the airport was backed up down the carriageway.

Robert sat in the car and watched a plane take off. He wished he was on it, flying away for Christmas, spending it on some warm beach without a trouble in the world. He smiled wryly. Next year maybe. The smile faded. What would the coming year bring? Where would he be this time next year: still with Kathy, still in business? The next couple of hours and days were going to determine the course of his future.

And Stephanie. What of her? There was still so much they needed to talk about. It couldn't just end so quickly, so abruptly. Only a couple of days ago, he had proposed to this woman. He had been planning to leave his wife and start again with Stephanie and she had been happy . . . but that was before she discovered that Kathy still loved him. That revelation had changed everything.

He needed to talk to her. He pulled out the overlarge XDA phone and hit the speed-dial that brought up Stephanie's home number. He was guessing she'd still be at home. The phone rang four times before the answer machine kicked in. Maybe she was screening her calls. Stephanie had recorded a new message recently: her voice sounded bright and cheerful, maybe even a little drunk.

"Happy Christmas, Happy Christmas, Happy Christmas! Leave a message."

"Stephanie . . ." He paused, waiting for her to pick up. "Stephanie, are you there? It's me." There was no response. "I want to talk to you, I need to talk to you . . . Please call me back. I'm in the car."

Where was she? A sudden thought struck him, chilling him to the bone. My God, what if Kathy was still there with her? His fingers trembled slightly as he hit the speed-dial that connected him to his wife's mobile. It rang twice before it was answered, and he felt a wash of relief when he heard the background noise of traffic. She was in the car.

"Yes?" she said shortly.

"Hi . . . I was just wondering . . . just wondering how you are."

"I'm fine."

"Where are you?"

"At the roundabout outside Swords. Where are you?"

"At the airport. I stopped to give Maureen her Christmas bonus."

"Good."

"She told me you'd spoken to her."

"Yes, I have."

Robert squeezed the steering wheel in frustration. She was deliberately making no contribution to the conversation. "How are you feeling?" he asked lamely.

"How do you think I feel, Robert?" Kathy snapped. "I've just been to see my husband's mistress. I've just learned some very ugly home truths. We'll talk later." She hung up.

Robert inched forward. Once he got past the turn-off for the airport, traffic should ease a little. He just needed to make a quick stop at The Pavilions in Swords and pick up a present for Kathy. He'd spent weeks choosing just the right present for Stephanie, but had left his wife's to the very last minute. As always. He was sure there was something symbolic in that.

Where was Stephanie? Surely she hadn't gone out? He hit another quick-dial key, this one for her mobile phone. The phone rang twice before it was answered,

"Yes?" The voice was muffled and for a moment, he thought he'd dialled the wrong number.

"Stephanie? Stephanie? Is that you?" He could hear background noise, voices, thumps. Where was she? "Steph . . ."

The call went dead.

Shit! He hit redial. The phone didn't even ring, it just went straight to her message service.

"You have reached Stephanie Burroughs. Leave your name, number and a brief message and I will call you back. Thank you."

"Stephanie? Stephanie, it's Robert. Look, we need to talk. We have to talk. About today. About us. About everything. Please call me back. I'm on the mobile."

Robert hung up, then sighed in exasperation. Why couldn't life be simple? There had been a time, a long time ago, when the world seemed to be a much simpler place: he'd no worries, no concerns . . . and, of course, no wife, no children, no mortgage. Maybe Maureen was right: maybe his time with Stephanie reminded him of what he'd once had . . . and lost. He'd been free: free of dependants, of mortgages and debts, free of worries. Then he married. The wedding had been a frustrating nightmare and they'd ended up paying for it for the first two years of their marriage. The mortgage on the first house was crippling, he struggled desperately to keep the business afloat, and then the children arrived. And as time went by it hadn't got any easier: the pressures increased and the bills were ever present. For the last eighteen years, in fact, he'd been running very fast just to stand still.

That wasn't to say that it had all been bad. There were happy times, lots of them, but somehow he found it harder to remember those. All that remained was the constant grind, the continual effort of just keeping going. And the frustration of doing it alone, of watching Kathy step further and further back from the business, leaving him to manage on his own. Oh, he knew she was raising the children and running the house, but she didn't have to worry about where the next contract was coming from. She didn't have to face a ninety-minute trek in and out of the city each day, she didn't have VAT and PRSI to worry about. He couldn't remember the last time she'd asked about the company – she'd even been shocked to discover that Maureen had been out sick. And he knew – just knew – that he'd mentioned it to her, though she claimed he hadn't. So, he'd ended up getting in a temp whose first language was not English when really Kathy should have been there to help …

Robert took a deep breath and tried to ease the knot of tension he could feel gathering at the back of his neck. He worked his head from side to side and rolled his shoulders, hearing muscles pop and crack.

Actually, if he was being honest – truly honest – he'd hired the temp before he'd told Kathy that Maureen was ill. The last thing he needed was his wife working in the building where he was conducting his affair.

Once past the airport roundabout, traffic melted away and he put his foot down. He needed to get to the shopping centre before it closed.

He'd been given a second chance, he realised.

He could choose to start again with Kathy. Come clean about his relationship – and the reasons behind it – clear the air and start again. Kathy wanted changes; well, so did he. Kathy said she would take him back and no doubt there would be conditions, but he'd lay down some conditions of his own too. He might have had an affair, but Kathy had been just as much to blame as he had. Naturally, Kathy wouldn't see it that way, but he'd be sure to remind her that she had first accused him of having an affair when he'd been perfectly innocent. She'd lost her trust in him when all he'd been doing was working every hour God sent to care for his family.

Robert turned off the carriageway into the car park of The Pavilions. This late on Christmas Eve, he expected to find it filled to overflowing, but it was surprisingly empty. He pulled into a space, turned off the engine and then sat, his head resting on the steering wheel. His thoughts were confused, whirling though dozens of permutations and he actually felt dizzy.

No, this wasn't Kathy's fault.

He'd had the affair. It was his choice. His decision. It was cowardly to even suggest that she'd somehow forced him into it. Circumstances, situations and opportunity had encouraged him to enter into the affair with Stephanie.

And he couldn't deny that it had made him very happy. Happier than he'd been with Kathy in a long time.

CHAPTER 21

Robert had been feeling increasingly nervous as he approached Swords and bile bubbled at the back of his throat as he turned into the estate and onto the road that led down towards the house. He was frightened – no, terrified might be a better description, of what the next few hours would bring.

The temperature had been falling throughout the afternoon and with the onset of night, ice had crept in, driven by a chill easterly wind. The footpaths and roads were sparkling and the Met Office was forecasting light falls of snow later on, and promising the possibility of a countrywide white Christmas.

Every house in the small estate was ablaze with lights. Many had now adopted the American custom of decorating the outside of the house, some to a rather vulgar extreme with a combination of Santas on the roof and full crib in the garden: all picked out in winking fairy lights. Most, however, had opted for dangling curtains of icicle lights running under the eaves, or had wrapped lights around trees in the garden.

In contrast the Walker house looked almost sombre: there were no lights on the exterior of the house and none in the garden. But the curtains in the sitting-room had not been drawn, and the Christmas tree, lights winking, tinsel glittering, looked suitably seasonal. Robert slowed, feeling the heavy Audi slip and shift on the icy street. Then he stopped: Kathy's Skoda was parked in the driveway, while behind it, parked at an awkward angle that took up the rest of the space was the enormous SUV belonging to Julia, Kathy's older sister.

Was she here by accident or invitation? Surely Kathy would not have asked her sister to come over for some sort of moral support? He shook his head slightly. He straightened the car and pulled it in to the kerb. No, he didn't think that Kathy would want her sister Julia – with her perfect twenty-seven-year marriage – to know about their problems.

Robert quietly let himself into the house and stood in the hall, head tilted to one side, listening. The TV was blaring in the sitting-room with what sounded like a game show and he could hear the low murmur of Brendan and Theresa's voices as they discussed the contestants. He eased open the door to the sitting-room and peered inside.

"Hi, guys," he said softly.

"Hi, Dad," they both said, without looking up. They were both watching TV: Brendan stretched out on the sofa, while Theresa was sprawled on the floor, chin cupped in her palms.

"Aunt Julia here?" he asked, addressing no one in particular.

"In the kitchen with Mum," Theresa said. "Mum asked me to leave, so I think there's a problem."

Robert felt his stomach twist. Maybe he'd been wrong about Kathy – again! Maybe she had called on her sister for support. If she had, then he knew he was in deep trouble: he knew Julia didn't like him.

"Keep the sound down, will you," he said, stepping out of the room. Then, taking a deep breath, and twisting his lips into an approximation of a smile, he stepped into the kitchen. "Hello, Julia," he said pleasantly, though his eyes were fixed on his wife's face.

"Julia's just telling me about Sheila," Kathy said immediately, her eyes flat and expressionless, but at least letting him know that Julia's presence had nothing to do with their personal situation. Sheila was the youngest of the three sisters.

Robert felt a wash of relief surge through him. "Is she OK?" he asked, stepping around the table to lean against the sink.

"She's having an affair with a married man," Julia said in hushed, appalled tones and then stopped, waiting for a response.

"So?" Robert frowned. "What's that got to do with

us?" He looked from Julia to Kathy and then back to his sister-in-law.

Julia Taylor was five years older than Kathy, and looked five years older than that. Short and unprepossessing, she dressed in the same sensible skirts and cardigans that her late mother had favoured and, since their mother's death, had assumed the role of the matriarch of the sisters.

"Oh, I should have known you would never understand," Julia said peevishly. "Men never do." Julia turned to look across the table at Kathy. "I phoned her today, just to confirm that she was coming on Stephen's Day for dinner. She said she would – on one condition: that she could bring her current young man with her. Well, I was delighted. Sheila is thirty-five now, it's about time she thought about settling down and if she's going to have children, then the clock is ticking." Julia took a deep breath and pursed her lips. Glancing briefly at Robert, she turned back to Kathy. "Turns out her young man is not so young; he's actually five years older than her."

Robert turned back to the sink and began to fill the kettle. He knew what Kathy was thinking: Stephanie was seven years younger than him.

"And then she gave me his name," Julia persisted. "Allan McLachlan. And I thought: I know that name. It's not a common name. So I said to her: 'I know an Allan McLachlan – he plays golf with my Ben.'" Julia nodded triumphantly. "And that was when she said that she didn't think she was going to be able to make it on Thursday after all."

Staring at Julia's reflection in the kitchen window, Robert asked, "So how did this lead you to suspect that he is married?"

Julia sighed. "She was quite happy for me to meet this Allan until she discovered that I might know him. It's not a common name, and, this Allan McLachlan who Ben knows has boasted about his little bit on the side. I put two and two together: it had to be Sheila."

"Dublin is so small," Kathy murmured. "Everyone knows someone who knows someone."

Robert plugged in the kettle, unsure if Kathy was talking to him or not.

"So I had a think about it," Julia continued, "and then I phoned her back."

"Julia, you didn't!" Kathy protested.

"Yes, I did."

"But it's got nothing to do with you!"

"Well, you may not think so, but I do, and I certainly didn't want an adulterer sitting at my table."

"That's a little extreme in this day and age," Robert said evenly.

Julia looked at him coldly. "I don't happen to think so. I phoned her. Asked her out straight. And do you know what she had the audacity to tell me?"

"That it was none of your business," Robert snapped, unable to keep the irritation out of his voice.

Kathy glanced at him, frowned and shook her head slightly.

"No," Julia said, not hearing the tone. "She admitted it. Brazen as you like: Allan McLachlan is married. So I

175

told her out straight that she would not be welcome in my house on Stephen's Day."

"Why are you telling me this?" Kathy asked.

Julia looked at her blankly. "Because . . . because . . ."

"This is Sheila's business. Hers alone," Kathy continued, surprising Robert. "Who she's seeing has got nothing to do with you or me."

"But he's married!" Julia protested. "She's breaking up a happy marriage."

"How do we know that?" Kathy asked. "How do we know the marriage is happy?"

For one of the few times in her life, Julia was stunned to silence.

"There are three people in an affair," Kathy said. "The mistress, the husband and the wife. Takes all of them to make it happen."

Julia pushed back her chair and stood up. "Well, this is not the attitude I expected to hear from you. And I don't know where you get such outlandish ideas – probably from those magazines you're always reading. The wives are always the innocents in these situations, always the last to know. I don't know why these women – these *mistresses* – are attracted to married men. I really don't!" She lifted her coat off the back of the chair and pulled it on. Then glancing at Robert, she was unable to resist adding, "I just hope you never have to go through what poor Allan McLachlan's wife is going through right now." Then, obviously misinterpreting the looks on Kathy's and Robert's faces as anger, she continued hastily, "Well,

I don't think that came out the way I meant it to. I'm sorry. I didn't mean to imply . . ." Looking embarrassed now, she turned to leave. "I'll let myself out." She paused before she stepped out of the kitchen. "You will come down on Stephen's Day for dinner, won't you?"

"We'll let you know," Robert said firmly, before Kathy could respond. "Good night, Julia. And do have a happy Christmas."

CHAPTER 22

In the silence that followed Julia's departure and the slam of the hall door, they both clearly heard the high-pitched squealing scrape of metal on stone.

"She's caught the edge of the pillar," Robert said, unable to keep the grin off his face. He poured water from the kettle into the teapot and glanced over his shoulder to where Kathy was also smiling. "She was parked at such an awkward angle," he explained. "I'm not sure I would have been able to get that big SUV out of the drive without hitting something either." He brought the fresh pot of tea to the table and sat down in the chair facing Kathy. Silently, he poured her a fresh cup.

"I'm thinking I might have given her a different response a couple of days ago," Kathy said quietly. "But when you become part of an affair, you discover a different perspective."

"Did you know?" Robert asked, just to make

179

conversation. "About Sheila," he added hastily, In truth, he couldn't care less about the youngest of the sisters and how she was living her life.

Kathy held the teacup in both hands and looked into the cloudy liquid. "She told me on Monday. We were sitting in her car in the carpark of a health club just off the M50. I sat there and watched my husband kiss another woman." She looked up and her expression made him sit back, suddenly frightened that she was going to throw the cup of tea in his face. She obviously had the same thought, because she carefully returned the cup to the saucer. "I phoned you," she said, her voice little more than a whisper. "I sat in a car not ten yards from you, and phoned you."

Robert nodded, remembering the call; he was standing in the car park having just spoken to Stephanie about children, then he had leaned over and kissed her, deeply, passionately. He felt himself colour and beads of icy sweat gathered in his armpits.

"I asked you what time you were coming home," Kathy continued.

Robert nodded. The idea that she had been trailing him around, following him, spying on him, was unsettling, even frightening. This was a Kathy he did not know.

"You told me you were just leaving the office and would be home in forty minutes." Kathy suddenly stood up, startling him. She dashed her tea into the sink and then began to clear off the kitchen table.

"How long . . . how long have you known?" he asked eventually. "About us? About me?"

"Not long. Why, did you think I was the sort of person who would turn a blind eye to my husband's affair?" Kathy's voice was calm, reasonable, conversational. She pulled a cookery book off the shelf and flipped through it until she found the recipe she was looking for.

"No. I never thought that," Robert admitted.

Pressing the book flat on the table, Kathy scanned the contents, then started to go through her presses, gathering the ingredients for the turkey stuffing.

"Will you sit and talk to me?" Robert asked. Kathy's constant movement around the kitchen, the banality of her actions contrasted so sharply with the extraordinary conversation that the whole experience was taking on a surreal dream-like aspect.

Kathy ignored his request. "I realised the truth last Thursday, when I was writing the Christmas cards. Once I suspected, it was relatively easy to put it all together. There was a speeding ticket upstairs in your office. You'd been caught speeding in Ballymun in October . . . and yet you were supposed to be in Belfast that night having dinner with a client."

Robert concentrating on adding sugar to his tea. He wasn't sure how many spoonfuls he poured in, but it didn't really matter. His throat felt closed and tight, and he knew he would not be able to drink it.

Kathy pulled the blender out from the press under the sink and plugged it in. Opening the kitchen press, she found the plastic bag of dried bread she'd been saving for the past couple of days. She started feeding the bread into the blender, grinding it to crumbs. When the blades were whirring, conversation was impossible and she only spoke when she stopped and cleared out the breadcrumbs. "Then I remembered all the other nights you'd stayed away, meeting with clients, wining and dining them . . . and you know something? I didn't remember the company getting any contracts from these clients. You were supposed to be having dinner with Jimmy Moran in Shanahan's on the Green last week. But do you know something? When I phoned to check, they had no record of your reservation."

"Actually, I really was supposed . . ." Robert began, and then shut up. No matter what he said, Kathy was not going to believe him – and why should she? She had lost trust in him; everything he said was suspect.

Kathy stuffed more bread into the blender and the blades whirred and stopped. "And then I discovered the phone records in the office." She turned to look at Robert. "Hundreds of calls, Robert. Hundreds. First call of the day. Last call at night. All to the same mobile number or the same house number. And I couldn't help but remember the mornings you left here without speaking to me, or the days when you were too busy to phone to see how I was, or those days when you got back late and I'd be in bed. Whole days would go by and we wouldn't speak more than a few words. And yet you could find time to phone your mistress several times every day, every single day."

"Maureen told me you'd seen the phone records," he muttered.

"She confirmed what I already knew. She just gave me the time frame. She thinks it's been going on for a year. Stephanie Burroughs said eighteen months. What is the truth?"

He nodded. "June of last year was the . . . the first time."

"The first time for what?" she snapped.

Robert glanced over his shoulder towards the sitting-room where the children's voices were just audible over the sound of the TV. "Could we discuss this somewhere more private?" he asked.

"Right now, this is the most private room in the house. If we go upstairs, the children will suspect that we're wrapping presents and be in and out every five minutes. Right now, they know I'm preparing the stuffing for the turkey and they've no interest in that."

Robert stood and came around the table to stand beside Kathy. "Can I help?"

"No," she said simply. She turned back to the blender. "I don't know what's going to happen between us, Robert. But it's going to take me a long time before I can trust you again . . . a long time before I can even look at you without feeling sick to my stomach."

He reached out to touch her, but she jerked away. "Don't!" she snapped.

Robert allowed his hand to fall loosely by his side. "I am sorry," he said. "I know it sounds like a cliché, but I

183

never wanted to hurt you. You have to believe me – that was never my intention." Folding his arms, he leaned against the counter and looked around the kitchen. It came into sharp focus and it was almost as if he was seeing it anew: the scraps of paper, the advertisements from the supermarkets, the flyers for chimney sweeps, the charity appeals pinned to the notice board, the unopened post on the counter, next year's calendar just visible beneath this year's. "I allowed myself to enter into the relationship –"

"Affair!" Kathy snapped. "Call it what it is – an affair, and you, an adulterer!"

Robert took a deep breath, suddenly conscious that he had to choose every word with care. "I began my affair with Stephanie June last year. I was lonely, Kathy, desperately lonely. I wanted someone to talk to, someone to share with, someone to show an interest in me. I tried to talk to you – tried I don't know how many times. But you never seemed to be interested. You never asked how things were going, never seemed to be in the slightest bit concerned with the ordinary day-to-day minutiae of keeping the company afloat. I'm not even sure you realised how much trouble we were in. We came close, so very, very close to going under."

Kathy stepped around Robert to remove fat tubes of sausage meat from the fridge.

"I was lonely," Robert repeated, aware of her movements, but not looking at her. "We'd stopped . . . stopped making love. When I tried, you'd turn your back on me or you'd come to me so reluctantly that I felt you were making love with me almost as a duty. There didn't seem to be any pleasure in it for you. And do you know how that made me feel? Small and dirty, that's how. I hated feeling like that. After a while I stopped making the effort, I'll admit it. But – and please don't take this as a criticism, it's just a statement of fact – you never made an effort either."

"So you're saying it's my fault you found yourself a mistress?" Kathy asked savagely.

"No," he sighed. "I'm not trying to score points here – I'm just trying to let you see how I ended up in this situation." When Robert had been driving home, he'd imagined several versions of the conversation he was having now. He'd visualised it taking place in the sitting-room, late at night, with the TV turned off or the pair of them sitting on either side of the big table in the dining-room, or upstairs in the bedroom, with both of them standing on either side of the bed. He'd never imagined it taking place in the kitchen, while Kathy stuffed the Christmas turkey as if everything was normal. "I allowed myself to have the affair, Kathy, because I believed – genuinely believed – that you no longer loved me." He held up his hand as Kathy rounded on him. "I know. I'm just telling you how I felt, telling you how I saw things. When you stood in Stephanie's sitting-room earlier and said that you loved me, no one was more surprised than I was."

"I never stopped loving you," Kathy said immediately.

"Even right now?" he asked, trying to lighten the sombre mood.

"I'm not sure how I feel about you at this moment. But the very fact that we're both standing in this room, even after all that's happened today, should suggest something."

"What?" he wondered.

"That maybe I do accept some responsibility for what happened," she said, surprising him. "I wasn't paying attention. And if a marriage is going to work, then both parties have to keep paying attention. You stopped paying attention to me, and I stopped paying attention to you."

"Would it help if I said I was sorry, truly sorry?"

Kathy glanced sidelong at him. "Sorry for what? Do you regret the affair?"

"I regret the pain and upset it caused you," Robert said carefully. In truth, he didn't regret the affair. His only regret was that he'd been caught and it was now at an end.

"Well, I'm glad you chose to tell me the truth," she said lightly.

"I would never knowingly hurt you," he continued.

"And yet you have hurt me, Robert. Hurt me and humiliated me. And it's going to take me a long time to forgive that."

"What's going to happen to us?" he asked.

"As I see it, we have two choices: we can stay together, make some new rules, start again, and really work at it this time. Or I can sue for divorce."

If Kathy sued for divorce, what happened then? If she got herself a good lawyer, he could end up losing his home, access to his children, and possibly even his business. He never realised that ending up in bed with Stephanie Burroughs could have such drastic consequences. "Well, look, let's talk about this later, or tomorrow maybe. We're both tired and probably not thinking too clearly. I know I'm not." Robert licked dry lips and glanced sidelong at Kathy. "I do have a favour to ask," he added.

Kathy looked at him, a mixture of amusement and disdain on her face. "A favour!"

"If you decide that you want me to go — and I can fully understand if you do — then can we keep this from the children for a while? I don't want to spoil their Christmas."

"I won't ruin their Christmas," she promised. "Let's try and get through the next couple of days like civilised people."

"Thank you," he said sincerely.

"When were you going to tell me, Robert?"

"Tell you what?" he wondered.

"Tell me that you were going to leave me."

"I don't know for certain," he mumbled. "Probably at the weekend."

"You don't sound so sure."

"I'm not," he admitted.

"And yet Stephanie seemed convinced that you were going to tell me after Christmas so that you could spend New Year's Eve with her."

"Yes, we spoke about that."

"Or were you going to give her an excuse and stay here?" Kathy guessed.

"Kathy," Robert said truthfully, "I've no idea what I would have done for certain. But yes, the plan was to tell you, probably on Saturday or Sunday, that I was leaving."

"Bastard!" Kathy hissed. She pushed him away from her. "You callous, uncaring bastard!"

Robert stepped away from her and moved around the table, "I'm sorry, Kathy, truly I am. But I made that decision believing that you did not love me. Before I knew the truth."

Kathy turned back to the turkey. "If we are going to rebuild our lives and our relationship, we're going to have to be honest with one another." She looked up, seeing his reflection in the window. "Will you be honest with me, Robert? Can you promise me that?"

"Yes. Yes, I can," he said.

"Then you have to promise me something."

"Anything."

"You have to promise me – swear to me – that you'll stay away from that woman."

"I promise," he said quickly. "In any case, I think you can tell from today that she'll want little enough to do with me." When he realised that Kathy wasn't going to speak to him again, he turned and left the room, stepped out into the hall and took the stairs two at a time. When he entered his office, he closed the door and turned the key in the lock. Then he lay back against the door and slowly slid to the floor.

This was a day he was not about to forget in a hurry. Thank God it was coming to an end. He reckoned the worst of it was over now.

CHAPTER 23

Sitting at his desk, it didn't look as if the papers had been disturbed; Kathy had obviously been very careful. He dug down through the pile of post until he found the speeding ticket. It was a fixed penalty ticket, two points on his licence, for driving 36 miles per hour on a 30-mile stretch of road in Ballymun last October 31, at 11.12pm.

He remembered the night, clearly remembered seeing the white van parked by the side of the road with its blacked-out back windows as he shot past it. The irony of it was, of course, that he had actually met with a client in Belfast and the plan had been for him to spend the night in the city and drive back the following morning. However, within about fifteen minutes of commencing the meeting, it became obvious that what Robert had assumed might be a potential client was nothing more than a time-waster. It happened all the time. He had concluded the meeting as quickly as politeness allowed, cancelled the dinner reservation and driven back down to Dublin. He had actually turned off the M1 and was heading into Swords and home when he'd picked up the phone and, on impulse, called Stephanie and asked her did she want him to stay the night. She said yes; Stephanie always said yes. So he drove through Swords and continued down the road towards the airport. There was an accident on the carriageway, so he'd driven around the airport roundabout and headed down towards Santry, before taking a right which took him along the side of the airport runway, then a left which led him into Ballymun and the speed trap. Usually, he was so careful with his speed. He was in a business that depended upon a car, and his insurance premium was so high that the last thing he needed were points to drive it even higher. But he reckoned his eagerness to be with Stephanie had edged the speed over the limit.

He checked through the rest of the post in his in-tray, but he could find nothing else incriminating in it – there was an MBNA bill, but it was for business expenses. He turned the page and frowned. Hmmm, had she seen this page? There were three items which might have given her pause for thought. A purchase from QVC, a bouquet of flowers and a meal in the White Orchid Restaurant. He could claim they were business expenses . . . but he doubted Kathy would believe him. Maureen was right: he was greedy. He should have conducted his affairs – he smiled grimly at the irony – on a cash–only basis. But he never thought he'd be discovered; he never imagined that Kathy would come searching, looking for proof.

How much did she know?

He looked at the bill in his hand. He doubted if she'd seen this: she would undoubtedly have brought it up in conversation. He pulled the second page off the bill and was just about to feed it into the shredder when he realised that the sound might alert Kathy to the fact that he was shredding documents on Christmas Eve. And it wouldn't take a genius to work out what he was doing.

He stood and opened the filing cabinet, then pushed the page to the very back of a folder marked *Revenue Comm*. She'd never find it there, and next time the house was empty, he'd shred it, and any other piece of evidence he could find.

How much had she discovered? He fully intended to tell her the truth, the whole truth and nothing but the truth . . . or as much of the truth as he dared tell her. He knew he could never tell her that he'd asked Stephanie to marry him. If he could tell her what she already knew, he rationalised, then he wouldn't cause her any more hurt.

Robert looked around the room, past the printers, faxes, scanners, a large desktop computer, the digital editing suite to the row of filing cabinets that took up the left wall. They were all work-related. There was nothing personal – nothing incriminating – in them.

And the computer?

Robert ran his fingers along the top edge of the screen. There was nothing on this computer. It was entirely business-related. There were no emails, no romantic letters that could link him to Stephanie. Besides, the machine was password protected and Kathy didn't have the password. When he wanted to send emails to Stephanie he used an online account, or his mobile phone, and when he talked to her using instant messaging, he never kept the IM logs. The laptop was also clean as far as he remembered. He'd check it out later. But it was also password protected.

Robert sat down at his machine and powered it on. Then he entered his password, 10101962 – his date of birth. As he did so he realised that the password offered little protection from Kathy – it was something she could easily guess if she thought about it. He really must get around to changing it.

He quickly checked his email. Some spam, an offer from a Nigerian to share fifty-two million dollars with him, offers for Viagra and Rolex watches, and a couple of emails from clients wishing him a Happy Christmas. Nothing from Stephanie.

Pulling out his phone, he called her mobile, but it went straight to her message service. Lowering his voice, he said, "Stephanie, it's me. Please give me a ring when you get this. I just want to have a few words about what happened today, about us too. Talk to me. Please."

Where was she?

He didn't think she'd had any plans for the evening.

She'd told him that her friend Sally was getting engaged, but she'd said it was a private party. He phoned the house. "Stephanie? It's me. I . . . I just need to talk to you. About today. About us. About the future. I know you're angry, but please call me. Let me know you're OK."

Somewhere at the back of his mind, an alarm bell started ringing. Where was she? Why wasn't she answering? He glanced at his watch. He'd try again in a couple of hours.

CHAPTER 24

Robert opened the hall door and breathed in the icy night air. It was so cold it burned his nostrils. It had snowed earlier, the merest dusting of flakes, but the sky was now completely clear, the stars hard and sharp in the heavens.

"Are you going out?" Kathy's voice sounded as cold as the night air, and did he hear the faintest hint of accusation in it . . . or was it just his guilty conscience?

"I just want to bring the car in," he explained. "I parked it on the street earlier." The kitchen door closed behind him, and he thought he heard Kathy's voice talking on the phone.

He stopped to look at the pillar on the way out. The edge of the stone cap was missing and there were flakes of blue metallic paint on the stonework. He grinned; he reckoned Julia had caught the back wing and probably the back door as well. Her little moral outburst had cost her a couple of grand at least. He hit the remote, the Audi's lights flashed and he climbed in and turned on the engine. Ice crystals had grown like mould along the edges of the windscreen and he leaned forward to stare at them, suddenly a boy again, remembering – with absolute clarity – that first terrible Christmas when his father left home. He'd spent Christmas Eve sitting at his bedroom window, fully dressed, with a blanket thrown over his shoulders, watching, hoping, praying that his father and brothers would come home for Christmas. They hadn't, and he'd sat through the night, watching the same ice crystals, intricate and delicate, creep across the window until they completely obscured the night.

Wheels spinning on the ice, he eased the car into the driveway, turned off the engine and then sat in silence, listening to the engine tick quietly to itself. He was beginning to realise that nothing was ever going to be the same again.

As he climbed out of the car, he caught the merest flicker of the bedroom curtain moving, and wondered if Kathy was watching him. Was this how the future was going to be: forever watched and spied on? He experienced the briefest snap of anger. Well, that wasn't going to happen. Kathy had every right to be angry with him but, as she'd admitted herself, she was not entirely blameless. She was talking about changes that she wanted to see . . . well, he wanted to see some changes himself.

He popped the boot, and pulled out the Dunnes and Carrig Donn bags. He'd barely managed to make it into

The Pavilions before closing and his choices for Christmas presents for his wife had been limited. He'd shop earlier next year, he promised himself, and then stopped: would there be a next year?

Shivering in the chill night air, Robert hurried back into the house.

This was now the third call and there was still no answer.

He'd been phoning Stephanie every hour on the hour. The calls kept going straight to her answer machine. Where was she?

He was beginning to get just a little frightened. Stephanie had always appeared to him as calm and sensible, not given to hysterics or emotional outbursts. She was the senior accounts manager in one of the biggest – if not *the* biggest – advertising agencies in Dublin, handling multi-million-euro accounts and even bigger egos on a daily basis. She didn't strike him as someone who would do something stupid.

And yet . .

And yet he had to admit that she had been slightly *off* over the past few weeks. He knew she was not looking forward to spending Christmas on her own and they'd come close to an argument on more than one occasion when she'd put pressure on him to leave Kathy and spend the time with her.

Robert continued wrapping Kathy's Christmas presents – an intricately beautiful, twisted white-gold necklace from Carrig Donn, and a trio of silk scarves from Dunnes – and tried to remember last Christmas. Stephanie had been a little down then too. They'd been seeing each other for six months and it would be true to say that it had been the happiest six months of his life. He'd felt young again. Young and alive. He had a young woman who was interested not just in him as a person, but in every aspect of his life, someone he could talk to about the business, someone he could make plans with. And then Christmas had arrived. It was the first big test of their relationship.

Stephanie wanted him to spend Christmas Eve with her – but he couldn't. She wanted him to call over on Christmas Day, but he couldn't do that either. Nor could he call to see her on Stephen's Day. And it was the same story with New Year's Eve and New Year's Day.

He'd spoken to her on several occasions over that week, and he knew how lonely and miserable she was. She promised she was never going to do it again. And yet here she was, a year later, in an even worse position. The future she had been happy to plan was in pieces, the man she'd hoped would move in with her and ultimately marry her, had left her, and she was alone once again over Christmas. He'd seen the look on her face earlier, a look of devastation, absolute loss. He could only imagine how she was feeling right now: lost, lonely, alone, depressed.

She had to be at home . . . where else could she be? But if she was at home, then why didn't she answer the phone? Sly and insidious, the thought that had been lurking at the back of his head all evening finally surfaced. She wouldn't have done . . . anything foolish, would she?

CHAPTER 25

Wednesday, 25th December

CHRISTMAS DAY

The house was still and silent.

The children had gone to bed and he'd heard Kathy move around her bedroom – funny, he'd always thought of it as *her* room, never *their* bedroom or his room – but now a deep silence had fallen over the house. The heating had just clicked off, and a chill was beginning to creep into the air.

Robert came out of his office and crept downstairs as softly as he could, moving silently in his stockinged feet on the heavy cream-coloured carpet. He checked the front door and slid the security chain across it, then went from room to room, unplugging the TV and the Christmas-tree lights. He noticed that Kathy had laid out the children's presents around the tree and he was embarrassed and just a little ashamed that, aside from the books, CDs and DVDs, he didn't know what she'd got them for their major present.

In the kitchen, he plugged out the small TV and the kettle, then checked the back door before turning off the lights. He stood in the darkened room and allowed his eyes to adjust to the gloom. The kitchen took on a vaguely milky glow and when he stepped up to the window, he could see that huge, silent flakes of snow were falling, swirling and curling around the back garden, painting one side of the trees in white, while leaving the other black and shapeless.

It was going to be a white Christmas, he smiled. And then the smile faded. Where was Stephanie?

Standing in the kitchen, he pulled out his mobile and hit redial. Hers had been the only number he'd been calling all evening. As before it went straight to her message machine, and he hung up without leaving a message. The snow hit the window, stuck briefly, then dissolved into icy tears, and he could see his own image reflected back at him, broken and distorted.

Where was she? He was getting seriously worried.

Maybe she'd drowned her sorrows in a bottle of wine and was even now sleeping it off. It would be totally out of character — he'd seen her tipsy, but never drunk — but today's events were totally out of the ordinary too.

Maybe she'd simply turned her phone off. He shook his head; he'd never known her to turn off her phone. Once she'd even stopped in the middle of lovemaking to take a call from a client.

Was she at home, with her mobile by her side, watching his number come up on screen again and again and choosing to ignore his calls? He went into the XDA's complicated menu and selected "Hide ID". Then he phoned again. If she was punishing him by not answering his calls and picked up now, he was going to give her a piece of his mind for worrying him.

The call went straight to the message machine.

He suddenly had a strong feeling that something was wrong. He looked up at the kitchen clock. Nearly one. If he left now, it would take him the best part of an hour to get to her place. But what was he going to tell Kathy? He couldn't exactly tell her the truth – I've gone to check up on my mistress, especially having just promised to stay away from her – could he? And yet he couldn't just walk out in the middle of the night . . .

He suddenly remembered the last time he'd been called away in the middle of the night. Pulling a page from the notepad by the phone, he scribbled, "*Office alarm has gone off – gone in to see if there's a problem.*" He was about to add, "*love, Robert*" but didn't. He might be a liar and a cheat, but he wasn't sure he was that much of a hypocrite yet.

The roads were deserted.

The carriageway was dusted with a thin layer of white snow, pristine and unmarked ahead of him, only his rapidly-disappearing car tracks behind. Even with the windscreen wipers doing double time, all they succeeded in doing was compacting the snow in either corner of the window and despite the heaters on full, frost was forming on the bottom edge of the windscreen. He could feel the heavy car shift and slide on the corners and kept dropping his speed until he was doing a little under twenty-five. At this rate it was going to take him at least ninety minutes to get to Stephanie's, though maybe when he got closer to the city, the roads would be free of ice. And where were the gritters and sanders? Maybe they didn't work at 1.15 on Christmas morning.

Even though he'd driven this section of road nearly every day of his working life, he found that the snow, now falling thick and fast, was removing all his usual landmarks. When it spun and eddied and blew directly towards the car, it gave the disconcerting impression that he was actually falling into it. And with the side and rear windows completely covered in a thick grey-white coating, his world was reduced to little more than an arc directly in front of his face. He was forced to pull off the road before he reached the Port Tunnel Works. He knew he daren't drive through that maze of bollards and roadworks with limited visibility. Forcing open the door, he was shocked by the bitter chill in the air and even more shocked by the amount of snow on the roof of the car and for the first time he wondered if he was actually going to make it back to Swords that night. What would Kathy say to that? Using a furled umbrella he scraped the snow off the roof, and cleared the back and side windows before climbing back into the car. The back and shoulders of his heavy leather coat were coated in snow and he could feel wet icy fingers clinging to the hair at the nape of his neck and beginning to trickle their way down his spine. OK, if he was stuck and not able to make it back up the carriageway, he would drive to the office and call Kathy, maybe even ask her to phone him back on some pretext. At least that way she'd know he was not with Stephanie.

Christ, what a mess!

The going was a little easier the closer he got the city. What had been snow in the suburbs was a dirty slushy rain in the city centre. The almost deserted city was bathed in sodium light which lent everything a slightly diseased-looking appearance. He slowed at the lights in Marlborough Street as a group of young men in dinner jackets and loose bow ties and women in too-light dresses conga'd their way across the street. They were all wearing reindeer headdresses. That's what Christmas should be like, he decided: young and free, without a worry in the world, full of dreams for the future and Christmases to come. Crouched in the doorway opposite, a shapeless, indeterminate figure in a filthy sleeping bag was huddled out of the icy sleet. As Robert drove away, he decided that the latter was probably a closer approximation of what Christmas was: lost innocence and shattered dreams.

Robert dipped his headlights as he turned into the

courtyard before Number 28, Stephanie's house. Ice crackled and crunched beneath his wheels and he swung into the parking space and parked beside her silver BMW. Her car was here, but he wasn't sure if that was a good or a bad sign. If she was going out to a party, she always left the car at home. Turning off the engine, he sat for a moment, composing himself.

The house was in darkness, unlike some of the others, which had miniature Christmas trees or menorahs in the windows. There was an illuminated *Santa Stop* sign in a window box of one of her neighbours, a string of icicles hanging on another. It was close to 2.30 and there was no movement in any of the houses and his were the only tyre marks on the cobbles. He pulled out his wallet and opened the little zip compartment. Nestled in the back of the pocket was a single unmarked key. Stephanie had given it to him on the occasion of the first birthday of his they'd shared in October, just over a year ago. "So you can escape, whenever you need to," she had explained. "And who knows, maybe I'll even come home one day and find you waiting for me in bed." But that had never happened.

Stepping out of the car he gently eased the door closed. The last thing he wanted to do now was to slam the door in the small courtyard: he knew from experience that it would echo around the little square and no doubt bring Mrs Moore, the nosy neighbour, to her window.

The moment he stepped into the hall, he knew the

house was empty. It wasn't the cold — the house was surprisingly warm — but it was the ambience. It *felt* empty.

"Stephanie!" he called from the bottom of the stairs. If she was upstairs, he didn't want to startle her, maybe have her hit the panic button beside the bed and have the police arrive. He grinned humourlessly; now wouldn't that just be the perfect end to a perfect day? "Stephanie?" He looked into the sitting-room: it was exactly as he had left it a couple of hours ago. The presents were where he had dropped them, the balloon floating close to the ceiling.

Robert climbed three stairs.

He was suddenly conscious that his heart was thumping in his chest. On the one hand he was hoping that the house was empty, because the alternative was almost too horrible to contemplate. What was he going to do if he did discover something?

He paused before he stepped onto the landing and took a deep breath. And then he realised that he was also unconsciously sniffing the air, smelling for . . .

The air smelled dry and warm, faintly perfumed by the flowers he brought earlier and a hint of something mint and floral from the bathroom. He couldn't smell anything else, anything noxious.

What if Stephanie had done something stupid in a fit of depression? What was he going to do if he opened the bathroom door and found her in the bath? Isn't that what women did: fill the bath with warm water and then use a razor blade to open a vein? It was just like falling asleep, he'd read.

Standing outside the bathroom door, he was conscious that his heart was hammering so hard he could feel the shake in his chest, his temples, even in his fingertips.

What would he do if he found the body? He'd have to report it to the police, and then they would want to know what he was doing here at 2.30 on Christmas morning, and then Kathy would know that he'd gone back to Stephanie's, and then . . .

What was he doing here, he suddenly asked himself. He'd phoned Stephanie; she hadn't answered. Why had he not been content to leave it at that? Why had he continued to phone and work himself up into a state of panic that actually drove him out of the house in the middle of the night to drive across the city to check up on a woman who had rejected him only a few hours previously?

The answer was very simple: he was here because he loved her. Still loved her, despite what had happened.

Pressing his hands flat against the bathroom door, he pushed it open. The bath was empty. Which left the bedroom. He took two quick steps towards the door and pushed it open.

The wave of relief that washed over him was a physical sensation that left him clutching the doorframe for support.

The bed was empty. It also hadn't been slept in, though the cover was rumpled as if Stephanie had sat on it, and it bore the outline of a rectangle. A small suitcase maybe? He pulled open the wardrobe and checked through Stephanie's dresses, skirts and coats. As far as he could tell everything was there.

But the handbag she normally used was missing as was her mobile, though her company laptop was shoved under the bed where it usually lived.

Robert sat on the edge of the bed and looked around the room. He was totally confused now; he wasn't sure whether to be relieved or even more scared. At least he hadn't found a body, but there was no evidence that she'd gone away. Maybe she'd simply gone out to an all-night party and was even now enjoying herself in the arms of a young man? The pulse of jealousy that rippled through him surprised him with its intensity. But if she'd gone out to a party . . . Robert stood and checked the opposite end of the wardrobe where Stephanie kept her party dresses. He remembered many happy occasions sitting or lying on the bed, watching her standing in her underwear going through the dresses looking for something suitable to wear. Inevitably, she ended up wearing black. There were four LBDs, all with different combinations of neck and hemlines on the hangers, all covered in dry-cleaning bags. There didn't seem to be any noticeable gaps on the rails. He pawed through the rest of the dresses; most he recognised and, as far as he could tell, none were missing. Nor were there any spaces in the lines of shoes that were arranged on their little shelf close to the floor.

So, maybe she hadn't gone to a party . . .

It looked as if she had simply walked out of the house. Where was she? His only hope was that she was with her friend Sally. If he hadn't heard from her by morning, he'd try and get in touch with Sally . . . and if Sally didn't know where her friend was, then he might have to go to the police.

He moved through the house, turning off the lights and closing the doors. He thought about turning off the heating, but he guessed that if Stephanie was out late partying, she would not want to come home to an icy house. Locking up, he climbed into his car and pulled out his mobile phone.

"Stephanie. I don't know what's happened. I don't know where you are. It's just after 3.00 a.m. and I'm just leaving your house. There's no sign of you. I'm leaving this message in the hope that you return, hear it and answer me. I'm hoping you're with your friend, Sally. I think I remember you saying that she was supposed to be getting engaged tonight . . . no, last night. My God, I've just realised it's Christmas morning."

It was 4.30 by the time he reached Swords. It was still snowing, quick flurries, followed by odd spiralling flakes, followed by another quick flurry, driven on by an increasingly icy wind. Driving alone along the carriageway, he felt as if he was the only soul in the world.

He was desperately tired, both physically and emotionally exhausted. He wanted to pull off the road and just close his eyes for a few moments, but he knew there were very real dangers in doing that. At one stage he cracked open the driver's window, slices of frozen snow caked on the glass falling into the car, and breathed in the bitter night air in an effort to stay awake.

By the time he turned down the road that led to his house, some of his neighbours were showing lights in the bedrooms and sitting-rooms. Santa always came particularly early to homes with young children. Climbing out of the car, he thought he saw the bedroom curtains twitch, but he was too tired to even care. Opening the hall door as silently as possible, he stepped into the hall, and wondered, for a moment, if he had enough energy to make some tea. Deciding it was too much of an effort, he climbed the stairs to his office, wincing as the third step from the top protested with a squeak. Still fully dressed, wearing his heavy leather coat and gloves, he slumped into his office chair, leaned his head back and closed his eyes.

The nightmare that followed was particularly unpleasant, although when he awoke, he could remember none of the details, only the incredible feeling of loss and searching, of travelling through a long grey-white tunnel where a figure, barely glimpsed, seemed to be constantly running away from him. He thought the shape in the distance might have been Kathy, but it could just as easily have been Stephanie.

CHAPTER 26

Robert came suddenly totally awake. And groaned aloud.

He was sitting in his chair in his office, wearing his leather coat, gloves and outdoor shoes. His feet were blocks of ice. Rising out of the chair and standing took an effort; he felt like an old man. Peeling off his gloves he dropped them on the floor, then shrugged off the heavy coat. He sank back into the chair to fumble with the laces of his shoes. His socks were damp, his shoes lined and stained from the snow. Padding barefoot into the bathroom, Robert found a towel and sat on the edge of the bath to dry his feet.

Christ, but he felt hungover. He felt exactly as if he'd spent a night drinking with Jimmy Moran. He tried arching his back and rotating his shoulders, but without success.

He wandered down to the kitchen and glanced up at

the wall clock as he put the kettle on. It was 7.30 and he was surprised the children hadn't come down yet: he smiled, remembering Christmases past when they would be up at three and four in the morning. He and Kathy would lie in bed, listening to Brendan and Theresa whisper excitedly together, wondering if Santa had come. They had been good times; happy times. But it had been a long time since the children had hurried downstairs on Christmas morning to fall upon their presents. It had been a long time since he and Kathy had been happy.

The kettle boiled and he made a small pot of tea. He was about to pour a cup for himself, then, on impulse, he poured a second cup for Kathy. He milked it with the low-fat milk she preferred and then carried both cups upstairs. Leaving his own cup balanced precariously on the banisters, he gently opened the door to the bedroom and peered inside. He immediately knew by the way she was lying that she was awake. Her posture was too rigid and normally, when she slept, she'd kick the clothes off, but now the bedclothes were tucked in tightly beneath her chin.

He moved around to her side of the bed and put the cup of tea on the small bedside locker, alongside the fat piece of historical fiction she was reading.

"Kathy," he whispered. "Kathy...?"

Her dark eyes snapped open and she looked at him.

"I brought you some tea."

Kathy continued to look at him, saying nothing.

"Happy Christmas," he said eventually, and thought about leaning in to kiss her, but decided not to.

"You went out last night." The simple statement held a world of accusation in it.

"The office alarm went on last night; I got a call from the alarm company. I had to go in." He kept his face impassive; but the irony wasn't lost on him: lying to his wife first thing Christmas morning, having promised only a few hours previously to be honest with her.

"You were gone for a long time," she said, pushing up in bed, pulling the covers up to her chin.

"Roads were terrible. I was the only car on the carriageway; I crept along. And then when I got there, I had to wait for the alarm company." That was the problem with lies: they built upon one another, a second lie bolstering the first, a third to add credence to the second.

"I take it there was no problem with the office."

He shook his head. "Probably snow or ice falling off a neighbouring building, hitting our roof and setting off one of the sensors. I could hear other alarms ringing out across Merrion Square as I drove home." More lies. Did you lie to a woman if you really loved her, he couldn't help but wonder. And yet he had lied to Kathy every day for the past eighteen months . . . and to Stephanie too, he realised. He had lied to her when he'd led her to believe that he was going to leave his wife to be with her. Because in the beginning he'd had no such intention. It was really only in the last couple of weeks when events had moved on, when Stephanie began pushing him for commitment, that he'd been forced to really consider leaving Kathy.

"Drink your tea," he said. "I'm sure the children will

be up soon." He padded silently out of the bedroom, retrieved his cup from the banisters and locked himself into his office.

Well – leaving aside the lies – that hadn't gone too badly. At least they were talking to one another.

While he was logging into his email, he checked his mobile for messages. There were none. He then checked both his office and online accounts, but aside from the usual rubbish, there was nothing from Stephanie. He started to scroll through his Outlook contacts, looking for Sally's name. He was sure Stephanie had given it to him at one stage and equally sure that he'd made a note of it. But where? The problem was he could not remember Sally's surname – Watson, Williams, Wilson, Wilton – something like that. He hunted under the word "Sally", but that returned zero hits. Perhaps Sally was short for something. Sarah? Sandra? He tried every combination, but nothing came back. He even tried the more drastic step of having the computer search every word file looking for the words *Sally* and *Stephanie*. But with no success. And now that he thought of it; he'd no idea of the names of any of Stephanie's other friends.

OK, so maybe she'd gone out to a party last night and had stayed over. If her friend Sally had got engaged then it was likely the party had gone on to the early hours of the morning. He knew Stephanie had her mobile with her and that she could use it to retrieve emails. He'd tried calling the house and her mobile: emails were all that was left.

Opening his Outlook email program, he composed a message to Stephanie.

Dear Stephanie,

I don't know what's happened to you. I am desperately worried. I've tried calling you at the house and on your mobile, but there's no response. You've just disappeared.

Please get in touch with me. Let me know you're OK.

I even went over to the house earlier this morning. I let myself in. I'm concerned there's no sign of you and yet I know you haven't gone away. I saw from the wardrobes that all your clothes are still there.

I am really concerned that something has happened or that you've done something.

I am at my wits' end.

I have no idea how to contact your friend Sally, and I realise I don't know any of your other friends. If I don't get in touch with you soon, I might try and contact Charles Flintoff. I'm half thinking I should contact the police and report you as missing.

If you get this, then please, please, please contact me.

I love you.

Robert

He read it twice over before he sent it. There was nothing but the truth in it and the only line that gave him any pause was the sentence, *I love you.* That was the truth, but he wondered how Stephanie would see it. Surely she'd realise that if he'd driven across the city in a snowstorm to check up on her, then he must have genuine feelings for her?

He hit *Send*.

He wondered how long it would take for him to get a response.

If only he could get in touch with Sally. He spent the next few minutes checking through his phone's address book, then he flipped through an old diary, wondering if he'd written it down somewhere. Damn it; he should have checked Stephanie's address book last night when he was over there. Maybe he'd slip away later this morning and drive back to get it. Christ: what excuse was he going to use this time?

The computer pinged, the sound like that of a door creaking open and then his Instant Message program, which usually ran silently in the background, popped up.

Stephanieburroughs is now online. Would you like to send a message to stephanieburroughs?

Thank God! Before he could type a letter, a single word appeared onscreen: *Yes?*

He was all fingers and thumbs, and practically misspelled every word in his haste to communicate with her. *Thank God. Are you all right? I was worried sick.* `

I'm fine.

But where are you? Was she home? She must be if she was online with him now. Could he call her, would she answer?

I'm fine.

He frowned in annoyance. What game was she playing now? *Are you not going to tell me where you are?* he typed, fingers moving more slowly now.

No.

Tell me you're all right? Surely that was the least she could do. If she was online, surely she had seen his email, surely she had to realise just how worried he'd been.

I'm fine.

Stephanie, please talk to me. We have a lot to talk about. OK, so she was angry with him, he could understand that. But could she not deal courteously with him?

We've nothing to talk about. I want my key back. Don't go near the house again. Stay away from my boss. I don't want to see you again.

That was like a slap in the face. He actually flinched away from the screen. *It doesn't have to be this way,* he typed quickly.

This is the way it is.

Please. I need to talk to you. I have to talk to you. About today. About the future.

We've no future together. Go back to your wife, Robert Walker.

A message box popped up: *stephanieburroughs* has signed off.

Robert sat in front of the screen, watching the cursor blinking rhythmically after the last sentence she had written: *Go back to your wife, Robert Walker.*

But on the long drive back across the city, Robert had arrived at a decision. Now that he and Kathy had got over the initial shock of discovery and had started to deal with it, he had slowly and inexorably come to the conclusion that he was not prepared to spent the next

221

couple of years constantly looking over his shoulder, wondering if his wife was checking up on his every move. He'd lived like that six years before: when Kathy had unfairly and mistakenly accused him of having an affair with Stephanie. He'd been conscious in the weeks and months that followed that she was spying on him. He remembered standing in the bedroom of the house they'd lived in at the time and watching Kathy climb out of the car with a pen and notepad in her hands. It took him ages to work out that she was noting down the mileage. He'd quickly realised that when he stayed away from home on business, Kathy always made a point of phoning the hotel or travel lodge with some excuse, question or query. It was a horrible, horrible feeling. He didn't want to live like that. He didn't want to spend the next few months knowing that his wife was watching his every move, not trusting a word he said, spying on him.

He wanted to get through Christmas, clear the air with Kathy, then talk to Stephanie. She was his future, he'd decided.

Except now she wanted nothing to do with him.

If he could only talk to her, he was sure he would be able to convince her that he genuinely loved her and wanted to be with her. If she knew that he was going to leave Kathy, he was sure she would come back to him. Wouldn't she?

Robert Walker nodded, the computer screen reflecting the movement: she would, he knew she would.

It was time to make changes, radical changes. At the

age of forty-two, he had the chance to start again. Over the next year, he'd concentrate on the business, build it up, really make it a force to be reckoned with. He'd work on those scripts he'd always been planning to write, maybe even apply to the film board for funding. He'd talk to Jimmy; although they'd often worked together in the past, maybe it was time they formalised their relationship – entered into a partnership. Jimmy could run the business, and he could look after the creative end.

And he would work with Kathy to make the separation as amicable as possible, but she would have to be reasonable, of course. He would do a deal with her for her portion of the house, if she was prepared to do a deal with him for her percentage of the business. He would make certain to let the children know that he would always be there for them, that he still loved them, would always love them. At least now they were that bit older, it would make it a little bit easier: he was sure they would understand.

And he wouldn't make the same mistakes with Stephanie that he'd made with Kathy. He'd pay attention to her and he knew she'd pay attention to him. They worked in the same type of business, so that would be a shared interest. He'd move into her home, help her with the mortgage, so there wouldn't be the distraction of establishing a home or looking after the house and although Stephanie had talked about children recently, she was thinking of them two or three years down the road. A lot could happen in that time. He'd had children, he'd done all that, knew the amount of time and effort they took and he didn't want to do it again. Once Stephanie started moving up the corporate ladder, she would not want children to distract her. It would be just the two of them, no distractions, no interruptions. They would be happy together.

A new beginning, a new future: that would be his new year's present to himself.

All he had to do was convince Stephanie that he was genuine. And the one way of doing that was to spend New Year's Eve together and start the new year with her.

CHAPTER 27

Most of the country awoke to a white Christmas. Two inches of snow had fallen across the entire east coast, while Donegal, parts of Sligo and Westmeath were coated in four inches with more forecast for the afternoon. Parts of Wicklow were impassable and the AA were advising drivers only to venture out if it was absolutely essential.

The sky had cleared with the dawn, and the sun was a flat gold disc that shed no heat, but touched everything with a thin veneer of amber light. The morning was spectacular and beautiful, and Robert thought it ironic that the last Christmas they would spend together should be so memorable. The children would be sure to remember that their last Christmas as a family was the time it snowed.

Robert and Kathy were outwardly polite to one another in the presence of the children, but when they were on their own, an icy gulf separated them. They went as a family to eleven o'clock mass, the only time of the year when the four of them attended church together. Although both Robert and Kathy had been raised Catholic, they had lapsed and were unwilling to force their children to join any organised religion. They hoped that when the children were old enough they would make their own decisions, though so far, neither showed an interest in any particular faith.

Robert felt deeply uncomfortable in church. He had never been particularly religious – but he did like to think of himself as honourable. When he'd stood at an altar eighteen years ago with Kathy by his side, he'd promised to love, honour and cherish her all the days of her life. No one was more proud that day. They were solemn promises that he never intended to break. And yet, here he was standing in church on Christmas morning, actively wondering how he was going to break those solemn vows without causing his wife too much pain. Maybe he didn't love Kathy enough to want to spend the rest of his life with her, but he still cared for her, she was the mother of his children, and he wanted her to retain her dignity. There was no stigma attached to divorce any more; people generally accepted that marriages – for any number of reasons – failed. At least now a situation existed so that couples could start their lives again. When his own father had left his mother all those years ago, there was no divorce in Ireland, and the couple had drifted into a legal limbo until their deaths.

"Let us share with one another the sign of peace . . ." The elderly priest's voice boomed across the loudspeakers.

Robert turned towards Kathy. While other couples around them were embracing or kissing, she stuck out her hand like a stranger. After a moment's hesitation, Robert fixed a smile on his lips and took her hand. "Peace be with you," he murmured.

Kathy didn't respond.

He was going to have to find himself a divorce lawyer. He'd call Jimmy Moran after Christmas; Jimmy would be sure to know.

"Dad, phone." Brendan didn't move from the couch.

Robert opened his eyes and blinked at the TV. His late night had finally caught up with him in the early afternoon and despite *Indiana Jones and the Temple of Doom* blaring from all five speakers, he'd fallen into a deep and dreamless sleep. "You get it," he mumbled.

"It'll be for you. It's always for you."

Robert rolled out of the chair, moved into the dining-room and grabbed the phone from its cradle before the call went to the answering machine. He licked dry lips and squinted at the clock, wondering who was phoning them on Christmas Day. Julia probably. "Hello?"

The line echoed and popped, ghost sounds clicking and whispering.

"Hello?" he asked again, squinting at the caller ID. *Unavailable*, it read, so either the call was from abroad or the caller had withheld their number.

"You may want to move away from the TV and find

someplace private where you can talk." Stephanie's voice, loud and clear in his ear, shocked him fully awake.

He swallowed hard. "Sure . . . sure," he said, forcing a smile onto his face, turning to look at the children, but they were both ignoring him. Kathy was working in the kitchen and he saw her glance curiously at him, obviously wondering who was calling. "And a happy Christmas to you too," he continued. "Let me just step out of the room away from the TV . . ."

"It's Jimmy Moran," he said to Kathy, the phone pressed against his chest, "just calling to wish us Happy Christmas."

Kathy nodded. Wearing a striped cook's apron, she was staring into the open oven, slowly sinking a skewer into the turkey. "Tell him I said Happy Christmas. Don't talk too long, I'll be serving dinner shortly."

Robert moved out into the hall. "I'll be a minute." He hurried upstairs, heart pounding, stepped into his office and locked the door behind him. Then he changed from the portable phone to his office line. "Are you OK?" he asked immediately, slightly breathless from his run upstairs and the shocking surprise of the call.

"Yes . . . no . . . I don't know." Her voice sounded strained.

He bet she had been out last night, and was probably hung over. No doubt she'd only now got around to checking her messages; maybe she was even a little embarrassed about her outburst earlier.

"I've been so concerned, and when I couldn't get

hold of you, I didn't know what to think, and then earlier, when we were instant-messaging earlier and you said you didn't want to see me again. I was devastated."

There was a long pause, then Stephanie said simply, "I think I'm pregnant, Robert."

There was a moment, a long moment, as the words sank in. Thoughts tumbled through his mind – she was mistaken, this was a joke, she was punishing him, she was lying – because he knew that she couldn't be pregnant. Simply couldn't.

Before he could reply, she snapped, "Nothing to say? No quick comment, no remark, no congratulations?" She was unable to disguise the bitterness in her voice.

"I . . . I . . . no, I don't know what to say."

"Well, think of something."

His mouth was dry and felt like it was stuffed with cotton wool and he had difficulty swallowing. He looked around the room, but could find nothing to drink. He finally cracked open one of the windows and dipped his fingers in the snow crystals, and then brought them to his mouth. Ice-cold, they burned their way down his throat. Staring out at the back garden, now sheathed in snow, he asked, "How did this . . . I mean, when did this happen?"

"Who knows? We've made love a couple of times now without using protection."

Pregnant. Dear God. She was pregnant. "I said you should have gone on the pill."

Stephanie didn't respond. She'd refused to go on the

pill, and they ended up using condoms, which he hated.

"Are you sure? Certain?" he asked carefully.

"Reasonably."

Reasonably? Reasonably! What exactly does *reasonably* mean, he wondered.

"I've just realised in the last few hours that my period is ten days late."

"Ten days isn't a lot, is it?" he said desperately.

"It's long enough."

"But you've done a test, haven't you? Confirmed it?"

"It's Christmas Day, Robert, just in case you've forgotten," she snapped. "Where am I going to get a pregnancy testing kit today?"

He licked his lips. "But you really think you could be pregnant?"

"Yes, I do."

Taking a deep breath, he asked, "Have you decided what to do about it . . . about the baby?"

"No," she said icily. "But you're the father. I wanted to talk to you first. Make some joint decisions. Real decisions."

"Yes, yes, yes, of course." Oh, this was a nightmare. A nightmare. If she was pregnant, they would have do something about it soon. He wondered how far gone she was. "Look, can we meet? Not today obviously. . ." he amended quickly. Getting out of the house now, with Christmas dinner about to be served, would be impossible. There would be too many awkward questions. "But tomorrow. Can we meet tomorrow? Where are you?"

"Tomorrow might be a little difficult for me . . ."

Robert shook his head in frustration. Why was she making things so difficult? "I really need to see you to talk to you," he said. "I can meet you. Anywhere," he added.

"Anywhere?"

He thought he heard a touch of amusement in her question. "I'll go anywhere," he insisted.

"Fine then. I'm at my parents' house."

Robert frowned, trying to make sense of the statement. "In Long Island?" he asked finally.

"Yes."

"What are you doing there?"

"Having a family Christmas," she snapped. "Robert," she hissed, "what did you expect me to do? Sit around in an empty house on Christmas Day reminding myself just how stupid I'd been?"

"Look, about yesterday . . ." he began.

"Dinner's ready!" Kathy's voice echoed faintly up the stairs.

"Not now," Stephanie snapped. "I don't want to talk about that. I want to talk about our child."

Our child. Robert felt a chill wash over him. *Our child.*

"You know, I had no intentions of ever seeing you again, of having anything to do with you. But all that's changed now. If I am pregnant, I have to see you."

"Yes, yes, of course you must." A child. Our child. Robert drew in a deep shuddering breath. "How sure?" he licked dry lips. "I mean how certain are you that you're pregnant?"

231

"You've asked me that before and I'll give you the same answer: reasonably sure."

"When will you know for certain?" He grasped at the straw: *reasonably sure* was not the same as *certain*.

"Tomorrow," she said.

"When are you coming home?" he asked.

"I don't know. I'd no plans to come back until the New Year, but I think this changes everything. I'll see if I can get back before the weekend. I'll check flights later."

"Let me know what flight you're coming in on. I'll pick you up. We can talk. Make decisions. See what you want to do with the baby."

Stephanie's voice was flat and unemotional, almost businesslike. "Robert, it's not what *I* want to do – this is our baby. It is all about what *we* want to do."

"Well, let's talk about options . . ."

"What do you mean by options?" she snapped immediately.

OK, this was definitely not something they should be discussing over the phone, this was something that had to be handled face-to-face. If she'd just discovered that she was pregnant, then she was bound to be emotional and upset. He needed to give her a little time to think about things. "I mean what's best for you and the baby. That sort of thing," he finished lamely.

"Dad, dinner's on the table!" Brendan called.

"Look, I've got to go," Robert said quickly. He didn't want the children coming up and finding the door locked and he wanted to take a few moments to compose himself before he went down for dinner . . . though right now, he had absolutely no appetite. "It's great to hear from you, and good to know that you're OK." He attempted a laugh, which sounded hollow even to his ears. "Though how you got to New York on Christmas Eve, I'll never know. What were you thinking?"

"I wasn't. Bit like when I began my affair with you, Robert. I simply wasn't thinking of the consequences." The phone went dead.

Robert stepped away from the window and hung up. Stephanie wouldn't want to keep the baby . . . would she?

CHAPTER 28

They had just finished their soup when the phone rang again.

The two children turned to look at Robert, but Kathy said, "Let the machine get it. This is one of the few meals this family sits down to together."

Robert nodded dubiously. What if it was Stephanie phoning back? The last thing he needed was her voice calling out into the room. "I'd best get it. I won't be a minute."

Kathy sighed as she carried the soup bowls out to the kitchen.

Robert snatched up the phone. "Hello?"

"Is that Robert Walker?"

"Yes, this is Robert Walker," he said, puzzled. The Caller ID showed a city centre number.

"This is Sister Holland at the Mater Hospital . . ."

"Good afternoon, Sister," Robert said, more puzzled than alarmed, "what can I do for you?"

Kathy came to the kitchen door, eyebrows raised in a silent question.

"I'm phoning on behalf of Mr James Moran . . ."

"James . . . I don't know . . . oh, you mean Jimmy Moran."

"Yes. Jimmy Moran."

"Is everything OK?"

"Mr Moran has just been admitted for observation. He's asked me to contact you. He said he would like to see you."

"Today?" Robert covered the mouthpiece and muttered to Kathy, "Mater Hospital. Jimmy's been taken in."

"But you were talking to him less than half an hour ago," Kathy said, but Robert wasn't listening to her. The nurse was speaking again.

"Mr Walker, are you there?" the Sister asked.

"Yes, yes, I'm here . . . it's just it's a little awkward at the moment. Christmas Day and all that."

"I fully understand," the nurse said, in a tone which suggested that she didn't.

"Is it an emergency?" Robert asked.

"Is Mr Moran a friend of yours?"

"Yes, yes, a good friend."

"Then I think you should come and see him."

"Tell him I'm on the way." He hung up and looked at Kathy. "I'm sorry, but I've got to go . . ."

"I know. You should go. But how did he sound when you were talking to him earlier?"

Robert looked at his wife blankly, then remembered that he'd used Jimmy's name as the excuse for the previous call. "He sounded fine," he said lamely.

"Go. Get your coat and gloves; I'll fill a flask with tea."

Once he got out of the estate, where the roads were still slick with ice and packed snow, the main roads were fine, though the two lanes of the dual carriageway had been reduced to a single central lane, with filthy slush piled high on either side. The late afternoon sunlight was blinding and Robert found himself squinting against the light, wishing he'd brought his sunglasses: he could feel a headache a combination of the light, lack of sleep and stress – beginning to throb behind his eyes.

Robert sipped the hot oversweet tea as he drove. What had happened to Jimmy, and why had he asked for him? Surely either Angela his wife or Frances his girlfriend would be with him?

He was surprised that Kathy had let him go so easily – though he had seen the expression of distrust in her eyes when she'd been questioning him about the previous call. Why had he used Jimmy's name? If he got a chance, he might have a quick word with his old friend and ask him for an alibi, just in case Kathy asked. He'd given Jimmy alibis often enough in the past, though he never thought he'd be needing a similar favour in return.

Actually, he was pleased to be able to get out of the house. The conversation with Stephanie had shocked him to his core, left him feeling slightly shaky and dissociated from the rest of the world, almost as if he was coming down with flu.

He was also astonished that following the dramatic encounter between Kathy, Stephanie and himself yesterday – was it only yesterday? – she'd managed to book herself on a flight back to New York. He didn't think it could be done – either she'd booked it earlier and said nothing to him about it, or she wasn't in the States. Maybe she was sitting at home, or in her friend's house, or somewhere down the west of Ireland, just spinning him this story to keep him away from her. And that also begged the question: was she really pregnant? They'd broken up only yesterday and suddenly she was pregnant. How likely was that? He'd tried to get a straight answer out of her, but all she'd said was that she *thought* she was pregnant, she was *reasonably sure* that she was pregnant. Well, either she was or she wasn't. She'd better phone him when she bought her testing kit tomorrow.

OK, let's assume she was pregnant. Well, she definitely wouldn't want to keep the child. She was too career-orientated. But supposing she went ahead and had the child before giving it up for adoption? Enough people now knew about their relationship to put two and two together and come to the conclusion that it was his child.

Consequences

And he couldn't help but wonder how this impacted on his new-year, new-start, daydream.

No matter how hard it tries, there is no place more lonely than a hospital on Christmas Day, Robert decided, following the directions the young woman manning the reception had given him. Although there were Christmas trees on every floor at the nurses' stations, decorations on the walls and Christmas cards and flowers everywhere, it had all the appearance of a movie set – everything was in place, but nothing belonged. Many of the wards he passed were half-empty, or held a single occupant, usually surrounded by a large family group and there were far fewer nurses than he would have expected. He saw no doctors.

Jimmy Moran was in a private room at the back of the hospital which looked out onto the stretch of waste ground that was used as a car park during the week. Robert checked the number on the half-open door and peered inside. It took him a single shocking moment to recognise the shrunken pallid figure in the bed as his friend and mentor. Jimmy's fine elegant features were sharply outlined against his skin, giving his face a skull-like appearance, and his flesh was the colour of off-white paper which highlighted the threads of broken veins in his cheeks. His jet-black hair – which he swore he didn't dye – was spread out on the pillow in a greasy swirl.

Conscious that his heart was hammering, Robert fixed

a smile on his face and tapped on the door as he stepped into the room.

Jimmy turned his head to look at his visitor, tired eyes struggling to focus. Then he nodded and stretched out his right hand. A tube attached to a drip was taped to his left hand. "Robert . . ." he licked dry, cracked lips. "Robert," he said a little more strongly, "thank you for coming."

Robert pulled over a chair and sat down beside the bed. He shrugged off his coat and laid it across back of the chair. He knew his friend was fifty-two years old – ten years older than himself – but today, he looked older, much, much older. "You knew I'd come."

Jimmy nodded. "I knew I could depend on you." He glanced sidelong at the bedside locker. "Pass me some water, would you?"

Robert stood to pour a glass of water. "I'm sorry I didn't have a chance to get you anything – lemonade or grapes, or something like that – but when the hospital phoned I just came straight here."

"Don't worry. I'm just glad you're here. And I'm sorry to have dragged you out on Christmas Day."

"There's no problem. Really, there isn't. Kathy sends her love." He held the glass to Jimmy's lips while he sipped, then helped him lie back on the pillow. When his friend was settled, Robert sat back down again and took his hand. "Dear God, Jimmy, what happened?"

"Looks like a heart attack." Jimmy grinned wryly. "I thought it was indigestion: I was cooking the turkey, and I'd been picking away at it all morning, just testing to see if it was cooked through. Plus, I'd had most of a bottle of an indifferent South African red."

"Oh Jimmy, you weren't cooking, were you? Do you remember that barbeque we had the garden of the Old Rectory when you'd finished renovating it? I spent a week on a loo after that."

Jimmy laughed, a quiet wheezing cough that seemed to catch in the centre of his chest. "I remember. You and me both, though the women were unaffected."

"I think they had more sense and didn't touch the sausages." Robert kept his tone light and the smile on his lips. The colour of Jimmy's skin, the blue of his lips was frightening him. "So how did you get in here?"

"I knew there was a problem when the indigestion didn't go away, and then I knew I was in deep trouble when it moved into my left arm. I'd a good idea what *that* meant. Shit, Robert, how many people in our business do we know who've had problems with the ticker?"

"Too many," Robert agreed. The lifestyle combination of too much business conducted over too many rich meals, coupled with incredible amounts of stress, meant that heart problems, high blood pressure and cholesterol problems were endemic in the business. He'd been meaning to have his own cholesterol checked recently, but he'd never had the time.

"I dialled 999," Jimmy went on. "And then I waited. And waited. And waited." He attempted a shrug, which hurt. "Of course it's Christmas Day, and the roads are lousy. I was waiting about forty-five minutes before they got to me." His eyes filled with tears. "It felt like an eternity. I think I may have had another attack sitting in the chair. Felt like I'd been stabbed in the shoulder."

"Where were you?"

"In the apartment in Temple Bar."

"Alone?"

Jimmy nodded.

"Jimmy, why didn't you say something to me the other night? You could have spent Christmas with us. I didn't even think to ask; I thought you'd go to Frances or that maybe Angela would have you home for the day." Frances was Jimmy's girlfriend who had borne him a son eighteen months previously. She now ran a small bookshop in the west of Ireland. Angela was Jimmy's long-suffering wife who was in the process of divorcing him.

"I didn't want to impose on you," Jimmy whispered. "Actually," he admitted, "I was hoping that Angela would have me back ... just for the day, as you say. But she's done with me. Really done this time. I tried phoning her from the apartment, but she wouldn't answer. Frances picked up her phone but put it down again when she heard my voice." There were tears on his cheeks now. "All I wanted to do was to say goodbye ... just in case."

"Why didn't you go down to Galway and stay with Frances?"

"I spoke to her yesterday morning and suggested it, but I could tell she wasn't keen on the idea. She said she was snowed in and that I'd never make it down. I wasn't sure whether to believe her or not, but I got the impression that even if she wasn't snowed in, she didn't want me around. I've a feeling," he added with a wry smile, "that she's found herself a nice young man, with the emphasis on young. More power to her."

"Jesus, Jimmy – what a mess."

"I always did have a flair for the dramatic."

"Have the doctors seen you yet?"

"I was checked in about two hours ago by some young fella who looked like he was about fifteen. All he'd tell me was there was some arrhythmia – as if I didn't know that – but that they'd take me in for observation and they'd have to do some tests, take some X-rays and scans to be sure. He said they'd have to wait for a little while because the alcohol in my system would mask the results, and it also means they could not give me any medication. Let me give you a piece of advice, son; don't ever come into hospital on Christmas Day. Any other day of the year, I reckon you're fine – but not Christmas Day."

"I'd come to the same conclusion myself. How do you feel now?"

Jimmy pushed himself up in the bed. Robert adjusted the pillows and helped him to sit a little straighter. "Actually, I'm not feeling too bad now. Better for seeing you. I'm feeling a little guilty now that I dragged you away from your family."

Robert shook his head. "I would have been annoyed if you had not."

Jimmy reached over and squeezed Robert's hand. "I

think I just got a fright, you know. Waiting for the ambulance to arrive, feeling the pain in my chest getting worse, watching black spots before my eyes . . . you know, I thought I was going to die."

"Why didn't you call me then?"

"Because if I did die, I didn't want you to find my dead body."

"Thanks . . . I think," Robert muttered. His own father had died fifteen years ago. Although he had been living on the other side of Dublin, less than an hour away from where Robert lived, they rarely saw one another. When he'd seen his father laid out in the open coffin in the funeral parlour, he hadn't recognised the bloated figure.

Jimmy tilted his head towards the grey window. "It's still snowing."

Robert crossed the room to look out over the patch of waste ground. There was a single car, lonely and forlorn, in the middle of the car park. Snow had banked high on one side of the car and the bonnet was completely covered, making it impossible to guess the make. The sky was leaden and the snow was falling heavily now, coating the piles of grimy slush in a new coat of white; heavy fat drops hit against the windows and curled slowly down to gather at the base of the frame in a lattice of ice-crystals. "A white Christmas," Robert said, glancing over his shoulder. "I don't remember the last one we had, do you?"

Jimmy shook his head. "Never forget this one though."

"Amen to that," Robert said grimly. He wasn't going to forget this Christmas holiday in a long time.

"Will you do me a favour before you go?" Jimmy asked.

Robert spun around. "Go? Go where? I'm not leaving."

"It's Christmas Day, Robert. You should be with your family."

"I'm happy to be here."

Jimmy nodded, suddenly unwilling to trust himself to speak. He concentrated on finishing the glass of water, then said, "Will you call Angela for me, please? Tell her where I am and that I'm OK."

"You're not OK," Robert reminded him.

"Aye, well, but there's no point in alarming her. Besides, what's she going to do? She's probably snowed in in Wicklow."

Robert took the number from Jimmy and stepped out into the hallway to call Angela Moran. He walked up and down the corridors, ignoring the glares from the few nurses on duty and the signs which said *switch off all mobile phones*.

Angela's phone rang nearly a dozen times before it was finally picked up. He could hear the clink of glasses and low muted music in the background.

A voice boomed, "Hello, hello?"

"Oh, hello." It was a man's voice, and Robert had been expecting Angela to answer. "I'm not sure if I've dialled the right number. I'm looking for Angela . . ."

"Yes, she's here."

Robert heard the clunk as the phone was dropped onto a hard surface, and then a slightly drunk male voice calling, "Angela, darling, phone for you!"

Footsteps rattled on wood, then clicked on marble. There was a time when Robert had been a regular visitor to the old Church of Ireland rectory which Jimmy and Angela had bought on the outskirts of Wicklow. The house was magnificent and the couple had restored it in exquisite taste. Robert could just imagine Angela – tall, thin, with an over-made-up brittle beauty – walking across the black-and-white marbled floor to pick up the phone. "Hello. Yes?"

"Angela. Good afternoon, and a Happy Christmas to you. It's Robert Walker."

There was a pause, no doubt as Angela tried to remember who exactly Robert Walker was. It had been about four years since he'd last spoken to her . . . the time of the infamous barbeque, in fact.

"Oh, Robert. What a pleasant surprise." Angela's cut-glass diction was perfect; she'd been a continuity announcer in the early days of RTE. "And the compliments of the season to you too, and to Kathy. How is she?"

"She's very good, thank you, Angela," Robert said quickly. "I'm phoning you on Jimmy's behalf."

There was a slight pause, and when Angela spoke again, there was a definite chill in her voice. "Has he asked you to telephone me?"

"Yes, he has . . ."

"I have no wish to speak to him or about him."

Robert bit back an angry response. "I'm in the Mater Hospital, Angela," he said firmly. "Jimmy was taken in earlier with a suspected heart attack."

There was a pause, then Angela said, "I'm not entirely sure I believe you, Robert. Is this another one of his pranks? He has broken my heart with his lies and his affairs, and I am afraid, Robert, that this may be just another of his tricks designed to fool me. Well, I'll not fall for it this time; I will not be taken in. If Jimmy is genuinely in hospital, then please give him my best wishes for a speedy recovery."

". . . and then she hung up," Robert finished. "She believed it was some sort of joke. Now where would she get that idea?"

"Ah well . . ." Jimmy said quietly. "Last Christmas I may have told her a little white lie to get back home."

"A little white lie?"

"I said the apartment was flooded — a burst water pipe. I painted a very graphic picture of frozen icicles of water hanging from the ceiling. And Angela — God love her, but she has a big heart — asked me home for Christmas dinner. I think that was the last meal we had together."

"But it was a lie."

"A slight gilding of the truth perhaps. She wasn't very happy when she found out."

"Why didn't you stay with Frances last year?"

"The baby was only a couple of months old, and her mother had come to stay. I'm afraid that the potent combination of post-natal girlfriend, mewling baby and girlfriend's mother was too much for me to contemplate, or bear. So I told her I spent Christmas in the apartment. And *she* was even *less* pleased when she discovered the truth that I'd spent Christmas Day with Angela."

"I know you didn't ask me to," Robert said, "but I phoned Frances."

"Ah," Jimmy muttered.

"She seems to think you had a fight the last time you were down with her and that she'd thrown you out and told you never to come back."

"There may have been some hard words said over her boyfriend," Jimmy admitted. "But you know me: quick to anger, even quicker to forgive."

"So the upshot of it is, Angela doesn't believe you're in hospital and your girlfriend doesn't care either. How do you end up in these messes, Jimmy?"

"Stupidity," Jimmy Moran said simply. "Just honest-to-God stupidity. I didn't realise how good I had it with Angela. I loved her – in my fashion – and she loved me, but I was prepared to throw it all away because a young one flashed her big eyes – and more! – at me." He patted Robert on the hand. "Learn from my mistakes, boy: you've a good thing going with Kathy, don't throw it all away for a quick piece of skirt."

Robert had opened his mouth to respond when the

door opened and an extremely harassed-looking young doctor appeared. "Now, Mr Moran," he began, then glanced at Robert. "If you could give us a few moments, I just need to run some tests on your father . . ."

CHAPTER 29

"They took him down for tests about two hours ago," Robert said to Kathy. "I keep asking them for results or a progress report, but the nurses on duty cannot tell me anything. They're run off their feet."

Kathy's voice cracked and hissed on the mobile phone. "And how did he look?"

Robert ran his fingers through his hair and sighed. "He looked terrible. Kathy, I got such a fright when I first saw him. I thought he was dead."

"He's as tough as old boots, Robert, you know that. He's going to pull through."

"I'm sorry for ruining your Christmas Day," he said eventually. He went back into Jimmy's room and closed the door. In the darkness, he stood at the windows, watching the snow fall, invisible until the moment it whirled around the streetlights.

"That didn't ruin my Christmas," she said quietly. "It was ruined a long time before Jimmy got ill."

He nodded, his reflection in the glass mimicking the movement. Then he said simply, "Yes."

"If you'd stayed at home today, we would probably have ended up in an argument."

"Probably," he agreed. He'd had the same thought himself. If Jimmy hadn't provided him with an excuse to leave the house, he knew he would have had to invent one. And he also knew that if he left the house for no reason, Kathy would immediately suspect that he was going to see Stephanie. Maybe he should tell her that Stephanie had gone home to America . . . though that might raise the awkward question: how did he know?

"Maybe this time apart has been . . . useful. Allows us both to get a little perspective."

"Yes, yes, you're right."

"Time to think," she added.

"I've been doing nothing but thinking," he said carefully, though he'd arrived at no conclusions. His head was still whirling with possibilities and opportunities – all he needed to do was to find a little quiet time to think them through. His lack of sleep was catching up with him, and he felt fuzzy, dissociated.

"We'll talk when you get home. I'll get the children up to bed. We might have a little supper together and talk."

"That would be nice . . . yes, it's been a long time since we sat down and talked. It'll be just like the old days." In the early days of their marriage and for the first few years after the children came along, they would sit together every night and talk. It didn't have to be about important things – events in their day, items on the news, television shows they'd seen, radio they'd heard. He wasn't sure when the ritual began to drift away: when the children got a little older, he thought, or maybe when he started working later and later. Then, by the time he got home, he was so exhausted the last thing he wanted to do was to *chat*. Looking back now, he realised how important those chats were.

"Do you think you're going to make it home tonight?" Kathy asked.

"I'd like to wait and see how Jimmy is. I don't want to leave him on his own."

"Why is he on his own? I thought Angela or Frances would be on the way? They're not snowed in, are they?"

"They may be snowed in, but that's not the reason they're staying away. They've both simply refused to come. Turns out Jimmy told them too many lies over too many years and that's finally caught up with him," Robert admitted. "I'd like to stay for a while longer . . . if that's OK," he added.

"Of course, it's OK. It's snowing heavily here: I'd almost prefer if you stayed there, rather than trying to drive on the roads. The hospital staff will hardly throw you out."

Robert leaned forward to stare down at the street. It was completely deserted. "You know, I might just do that. I'll kip down on one of the empty beds." His mobile started blipping and he swore softly. With all the excitement, he'd forgotten to charge the battery-hungry XDA. "I'm almost out of power on the mobile," he said quickly.

"Is there a phone in the room?" Kathy asked immediately.

Robert hit the switch over the bed, flooding the room with diffused yellow light, and squinted at the number taped beneath the telephone. "Here it is . . ." Even as he was reading out the number, he felt sure that Kathy would phone him on it at some stage in the next couple of hours. It was her way of checking up on him, one she had used before when she suspected him of lying to her about his location. Surely she didn't think that this was some sort of elaborate ruse to spend time with Stephanie? He felt anger bubbling . . . and then he remembered that he had used Jimmy's name to lie to Kathy earlier. "Look, I'd best go, and conserve what's left of the battery. You've got the number, call me anytime. I'll be here for the next couple of hours at least and if I do decide to stay here, I'll give you a call."

"Give Jimmy my love," Kathy said and rang off.

"And what about me?" Robert whispered quietly, staring at the phone.

Robert was dozing in the chair when Jimmy Moran was brought back to the room by a trio of green-suited

Consequences

nursing staff. He smiled wanly at Robert and attempted to lift a hand to wave at him, but couldn't manage more than waggling his fingers.

Robert stood awkwardly in the corner and watched as the staff lifted Jimmy onto the bed. Two bustled away pushing the trolley, while the third – a slender, olive-skinned woman – filled in the chart at the foot of the bed. She glanced up at Robert and smiled, her teeth startlingly white against moist red lipstick. "I'm Doctor Abnett."

"Good evening, doctor." He came over to the side of the bed and squeezed Jimmy's hand in his. "How is he?"

"Don't talk about me as if I wasn't in the room," Jimmy grumbled.

"Behave yourself," Robert snapped.

"Your father had at least one and possibly two minor heart attacks today," Doctor Abnett said, making the same mistake as the previous doctor and neither Robert nor Jimmy corrected her error. "They weren't the first, I might add, though he may not even have been aware of the previous ones himself. We did an angioplasty earlier, and I would imagine the surgeon will want to discuss a bypass – certainly a double and possibly a triple – within the very short term."

"How soon?" Robert asked.

"Within the next couple of months certainly. Maybe sooner."

Robert held a glass to water to his friend's lips and watched him sip. When Jimmy's lips were wet, he managed to ask, "When can I go home?"

The young doctor smiled. "Well, not today, and not tomorrow, that's for sure. Maybe before New Year – on condition that this will be the quietest New Year you'll ever celebrate. We'll keep you under observation for a few days, monitor your vitals and then our heart specialist will have a look at you. He'll make the final decision." She looked down at the chart. "It says here you live on your own."

"He can come home with me," Robert said immediately.

"I can't –" Jimmy began.

"I insist," Robert said.

"But Kathy –"

"Will be delighted to have you too," Robert said firmly. He looked at the doctor. "I'll look after him."

"Well, that makes it easier certainly." The doctor clipped the chart back onto the end of the bed and patted Jimmy's leg. "It's good to have family at times like this, isn't it?"

When she was gone, Jimmy muttered, "I hate doctors!"

Robert pulled over the chair and sat beside the bed. "What did she ever do to you?"

Jimmy did a passable imitation of her voice. "It's good to have family at times like this, isn't it? I'm fifty-two, not eighty-two. Give people a white coat and they think they're superior to everyone else on the planet."

"She was wearing a green coat," Robert reminded him with a grin.

"OK then, give someone either a white coat or a green coat . . ."

"And don't the surgeons, the misters, wear their own suits?" Robert grinned.

"OK, give someone either a white coat or a green coat or a three-piece suit, and they think they are superior to everyone else on the planet."

"And since when have I become your son?"

"I'm not sure whether to be annoyed or not about that," Jimmy muttered. "Do I look old enough to be your father?"

"Jimmy, right now, you look old enough to be my grandfather," Robert said sincerely.

Jimmy's smile faded. "I would have been proud to have a son like you, Robert. You know that."

"Hey, there's no need for that sort of talk. I'm proud to know you too. You've taught me so much. In fact I was thinking only this morning . . ."

"Was there drink involved in this thought?"

"Not a drop. And just as well, since I ended up driving across the city at three o'clock in the morning."

Jimmy's eyes widened. "This has to do with Stephanie?"

"Spot on first time. I'll tell you about that in a minute. First, let me tell you what I was thinking."

"Go on."

"I'm thinking that next year, I need to get my act together and crack this independent production lark. I really need to settle down and get some solid work done. You know, when I started out in this business, I had such high ideals; I was going to do cutting-edge controversial documentaries, hard–hitting exposés . . . and what have I ended up doing?"

"You did what I told you to do: anything and everything which puts food on the tables, gives you practical experience and you're not ashamed to put on the CV."

"I remember. I didn't agree with you when I first heard it. Then you told me that Ridley Scott started out in advertising."

"Shot the famous Hovis ad. Boy pushing a bike up a hill."

"So I've decided that I'm going to need a partner, someone I know and trust, someone who can look after the business while I concentrate on getting in some new work. If this pop video takes off, it could be massive and bring us in a lot of new business. I'll not be able to handle it on my own."

Jimmy lay in the bed and watched him, saying nothing.

"We've collaborated well together in the past. I was thinking it might be time to formalise our relationship and go into partnership together. We could set up a new company: Walker & Moran . . . or maybe Walker Moran. Well, say something," he added, when Jimmy didn't respond.

"I'd like . . . I'd like that very much," Jimmy Moran said, a catch in his voice. "But, Robert, you've got to realise that I'm damaged goods. There are a lot of people in this city who'd cross the road to avoid me."

"And many more who cross the road to ask your

advice," Robert persisted. "Will you at least think about it?"

"I'll think about it," he promised. "But only on condition that the name is Moran & Walker or Moran Walker," he smiled. "Have you spoken to Kathy about this idea?"

Robert stretched his forearms out on the bed and locked his hands together. "Not yet," he sighed. "I'm going to try and buy Kathy's piece of the company off her."

"Oh, that doesn't sound good," Jimmy mumbled. He reached over and hit the light switch, plunging the room in deep gloom. "The light was hurting my eyes," he explained.

The two men remained silent while the room gradually brightened with a dull metallic light reflected back off the snow outside. A streetlight cut a bar of warm amber high into the corner of the room. "Tell me what's happened, Robert," Jimmy said finally.

"In a nutshell: Kathy found out about Stephanie. The three of us had an encounter yesterday in Stephanie's house. If you'll pardon the expression: I thought I was having a heart attack when I walked into the room and found the two women there."

"Been there, son, worn that tee-shirt. It can go two ways – screaming or icy politeness."

"We had icy politeness."

"Oh, that's the worst sort. Nothing beats a good screaming match for clearing the air."

"And then Stephanie rejected me, told me to go back

to my wife." He shook his head; he was still not entirely sure why she'd done it.

"And Kathy took you back?"

"Yes."

"Always said she was a good girl. Takes guts to do that."

Robert remained silent. He remembered that Maureen had said exactly the same thing. Funny, he'd never thought of his wife in those terms before.

"That is what you want, isn't it?"

"Well . . . I've been thinking a lot about that," Robert said quietly.

Jimmy reached out and squeezed Robert's arm. "You've been given a second chance, son. Don't screw it up. Look at me – learn from my mistakes."

"I know I've got this second chance . . . but you know something: I want to take that chance with Stephanie."

"You don't throw away eighteen years of marriage so easily."

"I'm not. Six years ago, Kathy accused me of having an affair – I think that is when our marriage started to fall apart."

"You're the one who had the affair, Robert. Kathy stayed faithful to you."

Robert stood up and walked to the window, stuck his hands in his pockets and stared down onto the broad expanse of white below. His breath plumed a perfect circle on the glass.

"I'm forty-two, Jimmy. I've been given a chance to

start again with a women who loves me. I'd be mad not to take it."

"Kathy loves you. Loves you enough to fight for you. If she didn't want you, it would have been so easy to let you go to Stephanie."

Robert rested his forehead against the chill glass; he knew that. Even when he was making his new year's plans, that was always at the back of his thoughts: Kathy loved him.

"I take it you've not talked to either Kathy or Stephanie about this plan?"

"Not yet. Stephanie . . . Stephanie vanished after our encounter yesterday. I nearly drove myself frantic trying to find her – including driving out to her house in the middle of the night – but I managed to speak to her this morning: she's on Long Island at her parents' home."

"I thought she was spending Christmas in Ireland?"

"That was the plan, until Kathy ended up on her doorstep. Apparently when we left she decided she wasn't going to stay here on her own and managed to book herself a flight to the States."

"Resourceful girl. Getting there can't have been easy." Jimmy shifted uncomfortably in the bed. "You know, once you even hint to Kathy that you're still interested in Stephanie, she'll throw you out, have nothing further to do with you."

"I know that."

"So you need to be very, very sure of yourself and, even more importantly, very sure of Stephanie's reaction before you do anything drastic. You should not be even thinking about this right now. Emotionally, you're all over the place: your affair has been discovered, it's Christmas, you're worried about Stephanie . . . and, of course, now I've fetched up in the middle of it all, just to add another layer of complication to the situation. Please, please, please, make no decisions. Give yourself a little time, put a little distance between you and these events."

"There's another problem . . ." Robert looked over his shoulder. He could just about make out the shape of Jimmy Moran lying in the bed. In the grey half-light, his eyes were glittering brightly. "Stephanie thinks she may be pregnant."

"Ah, Jesus, Robert, and you tell me my life is a mess!"

Robert moved away from the window and started pacing up and down the small room. "Stephanie phoned me today . . ." A sudden thought struck him and he stopped, "Actually, could I ask you a favour?"

"Anything," Jimmy said immediately.

"If you're talking to Kathy and she asks if you called the house today, would you say *yes*? When Stephanie phoned earlier, I said it was you."

"I'll tell her," Jimmy said slowly.

"Stephanie is on her way home. She wants to talk to me about the child. Make plans."

"What sort of plans?" Jimmy's voice was an exhausted murmur.

"I don't know. I doubt she'll want to keep the child. I'm not even sure she'll want to carry it full term. If she's still early in her pregnancy, we could go to London."

"Sit down, for Christ's sake," Jimmy's voice snapped. "You're making me dizzy." Robert returned to the chair by the bed and Jimmy reached out to grab his arm. "Now, listen to me. I've never steered you wrong before, have I?"

"Never."

"Tell Kathy about the baby."

"Tell Kathy!"

"I didn't tell Angela that Frances was pregnant. That was the single biggest mistake I made. She could forgive me everything else, but not that. Tell Kathy. She needs to be involved now."

"I can't." Even the thought of it was unimaginable.

"If you don't tell her and she finds out – and she *will* find out – then you are finished."

"But, Jimmy, I want to finish with her."

"What! Why?" Jimmy demanded.

"Because . . ." Robert began.

"Does she still love you?" Jimmy interrupted.

"Yes, yes, she says she does."

"Did she go to Stephanie's to fight for you?"

"Yes."

"And did she offer to take you back?"

"Yes."

"Then, don't be a fool. These are your hormones talking. You want to walk away from a woman who loves you, from an eighteen-year marriage, a business you've spent the same number of years building up, a beautiful home, two gorgeous children . . . for what?"

"For Stephanie," Robert said quietly.

"For Stephanie. Tell me what Stephanie's ever done for you – besides bringing some jobs to the business and the sex, of course."

There was a long moment of silence, then Robert said, "She makes me feel good about myself."

"Robert, only you can make you feel good about yourself. Stephanie is younger than Kathy, yes, but what else has she got going for her? Let me tell you from bitter experience, the sex is never as good when you're living with the person. Nothing beats the thrill of an illicit liaison. You've told me she's not going to be able to put any more business your way for the moment, and once you're a couple, that door is completely closed. And you want to move into one of those tiny houses where there isn't room to swing a cat?" He stopped and started to cough, deep racking barks that doubled him over in pain. "If you leave Kathy," he gasped, his breath coming in painful heaves, "you will lose it all: wife, children and home, and maybe the business too. Maureen will walk: she is more loyal to Kathy than she is to you. You'll be left with nothing. Nothing. Trust me on this: this is one subject where I am an expert."

The producer's affairs were legendary. Robert had realised a long time ago that Jimmy genuinely loved women; he enjoyed the thrill of the chase even more than the capture, he'd once told Robert. And Robert couldn't help but wonder if Jimmy's attitude towards affairs had coloured his own mindset when he'd entered into his relationship with Stephanie. He'd remembered being almost shocked that he'd not experienced more pangs of conscience.

"Please rest, Jimmy," Robert said, becoming alarmed by the sound of Jimmy's cough. "Please. I'll think about everything you've said. I promise. Just relax now."

"Give me some water."

Robert poured a glass of water and held it to Jimmy's lips.

"Thanks."

"I won't make any drastic decisions, I promise. You've given me a lot to think about. As always," he added, attempting to smile.

"Kathy loves you," Jimmy murmured. "She's shocked, upset, puzzled. Telling her about the baby isn't going to be as big a blow as you might think. Be honest with her now. Tell her everything."

"I will," Robert said quickly. He would promise Jimmy anything now, just to calm him down.

"Good lad." Jimmy laughed. "You know, maybe I will go into partnership with you next year. You could be my junior partner."

"Hey – not so much of the junior!"

"I think I'd like that." Jimmy's voice was fading as he drifted into sleep. "Been alone for too long. We'd make a great team." His fingers were cool as he squeezed Robert's hand. "Don't make my mistakes, Robert. Don't walk away from a woman who loves you . . ."

It took Robert a few minutes before he realised that Jimmy Moran was never going to speak again.

CHAPTER 30

Saturday, 28th December

"It's time to go."

Robert Walker was sitting on the edge of the small bed in his office, tying his shoelaces. His wife was standing in the doorway, wearing her heavy black woollen coat.

"I didn't think it was that late," he muttered.

"The roads will be icy," Kathy reminded him. "We should leave a little early. The children have decided to stay here," she added. "They didn't really know Jimmy all that well."

Robert straightened. "Yes, yes, of course," he said distractedly. "I spoke to Lloyd, the brother in Australia, a couple of hours ago. He's not going to make it over for the funeral. He can't get the time off."

"That's a shame."

"Yes, but at least Mikey and Teddy will be here. I think Jimmy would have liked that."

Kathy stopped him at the door and brushed at the

collar of his black suit, then straightened his tie. "I think Jimmy would be very proud with everything that you've done for him over the past two days," she said. Then she turned and headed down the stairs.

Robert followed more slowly, realising that this was the first time she'd voluntarily touched him since she'd slapped him across the face in Stephanie's on Christmas Eve last Tuesday. It felt like a lifetime ago.

It was, he suddenly realised: it was a different lifetime entirely.

Later, when Robert Walker would try and make sense of the days immediately following Jimmy Moran's death, everything would shift and blur into a indiscriminate kaleidoscope of events. Trying to decide what actually happened and what he imagined happened became impossible – and there were whole swathes of time for which he had no memory.

He remembered sitting in the hospital bedroom holding the man's cooling hand in both of his, face pressed against the bedclothes and weeping, not only for the friend he'd lost, but for the father he'd never known. Jimmy Moran had such an influence upon so many areas of his life, good and bad. It was Jimmy who had taught him about the business; it was his enthusiasm and confidence which had encouraged Robert to go and establish his own business. But it was also Jimmy who introduced him to drink, who used him as an alibi for his various affairs.

Robert remembered being roused by a young nurse around midnight and then ushered out of the room. Nurses ran in and out of the room, and then a doctor he'd never seen before ambled — almost casually, he thought — into the room, and reappeared a couple of moments later, to tell Robert the lie that he was "sorry".

He had no idea how he got home.

None.

Later, much later, he would find a long scrape along the front passenger bumper of the car, but he'd no idea how he'd got it or what he'd hit. One moment he was brushing his car clean of snow outside the hospital in the early hours of the morning . . . and the next he was turning into the driveway in Swords . . . and the hall door was opening . . . and Kathy was standing waiting for him . . . and even without saying a word, she knew what had happened. He wanted — desperately wanted — her to take him into her arms, but she made no effort, and pride and shame and exhaustion ensured that he made no move either. He walked past her with just two words, "He's dead" and then climbed the stairs to his office, kicked off his shoes and dropped his jacket on the floor, fell into his chair and was asleep immediately.

The next forty-eight hours were filled with the confusion of trying to contact Jimmy's family, such as it was. Angela was quite happy to allow him to make all the arrangements, and Frances was initially uncontactable. He managed to find an address for Mikey Moran, the eldest brother, living in Toronto. From him he got addresses for Teddy in Pittsburgh and Lloyd living on the outskirts of Sydney. Mikey and Teddy immediately promised they would get home, if he could delay the funeral for a few days, but Lloyd could not give an immediate answer: he worked with the fire service and was on call over the New Year's holiday.

Robert made all the arrangements; choosing the funeral parlour, finding a church that would hold the service, picking the coffin, and arranging for Jimmy to be buried alongside his mother in Glasnevin. With Angela's permission, he went to the apartment in Temple Bar and found Jimmy's best black Armani suit and a white silk shirt and then chose a hand-painted Hermes tie, which he'd given him for a Christmas present the previous year. He'd never seen Jimmy wear it.

When he got home from the funeral parlour on Friday night, he found that Kathy had set up a bed in his office so that he wouldn't have to sleep in his office chair for another night. His black suit, a pale blue shirt and gold tie had been laid out over the back of the chair.

"Thank you," Robert said suddenly. He gunned the engine and turned the heaters to full, clearing the windscreen.

Kathy glanced sidelong at him.

"For the bed . . . and getting the suit . . ."

"I thought you had enough to worry about."

"Well, thanks anyway. And thank you for coming with me."

"I knew Jimmy, I liked him even though he was a rogue, and I wanted to pay my respects. And I also want to support you."

Robert nodded, unwilling to trust himself to speak. He pulled on a pair of sunglasses. The sky was cloudless and though the thin sunshine shed no heat, it sparkled and reflected off the banked snow and frozen water.

"How are you feeling?" she asked.

Robert concentrated on driving down the ice-locked road, conscious of the cars on either side of him. All he needed now was to sideswipe a neighbour's car to make this the perfect Christmas. "I'm a bit numb," he admitted finally, when he reached the end of the estate. The road that led into the village of Swords was glittering damply, sandy grit sparkling on the black tarmac. "Do you know," he said suddenly, "I realised yesterday . . . or maybe the day before, I'm not sure, that I've known Jimmy for more than twenty years. Nearly half my life."

"He was at our wedding," Kathy reminded him. "That's where you introduced me to him."

"I don't remember that."

"I do."

"There were times when I'd see him every day for a month . . . and then I wouldn't talk to him for weeks afterwards. But always, when we met up again, it was as if we'd never been away."

"There were times when I used to envy your

relationship with him. I was just glad that he wasn't a woman," said Kathy, stopping abruptly, realising what she'd said.

"Funny that, isn't it?" Robert said quietly. "A man can have a very close friendship with another man and no one even remarks upon it, but if it's with a woman, there are all sorts of questions raised."

"I used to think that a man and a woman could have a purely platonic relationship," Kathy said. "Now . . . now, I'm not so sure."

Robert carefully negotiated a roundabout, feeling the back of the heavy car shift on the gritty road, and headed out towards Malahide to the funeral parlour where Jimmy Moran's body had been laid out. "And yet Jimmy had a string of female friends who were never lovers. He used to say that once both sides realised that sex was never going to be an issue, a real friendship could develop."

"And what do you think?" Kathy asked.

"I don't know," he said truthfully. "Outside of business, I know very few women socially."

"Except your mistress!" Kathy snapped, and then immediately apologised. "I'm sorry. I didn't mean to bring that up today of all days. I know you're grieving. I'll respect that."

They drove in silence for a while, then Robert spoke. "I know we haven't had a chance over the past few days to talk about what happened."

"We'll talk about it when this is all over," Kathy said firmly. "I'm thinking we should go for counselling."

272

Robert frowned. "I'm not sure I want to let strangers know our business . . ."

"I'm not going to fight with you about this," Kathy said firmly. "Counselling is not optional. If you want to stay with me — if we want to stay together — then we have to start again. I want us to have counselling to clear the air, work through those issues which drove us apart."

"Work drove us apart," Robert snapped. "Me, working all hours God sent to pay the mortgage and put food on the table. If it comes right down to it, that was the only issue. If you had been a little more involved with the business — a little more involved with me — then you would have recognised that."

"You'd better not be saying that this was all my fault."

"I've told you before — it's not your fault," Robert said. "This whole sorry mess is entirely of my making. I put my hand up. I accept it." He took a deep breath, attempting to calm the bubble of rage that threatened to burst. "Let's talk about it in a day or two," he said, finally, quietly.

They drove the remainder of the distance to the funeral parlour in silence.

CHAPTER 31

Robert was astonished by the number of people who had turned up at the small funeral parlour just off the main street in Malahide. A lot of the entertainment industry were there, familiar faces from the world of TV and movies, theatre and radio. Even Angela had turned up, on the arm of a retired TV presenter. She kissed Robert on both cheeks and thanked him for all that he'd done. Neither of them mentioned their last conversation when he'd phoned from the hospital. There was no sign of Frances.

Laid out in his black suit, in the coffin Robert had chosen, Jimmy did not look as if he was sleeping – as it said on one of the wreaths: he looked empty. The skin on his face had tightened, highlighting his cheek and chin bones and he seemed almost shrivelled. Robert leaned in and gently kissed his icy forehead, not caring who saw him. "Good-bye, old friend. No worries now, eh?" and then walked away quickly, feeling the back of his throat burning fiercely. He knew if he caught anyone's eye, he was going to weep, so he kept his eyes firmly fixed on the checkerboard pattern on the floor.

Prayers in the funeral parlour were brief and then the coffin lid was screwed down. Robert was one of the six pall-bearers who carried the coffin out to the hearse. He knew all the others – senior figures in the Irish entertainment business, including Angela's companion – and when they stepped out into the crystalline morning air, there was a series of camera flashes as reporters and photographers grabbed interviews and images for the Sunday papers. When the back of the hearse slammed shut, he stood, suddenly unsure what to do, until Kathy caught his arm and urged him towards the car.

"Jimmy would have been pleased," she said.

Robert tucked his Audi in behind the mourning car and the hearse and glanced in the rear-view mirror. As far back as he could see a long line of cars were strung out along the Malahide Road.

"He would," he agreed.

"He knew a lot of people," Kathy said.

"Some came up through the business with him; and there were others – like me, I suppose – who he gave a start to in the business. I suppose there'll be more at the church, and even more at the funeral on Monday."

"I saw Angela," Kathy remarked.

"She just thanked me for taking care of things. She didn't seem too upset." He was more than surprised –

though not a little relieved – that Frances hadn't turned up with their son. To the best of his knowledge Angela and Frances had never met, though they'd featured alongside one another in the scandal sheets often enough, and the last thing he wanted was some unseemly catfight over the coffin. Maybe that was why the photographers were there. Ironically, Jimmy who had lived so much of his life in the public eye, had always attempted to keep his private life private. Without success.

"He knew everyone," Robert remarked. "I'd even thought about asking him to partner with me in the business," he added, and immediately recognised that he'd made a mistake.

"Without asking me?" Kathy said, sounding more surprised than angry.

"Well, I was going to talk to you about it first, of course," he lied.

"One of the things we need to get clear is my position in the business. I do own half of it," she reminded him.

And I own half the house, he thought, but said nothing.

"Well, it's all academic now," he said.

"We're going to make some changes, Robert," she said firmly.

"Yes, we are," Robert muttered.

Kathy nudged Robert. "Is that your phone?" Robert looked blankly at Kathy. They were slowly making their way out of the airport church after the brief service where the remains were received and welcomed by a severe-looking Jesuit, an old college friend of Jimmy's. "Something's buzzing," she insisted.

Robert patted his inside pocket and felt the vibrations through the cloth. "Oh, it's me." Gripping his left glove between his teeth, he pulled it off, then fumbled with the buttons of his overcoat before he got to his jacket pocket and pulled out the XDA . . . just as the call finished.

One Missed Call.

He hit the menu and scrolled to Records, looking for his Missed Call Log: *Burroughs, Stephanie.*

Robert felt a pulse begin beating along his jaw-line. Not now; he didn't need to deal with her just now. He just needed to get through this day without any more drama.

"Who was it?" Kathy asked.

"Friend of Jimmy's," he said quickly, "probably asking about the arrangements for Monday." He was slipping the phone back into his pocket when it buzzed again. Nervously, he glanced at the screen: *Private Number.* Moving away from Kathy and the throng, he hit the answer button and said very softly, "Yes?"

Stephanie Burroughs' voice was icy. "Why didn't you answer my previous call?" she snapped.

"Sorry," he whispered, "the phone was in my inside jacket pocket and I had to pull my gloves off to unbutton my overcoat. By the time I got it, you'd gone. I was just putting it back in my pocket when you phoned again. Sorry." He was aware that he was babbling, and conscious too that Kathy had stopped and was looking back at him, looking vaguely annoyed that he had taken the call, even though they were now outside the body of the church and making their way around the rectangular courtyard towards the exit into the carpark.

"Did you get my email, telling you I was coming home?" He could hear background noise behind Stephanie's voice, as if she was in a car.

"No, no, I've not been near a machine."

"Now that I simply do not believe," she snapped.

"Honestly," he sighed, "things have been crazy. Look, I cannot talk now. I'll phone back later."

"You'd better!"

"I'll talk to you later," he said firmly. "I've got to go. I'm at Jimmy Moran's removal," he said finally, desperately, as Kathy began to make her way back towards him.

"What? I can't hear you. What did you say?"

Robert's voice hardened. "I said I'm at Jimmy Moran's removal of remains. Jimmy died on Christmas Day," he added, just to make it absolutely clear, and then he hung up.

"Who was that?" Kathy asked.

"Someone who'd not heard the news."

"How did they take it?"

"I don't know," he said truthfully. "I didn't wait for a response."

It was close to noon by the time they got back to

Swords. Robert pulled into the drive, but did not turn off the engine.

"Are you not coming in?"

"I want to head into the office, check up on things. Maybe do a little work, distract me."

Kathy looked as if she was about to respond, but instead all she said was, "You could come in and catch up on your sleep. You look wretched. I doubt if you've eaten properly and I know you haven't really slept."

"No, let me do this. I meant to get in to the office yesterday, but events caught up with me. I'll get home as early as I can. I'm exhausted." It was true, a combination of the emotional trauma of the last week, coupled with the physical exertions and too little sleep, had left him feeling physically ill, with every muscle aching and a solid bar of tension sitting across his shoulders. The last thing he wanted to do was to drive across the city and face Stephanie's wrath, but it was preferable to her phoning the house again or − worse still − turning up on the doorstep. "I won't be long," he promised.

When Kathy climbed out of the car, Robert turned around and began the long drive into the city. He cracked the window open to allow a little of the chill air to blow onto his face to keep him awake, and desperately began to rehearse the words he would use with Stephanie. All he had to do was to make her see sense, and he didn't think that was going to be too difficult. Once they'd made some plans, that would be a little pressure off him.

CHAPTER 32

"Hello, Stephanie."

Even in his exhausted state, Robert recognised that the woman standing in the doorway before him looked stunning. She was wearing a cream-coloured silk blouse over black trousers with her usual discreet jewellery that he knew, from having bought some of it, was platinum. She was simply and elegantly made up, lips bright with a shade of lipstick that he hadn't seen before, eyes sparkling.

She stepped back and allowed him to walk into the sitting-room. Was it only three nights ago he had stood in this same room, looking at the presents he'd delivered, and wondering if he was going to find a body waiting for him upstairs? Only the wilting flowers were missing; the balloon still lay deflated over the back of the chair. He heard her come into the room behind him and he turned to look at her. He saw what might have been concern dart across her face.

"It's good to see you again," he said, his voice flat, emotionless.

Stephanie nodded. She looked cool and distant, completely confident, self-assured and relaxed and he found himself wondering, yet again, if she really had flown home for Christmas. She certainly showed no signs of it. "Would you like some tea?" she asked.

"Tea. Yes, that would be wonderful, thank you."

He waited until she had disappeared into the kitchen and then took up his usual position in the doorway, leaning against the frame, arms folded across his chest. There were tiny black spots spinning before his eyes and it took a monumental effort of will to keep his eyes open. He watched Stephanie fill the kettle with water from the filter jug and slowly came to the realisation that the only question she'd asked him since he stepped into the house was whether he wanted tea or not.

"You got back this morning?" he said finally, when he realised that she wasn't going to break the silence.

"A couple of hours ago," she said shortly.

"I'm sorry I wasn't there to meet you . . . I hadn't thought to download my emails." And even if he had, what would he have done: gone to the removal of Jimmy's remains or collected Stephanie from the airport? By not collecting his emails, he'd been spared being placed in that difficult decision.

"That's perfectly understandable given the circumstances."

"Flight was OK?"

282

"Fine. I came in via Paris, so it was a bit of the trek, but I'd booked First Class, so I could sleep on the transatlantic leg and that helped."

"Good. Good."

He watched as she took out a cup for herself and a mug for him – he preferred mugs to cups – and he smiled, curiously pleased that she'd take the care to make the distinction.

"How was the removal? Were there many there?"

"Yes." Robert drew in a deep shuddering sigh. "I was surprised by how many. Shocked. I think Jimmy would have been too. He made a lot of enemies over the years, but far more friends it seems. They all came out today." His voice broke, catching him unawares, and then suddenly, surprisingly, for the first time since he had cried by his friend's hospital bed, there were tears on his face. He tugged a handkerchief out of his pocket and quickly patted his eyes. He didn't want her to see him like this. Then the kettle started to boil and she busied herself with that, and he was sure she wasn't aware of his breakdown.

"Tea's ready." But when she turned to hand across the mug of tea, he saw the expression on her face – a cross between pity, embarrassment and concern – and he knew she'd heard him cry. He was glad she hadn't discomfited him further by turning around to look at him. "I've added two sugars."

"Sorry," he mumbled. "Been an intense few days; I've not got much sleep."

He followed her into the sitting-room, taking up his usual position on the couch facing her. He glanced to the opposite end of the couch; only a couple of days ago, Kathy had sat on this couch with him.

Stephanie cradled a tiny porcelain cup in the palms of her hands and sipped what he recognised from its distinctive odour as liquorice tea. "Tell me what happened," she said.

What had happened? Events had moved so quickly, he'd been acting and reacting without pausing to think and it took him a few moments to put his thoughts in order.

"I got a call on Christmas Day . . . not long after yours," he added, not looking at her. "Jimmy Moran had been taken to hospital with a suspected heart attack. I immediately went in to see him. Oh, Stephanie, he looked ghastly . . ." He breathed deeply and took a mouthful of tea, remembering the sight of Jimmy lying in the hospital bed. "He said that at first he was trying to make light of it, thinking it was nothing more than indigestion. He was cooking his own Christmas dinner and had sampled the turkey. He reckoned it hadn't been cooked through. It was when he felt the pain move into his left arm that he realised it was serious and dialled 999. But it was Christmas Day and it took the ambulance ages to arrive." He sipped a little more of the hot tea. This was the first time he had put the sequence of events into words. "They'd put him in a room on his own. He looked old, so old and frail . . . and the moment I looked at him, I knew he wasn't going to make it. It was almost as if he had given up. The spark had gone. Turned out he'd tried phoning Angela but she wasn't taking his calls, nor was Frances. He asked me to contact Angela. She spoke to me, but she wouldn't come in to see him. She was finished with him, she said. He'd broken her heart with his lies and his affairs and she was afraid that this was just another of his tricks." He fell silent; he found it hard to forgive Angela for not coming in to see Jimmy. He knew she had any number of reasons, but she should have been there. There were tears in his eyes now, but he was unaware of them. "I phoned Frances," he continued, his voice barely above a whisper. "She wouldn't come either. They'd had a fight and she had thrown him out. I think she thought it was a trick too. He was incredibly manipulative, I think."

"So you stayed with him?" Stephanie asked.

"I stayed with him throughout the day and into the night until . . . until he died," he finished simply. "He died." There were tears on his face now, rolling down his cheeks. "He squeezed my hand and then . . ." He drew in a deep sobbing breath. It was a moment he would carry with him to his grave. That and Jimmy's last words: *Don't walk away from a woman who loves you.*

"I'm sorry, Robert. So sorry." Stephanie said coolly. "I know you and Jimmy were very close."

"He died alone, Stephanie," Robert said very softly. *That* was what he couldn't forgive Angela for, nor Frances either.

"Not alone. You were there."

"But his wife . . . his miss . . . his girlfriend should have been there. Someone more . . . more significant than me. Someone who loved him."

"You loved him, Robert," Stephanie said firmly. "In the same way that he was very significant to you, then you too must have played a significant part in his life. Why else would he contact you when he went into hospital?"

Robert nodded automatically. "Yes, yes, you're right. Thank you for reminding me." Kathy had said the same thing to him, but he hadn't believed her either. Finishing his tea in one quick swallow, he put the cup on the floor. "I'm sorry, I guess I'm all over the place. Since everything that happened here on Tuesday. . ." he waved his hand around the room, "then frantically looking for you, and then your call on Wednesday, and *then* Jimmy's death, it's just been an incredibly emotional time."

"Yes, I can see that. And Christmas is the most stressful time of the year too."

He smiled grimly, "There were times I thought I was having a heart attack myself." Then he pressed the palm of his right hand against his chest. "I think it was just stress."

"You should get it checked out, just in case," she said immediately.

"I will. I promise. Jimmy was fifty-two – only ten years older than me." As soon as the local GP's surgery opened in the new year, he was going to book an appointment. Jimmy's death had frightened him more than he cared to admit.

"He lived a completely different lifestyle," Stephanie remarked.

"Not that different," he said quickly.

"But he did smoke."

"He did. And he liked rich food," he added.

"And he drank," Stephanie reminded him, "much more than you."

"Yes, he did that too. I'm only sorry now that we didn't get a chance to have that meal in Shanahan's on the Green before Christmas. We had drinks around the corner in the Market Bar instead — you suggested that, remember? That was the last time I saw him until . . . until I saw him in the hospital on Christmas Day."

"At least you had the chance to see him."

Robert nodded. "Yes. I'm glad." But dead at fifty-two was simply wrong; he was determined it was not going to happen to him. Next year would be different, he promised himself. He'd already determined to make changes in work; well, he was going to make them in every area of his life. He was going to start eating healthier, drinking less . . .

"Would you like some more tea?" Stephanie asked, breaking into his reverie.

"Yes. Thank you." He picked his cup up off the floor, handed it across, then sank back onto the sofa, resting his head on the back of the chair and closing his eyes as Stephanie moved into the kitchen.

He was going to start exercising. Maybe he'd bring a bike into town and cycle around Merrion Square or up and down the Canal at lunch . . .

As if from a great distance, he heard Stephanie's voice, "Jimmy's life was also incredibly stressful, and I'm quite sure he didn't take a whole lot of exercise." He tried to respond, but all that came out was an indeterminate grunt. "Plus, the whole issue with Angela and Frances must have taken its toll on him, and I'm sure the prospect of the looming divorce just added to the stress level."

His phone brought him shockingly, suddenly awake. There was a moment of complete disorientation when he didn't know where he was, and then he saw Stephanie's face, staring at him, and for an instant he imagined that it had all been a dream, a shockingly vivid nightmare. He pulled the phone out of his pocket, regretting now having taken it off vibrate earlier. "Hello . . ." he began, then licked dry lips and tried again, "Hello . . ."

He heard Kathy's voice, and in that instant it all came flooding back: this was no dream, though it was still a nightmare. "Kathy . . . yes, I'm fine. I'm in the office . . ." He was aware that Stephanie was watching him, her eyes hard and cold in her face. "Yes, I'll be home soon," he said quickly and rang off.

"Why did you lie?" Stephanie asked what he considered to be a very stupid question.

"Well, I could hardly tell her where I was, now could I?"

"You could have said we had some unfinished business."

"I promised Kathy I would never see you again."

"And you're breaking that promise already?" she said evenly.

"Well, I made that promise before . . . before I knew about . . . about you and . . . and . . ."

"About me being pregnant?"

"Yes. That." It was nearly sixteen years ago that Kathy had last told him she was pregnant and it wasn't something he thought he'd ever be hearing again.

Stephanie stood. "I'm going to make that tea now. Why don't you go and grab a shower, freshen up?" she said briskly. "I need you awake and alert when we talk and right now you're about dead on your feet. You've got some clothes upstairs, and there's a toothbrush and a razor of yours in the bathroom cabinet. Shower and change: you'll feel much better."

He was about to refuse, but suddenly the thought of a shower was incredibly inviting. "Yes, I will, thank you." He stood up and caught a hint of his own stale sweat. "Gosh, I stink," he said in disgust.

"Yes, you do," Stephanie said and turned away quickly. He wasn't sure if she was talking about him as a person or his bodily odour.

It took an effort to lift one foot in front of the other as he climbed the stairs. He'd been running on adrenalin for the past couple of days, and was beginning to pay the price. He'd grab a quick shower, then talk to Stephanie about the pregnancy, then head home. He glanced at his watch. He could be home before five . . . six at the latest. Then he was crawling into bed and not getting up until Monday morning.

CHAPTER 33

"Robert. Robert."

Robert Walker opened his eyes and looked around. He knew where he was . . . in the bed of his lover, Stephanie Burroughs. He smiled as her face leaned in towards his, "Hi . . ."

"Hi."

Then the bubble burst. The smile faded as his eyes moved towards the curtains, which were pulled against the night outside. "My God, how long have I been asleep?"

"A few hours. It's just nine."

Nine. Where had the afternoon and evening gone? He remembered having a shower, the hot water an incredibly sensuous and satisfying experience. Then he'd wrapped himself in a robe just to dry off and then . . . He'd no idea how he ended up in bed with a thick duvet over him. He sat bolt upright in the bed. "I've got to go . . ."

"You've got to eat first," Stephanie said firmly. She was sitting on the edge of the bed with a tray in her hands. It held a broad flat pizza flanked by a bottle of red wine and two glasses. "It's only takeout, I'm afraid. I'd no food in and I didn't want to leave you on your own."

Robert looked at the ham-and-pineapple pizza and started to shake his head – he had to get back, Kathy would be frantic and furious – but then his stomach betrayed him, and rumbled loudly, and he suddenly realised that he was hungry, ravenously hungry. "Just a slice then," he said with a grin.

He ate quickly, though he barely touched the wine; he didn't want to risk getting stopped on the way back to Swords. He was already working out his excuses: he'd called on a few friends in the business and they had ended up talking about Jimmy. That had led to a couple of drinks and then a meal. He hadn't been able to phone her because his battery had run out. Would she believe it? It was plausible enough. Like all good lies.

"When did you last eat?" Stephanie asked eventually.

He shook his head. "I've grabbed a few bits and pieces on the run. When Jimmy . . . Jimmy died, I was left to make the funeral arrangements and contact his family. Two of his three brothers are coming home. They're spread all over the world: Lloyd is in Australia, Mikey's in Canada, and Teddy is in Boston. I spoke to Mikey, the oldest. He told me to go ahead with the removal, but to delay the funeral until they arrived."

"When will the funeral take place?"

"Monday the thirtieth, in Glasnevin. Teddy and Mikey are coming in tomorrow morning, but Lloyd's not going to be able to make it."

"That's a shame."

"I know. But they've never been close. Jimmy never really told me the full story, but I know he went to live with his mother when the family broke up, while the older brothers chose to live with his father. When his parents separated, it destroyed all their lives and shattered the family. A bit like my own childhood experience." He glanced up at Stephanie and smiled. "I'm sorry, I've done nothing but talk about me. Tell me what you did over Christmas. You went home?"

Stephanie nodded. She lifted the tray and moved around the room to put it on the bedside locker. Then she leaned back against the windowsill and folded her arms. "I went home. It was a last-minute rush, and I had to go in via London, but I made it back late on Christmas Eve and I'm glad I went. It was good to see Mom and Dad again. Made me realise that they're getting on a bit, Dad especially. I know people say that time slips by – it doesn't: it races. I'm going to try and get home regularly, maybe every second or third month to keep in touch with them."

"That's a good idea." Robert pushed away the duvet and slid his legs out over the edge of the bed. He glanced sidelong at the clock on the bedside locker. It was after nine and the roads were probably icy. It would be after ten before he got back. "I really should be going." He tugged on his underwear, pulled on his socks and stepped into his trousers.

And then Stephanie suddenly, shockingly, exploded. "Hang on a second! We've talked about everything, but the most important thing: us. *Me.* And the fact that I might be pregnant."

He opened the wardrobe and pulled out one of the shirts he'd left there for emergencies. He was surprised by her reaction. He'd thought when she hadn't brought it up earlier that it was no longer an issue. He assumed that she'd come to a decision. He turned to look at her as he did up the buttons. "How sure are you?" he asked.

"Sure?"

"Sure that you're pregnant.

"Almost positive. I'm nearly two weeks late now."

"Did you do a test?"

"Yes. It came back positive. That's why I came home."

He nodded as he tucked his shirt into his trousers. He was no expert, but while two weeks was *late*, he didn't think it was *that* late. "So, let's say you are: what are you going to do about it?"

Stephanie came off the window ledge to stand directly in front of Robert. She was radiating anger. "What do you mean by that?"

He blinked in surprise. "I mean, you can't seriously be thinking of having it?"

"Yes, I am," she whispered.

This was madness! What was she thinking? Well, obviously, she wasn't. Surely she wasn't going to throw away everything she'd spent years acquiring? Maybe it was her jet-lag and a highly emotional state that were confusing her thinking. "But you can't," he said, keeping his voice reasonable. "You've got this place . . . and then there's your job. You can't have all that and a baby."

"I could if I had a partner."

At no point in Robert Walker's New-Year New-You plan was there room for a baby. He'd had his children seventeen and fifteen years ago; he'd done all that, he didn't need to do it again. Gathering his thoughts, concentrating on his cuffs, he said carefully, "If I'm the father of this child . . ."

She cracked him across the face, the force of the blow snapping his head to one side, shocking him, further chipping his already damaged tooth, the pain and surge of his own anger surprising him.

"How dare you! You *are* the father. There's been no one else."

"I'm sorry," he said, drawing in a deep breath, pressing the palm of his hand to his stinging cheek. This was obviously his week for getting slapped in the face – and on the same cheek too. "Maybe that was an ill choice of words. I'm sorry. I didn't mean to imply anything." He wasn't trying to suggest anything: he had no doubts that there was no one else in Stephanie's life. "I mean, let's be logical about this. I've reared my family, I don't want to start again. And you're on the corporate ladder – a child would stop that dead. Neither of us can afford to have a screaming child in our lives." If he could just appeal to her common sense, he was sure he could make her see reason. "And what would I tell Kathy and the kids?"

Stephanie remained silent, and he guessed that he was getting through to her. He knew she'd see sense in the end. He'd got her into this situation, so he was quite willing – eager! – to help her get out of it.

"I mean, if you want me to help you make a decision about what you should do with the baby, I'd suggest an abortion. I'll pay for it, of course, and I'll accompany you to the clinic." He smiled as a sudden thought occurred to him. "We'll have a weekend in London and the problem will be solved. We might even get a chance to take in some of the sights. When we return to Dublin, we can go back to our lives again." Somewhere at the back of his mind, he was wondering when he was going to find the time to slip away to London – middle of January maybe, end of January certainly. Then he realised that he hadn't told her the news yet – that he was going to move in with her. They would be living together in January, he wouldn't have to make any more excuses. He opened his mouth to speak . . .

But Stephanie spoke first, her voice so low that he couldn't make out what she was saying. Was she agreeing with him, thanking him?

"Well, what do you think?" he asked.

And then she screamed, the sound shocking him with its raw savagery. *"Get out! Get out! Get out!"*

Dumb with surprise, Robert backed away from her.

Stephanie reached for the nearest item – the pizza plate – and flung it at him. It missed and shattered against the wall, leaving a bloody smear of sauce. "You bastard!" she gasped. "You bastard!"

"Stephanie . . . I'm just suggesting . . ." This was a woman he did not know. This was a stranger . . . and she was terrifying.

"You've got a key to this house. Give it to me," she demanded.

There was no point in arguing with her at this point. As he took the key from his wallet and dropped it on the bed, she was flinging his shirt, his tie and his patent leather shoes across the room at him. "Stephanie. Let's talk. I know you're upset now, but –"

"We're finished," she said icily. "Don't you ever speak to me again."

He'd talk to her in a day or so, he decided, but right now, her face was set in a mask that robbed any beauty from her features.

"I loved you. I loved you with all my heart. Now, I see you for what you are: just another egotistical bastard. This isn't a problem to be solved: this is a life and a future we're talking about. And you think an abortion will sort everything! A quick abortion, then we take in the sights as if nothing has happened? I hate you, Robert Walker. No, more than that. I despise you. Now get out. Don't come back."

Still not entirely sure what had happened to set her off like that, Robert hurried from the house, pulling the door closed behind him. He threw the shirt, tie and shoes on the passenger seat as he climbed in and started the car. As he pulled away, he thanked God that he hadn't told Kathy that he'd intended leaving her on Monday after Jimmy Moran's funeral.

BOOK 3

The Wife's Story

When I discovered the truth about the affair, I hated him.

He had betrayed me, betrayed my love, betrayed eighteen years of marriage.

But I still loved him.

And he said he still loved me.

But did I believe him?

And could I ever believe him again?

CHAPTER 34

Tuesday, 24th December

CHRISTMAS EVE

Jingle bells . . . jingle bells . . .

The irritatingly cheerful polyphonic version of "Jingle Bells" her son had put on her mobile phone jerked Kathy Walker out of her reverie. Keeping her eyes on the road, she rummaged through her handbag on the passenger seat, probably one of the children wondering where she was. She fished the phone out of her bag, but before she answered, she glanced at the screen: *Robert Mobile*.

She didn't want to speak to him.

Jingle bells . . . jingle bells . . .

At this particular moment, Robert was the last person she wanted to talk to, but she still hit *Answer* and switched the phone to speaker. "Yes?" she said shortly.

Her husband's voice sounded flat and echoing, the speaker robbing it of all emotion and inflection. "Hi . . . I was just wondering . . . just wondering how you are."

"I'm fine," she said shortly. Under the circumstances, that was probably the most stupid question she had ever been asked. How did he think she was?

"Where are you?"

"At the roundabout outside Swords. Where are you?"

"At the airport. I stopped to give Maureen her Christmas bonus."

"Good." Well, at least he'd had the good manners to do that. She'd been disgusted to learn that he hadn't even bothered to call on Maureen when she was out sick over the past number of weeks.

"She told me you'd spoken to her." He made the simple statement sound like an accusation.

"Yes, I have." She could understand now why he wouldn't want her talking to Maureen – or indeed any of their very few mutual friends. She also understood why he hadn't invited her along on any of the social events or business dinners over the past months: he was probably terrified that someone would say something to her about his mistress. Or, worse still, that Stephanie Burroughs would be there.

"How are you feeling?" he asked, voice popping in and out as the signal wavered.

"How do you think I feel, Robert?" she snapped. "I've just been to see my husband's mistress. I've just learned some very ugly home truths. We'll talk later." She hung up.

Truthfully, she wasn't entirely sure how she felt. She thought she'd feel worse, but if she could put a name to one overall emotion, it was one of relief. His affair was out in the open; now they could move beyond the suspicions and lies, deal with them and go forward. And mingled with the relief was something else: shock and astonishment. And pride. She had fought for Robert. And won.

And no one was more surprised or more proud than she was. She hadn't thought she had it in her.

The anticipation of the encounter with Robert's mistress had definitely been worse than the actual event. She'd built up an image of Stephanie Burroughs in her mind as a scheming, manipulative home-wrecker, who'd deliberately set out to steal Robert away from her. Yet the truth could not have been more different. If Stephanie was to be believed – and Kathy *did* believe her – then the woman had only allowed herself to have a relationship with Robert because she believed that his wife didn't love him. Kathy had been watching her when Robert had admitted before them both that he still loved his wife; she had seen the look of genuine anguish in the woman's eyes. It was at that point that Stephanie had backed away, admitted that she'd made a mistake, a terrible mistake, then told Robert to go back to his wife . . . "If she'll take you, that is . . ." she'd added. In that moment, Kathy had liked – even admired – the woman.

In other circumstances, Kathy thought, they might have been friends.

When she'd set out for Stephanie's address, Kathy hadn't known how the day would finish up. On the drive over she had prepared herself for the worst: that Stephanie would fight for Robert . . . and that Robert would want to go to his mistress. Kathy had even prepared the little speech she would give the children. Having Robert walk in on the conversation was both terrifying and disgusting. He'd turned up to the house laden down with an armful of presents and flowers. When was the last time he had brought *her* flowers, when was the last time he had taken his time over choosing a present for her, rather than just grabbing something at the last minute in The Pavilions in Swords? Luckily, there was never any problem changing items in Dunnes.

But Kathy wasn't going to need the speech for the children – not yet anyway – because Stephanie had done the honourable and decent thing. She had walked away. In fact, the only one of the three of them who came out of this affair badly – she smiled bitterly at the unfortunate phrase – was Robert. He'd lied to her, lied to Stephanie . . . probably even lied to himself. How did he think the affair was going to end, or was he one of those men who thought that he could have his cake and eat it, that he'd be able to manage his wife and mistress without someday having to face the consequences? But he hadn't been thinking: at least not with his brain.

Kathy came off the roundabout and turned into the main street of Swords, but it was at a standstill with Christmas Eve traffic, and she cut off to the left, down one of the narrow lanes. She was eager to get home now; she still had the turkey to prepare for tomorrow's dinner, though she didn't think she was going to have any appetite. Her stomach had been upset from the moment she left

Swords to drive to Robert's mistress. Once they got through Christmas, she would insist that they go to a marriage guidance counsellor. A problem like this obviously needed professional help. Robert wouldn't like it, she knew that – he was an intensely private person – but she'd make it one of her conditions. If they were going to stay together, then things would have to change. *He* would have to change. And she would change too, she vowed. There was no denying that if she'd been paying attention, to him, to the business, to their relationship, then he would never have found either the time or the opportunity to start and then maintain an affair with Stephanie.

As she turned into her small estate, Kathy suddenly smiled. A bizarre thought had just crossed her mind: that she should be grateful. At least she now knew that there was a problem in their marriage and she had an opportunity to fix it before the problem became insurmountable. Her late mother had always said that Kathy could find the good in every situation. She had been dead for the past eighteen months . . . just about the same length of time Robert had been having his affair. Kathy wondered if the two events could, in any way, possibly be connected, though she couldn't see how. She wished her mother were alive now; she desperately needed someone she could talk to.

Kathy slowed as she turned down her road. Although the weather had turned bitterly cold, there were plenty of young children running about, bundled up in thick anoraks, hats and hoods. Wrapped up like that she knew all sounds were muffled and their range of vision was strictly limited. She kept reminding Robert of that every time he drove down this road – she was convinced that he drove too fast through the estate; not that he listened to her . . . in fact it had been a long time since he had sought her opinions on any subject. Her lips twisted in a smile: it had been a long time since she had volunteered an opinion. What had happened to the self-confident, self-assured young woman who'd wanted to set up her own production company and make documentaries and features? Eighteen years of marriage, children and keeping a home together, that's what had happened.

Maybe it was time to start again.

The situation was serious, but she reckoned that they'd weathered the worst of it and managed to come through with a reasonable amount of dignity. There would be some tough times ahead, and she still loved Robert – though she didn't really like him at the moment – and he'd said that he loved her. If that was true, then they could start again, and go forward together.

There were more cars than usual parked on the kerbs and in the drives; Christmas was a time for family and visitors. As she was indicating and turning into her drive, she caught sight of a big dark-blue SUV making its way gingerly down the road behind her. Kathy's wry smile faded; it looked as if she was about to have a visitor of her own, someone she would definitely not be sharing her latest bit of news with: her older sister, Julia.

CHAPTER 35

"We have to talk."

"That sounds serious," Kathy said lightly, moving over to the sink, to fill the kettle.

"It is," Julia said. She sighed dramatically as she assumed her usual seat at the kitchen table.

Although Julia was only five years older than her sister, she looked, dressed and acted a lot older. It still gave Kathy a slightly guilty pleasure that the last time the two of them were out together, a shop assistant had mistaken them for mother and daughter.

Kathy's mind was racing: surely Julia hadn't somehow found out about Robert's affair? If she had, it would be just like her to rush over and break the news in person; she'd want to see the expression on Kathy's face.

"It's about Sheila," Julia said, dropping her voice to a whisper, when it became apparent that Kathy was not going to ask her the obvious question.

And Kathy immediately knew what Julia was about to tell her, knew why her sister have driven out on Christmas Eve. She dispensed good news on the phone, but she liked to deliver bad news in person. "Sheila?" she said, her voice carefully neutral. "What's she done now?"

"Sheila. She's seeing someone . . ." Julia began, and then stopped.

Both women heard the hall door open, then Robert's voice drifted in from the next room as he talked to the children. He stepped into the kitchen and said, "Hello, Julia," though his eyes were fixed on Kathy's face. He walked around her to stand by the sink, where he could look at them both. Was that fear she saw in his eyes? Then she realised that he thought she'd asked her older sister over to talk about his affair. Did he really know so little about her? She was half-tempted to let him sweat for a while, but then she realised that he might say something to alert her sister. "Julia was just about to tell me about Sheila," she said, her eyes never leaving his face. She actually saw his features relax as the tension flowed out of them and when his fingers gripped the edge of the sink, she could see the white-knuckled tension in them.

"Is she OK?" he asked casually.

"She's having an affair with a married man," Julia said in hushed, appalled tones and then stopped, waiting for a response.

Kathy was watching Julia as she made the announcement. Was this how Julia – and those women like her – spread the news about Robert's affair? Would they each have the same shocked and horrified expressions, but yet be unable to keep the tiniest note of glee from their voices as they passed on the news over tea and biscuits?

"So?" Robert frowned, adding quickly, "What's that got to do with us?"

Kathy saw him glance at her before turning back to his sister-in-law.

"Oh, I should have known you would never understand," Julia said peevishly. "Men never do." Julia turned her full attention on Kathy. "I phoned her today, just to confirm that she was coming on Stephen's Day for dinner."

Kathy abruptly decided that she did not want to go down to Julia's for the endless ritual of dinner on Stephen's Day. She needed to spend time with Robert and she was guessing that she would not really get a chance to talk to him tonight; tomorrow was out of the question, so she'd keep Stephen's Day free for them to talk and plan.

"Well, she said she would," Julia continued, "on one condition: that she could bring her current young man with her. I was delighted, of course. Sheila is thirty-five now, it's about time she thought about settling down, and if she's going to have children, then she'll have to start soon – that clock is ticking." Julia took a deep breath and pursed her lips.

Julia and Ben, her husband, had never had children and Kathy knew that she overcompensated by mothering her two younger sisters and her nephew and niece. Glancing briefly at Robert, Julia turned back to Kathy. "Turns out her young man is not so young; he's actually five years older than her," she said breathlessly.

Kathy didn't need to do the calculation: Stephanie Burroughs was seven years younger than Robert, five years younger than she was. She supposed she should at least be grateful that he'd not ended up with a twenty-year-old blonde bimbo.

"And then she gave me his name," Julia persisted. "Allan McLachlan. And I thought: I know that name. It's not a common name. So I said to her: 'I know an Allan McLachlan – he plays golf with my Ben.'" Julia nodded triumphantly. "And that's when she said that she didn't think she was going to be able to make it on Thursday after all."

Robert was standing behind Kathy's chair, staring out into the garden. Kathy heard him ask, "So how did this lead you to suspect that he is married?" She was aware of the tiniest undercurrent of anger in his voice.

Julia sighed. "She was quite happy for me to meet this Allan until she discovered that I might know him. It's not a common name, and this Allan McLachlan who Ben knows has boasted about his little bit on the side. I put two and two together: it had to be Sheila."

"Dublin is so small," Kathy murmured. "Everyone knows someone who knows someone." She wasn't sure if she was speaking to her sister or to Robert.

"So I had a think about it, and then I phoned her back."

"Julia, you didn't!" Kathy protested.

"Yes, I did."

"But it's got nothing to do with you." When did Julia take over the role of matriarch and moral guardian of the family, Kathy wondered, suddenly conscious that she too was beginning to get annoyed with her sister.

"Well, you may not think so, but I do, and I certainly didn't want an adulterer sitting at my table."

"That's a little extreme in this day and age," Robert said evenly.

Julia looked at him coldly. "I don't think it is. I phoned her. Asked her out straight. And do you know what she had the audacity to tell me?"

"That it was none of your business," Robert snapped. The irritation was clearly audible in his voice.

Kathy caught him looking at her, frowned, and shook her head slightly.

"No," Julia continued, "she admitted it, brazen as you like. Allan McLachlan is married. So I told her out straight that she would not be welcome in my house on Stephen's Day."

"Why are you telling me this?" Kathy asked, feeling a sudden wave of exhaustion washing over her. Whether Sheila was having an affair was none of her business, none of Julia's either. What gave Julia the right to sit in pious judgment on her and, more importantly, what gave her the right to spread the gossip?

Julia looked at her blankly. "Because . . . because . . ."

"This is Sheila's business. Hers alone," Kathy continued,

struggling now to keep her own rising anger in check. "Who she's seeing has got nothing to do with you or me."

"But he's married," Julia protested. "She's breaking up a happy marriage."

"How do we know that?" Kathy snapped. "How do we know the marriage is happy?"

Julia looked at her blankly, mouth opening and closing in stunned silence. Whatever response she had been expecting from her younger sister, it hadn't been this. Colour touched her cheeks.

"There are three people in an affair," Kathy said. "The mistress, the husband and the wife. Takes all of them to make it happen."

Julia pushed back her chair and stood up. "Well, this is not the attitude I expected from you. And I don't know where you get such outlandish ideas; probably from those magazines you're always reading. The wives are always the innocent in these situations, always the last to know."

Maybe always the last to know, Kathy agreed, but perhaps not entirely innocent.

"I don't know why these women – these *mistresses* – are attracted to married men, I really don't." Julia lifted her coat off the back of the chair and pulled it on. Then she was unable to resist adding, "I just hope you never have to go through what poor Allan McLachlan's wife must be going through right now!"

Kathy could feel the colour draining from her face, as

anger gave way to guilt and bitter exhaustion. She later realised that Julia must have completely misinterpreted the looks on both of their faces as anger and disgust.

"Well, I don't think that came out the way I meant it to," Julia continued hastily. "I'm sorry, I didn't mean to imply . . ." Looking embarrassed now, she turned to leave. "I'll let myself out." She paused before she stepped out of the kitchen. "You will come down on Stephen's Day for dinner, won't you?"

"We'll let you know," Robert said firmly, before Kathy could respond. "Good night, Julia. And do have a happy Christmas."

No, she definitely was not going down for dinner, Kathy decided. She glanced sidelong at Robert, wishing he would leave her alone. She wanted a little time to think . . . and she wanted to talk to Sheila. She was brought out of her reverie by the high-pitched squealing scrape of metal on stone. She immediately knew what had happened; served the nosy old bitch right!

"She's caught the edge of the pillar," Robert said. He was standing at the sink making tea. "She was parked at such an awkward angle. I'm not sure I would have been able to get that big SUV out of the drive without hitting something."

He was talking just to fill the silence, she knew, chatting inconsequentially so that he could avoid discussing the major issue. He placed a fresh pot of tea on the table between them and sat down in the seat so recently occupied by Julia. He poured her a fresh cup.

"I'm thinking I might have given her a different response a couple of days ago," Kathy said quietly. "There was a time – in the very recent past, days ago, a week ago – when I might have agreed with Julia. But when you become part of an affair, you discover a different perspective."

"Did you know about Sheila?" he asked.

Yes, she knew. It had been another shock in a week of shocks. Kathy held the teacup in both hands and looked into the cloudy liquid; he always made the tea too strong. "She told me on Monday," she said evenly. "We were sitting in her car in the car park of a health club just off the M50." She saw him start; the health club and gym he attended were just off the M50. "I sat there and watched my husband kiss another woman."

That, for her, had been the defining moment.

Up until that point, Robert's affair had not been entirely *real*. Oh, she knew it was happening, she had the proof, but it was all hearsay and circumstantial evidence. But watching her husband of eighteen years take another woman in his arms, and kiss her on the lips, was like being stabbed. The pain was physical; it was real and it hurt. How it hurt!

And suddenly she wanted to hurt him back, to make him pay for what he'd put her through. Something must have shown in her eyes or on her face because Robert suddenly sat back, away from her. Kathy wondered if he thought she was going to throw the hot tea in his face . . . because in that instant that is precisely what she wanted to do. But she carefully returned the cup to the saucer; it was part of a set her grandmother had given her for a wedding present.

"I phoned you," she said. "I sat in a car not ten yards from you, and phoned you." She saw him nod, saw the flush of colour on his cheeks. "I asked you what time you were coming home," she continued and watched him nod again. "You told me you were just leaving the office and would be home in forty minutes."

She suddenly stood and turned away from him so that he would not be able to see the tears in her eyes. She busied herself at the sink, carefully washing and drying the cup, then, when she had composed herself, she turned around and started to clear off the kitchen table.

"How long . . . how long have you known?" Robert asked, not looking at her. "About us? About me?"

"Not long. Why, did you think I was the sort of person who would turn a blind eye to my husband's affair?" Kathy was pleased that she'd managed to keep her voice calm and without a tremor.

"No. I never thought that," Robert said.

Once she'd discovered his affair, there had been no other course of action but to confront him. She was not prepared to let it continue in the hope that he would come to his senses. She would not have been able to live with herself, not even able to look at him, if she'd known he was carrying on and did nothing about it.

She pulled a cookery book off the shelf and flipped it open, then pressed it flat on the table and quickly scanned the list of ingredients. This was part of the ritual of preparing Christmas dinner. The recipe book had belonged to her mother and, written into the margins, in Margaret Child's tiny precise handwriting, were her additions and corrections to the recipes. Kathy knew her sister Julie desperately coveted the book; every Christmas she tried to borrow it, and every year Kathy refused and presented her sister with a handwritten copy of the turkey, ham and pork recipes. Kathy turned back to the presses and started to pull out the ingredients that would go into the turkey stuffing.

"Will you sit and talk to me?" Robert asked suddenly.

Kathy didn't answer the question, but continued her previous topic of conversation. "I realised the truth for the first time last Thursday, when I was writing the Christmas cards. Once I suspected, it was relatively easy to put it all together." She'd found the evidence because he had become careless, she knew that. He'd become just a little complacent; he'd got away with his affair for so long he'd stopped taking precautions. "There was a speeding ticket upstairs in your office. You'd been caught speeding in Ballymun in October . . . and yet you were supposed to be in Belfast that night having dinner with a client."

Kathy started feeding bread into the blender, grinding it to crumbs, taking a certain pleasure at the expression on his face when the blades were whirling. It sounded not unlike a dentist's drill, and she knew how much he hated going to the dentist's . . . though that hadn't stopped him having a lot of very expensive work on his teeth done recently. She wondered if that had been at Stephanie's insistence; and what about the gym, the new clothes, the extra attention he'd started paying to his grooming? Wasn't that supposed to be one of the first signs of an affair?

"Then I remembered all the other nights you'd stayed away, meeting with clients, wining and dining them," she continued. "And you know something? I don't remember the company getting any contracts from these clients. You were supposed to be having dinner with Jimmy Moran in Shanahan's on the Green last week. But do you know something? When I phoned to check, they had no record of your reservation."

"Actually, I really was supposed —" Robert began, but she hit the blender again and the blades howled.

"And then I discovered the phone records in the office." Kathy turned and the only expression on her face was one of disappointment. "Hundreds of calls, Robert. Hundreds. First call of the day. Last call at night. All to the same mobile number or the same house number." She remembered a time, many, many years ago, before they married, when he would always phone her late at night, just to say good night. She'd always thought that was so romantic. "And I couldn't help but remember the mornings you left here without speaking to me, or the days when you were too busy to phone to see how I was, or those days when you got back late and I'd be in bed. Whole days would go by and we wouldn't speak more than a few words. And yet you could find time to phone your mistress several times every day, every single day."

"Maureen told me you'd seen the phone records," he muttered.

"She confirmed what I already knew. She just gave me the time frame. She thinks it's been going on for a year. Stephanie Burroughs said eighteen months. What is the truth?" She already knew the truth, but she wanted to hear him say it.

"June of last year was the . . . the first time."

"The first time for what?" she snapped.

She saw Robert look over his shoulder towards the sitting-room. Brendan and Theresa's voices were audible as they chatted happily together. She didn't even want to think of the effect this revelation would have on the children. They both idolised their father; how would they regard him if they knew he had betrayed them all? Would they blame him, or would they blame Kathy, thinking that it must have been partially her fault for driving him away?

"Could we discuss this somewhere more private?" Robert asked.

Kathy shook her head firmly. "Right now, this is the most private room in the house. If we go upstairs, the children will suspect that we're wrapping presents and be in and out every five minutes. Right now, they know I'm preparing the stuffing for the turkey and they've no interest in that." She caught his reflection in the glass and was aware that he was moving around to stand beside her.

"Can I help?" he asked.

"No," she said. Kathy hit the button on the blender and it howled. When it stopped she said, "I don't know what's going to happen between us, Robert. But it's going to take me a long time before I can trust you again . . . a long time before I can even look at you without feeling sick to my stomach," she added bitterly. She saw his hand move towards her and she jerked away. "Don't!" she snapped. She didn't want him to touch her, to lay a finger on her. The knowledge that he had kissed Stephanie, touched her, slept with her made her physically nauseous.

"I am sorry," he said eventually. "I know it sounds like a cliché, but I never wanted to hurt you. You have to believe me – that was never my intention."

Well then, what had been his intention? And yes, it was a cliché; it was, she imagined, what every man said when he was caught. He hadn't been thinking: that was the problem. He was prepared to sacrifice eighteen years of marriage, eighteen years of memories, of love and trust, for what . . . a brief moment of passion. Was that all their marriage was worth?

"I allowed myself to enter into my relationship . . ." Robert began.

"Affair!" Kathy snapped. "Call it what it is – an affair, and you, an adulterer." Julia had used the word earlier, and Kathy remembered thinking that it had been a long time since she'd heard it. It was an old-fashioned word, from an earlier age, a simpler age, with different morals and a clearly defined sense of right and wrong. And it was a word which perfectly described Robert: he was an adulterer.

"I began my affair with Stephanie June last year. I was lonely, Kathy, desperately lonely. I wanted someone to talk to, someone to share with, someone to show an interest in me, in the company. I tried to talk to you . . . tried I don't know how many times. But you never seemed to be interested."

Kathy concentrated on the recipe, saying nothing, listening intently to what he was saying. Was it true; had she not been interested? It cut both ways, of course: he had only been vaguely interested in the house and the children. But she kept coming back to his statement and, try as she might, she found she couldn't deny it. She had to admit that she had not really been interested in the company or how he was coping.

"You never asked how things were going, never seemed to be in the slightest bit concerned with the ordinary day-to-day minutiae of keeping the company afloat. I'm not even sure you realised how much trouble we were in. We came close, so very, very close to going under."

Maureen had hinted at something similar and Kathy suddenly felt extraordinarily guilty. Had she been so wrapped up in her world of home and children to the exclusion of everything else?

She pulled open the fridge and stared inside, looking for the sausage meat.

But if the situation had been that serious, why hadn't he made a point of sitting down and talking with her?

She guessed that if she asked him that he would say that he hadn't told her because he didn't want to worry her.

"I was lonely," Robert repeated. "We'd stopped . . . stopped making love. When I tried, you'd turn your back on me or you'd come to me so reluctantly that I felt you were making love with me almost as a duty."

At the end of a long day, a day which started at seven o'clock when Robert got up and only finished when the dishes were washed up and put away, and the following day's lunches prepared, she had no energy left for making love.

"There didn't seem to be any pleasure in it for you. And do you know how that made me feel? Small and dirty, that's how. I hated feeling like that."

And she hated refusing him, but it had become apparent to her a long time ago that their rhythms were different. She liked to make love in the early morning; she loved the burst of energy it gave her. It lifted the entire day. Whereas he liked to make love late at night and then fall into a sound, motionless sleep.

"After a while I stopped making the effort, I'll admit it," Robert continued. "But – and please don't take this as a criticism, it's just a statement of fact – you never made an effort either."

"So you're saying it's my fault you found yourself a mistress?" Kathy asked savagely, but at the back of her mind she knew the point he was making was true. She could not remember the last time she'd initiated their lovemaking. A long time ago; too long.

"No," he sighed. "I'm not trying to score points here – I'm just trying to let you see how I ended up in this situation. I allowed myself to have the affair, Kathy, because I believed – genuinely believed – that you no longer loved me."

Kathy spun around to face him, mouth open, but he held up his hand.

"I know. I'm just telling you how I felt, telling you how I saw things. When you stood in Stephanie's sitting-room earlier and said that you loved me, no one was more surprised than I was."

"I never stopped loving you," Kathy said immediately, though in the last couple of days she had stopped liking him.

"Even right now?" he asked, attempting a smile.

"I'm not sure how I feel about you at this moment," she said truthfully, "but the very fact that we're both standing in this room, even after all that's happened today, should suggest something."

"What?" he wondered.

"That maybe I do accept some responsibility for what happened," she said simply. "I wasn't paying attention. And if a marriage is going to work, then both parties have to keep paying attention. You stopped paying attention to me, and I stopped paying attention to you."

"Would it help if I said I was sorry, truly sorry?"

She looked at him. "Sorry for what? Do you regret the affair?" she asked lightly, though she was deadly serious

"I regret the pain and upset it caused you," was all Robert would say.

At least he hadn't lied and said that he regretted the affair, because she knew he didn't. She could see it in his eyes and he'd said only a few short hours ago that he loved Stephanie. "Well, I'm glad you chose to tell me the truth."

"I would never knowingly hurt you," he murmured.

"And yet you have hurt me, Robert," she said simply. "Hurt me and humiliated me. And it's going to take me a long time to forgive that."

"What's going to happen to us?" he asked.

She'd thought about nothing else on the drive home, creating all sorts of possibilities, and she kept coming back to the same conclusions. Taking a deep breath, she said quickly, determined that her voice would not shake: "As I see it, we have two choices: we can stay together, make some new rules, start again, and really work at it this time." She finished quickly, "Or I can sue for divorce."

She watched him assimilate that. The thought of divorce was terrifying - she had no idea of the practicalities involved: splitting the assets, maybe selling the house and the business, moving the children to different schools. She would have to find a job.

"Well, look, let's talk about this later, or tomorrow maybe," Robert said, unable to disguise the tremble in his voice. "We're both tired and probably not thinking too clearly. I know I'm not," he added. He took a breath. "I do have a favour to ask."

"A favour!"

He nodded. "If you decide that you want me to go — and I can fully understand if you do — then can we keep this from the children for a while? I don't want to spoil their Christmas."

Kathy bowed her head and looked away. She had been about to make a similar request. "I won't ruin their Christmas," she promised. "Let's try and get through the next couple of days like civilised people." If they could get through this, then the children would never have to be told.

"Thank you," he said sincerely.

"When were you going to tell me, Robert?" she asked him suddenly.

"Tell you what?"

"Tell me when you were going to leave me." She already knew the answer, but she wanted to hear him say it.

"I don't know for certain," he mumbled. "Probably at the weekend."

Something cracked and broke inside her. "You don't sound so sure."

"I'm not," he admitted.

"And yet Stephanie seemed convinced that you were going to tell me after Christmas so that you could spend New Year's Eve with her."

"Yes, we spoke about that."

"Or were you going to give her an excuse and stay here?" Kathy guessed. She was surprised that she was not hearing a tremendous amount of conviction in his voice.

326

"Kathy, I've no idea what I would have done for certain. But yes, the plan was to tell you, probably on Saturday or Sunday, that I was leaving."

"Bastard!" Kathy hissed. She felt a terrible rage bubble up inside her. She wanted to scream and shout and howl. She wanted to hit him, and claw at his face with her fingers. How could he walk away from eighteen years together in such a cavalier way? She put her palms on his chest and pushed him hard away from her. "You callous, uncaring bastard!"

Robert stepped back. "I'm sorry, Kathy, truly I am. But I made that decision believing that you did not love me. Before I knew the truth."

Kathy turned away from him. She concentrated on the stuffing, clamping down hard on her anger. When she was sure that she could control her voice, she said, "If we are going to rebuild our lives and our relationship, we're going to have to be honest with one another." She looked up, and found that he was staring at her reflection in the window. "Will you be honest with me, Robert? Can you promise me that?"

"Yes. Yes, I can," he said.

"Then you have to promise me something else."

"Anything."

"You have to promise me – swear to me – that you'll stay away from that woman."

"I promise," he said quickly. "In any case, I think you can tell from today that she'll want little enough to do with me." Then he turned and left the room.

Kathy continued leaning against the sink, staring out into the night, seeing only her own reflection, broken and distorted in the window. Stephanie had said that she was finished with him . . . but the real question was: would Robert accept that? Would he finish with Stephanie?

CHAPTER 36

Kathy sat with both elbows on the kitchen table, forehead pressed into right palm, while her left hand held the portable phone pressed to her ear. "Answer, answer," she murmured.

An answering machine clicked in, and a polite, accentless male voice said, "*There is no one available to take your call at the moment. Please leave a message after the tone. Thank you.*"

"Sheila? Sheila, are you there?"

There was a click and then Sheila's slightly amused voice cut in. "I'm here. I was just screening my calls. Julia's looking for me."

"I guessed she might. She called down here this evening."

"Ah."

Kathy heard a series of rustling noises, then a thump, and when Sheila spoke again, her voice was slightly

329

muffled, "Sorry," she said. Then the sound cleared, "I'm in bed – I was just lying down. Tell me what she said. But before you get to that, tell me: did you go and see Stephanie Burroughs?"

"Well," Kathy said slowly, "it's certainly been a Christmas Eve to remember. And yes, I went to see Stephanie."

There was a tiny pause, then Kathy heard the rustling again and guessed that her sister was now sitting up in the bed. "Oh my God . . . I wasn't sure if you were joking or not when you told me!"

"I had to." Kathy stopped suddenly. She heard the door to Robert's office close overhead, then a stair creaked. "Hang on a sec," she said quickly, putting down the phone. By the time she got to the kitchen door, Robert had already stepped out the front door into the night.

Kathy stepped out into the hall. "Are you going out?" she asked, her voice carefully neutral.

"I just want to bring the car in," he said. "I parked it on the street earlier."

Kathy didn't wait for the rest of the explanation. She stepped back into the kitchen, shut the door and grabbed the phone. "Sorry," she said to her younger sister. "I thought I heard Robert leaving, but he was just bringing the car in."

"Stop, stop, stop, stop! You've just told me you went to see the Burroughs woman, and now you're saying that Robert is still there. What happened?"

Kathy quickly filled Sheila in on the day's events. As

she spoke on the portable phone, she darted upstairs and slipped into the bedroom. Standing well back from the net curtains, she looked down into the front garden. Robert was slowly and carefully manoeuvring the car into the drive. So he hadn't been lying. She watched him for a moment and wondered if she would ever trust him again. Could she afford to? Was she going to be constantly on edge every time he left the house, would she end up checking and double-checking his whereabouts, noting his mileage, verifying every reason he gave to her when he stayed out at night? She couldn't live like that; no-one could.

And she wouldn't.

Kathy turned and hurried back downstairs to the kitchen and was just closing the door behind her when she heard the hall door shut as Robert came back into the house. The stairs creaked, then she heard his office door close and the creak of floorboards as he moved about the room.

"So you took him back," Sheila said, her voice carefully neutral.

"It was a little more complicated than I thought," Kathy said.

"It always is," her younger sister said. "In an affair, there are no black and whites, only shades of grey."

Kathy nodded. She was beginning to understand that now.

"So what happens now?" Sheila asked.

"I don't know," Kathy said truthfully. "Robert and I

need to talk, we need to really, seriously talk. I want to get counselling, I want to get back into the business, to start taking control again ..." And suddenly, with the flood of words, came the tears. The sobs came from deep in the pit of her stomach, tearing at her very being and, for a moment, she thought she was going to throw up.

"Kathy, oh, Kathy," Sheila said miserably, "I'm coming right over."

Kathy took a deep shuddering breath and attempted to compose herself. "No. No, I'll not allow it. Please stay where you are, Sheila. The roads are too bad. I'd never forgive myself if anything happened." She pressed the heels of her hands against her eyes and rubbed away the tears. "I'll be fine," she promised, knowing it was a lie. It was going to be a long time before she would be fine again. "Give me a little time to deal with this."

"Would you rather not have known?" Sheila wondered.

Kathy's response was instant. "No. This was something I needed to know. But I'm glad I found out myself. Discovering the truth, piece by piece, has, I think, allowed me to deal with it. I would hate to have had it sprung on me."

"The sort of news our delightful sister would like to break," Sheila said grimly.

"Exactly." With the phone propped between her head and shoulder, Kathy started to clear off the table, loading the cups and plates into the dishwasher. She needed to start preparing the vegetables for Christmas dinner and it would be nice to get the children up to bed at a reasonable hour for once. She wanted them up early in the morning; Christmas Day was the one day of the year when the entire family attended church and it was always preferable to get one of the early Masses. They were shorter for a start and there were fewer children present. Floorboards creaked overhead and she suddenly glanced up: would Robert be attending church with them tomorrow?

Questions. That's what an affair raised, she realised. In the few days that had passed since she discovered Stephanie Burroughs' name in Robert's phone and begun to suspect that he was engaged in an affair, she had found herself asking so many questions. Suddenly everything that she had taken for granted was open to doubt. All the certainties of eighteen years of marriage lay shattered about her. "Why?" she said, and didn't realise she had spoken aloud until Sheila answered her.

"Why what?"

"I suppose I was just wondering why he had the affair."

"Because he could," Sheila said immediately.

"I keep asking myself if I could have stopped it, prevented it by being more . . . I don't know, more *present*," she said eventually.

The portable phone began to blip softly and Kathy realised it was running low on battery.

"Quickly," she said, "before the phone dies; what possessed you to tell Julia about Allan?"

Sheila's laugh was completely without humour. "He

333

was here at the time. He said he was going to tell his wife tonight that he was leaving her for me . . ."

"Sheila!"

"I was pleading with him not to. Allan is fun and charming and sophisticated, but he can also be just a little bit pompous and more than a little boring. I enjoy his company, but he's definitely not someone I want to spend the rest of my life with. Over the past couple of weeks, he's been promising me an extra special Christmas present. Well, he was unable to contain himself today: he was going to tell his wife tonight, and then drive straight over here so that we could see in our first Christmas together. That was his present to me!"

"Very romantic," Kathy said bitterly.

"Very. I kept telling him not to make an announcement at Christmas, where every emotion is heightened. Then he accused me of being ashamed to be seen with him. I'd never even introduced him to my family, he was saying, and right at that moment Julia phoned. I've no idea what got into me, but I actually heard myself saying that I would come over for dinner if I could bring my boyfriend. I'm not sure who was more surprised, Julia or Allan."

"But she recognized his name," Kathy said.

"I know. Dublin is so small. She recognised the name, obviously thought about it and then phoned me back, asked me point blank if he was married and then started asking me if his wife knew we were having an affair, saying she wasn't going to be able to let this pass. I mean, what has it got to do with her?"

"I know. Robert asked her exactly the same question."

"Anyway, she's been phoning me on and off throughout the evening, obviously wanting to talk to me about the *situation*."

"And is Allan still there?"

"No, I convinced him to go home and say nothing."

"What are you going to do?"

"I've no idea. Try and stall him till after Christmas. And then dump him. Nicely if I can, but I'm prepared to be brutal too."

"And will you bring him to Julia's for dinner?"

"No way! Can you imagine how much fun that would be? Actually, I doubt she'd even let him in the door."

The phone gave a final whine and Sheila's voice faded into the distance as the battery died. Kathy replaced the phone on the cradle and contemplated going up to the bedroom to phone Sheila back, but she decided that could wait. She had a lot to do before she went to bed and she wanted to bury herself in the simple Christmas Eve routine. Talking to Sheila, knowing that she was involved in an affair with a married man, was a constant reminder of her own situation. And right now she wanted to forget about it, just for a few minutes. She wanted things to be the way they were last Christmas.

And then, bitter and foul, she realised that Robert had been having his affair last Christmas too. Pressing both hands to her mouth, she raced out to the downstairs toilet, where she knelt on the floor and retched in great heaving gulps.

CHAPTER 37

Wednesday, 25th December

CHRISTMAS DAY

Kathy Walker opened her eyes, suddenly awake and alert. What had awakened her?

She'd gone to bed alone just after midnight when she'd finished in the kitchen, leaving it rich with the smell of Christmas – odours of spice and cinnamon, cooking and candlewax, odours which she would forever afterwards equate with betrayal. Rolling over, she glanced at the clock: just before one.

The house was absolutely still and silent and she knew, even before she rolled out of bed and pulled back the curtains, that it had snowed. The world outside the window was solid white, crisp, magical and clean. Later cars would churn the road to filthy black sludge and children would turn the paths into glistening ice-sheets, but right at this moment the world had lost all its sharp edges and everything looked spectacular and new.

Kathy slid back into the warm bed, lay on her back and

stared at the ceiling. The room should have been in total darkness, but the snow reflected grey alabaster light onto the ceiling.

A white Christmas.

She'd been a child the last time it had snowed on Christmas Day. It should be something to celebrate – but not this Christmas, not today.

Yesterday – was it only yesterday? – she had confronted her husband's mistress.

Yesterday, she had walked up to a woman she did not know and slapped her across the face.

Yesterday, she had drunk tea with the woman who was sleeping with her husband.

Yesterday, that woman had given up her husband.

Yesterday, yesterday, yesterday.

Less than twelve hours and yet it seemed a lifetime ago.

Kathy pressed both hands to her churning stomach. From the moment she had set out to drive from Swords across the city to Stephanie Burroughs' townhouse on the canal, her stomach had started to twist and coil, and burn with acid indigestion. When she'd climbed out of her car before the woman's house and rested her finger on the bell, she'd actually thought she was going to throw up.

On the drive home, away from Stephanie's townhouse, she'd had to pull off the road twice and roll down the window to breathe in great heaving breaths. The cramping pain had come back at her again throughout the remainder of the day. It had grown worse in the late evening and into the night. With the sights and sounds of the encounter with her husband's mistress running and rerunning through her head, she'd felt her stomach protest and she'd thrown up until there was nothing left but bitter bile. In desperation, she'd drunk Maalox – which she hated – straight from the bottle, the chalky liquid coating her tongue and mouth with its milky residue.

Kathy glanced across the bed.

Robert's side was empty. He'd made no attempt to come to bed with her and she guessed he'd spent the night sleeping in the chair in his study. She wasn't sure what she would have done if he'd attempted to climb into bed alongside her. Got out and slept downstairs, she supposed. But she should have known he wouldn't want to put himself in a position where they would have to talk.

She knew he didn't want to do that just yet. They'd had arguments and disagreement in the past, just like every other couple. His usual tactic was to state his position and then simply refuse to discuss it further. After a few vain attempts to raise the topic of conversation, she would normally let it drop, allowing him to win by default. That was not going to happen this time: they needed to discuss the future.

If there was going to be a future.

Then she heard it: the quiet closing of a door followed by the irregular creaking of the stairs. Every sense tingling, she heard him move around downstairs, then the click as he pulled a plug from the wall in the sitting-room below and the rattle of the kettle as he moved into the kitchen. There was a long silence and then she heard the kitchen door close. Footsteps hurried upstairs and she heard his office door open, then close again moments later. This time when the footsteps descended the stairs they sounded more solid . . . as if he had put on his shoes.

Kathy sat bolt upright in bed, heart thumping. Surely he wasn't going out?

The chain on the front door rattled, then the door was gently eased open and pulled closed with a click.

Leaping out of bed, she stood in the chill and watched him back the car out of the drive. He hadn't put on his headlights because they would light up the bedroom, she realised, but his break lights painted the snow blood-red.

He was going to *her*.

She'd thought . . . she'd thought . . . When he'd come back with her, he had seemed genuinely contrite, and she was hopeful that once they got through these few days, they would be able to move on. She'd asked him to promise not to see Stephanie again, and he had, but without a huge amount of conviction, she'd thought. Talking about Stephanie, he'd said, "In any case, I think you can tell from today that she'll want little enough to do with me."

He'd lied to her.

There were no tears now, just a cold anger . . . coupled

with a feeling of absolute helplessness. What was she going to do? What could she do? Throw him out? Gather all his clothes, stuff them into the suitcases and fling them out into the front garden? Phone Stephanie now and tell her that he was on the way and not to send him back?

Was he coming back?

Pulling on her dressing-gown, she wandered out of the bedroom and into his office. It felt hot and stuffy, the air slightly stale with a hint of his old aftershave overlaying sour perspiration. Everything seemed in order – perhaps in a little too much order. The pile of post on the desk was certainly a lot neater and she guessed that if she went to it she would find that the parking ticket and the Visa bill would be missing.

She wandered down into the kitchen where she found the note beside the phone. "*Office alarm has gone off; gone in to see if there's a problem.*"

Her first instinct was to pick up the phone and call the alarm company to confirm. She'd actually lifted the receiver when she changed her mind and put the phone down again. If she and Robert were to begin again, then she had to start trusting him. She'd been wrong about him before, when she suspected that he'd been having an affair six years before. Her accusations then had desperately damaged their marriage and she didn't want to make that mistake again. Maybe the office alarm had genuinely gone off . . . but she hadn't heard the phone ring and when she checked the caller ID, there had been no calls since Julia's much earlier that evening. If the alarm company were calling, would they have contacted Robert's mobile number first, and then the house second, or the other way around? Feeling a little relieved now, she returned the note to where she'd found it, then went back upstairs and climbed into the cold bed.

Lying in the silence, she heard the snow hiss and spit against the window and suddenly found herself praying for his safe return.

But at the back of her mind, faint but insistent, was the thought that he had gone to Stephanie. And if he had, she knew, then they were finished.

Finished.

She was still awake at four-thirty when he returned.

The minutes had crawled by, second by agonising second, each one accompanied by an equally terrifying scenario: Robert dead by the side of the road . . . the car on its roof in a pile-up on the motorway . . . Robert in the arms of his mistress.

Several times she had reached for the phone to dial his number or the office number or even Stephanie's number. But each time she pulled back. If he had gone out for a genuine reason, she didn't want him to know that she was checking up on him.

When she saw the splash of headlights on the road and heard the car slowly crunch its way down the ice-locked street, she knew it was him and experienced a wave of relief that left her shaking with emotion.

Climbing out of bed, she stood and watched the Audi approach and then the lights click off so that they would not illuminate the front of the house before he turned into the drive. Leaning forward, straightening the net curtains, she watched him climbing out of the car, and the look of leaden exhaustion on his face convinced her that he had not gone to Stephanie. If he'd gone to his mistress, surely he would have spent the night and even if he had decided to return home before Brendan and Theresa got up to open their presents, then he would be looking a whole lot happier.

She heard the hall door open and, for a moment, thought about going down and asking about the office alarm, but then she decided that she didn't want him to be aware that she knew he'd been out. Stairs creaked, his office door opened and closed, then she heard the pneumatic hiss as he sat back in his chair.

Then silence.

Kathy sat on the edge of the bed for what seemed like a long time, then she padded out of the room, down the landing and stopped outside his door. She opened the door and peered inside.

Still wearing his leather coat and gloves, Robert was slumped in his office chair, fast asleep. His face was ashen and, even in sleep, lined with exhaustion. He must have been into the office, she decided. And she felt vaguely guilty then for ever having her suspicions.

She was going to have to learn how to trust him again. She would, she promised. Standing in the doorway, watching him sleep in his clothes, Kathy Walker made an early New Year's resolution: she was going to work to save this marriage because despite the pain and anguish he had put her through, despite how small he had made her feel, she still loved him.

God help her, but she still loved him.

CHAPTER 38

She dozed rather than slept for the next couple of hours.

Whenever she closed her eyes, events and incidents from the previous hours came rushing back. Suddenly she would find herself remembering the look in Stephanie's eyes when she'd opened the door and found her standing there. Somehow she hadn't seemed to be in the least surprised; maybe she too was relieved that events were coming to a head.

In an affair time stopped, Kathy suddenly realised. The affair existed in a bubble. It was only when it was discovered or ended that people could go on with their lives. In her own situation, she had been trapped in a world of lies, half-truths and evasions, while Stephanie was equally trapped by the same lies for the past eighteen months. And in the middle was Robert, spinning the lies, trying to balance both worlds, telling both women what he thought they wanted to hear.

When she'd visited Stephanie yesterday, time started moving again and she was glad that Robert had turned up. It had spared her the ordeal of having to confront him herself, and maybe having him lie and cast doubts on her every piece of evidence. She had absolutely no doubts that's what would have happened. Robert always had an answer for everything.

She heard movement. At first she though it was the children rising to see what "Santa" – in the shape of Mom and Dad – had brought them or, more correctly, checking to see if "Santa" had brought them exactly what they'd asked for.

The bathroom door opened, then footsteps, slow and heavy – so she knew they were not the children's – went downstairs. Maybe he too couldn't sleep.

Kathy got out of bed and went to stand by the window. The garden and road looked like a traditional Christmas card. No-one was moving yet, and no tracks broke the pristine snowy surface; even the tracks left by Robert's car three hours previously had been covered over. Some of the houses had lights on; she could see dressing-gown–clad children in the sitting-room of the house opposite, clustered around the Christmas tree ripping paper off their presents.

She found herself remembering her own childhood, and in particular that morning when she awoke to find that it had snowed overnight. She shared a bedroom with Sheila and she'd shaken her sister awake. They would have been about ten or eleven, she thought, old enough to begin to suspect the existence – or non-existence – of Santa Claus, but not prepared to question it too deeply. Just in case. Together, the two girls had huddled in the window, with the quilt pulled around their shoulders and simply looked at the snow and the world that they knew so well, now changed out of all recognition. They'd scanned the roofs of the houses opposite looking for reindeer tracks in the snow and then decided that magical reindeer probably didn't leave tracks in the snow.

She remembered, with absolutely clarity, what she had got for her Christmas presents that year. The big curly-haired doll with the eye that always stuck, the painting-by-numbers art set of a seascape that she'd never finished, *Bunty* and *Mandy* annuals and two blouses – one of which still had a Boyers tag on it . . . which she'd remembered thinking was a strange place for Santa to get his clothes from.

She couldn't remember the following Christmas, nor the previous one. It was the snow which made it special and memorable.

Other Christmases stuck in her memory; the first Christmas after her father died, the first year she was married, the year Brendan was born, the year Theresa arrived, their first year in this house. The rest melted into one vaguely similar event, with the same food, the same movies on TV, the same "Is that all?" feeling at the end of the day.

And now this Christmas. She would certainly be adding this to her list of memorable Christmases. This was one she would never forget and, she was afraid, would forever taint all future Christmases.

A creak on the stairs disturbed her reverie, and she turned away from the window and quickly slipped back into bed.

The bedroom door cracked open, yellow light from the landing spilling into the room. She heard Robert move around to her side of the bed and then the rattle of a cup and saucer as it was put down. She didn't remember the last time he had brought her up a cup of tea. "Kathy," his voice was a hoarse exhausted whisper, "Kathy?"

She opened her eyes. He looked wretched. There were deep bags beneath his eyes and the skin on his face seemed to have sagged. She fought to quell her rising concern.

"I brought you some tea," he said, then added, "Happy Christmas."

"You went out last night." It wasn't what she intended to say, nor was it what she wanted to ask, but she had to know, she had to ask the question and she had to hear his response. She had worked hard to keep her voice carefully neutral.

"The office alarm went off last night – I got a call from the alarm company. I had to go in."

She searched his face, looking for the truth. But would she even know if he was lying? He'd spent the past eighteen months lying to her and she hadn't picked that up; he must be an expert at it by now. "You were gone for a long time," she said, pushing up in bed, pulling the covers up to her chin.

"Roads were terrible. I was the only car on the carriageway. I crept along. And then when I got there, I had to wait for the alarm company." He'd moved around to stand by the window and look out at the dawn. Was that because he couldn't bear to look her in the face, she wondered. But no, he'd stared into her eyes countless times lately and lied to her.

"I take it there was no problem with the office."

He shook his head. "Probably snow or ice falling off a neighbouring building, hitting our roof and setting off one of the sensors. I could hear other alarms ringing out across Merrion Square as I drove home."

Kathy nodded. It had the ring of truth to it; especially the reasons for the alarm to go off in the first place. Surely he wouldn't be able to make up that detail himself?

"Drink your tea," he said. "I'm sure the children will be up soon." He padded silently out of the bedroom, and then she heard his office door close.

Kathy sat up in bed drinking the cooling tea, feeling guilty that she'd ever suspected him of sneaking off to Stephanie's in the first place.

They missed ten o'clock Mass.

When Kathy finished her tea, she closed her eyes – just for a moment – and then woke again at ten minutes to ten with a start, convinced that it had all been nothing more than a dream, a terrible, terrifying dream. All she had to do was to open her eyes and look around, and there would be Robert asleep beside her, and Stephanie and the last twenty-four hours, the last week would all be nothing more than a . . .

She opened her eyes.

It was no dream.

She could hear muted sounds coming from below and although she'd been bright and alert earlier, now she felt as if she was moving in slow motion. Robert and the children were up. Pulling on her dressing-gown, she padded silently downstairs. The children were in the midst of opening their presents and Kathy arrived just in time to hear Theresa say, "Thanks, Dad, how did you know I was looking for this one?"

Robert, standing beside the tree, while the children scattered Christmas paper across the floor, had the grace to look embarrassed as Kathy paused by the door. "Don't you know I had a little help? As always."

Kathy turned away and headed into the kitchen and was aware that Robert was coming in behind her. He had two badly wrapped presents in his hands. "Happy Christmas," he said awkwardly, holding them out.

And what had he got his mistress, Kathy wondered. She couldn't help but compare the two small items he was holding with the carefully wrapped and beautifully presented boxes he'd carried into Stephanie's house yesterday. And where were the flowers and the balloons? For a moment, she was going to refuse them. Whatever they were, she would never wear or use them: she wanted no memories of this particular Christmas. But then she relented and took them from his hands. "Thank you," she said simply. She thought he was leaning in to her, perhaps expecting a kiss or a hug, but she turned away quickly. "I'll give you yours later," she said, without turning around. "It's upstairs in the wardrobe. Now, come on, we'd better hurry or we're going to miss eleven o'clock Mass too. And midday Mass goes on forever."

Next year, Kathy promised herself, walking down the steps as she left the church, she was getting early Mass. Very early Mass. The service had been interrupted every few minutes by the blips and pips of some hand-held computer game or the irritating ringtone of a newly acquired phone and every so often a doll would cry realistically or an Action Man toy would fire off his gun.

As they filed out through the gates, they bumped into Julia who was holding court to a group of women, all of whom seemed only too delighted to make their escape when Kathy appeared.

"There you are, I was hoping to see you," she began, then quickly kissed Kathy and Robert on the cheeks. "Happy Christmas . . . Happy Christmas. And it's a white Christmas too, isn't it lovely." She made the question into a statement. "And you look lovely too – though you shouldn't have worn those trousers in this weather."

Kathy had dressed simply in her woollen trousers, worn over black square-heeled boots and, although she knew it made her look small and dumpy, she'd pulled on her heavy navy-blue coat. It was like wearing a blanket, but the open-plan, high-ceilinged church could be draughty. Julia, on the other hand, was wearing what Kathy called her country-lady look: tweed skirt, sensible brogues, a long hacking jacket and a hat with a short feather in it. And this was the lady giving her fashion advice! Kathy suddenly found herself biting the inside of her cheek to keep a straight face.

"Now, about tomorrow," Julia began, "we're going to start about –"

"We won't be down," Kathy said suddenly.

Julia looked blankly at her, then turned to look at Robert. "We're starting about four –"

"I'm not sure if you heard Kathy correctly," Robert said with a smile, "but we've decided not to come down this year."

Julia's mouth opened and closed. "But it's a tradition."

"We're breaking with tradition," Robert said.

"Starting some new ones," Kathy added. "Have a happy Christmas, Julia. Give our love to Ben." Then she turned and walked away.

Robert nodded to his dumbstruck sister-in-law and hurried after Kathy.

"Thank you," Kathy said.

"For what?"

"For supporting me."

"We should have done it years ago," he said.

"You're right. But it's time to make some changes," she said, glancing sidelong at him.

Robert nodded, eyes distant and lost. Then he blinked

and tried a smile. "And what was she wearing on her head? She looks like that woman in *Keeping Up Appearances* – the lady-of-the-house, Mrs Bucket." He pronounced it *boo-kay*.

"*Bucket*," Kathy corrected him and then she laughed, and Robert laughed with her. Climbing into the car, she couldn't remember the last time they had laughed together so easily.

CHAPTER 39

The moment the telephone rang, Kathy felt her insides twist and the little bubble of good humour that had remained with her since Mass instantly evaporated. She moved away from the oven and heard Brendan call out, "Dad, phone!"

"You get it," came the mumbled response.

"It'll be for you. It's always for you."

Rubbing her hands on her striped apron, Kathy started to move into the dining-room to get the phone when Robert – looking bleary-eyed and haggard – appeared and grabbed the phone out of the cradle. "Hello?"

She wondered who would be calling at this time on Christmas Day, and immediately thought: Julia. No doubt she'd spent the past couple of hours working herself up into a self-righteous frenzy and now had a dozen cast-iron reasons why they should come down for dinner tomorrow.

At some point in the conversation she'd play the "it's what mother would have wanted us to do" card.

"Hello?" Robert asked again.

Kathy glanced at him, eyebrows raised in a question. She saw him swallow and lick dry lips and then he smiled.

"Sure . . . sure," he said, and then he added, "And a happy Christmas to you too." He took a breath. "Let me just step out of the room away from the TV . . ."

"It's Jimmy Moran," he said, phone pressed against his chest, "calling to wish us Happy Christmas."

Kathy nodded as she sank the skewer into the turkey. "Tell him I said Happy Christmas. Don't talk too long, I'll be serving dinner shortly."

Robert moved out into the hall. "I'll be a minute."

She heard his footsteps on the stairs and knew he'd be more than a minute. He always was. She glanced over at the worktop, checking to ensure that everything was in place. This was the one big meal she cooked every year. When the children were younger she'd cooked what she called a proper meal every night, and then something special – like a roast, or a leg of lamb – every weekend, but as they'd grown up and Robert often found himself working on Saturday mornings, she'd fallen back on quickly prepared convenience foods. By the time the children were into their teens, they simply had no time to sit at the table and eat, and often she found herself cooking just for Robert and herself. More recently, she found she was eating alone. Robert would come home "not hungry" or having "had a big lunch"; now she wondered how much of that was true, or was he not hungry because he'd been eating with *her*?

Kathy veered away from that thought.

If they weren't going down to Julia's tomorrow – and she was determined that they were not, then maybe they should have Jimmy Moran around, and Sheila too. Kathy stopped and straightened: and what if Sheila wanted to bring her boyfriend? She took a deep breath: she could bring him. She was in no position to stand in judgment over someone else's relationship, nor should she.

She heard the door to Robert's office close and, when he came down, he looked ghastly. There was no colour in his face, and the bags beneath his eyes looked like physical bruises.

"Is everything all right?"

"Yes, he's fine," Robert said, licking dry lips.

"Not with him – with you."

"Yes, yes, I'm fine. I'm just exhausted," he admitted. "I might try and grab a nap after dinner. If that's OK," he added.

"It's what you do every year," she reminded him.

The long table in the dining-room had been opened out and covered with the Irish linen tablecloth that only saw service one day a year. Four full place settings had been laid out, Theresa having taken great care to ensure that the correct knives and forks were in the right position, while Brendan organised the plates and side plates.

Robert sat at the head of the table, Kathy at the opposite end, facing him, while the two children sat at either side. Kathy looked around the table, deliberately and consciously impressing every detail into her memory. Maybe this would be their last year at home for Christmas. Every year – usually on Christmas Day and at about this time – she would come up with the idea they would go away for a holiday next year. Enjoy Christmas in some warm and sunny climate. Ever since she'd been a child, and discovered that the seasons were reversed in the southern hemisphere, she'd wanted to spend Christmas on a beach in Australia. Next year, she promised herself, next year.

She had little appetite for food – nor had Robert, she noticed, and it gave her some little satisfaction to realise that he was feeling as bad as she was, but the children quickly finished the home-made tomato soup and Brendan finished off his father's barely touched bowl.

Kathy stood up and had started to gather the bowls when the phone rang again. She caught a glimpse of something move across Robert's face – some emotion she could not identify. "Let the machine get it," she said quickly. "This is one of the few meals this family sits down to together."

Robert nodded dubiously even as he was standing up. "I'd best get it. I won't be a minute."

Kathy sighed as she carried the soup bowls out to the kitchen. Next year they were definitely going away. She dropped the soup bowls in the sink and turned to the turkey which she'd left cooling on the draining-board.

Consequences

Peeling back the silver foil, she breathed in the distinctive aroma of turkey and spices.

"Hello . . . Yes, this is Robert Walker . . ."

Half-listening to Robert's conversation she plugged in the electric knife and prepared to start slicing into the bird. Brendan would take a leg, while Robert preferred the white breast meat and sausage stuffing. Theresa was going through one of her periodic vegetarian phases and had said she was only having vegetables.

"Good afternoon, Sister, what can I do for you?"

Sister? Kathy put down the knife and stepped over to the kitchen door, eyebrows raised in a silent question. A nun? A nurse? She could tell by Robert's voice and expression that he was just as confused as she was.

"James . . . I don't know . . . oh, you mean Jimmy Moran."

Kathy frowned. Jimmy Moran? But Jimmy had just been on the phone to Robert.

"Is everything OK?" Robert asked. He looked at her and shrugged and then said into the phone, "Today?" He quickly covered the mouthpiece and muttered to Kathy, "Mater Hospital. Jimmy's been taken in."

"But you were talking to him less than half an hour ago," Kathy said.

But Robert had turned back to the phone. "Yes, yes, I'm here . . . it's just it's a little awkward at the moment. Christmas Day and all that."

Kathy turned away and unplugged the knife; if Jimmy was in trouble, then she knew Robert would go to him.

"Is it an emergency?" Robert asked, then added, obviously responding to a question from the nurse, "Yes, yes, a good friend."

Kathy watched his expression change; there was something like fear in his eyes now.

"Tell him I'm on the way." He hung up and looked at Kathy. "I'm sorry, but I've got to go ..."

"I know. You should go. But how did he sound when you were talking to him earlier?"

"He sounded fine," he said simply.

"Go. Get your coat and gloves. I'll fill a flask with tea."

Kathy stood at the door and watched Robert gingerly inch the car out of the drive. She found herself waving out of habit, and then turned and closed the door behind her. She wondered when she'd see her husband again. When she got back into the dining-room, the children had drifted away to the television and she hadn't got the heart to call them back to the table. Having a Christmas dinner without Robert seemed *wrong* somehow.

As she passed the phone, she stopped and looked at the caller ID. The last call showed a city centre number 8032000 – she'd no doubts that was the Mater Hospital – but the call before that read *Unavailable* ... which was strange, because that usually only came up when it was a foreign call. Jimmy Moran had an apartment in Temple Bar; she seemed to remember that he had a city centre number, beginning with 67 or 69. Maybe he'd gone ex-directory. But ex-directory numbers came up as *Private* on the caller ID.

Suddenly realising what she was doing, and feeling guilty that she was checking up on Robert, she turned away and started to busy herself tidying the kitchen, putting away the meats, wrapping up the vegetables, pouring the sauces – apple, cheese and cranberry – into small containers. Just about everything would keep. Knowing that the children would be looking for something to eat in a couple of hours, she cut slices off the turkey and ham onto two side-plates, covered them in cling film and left them in the centre of the table.

"I've left some meat out if you want to make yourselves sandwiches later, and listen out for the phone, will you?" she told Brendan and Theresa, who were sitting on either end of the couch, playing one of the new games Brendan had got for his X-Box. "Your dad's gone to visit Uncle Jimmy in hospital. I'm just going upstairs for a lie-down. I didn't sleep too well last night."

"When is Dad coming back?" Theresa asked, without looking away from the screen.

"I've no idea," Kathy said truthfully. "Depends on what he finds when he reaches the hospital. He'll phone as soon as he has news."

"They took him down for tests about two hours ago," Robert said, his voice echoing slightly as if he was standing in a corridor. "I keep asking them for results or a progress report, but the nurses on duty cannot tell me anything. They're run off their feet."

Kathy lay on the bed and stared at the ceiling. An outsized paperback lay on the bedspread beside her; she'd tried reading but the words kept shifting and moving on the page and made no sense to her. "And how did he look?"

"He looked terrible. Kathy, I got such a fright when I first saw him. I thought he was dead."

She could hear the genuine fear in his voice. Although Robert would probably never admit it, she knew he had come to regard Jimmy Moran as a father figure. Kathy liked the older man, but was also wary of the influence he had on Robert and had little time for his attitude towards women. He was of the generation that regarded them as objects to be conquered, bedded and then chained to a kitchen sink. "He's as tough as old boots, Robert, you know that. He's going to pull through."

There was a pause and she could hear the ambient sound change, the echo of the corridor dying away.

"I'm sorry for ruining your Christmas Day," he said suddenly.

"That didn't ruin my Christmas. It was ruined a long time before Jimmy got ill."

"Yes." His voice hissed and popped across the line.

"If you'd stayed at home today, we would probably have ended up in an argument," she said eventually.

"Probably," he agreed.

"Maybe this time apart has been . . . useful. Allows us both to get a little perspective." Lying in the darkened bedroom, listening to the muted rumble from the TV below had been vaguely comforting. She hadn't realised just how on edge she'd been until she lay back on the bed and felt the rigid bar of pain across her shoulders that had been building throughout the day begin to ease.

"Yes, yes, you're right."

"Time to think," she added.

"I've been doing nothing but thinking," he said.

"We will talk when you get home. I'll get the children up to bed; we might have a little supper together and talk."

"That would be nice . . . yes, it's been a long time since we sat down and talked. It'll be just like the old days."

Kathy sat up on the bed and looked out into the street. Heavy banks of grey black clouds had been rolling in all afternoon and it had started to snow again. The world outside was white and still. "Do you think you're going to make it home tonight?" she asked.

"I'd like to wait and see how Jimmy is. I don't want to leave him on his own."

Kathy frowned. That didn't sound right; Jimmy was one of the most sociable and gregarious men she knew. "Why is he on his own? I thought Angela or Frances would be on the way. They're not snowed in, are they?"

"They may be snowed in, but that's not the reason they're staying away. They've both simply refused to come. Turns out Jimmy told them too many lies over too many years: that's finally caught up with him," Robert said.

Kathy nodded. She'd always known that sooner or later Jimmy Moran would have to pay for a lifetime of sailing far too close to the wind with his relationships and too-close friendships with women. And his treatment of his wife and, latterly, his mistress, was shameful . . . not unlike Robert's, in fact, she couldn't help but add.

"I'd like to stay for a while longer . . . if that's OK?"

"Of course, it's OK. It's snowing heavily here: I'd almost prefer if you stayed there, rather than trying to drive on the roads. The hospital staff will hardly throw you out."

"You know, I might just do that. I'll kip down on one of the empty beds."

Kathy heard a sudden high-pitched blipping sound and then Robert swore. "I'm almost out of power on the mobile," he said quickly.

"Is there a phone in the room?" she asked immediately.

She heard movement and then a click, as if he'd turned on a light. "Here it is . . ."

She copied down the number onto the notepad beside the bedroom phone. "Look, I'd best go, and conserve what's left of the battery. You've got the number, call me anytime. I'll be here for the next couple of hours at least and if I do decide to stay here, I'll give you a call."

"Give Jimmy my love," Kathy said and rang off.

She sat for a little while longer and watched it snow.

Then she opened the presents Robert had given her.
The necklace was lovely, though remarkably similar to
one he had bought her a couple of years ago, and the
scarves were nice, if rather ordinary. She only had about
two dozen similar ones. He'd probably picked up both gifts
in The Pavilions, and she wondered if she could return
them next week.

Then she realised that she hadn't given him his
present. Opening the bottom of the wardrobe, she took
out the large rectangular box, now wrapped in several
sheets of three-euro-a-sheet Christmas paper. Inside was
a pigskin briefcase, with his initials RW embossed in gold
onto the front. There was a Christmas card attached to
the box. She'd written it before she'd discovered his affair
and thought for a moment about removing it. In the card
she had added a little note about how much in love she
was, and thanking him for everything he had done for
them all over the past year. She decided to leave it. His
card to her had been a generic *To My Wife* card with an
insipid verse to which he had added, *"With all my love"*
and signed with an indecipherable flourish.

She carried the box into his office and laid it on the
table alongside his computer. She glanced at the machine
and, for a single moment, thought about turning it on to
check his emails, but then she turned away, feeling
disgusted with herself.

She was dozing in the sitting-room with the TV off and

the fire burnt down to embers when he returned. Although it was not yet midnight, the children had gone to bed, and his absence had cast a pall over the day. The phone had rung twice and she'd jumped on each occasion. Recognising Julia's number on the caller ID she'd allowed her two calls to go to the answering machine. But there had been no message. She was in no humour to speak to her sister; it would be bound to end in an argument. She thought about phoning Sheila or Maureen, just for a chat, but in the end called neither of them. She wanted the time to think and plan for the future, but found she couldn't do that either. Her thoughts were chaotic and she found herself quickly shifting between anger at Robert's behaviour and sympathy for his current situation, coupled with her own doubts and self-loathing. Surely there was something she could have done to prevent this happening?

The flare of headlights against the sitting-room window alerted her to his return and she had the hall door open before he had climbed out of the car. And if he'd looked tired and ill before he left, now he looked positively pitiful. His skin was the colour of parchment, his shoulders were rounded as if he carried the weight of the world on them, his eyes half-closed. When he came into the house, she wanted to gather him into her arms and hold him close, tell him that everything was going to be OK, but the look on his face was so off-putting, so forbidding that she backed away and she knew, even before he opened his mouth, and said, "He's dead" that Jimmy Moran was gone.

Robert climbed the stairs and closed the office door

behind him, without saying another world. She heard the double-thump as his shoes hit the floor, then silence.

Kathy Walker closed the door, locked up and turned off the lights. She was feeling weary, stiff and aching, almost as if she was coming down with flu.

Climbing the stairs, she stopped outside Robert's door, head tilted to one side, and listened for several long moments before she cracked the door open and peered inside. Robert was slumped in the chair and, although he was asleep, his brow was furrowed and his eyes were twitching furiously behind closed lids. In that moment, her heart broke for him and she resolved that things would be different. He shouldn't be here, sitting in an uncomfortable chair, still in the clothes he'd been wearing all day. He should be in bed, beside her, and she should be holding him, comforting him.

She went to the airing cupboard, found a heavy blanket, carried it into his room and tucked it in around him. He moaned in his sleep, but didn't awaken.

Before she left the room, she looked back and came to the decision that they could – they *would* – put all this behind them; they would work to rebuild their marriage and relationship; they would start again.

CHAPTER 40

Thursday, 26th December

"Thank you for the briefcase . . . and the card," Robert said, accepting the mug of tea from Kathy's hand.

"I thought it was about time you got a new one; that old case is the same age as Brendan, and beginning to look it." She noted that he'd put her Christmas card on top of the computer screen.

Robert turned to look at the fine-grained pigskin case on the table. "I'll take good care of it," he promised.

"How are you getting on?" she asked, looking around the office. As if it mirrored his mental state, the once-neat room was in disarray: there were clothes piled over the back of the chairs, the blanket she'd covered with him was tossed on the floor and there were papers and files everywhere.

"I've been looking for addresses," Robert said, turning back to the computer and nodding at the screen. Kathy noted that he had Outlook open to the Contacts page. "Angela said she was too *distraught* to get involved in the

369

funeral arrangements," Robert said bitterly, "though she didn't sound that upset when I phoned her yesterday and told her that he was dead. I could hear some sort of party going on in the background."

"It is Christmas, Robert," Kathy gently reminded him.

"And I'm not getting any sense out of Frances. The last time I spoke to her, I thought she was drunk or stoned. She didn't seem especially upset either by the thought that the father of her child was dead."

"Their relationship had more or less foundered though, hadn't it?"

"I think he loved her more than she loved him," he continued. "She lost interest in him when she realised that he was never going to make her a star."

"He spent a long time lying to her, making her promises that he could never keep."

"I know that!" Robert snapped. "I'm sorry," he said immediately. "I know what he was like. I spoke to him about it often enough and you're right; his lies turned her against him. But I would have thought that his death changes things."

"Doesn't change how you feel about a person," Kathy said. "Just because someone dies, that doesn't make them a better person."

"No . . . no, I suppose you're right. But he was always a friend to me, and I liked him, liked him a lot . . . despite his faults."

"I know that."

"Anyway, the upshot of it is that I'm trying to coordinate with Angela, and she's doling out information in dribs and drabs. I finally found an address for Michael – Mikey – Moran, the eldest brother. He's living in Canada. I've just been hunting through the online Canadian phone directories looking for a number for him. And even if I do get a number, I'll have to wait before calling: Toronto is five hours behind us."

"Do you know what sort of relationship they had?"

Robert shook his head. "Not really. Distant, but friendly, I think." He suddenly turned away from the machine. "Once I get him, I can sort out the funeral arrangements, and then I'll start contacting people in the industry. I'll write a press release too, I think." He looked up at Kathy. "I'm sorry, I guess I'm not going to be much use to anyone today."

"Do what you have to do," Kathy said. "But do try and get some rest. You look exhausted."

"I am tired," he admitted. "I'll take a nap later. What are you going to do?" He smiled. "Go down to Julia's?"

"Over my dead body," she said, and then coloured, realising what she'd said. "I'm sorry. That was thoughtless."

"Yes, but funny, you have to admit. You know, if you don't go down to her, she's more than likely to turn up at the door."

"She'd pick a bad day for an argument," Kathy said grimly.

"Why, Kathy, how wonderful to hear from you!"

"Maureen . . . Happy Christmas to you," Kathy said carefully.

"Is everything all right?" Maureen asked immediately, obviously picking up something in Kathy's reserved tone.

"Not really," Kathy said carefully. "Jimmy Moran died yesterday."

There was a long silence, then Maureen sighed and said, "Poor Jimmy. My God," she said suddenly, "he was younger than me. What happened?"

Kathy stood at the kitchen window and watched Brendan and Theresa build a lopsided snowman in the back garden. Overhead, the sky was cloudless, the brilliant sunlight catching painfully bright reflections of every surface, but massing in the distance she could see enormous blue-black clouds boiling up out of the north. There would be more snow later.

"Kathy?" Maureen said, breaking into the long silence.

"Sorry," she said quickly. "It was a heart attack. Robert got a call yesterday, early afternoon, from the hospital. He went in, of course. He was with him to the end."

"And how is he taking it?"

"Badly," Kathy said simply.

"I never understood that relationship myself. Jimmy usually drove away younger talent. I think he was a little fearful of it, envious too, but he and Robert just connected."

"I just wanted to let you know about Jimmy," said Kathy. "I know you knew him."

"I've known him for more than twenty-five years, I

372

think," Maureen said softly. "There were times when I even liked him. We got on because I was the one woman who would never sleep with him, he said. He was so charming," she added with a sigh. "He was also the most wonderful and outrageous liar. That made him the perfect producer," she added with a small laugh. "When is the funeral?"

"I don't know yet. Robert is trying to make the arrangements. Apparently neither Angela nor Frances want anything to do with him. They wouldn't even come in to the hospital."

"I'm not surprised."

"Robert is trying to contact Jimmy's brothers . . ."

"I didn't know he had family," Maureen exclaimed.

"Three brothers, in America, Canada and Australia, as far as I can make out. Robert is not making a lot of sense this morning. He's physically and emotionally shattered."

"He called here on Christmas Eve. He told me about your encounter with Stephanie. So, how are you?" Maureen asked softly.

"I'm OK," Kathy said quickly.

"Truthfully," Maureen persisted.

"I'm feeling a little shattered myself."

"Hardly surprising. You know, if you want someone to talk to, someone who's been there and has gone through what you're going through right now, all you have to do is to give me a call."

"I know. Thank you." There were tears in her eyes now, fragmenting the garden into rainbows of bitter light. Then she said suddenly, "What are you doing this afternoon? Are you free?"

"I've no plans," Maureen said, sounding surprised.

"We had no Christmas dinner yesterday; Robert got the call before I could serve it up. Would you come over? My sister Sheila is coming too – you remember Sheila? – I could phone her and ask her to pick you up, so you wouldn't have to drive. Say yes, please!"

"I'd be delighted to," Maureen said without hesitation.

"Good. Thank you. I'd just really like some company," she admitted, "someone to talk to. Robert is busy at the moment organising Jimmy's funeral and I think he might just crash later. It'll just be the three of us."

"I'll be there," Maureen promised.

"I'll have Sheila call and collect you about three."

"I'll be ready."

CHAPTER 41

It was only when she saw the two women standing at the door that the tears came. The deep racking sobs came from deep within and left her shuddering with emotion. Sheila and Maureen gathered her into their arms, and hugged her closely, letting her cry out her pain and terrible anguish.

Then Maureen eased them all away from the door and in towards the kitchen and sat her down in a chair. "Make some tea," Maureen suggested to Sheila, while she dug in her tiny handbag and produced a linen square, which she used to pat Kathy's eyes as if she were a child.

Kathy drew in a deep shuddering breath. "I'm sorry. I don't know what came over me."

Maureen crouched beside her. "There's nothing to apologise for. You've been through a lot over the past couple of days."

"Where are the children?" Sheila asked.

"They've both gone out – to different parties."

"And Robert?"

"Upstairs. Asleep. At least I think he's asleep. I haven't heard any movement in the last hour or so." She stood up and carefully wiped at her eye make-up. "Well, putting this on was a waste of time, wasn't it?"

"You look wonderful," Sheila said.

Kathy was wearing a simple wine-coloured suit that she'd bought about six months ago for an entertainment-industry function dinner, but which she'd never worn. Robert had been forced to cancel at the last minute . . . she hadn't thought too much about it at the time, but now, of course, she could think of any number of reasons why he would want to cancel.

Sheila was wearing an oyster-coloured silk dress with just the hint of a pattern in the cloth and Maureen was, as always, elegant and sophisticated in black trousers and a white roll-neck sweater.

"Thank you for coming, both of you," Kathy said sincerely. "I think I was beginning to go crazy here. And, you're the only two people I can talk to about the situation. But I won't," she added quickly. "I promised myself that we would have a little food, a little drink, but we wouldn't discuss . . . Robert and me."

Maureen pulled over a chair and sat down beside Kathy. The older woman's almost translucent eyes had taken on the grey of the afternoon sky and made her look older, sterner than usual. "Oh, but I don't think either of us will hold you to that promise."

Sheila put a cup of tea on the table in front of Kathy. "I spoke to Maureen on the way over," she said. "She knows my own peculiar situation too."

"No secrets, eh?" Kathy asked.

"Not between us," Maureen said. She nodded her thanks as Sheila put a cup of fragrant Earl Grey down in front of her. "You remembered," she said delightedly.

"I remembered."

When the girls' mother had died about eighteen months previously, Maureen had stepped in and helped organise everything. She had turned up at Julia's house, where the wake was going to be held, with a box of Earl Grey tea.

"I've got plenty of food — too much food. No one had a proper dinner yesterday," Kathy said. "I know Brendan and Theresa ended up making themselves some oven chips last night. Some Christmas dinner, eh?" She looked from Maureen to Sheila. "We can eat out here or go inside."

"Let's do it properly," Maureen said. "Let's go inside."

The dining-room smelled of Christmas tree and incense mingled with the peaty tang from the turf on the fire. The three women carried in platters of cut meat, deep bowls of vegetables and a bottle of white wine from the fridge. An opened bottle of red wine sat breathing by the fire. Kathy assumed her usual position at the table and the two women sat down at either side in the places normally occupied by the children. While Kathy served the food, Sheila poured the wine — red for Maureen and herself, white for Kathy – and then they raised their glasses in a toast.

"What will we toast?" Sheila asked.

"Christmases to come," Kathy said.

"Lots of them," Maureen said, "and all of them better than this one!"

"Amen to that," Kathy agreed.

They ate in companionable silence for a while. Kathy suddenly discovered that she had an appetite, and then she realised that she hadn't eaten properly since . . . well, Monday night, she thought, before she had seen her husband kiss another woman. She'd hadn't been able to stomach anything solid since then.

"I'm really glad we're doing this," Sheila said. "I was going crazy at home. Since I'd decided not to go to Julia's for her traditional Stephen's Day leftovers, all I'd got to look forward to was *The Sound of Music* and a Marks & Sparks turkey dinner. With stuffing," she added significantly. She glanced sidelong at her older sister. "You didn't invite Julia?"

"No. I wanted to enjoy this in the company of people I loved."

"She *is* your sister," Maureen reminded her gently.

"As you get older, I realise that you get to pick your own family; they become more important than the family of your birth."

"Hey . . ." Sheila said, mock indignantly.

Kathy reached over and held her sister's hand. "Sometimes, they are one and the same."

"Thanks."

"Julia feels that she has a role to live up to," Maureen explained. "She thinks you all need a mother, so that's the role she's assumed for herself. She has no children of her own, has she?"

Kathy and Sheila shook their heads.

"Just be firm with her. I would imagine you've both deferred to her all your lives."

The sisters nodded.

"Reminds me of my own sister," Maureen remarked.

"All this time I've known you and I never knew you had a sister," Kathy said.

"My sister Marion. Four years younger than me. I thought of her today for the first time in ages." Maureen smiled wistfully. "She used to be a friend of Jimmy Moran's, a very good friend," she added significantly.

"Where is she . . . what happened?" Sheila asked, glancing sidelong at her sister.

"She's in LA. Married, twice – three times maybe – and now runs a hugely successful casting agency. When Jimmy was trying to get his Irish films off the ground, Marion was his Hollywood connection. We had a falling out – not about Jimmy, but he was part of it – and just drifted apart."

"Do you miss her?" Sheila asked.

"Sometimes." Then she shook her head. "I rarely think of her, to be truthful. She could be such a bitch sometimes." She shook her head. "Old memories and not particularly pleasant ones. I thought about phoning her and telling her about Jimmy, but I didn't want to enter her world again, or allow her back into mine." She sipped her wine, her garnet-coloured lipstick leaving a perfect impression of her lips on the glass. "But Kathy is right: as you get older, the family you choose to surround yourself with can be just as important as those that are accidents of birth." She looked over at Sheila. "You'd started to tell me in the car about Allan."

"Oh, poor Allan," Sheila laughed wistfully. "He's so much in love with me . . . or he thinks he's so much in love with me."

"For men that is the same thing," Maureen remarked.

"I am the love of his life apparently. After rugby and sports cars. Well, before I finally managed to get rid of him on Tuesday, I made him promise that he wouldn't say anything to his wife. Made him swear. Told him we needed to talk and plan."

Kathy concentrated on her wine, feeling uncomfortable with the conversation. Robert and Stephanie must have had a similar chat when they were working out the best days to tell her that he was leaving her.

"So he's agreed to say nothing to his wife. I'm going to finish with him as soon as I can. Problem solved. Except . . ."

"Julia?" Kathy guessed.

"Julia! She is now threatening to tell his wife . . . who will throw him out . . . and he'll come crawling around to me!" She shook her head. "I'll talk to Julia about it. It'll cause a row, but I've no choice. However," she added, "I have come to a decision."

Both women looked at her.

"I'm finished with married men or men with partners, lovers or girlfriends, ex- or otherwise. I'd never really thought about the other women before." She reached out and touched her sister's hand. "But watching you . . . seeing what's happened . . . made me realise just how devastating an affair can be, how painful it can be. I'd never thought of that before. I just assumed that if the men were wandering it was because there was something wrong at home."

"There was. There is," Kathy said bitterly.

Maureen stepped in quickly. "It's a good decision," she said. "I've had my share of relationships. I've been cheated upon, I cheated and I've been the mistress . . . and you know something: it never works out. Never."

"Can a marriage survive an affair?" Kathy wondered seriously.

"Yes. It can. And it can sometimes be stronger because of the affair," Maureen said, "but in my experience, the affair can never survive the discovery. The men inevitably go back to their wives, who invariably take them. The mistress is nearly always abandoned." She saw Sheila watching her closely across the table and nodded. "And you don't want to get a reputation as a mistress. After a while you stop getting the invites to the parties, just in case you try and seduce all the married men. And when you do go all the old letches come around, thinking they're in with a good chance." She held up her glass and Sheila refilled it. "Men – who needs them!"

Kathy pushed away her plate, suddenly no longer hungry. She looked at Maureen. "You know Robert. How do I keep him?"

The older woman rested her chin on her right hand and gazed at Kathy. "Do you want to keep him?"

"Yes."

"Why?"

"Because I love him . . ." She stopped, thinking hard, then tried again. "He's the children's father."

"Does he make you happy?" Maureen asked.

"Yes . . . once he did. But we were younger then, with fewer responsibilities . . ."

Maureen shook her head firmly. "With *more* responsibilities. A young couple, newly married, children on the way, business to grow, house to pay for. You should have been under even more pressure and yet, I'll bet, you were never closer."

Kathy nodded. It was true.

"But then you got used to one another, maybe a little bored. You allowed your relationship to slip into a routine."

Kathy nodded again.

"It's the routine that's the killer. Boredom." She squeezed Kathy's hand. "I know you're going to get through this. You love him, that's a start, and he says he loves you."

"He did say that."

"He just has to be honest with you now. You both have to be honest with one another. No more secrets, no more lies."

"Plus he has to guarantee to stay away from her," Sheila added.

"He's already promised me that." Kathy heaved a sigh. "You're right. I'd hoped we would have had a chance to talk, but so far everything has conspired to keep us apart. And he's so tired at the moment; he's just emotionally and physically exhausted. Driving into the office on Christmas night really flattened him."

Maureen's eyes flickered across to Sheila. "Why did he go out on Christmas night?" she asked casually.

"He got a call from the alarm company; the office alarm had gone off. Turned out to be a false alarm — literally — in the end: snow falling onto the roof. He was gone for about three hours. Driving in the snow on the icy roads must have been a killer. He was exhausted when he came home, and then, of course, he had to go out again on Christmas Day."

Maureen sipped her wine. "Wonder why the alarm company didn't phone me," she murmured. "I'm on that call list too. And my name is first on the list because I'm closer." She saw the suddenly distraught look on Kathy's face and said slowly, "But maybe Robert had me taken off the list when I fell ill."

"Maybe," Kathy said, though no one at the table believed it. She stood up suddenly, and started to gather up the plates. "Now, who wants some Christmas pudding?"

"With brandy butter?" Sheila asked.

"Freshly made," Kathy said, far too cheerfully.

CHAPTER 42

Friday, 27th December

Kathy waited until she heard the bathroom door close, the lock click shut and the shower start to thrum, before she moved. She had maybe six or seven minutes at most. Moving quickly from her bedroom, she padded silently down the corridor and slipped into Robert's room. His computer was still on, a digital clock slowly rotating on the screen.

She had to know.

Previously, she'd felt guilty when she'd had her suspicions about him. No longer. Now she just needed to know the truth, and she would do whatever it took to discover it. There was a quote she remembered. *"The truth will set you free."* Maybe that was right, because now not knowing had her trapped like a fly in a web, and the lies, the suspicions, the doubts and the constant questions were destroying her.

Still listening for the shower, she sat in the chair before the screen and moved the mouse.

Please enter password.

Kathy blinked in surprise. That was new. She'd never known Robert to add a password to his screensaver before. Her instinct was to turn and flee – she definitely didn't want to be caught doing this – but she sat and stared at the black letters on the grey rectangle.

Please enter password.

She knew he used his date of birth as the password for the machine log on; he'd hardly use the same password for the screensaver too, would he?

He had.

She entered 10101962 and the screen cleared. Outlook, the email program, was still open, a message from Jimmy's brother open on screen. Kathy clicked on the Inbox, looking for something from Stephanie.

There was nothing.

Kathy moved the cursor down and clicked into Sent Box and then blinked in surprise. He had sent out scores of emails over the course of the past twenty-four hours, a simple *"I am terribly sorry to inform you that our good friend . . ."* They were to Jimmy's friends, colleagues, industry journalists, and scattered amongst them were emails to all three of the Moran brothers.

She finally found what she was looking for – and hoping not to find – at the bottom of the screen. An email sent to Stephanie Burroughs on Wednesday morning – Christmas Day – at 8:15am.

Consequences

Dear Stephanie,

I don't know what's happened to you. I am desperately worried. I've tried calling you at the house and on your mobile, but there's no response. You've just disappeared.

Please get in touch with me. Let me know you're OK.

I even went over to the house earlier this morning. I let myself in. I'm concerned there's no sign of you and yet I know you haven't gone away. I saw from the wardrobes that all your clothes are still there.

I am really concerned that something has happened or that you've done something.

I am at my wits' end.

I have no idea how to contact your friend Sally, and I realised I don't know any of your other friends. If I don't get in touch with you soon, I might try and contact Charles Flintoff. I'm half thinking I should contact the police and report you as missing.

If you get this, then please, please, please contact me.

I love you.

Robert

Kathy looked at the screen and watched the words dissolve and fragment as bitter tears stung her eyes. Here it was: proof, if proof she needed that he was still in touch with Stephanie. She brushed away the tears and read the email again . . . and then she frowned. Something wasn't right. He'd sent this email *after* his return on Christmas night. She realised he must have gone to her home searching for her.

Kathy heard the water pipes clank and then the

shower was turned off. She was tempted to hit print, but she was unsure how long it would take the printer to warm up. Scrolling back up to the Inbox, she positioned the cursor on the email from Jimmy's brother, then slipped out of the room. She hoped that the screensaver would have kicked in before Robert returned from the bathroom.

Stepping into her bedroom, she shut the door behind her and turned the key in the lock. Whatever type of email she had been expecting to find from Robert or Stephanie, it certainly hadn't been this one. She didn't need to print up the email. Every word was imprinted on her consciousness.

I even went over the house earlier this morning. I let myself in.

So he had lied to her and gone over to Stephanie's house on Christmas Eve night . . . but she wasn't there, and he was concerned that something was wrong.

I don't know what's happened to you. I am desperately worried.

This would have been only hours after she had made him promise that he would not see Stephanie again. Even as he was making that promise he was obviously worried about Stephanie's disappearance, which suggested that he'd tried to get in touch with her earlier in the evening. He'd obviously been so worried that he'd driven across the city in a snowstorm to check up on her. She wondered what he thought he'd find – a body? He was flattering himself. Women like Stephanie didn't kill themselves over men like Robert.

Kathy was surprised by how calm she felt. She'd just discovered more evidence of Robert's infidelity, more evidence of lies. She should be angrier... instead she just felt sad. Sad and exhausted.

Well, since she'd started down this path...

Sitting by the side of the bed, she riffled through her old diary until she found the number she was looking for.

"Pro-Alarms. Tony speaking. How may I help?"

"Good morning, Tony. This is Kathy Walker, R&K Productions. We're one of your clients."

"Good morning, Mrs Walker. Do you have a security reference number?"

"A security reference number?"

"We ask our clients to supply us with a number known only to them. When they get in touch with us we use the number to verify that it really is them."

"Oh." Kathy looked at the diary again. There was nothing beside the Pro-Alarms number. Then a sudden thought struck her. "The only number I have here is 10101962."

"Thank you. We just have to be sure it's a genuine call."

"I understand. Tony, could you tell me if the R&K Productions' office alarm was activated early on Christmas morning, December 25th?" She heard fingers tapping a keyboard. "Some friends were coming home from a late party and thought they heard our alarm ringing out."

"I have nothing on record. No, definitely not. Could have been a nearby building."

"Probably. Before I go, could you confirm that you have Maureen Ryan and Robert Walker on your call-out list in that order?"

"Yes, Mrs Walker. We contact Ms Ryan first. Then, if she is unavailable, we contact Mr Walker."

"And you have two numbers for him: mobile and home?"

"Yes. It would be our policy to contact the home number first, particularly for a late-night call, then we try the mobile number."

"That's great. Thank you, Tony – you've been very helpful. Have a happy Christmas."

"And a Happy Christmas to you too, Mrs Walker."

So now she knew.

She'd contacted the alarm company just in case Robert had received a call-out and had then driven from the office to check up on Stephanie since he was on that side of the city. He hadn't. He'd risked the dangerous drive just to check up on his mistress.

Exhaustion settled over her in a leaden blanket. She felt her eyelids close and her shoulders slump. All she wanted to do right now was to crawl into bed, curl up in a warm cocoon and drift into a deep and dreamless sleep. But what was that going to achieve? Nothing would have changed when she got up.

Could she blame him for doing what he had done?

The sudden thought caught her unawares and she sat,

still and unmoving on the edge of the bed, looking out over the snow-locked streets.

I've tried calling you at the house and on your mobile, but there's no response. You've just disappeared . . . I don't know what's happened to you. I am desperately worried . . . I am really concerned that something has happened or that you've done something.

He was concerned for the woman. He had been in love with her – she had to accept that. And love wasn't something you could turn on and off like a tap: she knew that. Even after all he'd done to her, she still loved him. It stood to reason that Robert must still have feelings for Stephanie. He'd admitted as much when they spoke on Tuesday; he'd said then that he still loved Stephanie.

So he'd tried to get hold of her and failed, and then risked a drive across the city to see if she was all right. He hadn't abandoned her. She had to admire that loyalty, to recognise that commitment. And then she remembered that they were the qualities of the man she had originally fallen in love with.

She heard the bathroom door open. Then the door to Robert's office clicked shut.

The man she married eighteen years ago had been kind and gentle, caring, honest and loyal. Especially loyal. She liked to think that he still had most of those qualities. On impulse, she climbed off the bed, knelt on the floor and pulled open the drawer under the bed. At the bottom of the drawer, almost lost under piles of T-shirts that she would never wear was a small cloth suitcase. Dropping the case on to the bed, she pulled the curtains closed and turned on the lights before she turned back to the bed and opened the case. Inside there were hundreds – maybe thousands – of pictures, either six-by-four or ten-by-eight prints of every Christmas and birthday, first days at school, visits to the zoo, Christenings, Communions and Confirmations. At the bottom of the case was the white linen box which held her wedding album. She opened the box and lifted out the heavy leather-bound volume with the gilt-edged pages. A sprinkling of eighteen–year–old confetti fell to the bed covers.

Kathy didn't remember the last time she had looked at the album. A couple of years ago, she thought, when Theresa had asked out of the blue what her dress had been like.

She turned to the back of the book. The early pages, which held all the photos of her late mother and father, were filled with too many sad memories and she knew if she started with them, she would end up weeping. The last few pages contained the images of the wedding reception.

Kathy smoothed down the slightly crumpled tissue guards and looked at the first picture she came to: the happy couple dancing in the centre of an empty floor. Robert, tall, handsome and elegant in an Edwardian morning coat, with his eyes fixed on her face, holding her as if she were a delicate piece of china. She looked so young – she was only twenty-two, but looked maybe eighteen – wide-eyed, innocent and ecstatic. She was wearing the wedding dress that now lay wrapped in tissue paper in a suitcase in the attic. Eighteen years later, she could only remember fragments of the day with absolute clarity: her father crying the first time he saw her come down the stairs in her dress, the moment she stepped out of the car in front of the church, the instant she said "*I do*", and then later, this particular photo, the first time she'd danced in the arms of her husband. She had never felt so beautiful, so loved.

And she was proud to be Mrs Walker. Robert was kind, caring and compassionate, someone his friends and family could depend on to lend a hand when it was needed. She loved him for those qualities, and he hadn't lost them either. When the call came in from the hospital, he hadn't thought twice about going in to be with his friend. She understood that. And then she recognised that it was the same quality that had driven him out of the house to see if Stephanie was all right. And, thank God, he had found nothing when he got there.

But he should have said something. He should not have lied to her. She smiled as she turned the page, trying to imagine the conversation. "*Oh, Kathy, I know you've just discovered that I'm having an affair, but I just want to pop over to Stephanie's to see if she's OK. She's dropped out of sight and I can't get in touch with her.*" She was hardly likely to say, *Go right ahead,* was she?

The next-to-last image in the back of the album was a group photo of all their friends. She was shocked to discover how few of them she could name. There was

Jimmy Moran standing behind Robert. She'd met him for the first time at the wedding. On the other side, looking exotic in a dress that exposed far too much flesh, was Maureen Ryan. But who were the rest, and where had they all gone? The girl in the pink dress was someone she had gone to college with, and the boy with the pitiful attempt at a beard was a young director working in RTE at the time. He was still there as far as she could remember.

Loss of friends . . . that was one of the hidden costs of marriage. Oh, they'd all kept in touch for the first year or so, and then slowly, one by one, as they'd married, or emigrated or moved on to different careers, they'd slipped away.

New friends had come along, neighbours she'd grown friendly with as she'd gone up and down to the school, colleagues of Robert's they sometimes socialised with, but they weren't deep friendships. She'd realised that yesterday when she'd discovered that she desperately wanted someone to talk to, someone who understood the nuances and moods of an affair, someone discreet enough not to talk about it. The only names which had come to mind were Sheila and Maureen. She'd thought about asking in her friend and neighbour, Rose, but much as she liked Rose, she didn't think she could be trusted to keep her mouth shut.

The last picture in the book was a portrait of Robert and Kathy in an oval-shaped frame. They were smiling into the camera, shy, slightly scared-looking smiles. They'd promised to love, honour and cherish one another. Kathy remembered that her mother had been scandalised that she was not going to use the work "obey" in the service.

And although Robert had broken every one of those vows, she still loved him and cherished him, thought she was unsure if she still honoured him. Whatever that meant.

But she'd never betrayed him, never even looked at another man over the course of their marriage, couldn't even contemplate it.

Kathy closed the book with a snap, and decided that, no, she could not fault him for checking up on Stephanie Burroughs. The man she married would have been concerned enough to do that and she was pleased that that, at least, had not changed.

What she found unforgivable however, was the last line in the email: *I love you.*

She tried to dismiss it 'I love you' was such an overused sentiment these days. People signed off emails and letters with "love" and "all my love" and "give my love" without a second thought.

I love you.

No, Kathy had no illusions about what he meant. He still loved Stephanie. The only consolation left to her was her memory of her conversation with Stephanie on Christmas Eve. She'd watched Stephanie turn to Robert and say, "I love you, Robert, as much as Kathy loves you. But I cannot have you."

Maybe Robert still wanted Stephanie, but she was sure – almost sure – that Stephanie didn't want Robert.

CHAPTER 43

Saturday, 28th December

Kathy stood in the doorway watching her husband. He was sitting slumped on the small bed she had set up in the office for him. He'd aged in the past few days, she realised that, or maybe she'd simply started looking at him with new eyes. She'd met him when he was in his early twenties and that was more or less the age she always imagined him. Looking at the photos in the album yesterday had brought it home just how much time had passed: they were getting old, heading towards middle age. She finished buttoning up her heavy black woollen coat and said gently: "It's time to go."

Robert looked up, eyes momentarily blank. "I didn't think it was that late," he muttered.

"The roads will be icy. We should leave a little early. The children have decided to stay here — they didn't really know Jimmy all that well." That wasn't entirely true; she had more or less encouraged the children to stay, just in case Jimmy's wife and mistress turned up at the removal and there was a scene. There was another reason, one she was even more reluctant to acknowledge. She guessed that some of the people in the industry knew about Robert's relationship with Stephanie. She didn't want to run the risk that the children might overhear anything.

Robert stood up. "Yes, yes, of course," he said distractedly. "I spoke to Lloyd, the brother in Australia, a couple of hours ago. He's not going to make it over for the funeral. He can't get the time off."

"That's a shame." She kept her voice carefully neutral.

"Yes, but at least Mikey and Teddy will be here. I think Jimmy would have liked that."

Kathy stopped him at the door and brushed at the collar of his black suit, then straightened his tie. "I think Jimmy would be very proud with everything that you've done for him over the past two days," she said, before she turned and headed down the stairs. She looked in on the children.

"We're off now. We won't be too long," she promised.

"Bye, Mom, bye, Dad!" Theresa called. Brendan couldn't speak. He was too busy negotiating a busy chicane on the Monte Carlo track on his Xbox.

Kathy followed Robert out of the house, pulling the door closed behind her, then smiled as he held open the car door for her. That was the old Robert: maybe things would change.

Robert came around the front of the car and climbed

in. He revved the engine and turned the heaters to full, clearing the windscreen.

"Thank you," he said suddenly, surprising her. "For the bed . . . and getting the suit . . ."

"I thought you had enough to worry about." She didn't add that when she was setting up the bed in his office when he was at the funeral parlour yesterday she'd taken the opportunity to go through his post again, and log back into his email. She'd found nothing.

"Well, thanks anyway. And thank you for coming with me."

"I knew Jimmy, I liked him even though he was a rogue, and I wanted to pay my respects. And I also want to support you."

Robert nodded, saying nothing, but she could see that he was touched. He pulled on a pair of sunglasses and she fished her own out of her small black bag. She loved the wan winter sunshine, loved the myriad reflections on the banked snow and the crisp shadows. Maybe next year, instead of Australia, they could go away for some winter sunshine. Skiing in Austria; she'd always wanted to do that. "How are you feeling?" she asked.

"I'm a bit numb," he said, after a moment's thought. He drove in silence, then said, "Do you know, I realised yesterday . . . or maybe the day before, I'm not sure, that I've known Jimmy for more than twenty years. Nearly half my life."

"He was at our wedding," Kathy said, remembering the photo. "That's where you introduced me to him."

"I don't remember that."

"I do."

"There were times when I'd see him every day for a month . . . and then I wouldn't talk to him for weeks afterwards. But when we met up again, it was as if we'd never been away."

"There were times when I used to envy your relationship with him. I was just glad that he wasn't a woman." Kathy stopped abruptly, realising what she'd said.

"Funny that, isn't it?" Robert said quietly. "A man can have a very close friendship with another man and no one even remarks upon it, but if it's with another woman, there are all sorts of questions raised."

"I used to think that a man and a woman could have a purely platonic relationship," Kathy said. "Now . . . now, I'm not so sure." But a woman could also have a deeply personal relationship with another woman and no-one ever gave it a second thought either, she realised. Robert was right: put a male and female together and eyebrows were raised and tongues would wag.

"And yet Jimmy had a string of female friends who were never lovers. He used to say that once both sides realised that sex was never going to be an issue, a real friendship could develop."

Kathy wasn't entirely sure that Jimmy had been telling the truth. As far as she knew, he had tried it on with just about every female he met. Though, to be fair, he'd never been anything but the complete gentleman with her. "And what do you think?" she asked.

"I don't know," he said. "Outside of business, I know very few women socially."

"Except your mistress!" Kathy snapped, surprised and dismayed that that she'd blurted out what was obviously so close to the surface. "I'm sorry. I didn't mean to bring that up today of all days. I know you're grieving. I'll respect that."

When Robert spoke, his voice was cautious, as if he was choosing his words with care. "I know we haven't had a chance over the past few days to talk about what happened."

"We'll talk about it when this is all over," Kathy said firmly. "I'm thinking we should go for counselling."

"I'm not sure I want to let strangers know our business . . ."

She'd known that would be his reaction. But this was one item which was non-negotiable. "I'm not going to fight with you about this. Counselling is not optional. If you want to stay with me – if we want to stay together – then we have to start again. I want us to have counselling to clear the air, work through those issues which drove us apart."

"Work drove us apart!" Robert snapped, genuine anger in his voice now. "Me, working all hours God sent to pay the mortgage and put food on the table. If it comes right down to it, that was the only issue. If you had been a little more involved with the business – a little more involved with me – then you would have recognised that."

Kathy deliberately allowed a little of the bitterness that curled inside her to colour her words. "You'd better not be saying that this was all my fault."

"I've told you before – it's not your fault," Robert snapped. "This whole sorry mess is entirely of my making. I put my hand up. I accept it."

She watched him deliberately take a deep breath, calming himself.

"Let's talk about it in a day or two," he said, eventually.

She was content to leave it at that. For the moment.

Robert offered her his arm as she climbed out of the car outside the funeral parlour in Malahide. She hesitated only for a moment, then took it, and immediately realised that he was the one needing support. She could feel the tremble of his fingers through the heavy wool of her coat.

She spotted scores of familiar faces from the world of entertainment– and was astonished that so many of them knew Robert on a first-name basis. She didn't realise he was so well connected in the business. He introduced her as his wife and although she was sensitive to any knowing glances or untoward comments, there was nothing. It also made her realise just how out of touch with the business she was. Angela swept over at one point, on the arm of a famous TV presenter, kissed Robert perfunctorily on both cheeks and thanked him for all that he'd done, then enveloped Kathy in a cloud of cloying musky perfume more suited to an evening at the theatre than a morning funeral. There was no sign of Frances.

Kathy hung back as they entered the funeral home. She'd stood in a room just like this just over eighteen months ago when her mother had died, and the memories were still fresh and raw. "You go," she murmured to Robert, and urged him forward. Standing against a wall, she watched her husband approach the coffin where Jimmy was laid out in his black suit, and was shocked when he bent over and kissed Jimmy's forehead. There were suddenly tears in her eyes. This was a side of her husband she had never seen before. She saw his lips move and wondered what last words he was whispering to his old friend. When he came back into the crowd, he was moving stiffly, like an old man, and she slipped her right arm into the crook of his arm and then held onto his arm with her left hand, supporting them both.

Prayers were brief and anonymous, and virtually identical to the prayers they had used for her mother's funeral. Then Robert was called forward as the coffin, which looked surprisingly heavy, was hoisted onto the shoulders of six pall-bearers who carried it out of the funeral home. Kathy trailed along behind, eyes firmly fixed on Robert, watching for any sign that he was going to collapse. She saw him physically flinch when the press photographers shot some images of the coffin being loaded into the back of the hearse. When he was relieved of the burden of the coffin, Kathy immediately darted forward, caught his arm and turned him towards the car. She was going to offer to drive, but she imagined that he probably needed the distraction of driving right now. "Jimmy would have been pleased," she said.

Robert didn't speak until he had manoeuvred his Audi in behind the mourning car and hearse. "He would," he agreed.

"He knew a lot of people."

"Some came up through the business with him; and there were others — like me, I suppose — who he gave a start to in the business. I suppose there'll be more at the church, and even more at the funeral on Monday."

Kathy glanced sidelong at Robert. "I'm glad Angela came," she said. They could both see the back of her head in the mourning car directly in front of them.

"She just thanked me for taking care of things. She didn't seem too upset. He knew everyone," Robert continued his previous train of thought and she realised that he was rambling. "I'd even thought about asking him to partner with me in the business," he added, stopping abruptly.

The revelation stung — but all she said was, "Without asking me?"

"Well, I was going to talk to you first about it, of course."

"One of the things we need to get clear is my position in the business. I do own half of it," she reminded him.

"Well, it's all academic now," he said, and she hoped he was still talking about Jimmy.

"We're going to make some changes, Robert," she said firmly.

"Yes, we are," Robert muttered.

There was something in his tone which bothered her, though she could not put her finger on it. She was about to press him further when they turned into the airport and took the slip road that brought them around by the church.

Kathy nudged Robert. "Is that your phone?" Robert looked blankly at her. They were slowly making their way out of the airport church after the brief service to receive the remains. "Something's buzzing," she insisted. She hadn't actually heard any ringtone, but had felt the vibrations through her arm, where she linked him. She smiled at faces she vaguely recognised and watched Robert pat his coat.

"Oh, it's me," he muttered. He pulled his left glove with his teeth and fumbled with the buttons of his overcoat before he finally fished out the buzzing silver XDA. It stopped.

"Who was it?" Kathy asked, watching him scroll the buttons, looking for the Missed Call log.

"Friend of Jimmy's," he said quickly, "probably asking about the arrangements for Monday." He was in the process of putting the phone back into his inside pocket when it buzzed again.

Kathy had actually moved on a couple of steps before she realised that her husband was no longer beside her.

Glancing back, she saw him standing against one of the pillars surrounding the small square courtyard before the church, with the phone pressed to his ear. She could see his lips moving. At one point he looked up at her and smiled.

Kathy turned around and began to make her way back towards him. She could hear his voice now, bouncing off the pillar behind him, throwing back his words, and she tilted her head to one side to catch some of them. "Jimmy died on Christmas Day."

"Who was that?" Kathy arrived just as he hung up.

"Someone who'd not heard the news."

"How did they take it?"

"I don't know. I didn't wait for a response."

Something about the reply bothered her. It was too quick, too glib. It felt wrong. If you were telling a person that someone died, then it stood to reason that you would fill in the details.

Unless you simply wanted to get them off the phone.

God – why couldn't she just accept the call at face value? If she didn't resolve this situation with Robert soon, it was going to drive her insane. She shouldn't be spying on her husband, checking his mail, reading his emails, trying to eavesdrop on his phone conversations.

She'd speak to him tomorrow. She wouldn't accept any excuses. He would simply have to make time. He'd prioritised his friend – and she understood and accepted that – now he had to make her a priority in his life once again.

CHAPTER 44

The noon news was just finishing as Robert pulled into the driveway in front of the house. Kathy leaned forward and turned off the radio but, surprisingly, Robert made no move to turn off the engine. She turned to look at him, her hand on the door handle, and although her face was impassive, her voice calm and unemotional, she knew with a terrible chilling certainty that he wasn't going to come in and he was going to give her an excuse that would take him across the city.

"Are you not coming in?"

"I want to head into the office, check up on things," he said, adjusting the rear-view mirror, then using the rear wiper to clean the window. Anything but look her in the eye. "Maybe do a little work, distract me."

"You could come in and catch up on your sleep," she suggested. "You look wretched. I doubt if you've eaten properly and I know you haven't really slept."

"No, let me do this. I meant to get in to the office yesterday, but events caught up with me. I'll get home as early as I can. I'm exhausted." He added, "I won't be long."

She could have protested, she knew that. She could have insisted that he come into the house, but instead Kathy Walker climbed out of the car without saying another word.

She knew he was lying to her.

She knew where he was going.

Kathy opened the door, stepped into the hall and closed the door behind her without looking back. She immediately checked in on the children. They looked as if they hadn't moved in the past couple of hours: Brendan still concentrating furiously on his driving game, with Theresa crouched beside him, muttering words of advice. "Left . . . left . . . left . . . watch out for the German car on the right."

"I'm home," said Kathy.

There was no response other than a couple of vaguely welcoming grunts.

"I've just going to pop out again for a hour or so. Will you be OK on your own for a while?"

That got a response. Both children turned to look at her, their expressions that particular mixture of disgust and astonishment that teens perfected from about the age of thirteen.

"I'll be back as quick as I can. Your dad's gone in to the office. He should be home soon too."

Kathy turned away and snagged her keys off the hall table. Checking to make sure she had her phone in her pocket, she turned and walked out of the house.

She was in no hurry as she reversed the Skoda out of the drive. This wasn't a race. The light car skidded a little at the bottom of the road and she felt her heart leap; wouldn't it be wonderfully ironic to be killed in a car crash right now? That would certainly solve all of Robert's problems. There could be a brief period of mourning and then no one would be at all surprised when the young widower married Stephanie Burroughs who had consoled him in his grief. She supposed they'd sell Stephanie's house and move into Swords.

If she was killed in a car crash right now, she'd be sure to come and haunt him and his mistress.

However, there was no ice once she got onto the main roads and in places it was hard to tell that it had ever snowed. Traffic was unexpectedly heavy, and she was surprised by the amount of it, especially Northern registered cars, on the motorway. She knew that some of the January sales had started early, and no doubt the northern buyers had come down to get the advantage of very strong sterling against the euro. She eventually turned off the motorway and headed into the city along the Malahide road. As she approached the city, the big Traffic Information signs were showing that all the major city-centre car parks were full.

Sitting in traffic in Amiens Street, she lifted her phone off the passenger seat. She quickly checked to ensure that there were no police around before she dialled Sheila's number. It was picked up on the first ring.

"I was just about to call you," Sheila exclaimed.

"Great minds."

"How did it go this morning?

"OK. There was a good crowd there. Jimmy's wife, Angela, turned up, but no sign of the mistress, so we were spared any unpleasant scenes. Maybe Monday."

"And how was Robert?"

"Distracted. A little upset. Hang on a sec . . ." she said, dropping the phone onto her lap and changing gear as a LUAS crossed her path. She then sent the call to speaker. "Can you hear me?"

"You've gone distant. Are you in the car?"

"Yes," Kathy said shortly. "After the removal, when we got back to the house, Robert announced that he was going in to the office."

"Ah," Sheila breathed. "Do you want me to meet you?"

"No . . . no, thank you, not this time." Sheila had accompanied her the last time she had spied on Robert and his mistress. "But you can do me a favour. I know they're fifteen and seventeen, but could you call over to the children and wait until I get back? They were talking about having a few friends over for a bit of a party and I don't want it getting out of hand without an adult present. I don't know how long I'm going to be."

"Of course, I'll do it; I should be there in an hour maybe."

"He may have gone in to the office," Kathy said, more to herself than to Sheila.

"Maybe," Sheila said non-committally, though neither of them believed it.

"Thanks. I'll keep in touch on the phone."

"You do know you cannot go on like this, Kathy," Sheila said gently.

"I know that," she sighed. "But I just need to be sure."

"You're already sure," Sheila reminded her.

"I know," Kathy said, but she'd ended the call by then and was talking to herself. "One last chance."

There was no car outside the office, no sign of tyre marks on the unblemished snow piled up outside the door. Truthfully, she hadn't really been expecting any. Kathy stood outside the office, the keys held so tightly in her hand that they were pressing painfully into the flesh, staring at the small brass plate to the left of the bell. *R&K Productions.* The brass was tarnished and smudged and the K was practically invisible. Maybe it was an omen. She nodded; she had been invisible in their relationship for far too long. Turning away from the office, she headed down the lane to the Peppercanister Church where she'd parked the car.

Kathy drove the rest of the way to Stephanie's house with the radio turned to a hard rock station and the volume turned all the way up so she wouldn't have to think.

Kathy pulled into a parking spot on the canal, turned off the radio and rolled down her window, blinking as the bitter air stung her cheeks and eyes, ears still ringing from the too-loud music. Though the decorative wrought-iron gates that protected the little courtyard from casual visitors she could clearly see Stephanie's house, Number 28.

Robert's Audi was parked outside the house, alongside his mistress's silver BMW. There were lights burning in the sitting-room, shedding a warm golden light out into the early afternoon.

Kathy knew that room well; she knew she would remember every detail of it to the day she died. Stephanie would be sitting in her chair facing the window and Robert would be on the settee facing her. They would be drinking wine . . . no, Robert wouldn't risk wine in case he was stopped on the way home. He would be drinking a mug of tea and they would be talking, making plans, deciding on their futures, deciding what to say to Kathy, how to tell the children.

Kathy turned off the car and continued to stare at the house, unaware that there were tears on her cheeks and that she was sobbing. After all the promises he'd made, all the chances she'd given him. She was heartsick; she'd never understood exactly what the expression meant before. She did now.

The phone rang and she answered it, without looking at the caller display. It was Sheila. "I was just checking in. I'm on my way to Swords now, but the traffic is terrible. Where are you?"

"Outside her house," she whispered.

"And is he . . .?"

"Yes, he's there."

"Well, then you know all that you need to know. Drive away or, better still, let me come and collect you."

"No. Just leave me be. I need to do this. I need to see this through."

"Kathy, please?" Sheila begged.

"Let me do this."

Sheila sighed. "I understand."

"Sheila," Kathy said suddenly, "you said the other night that you would never be responsible for putting another woman through what I'm going through now. Did you mean it?"

"Believe me, I meant it. I've already told Allan we're finished."

Kathy nodded. "Thank you. I'll call you later." She hung up and immediately hit the speed-dial.

"Hello . . . hello?"

Robert's voice was hoarse and croaking, sounding slightly breathless, and she wondered what he'd been doing before she called. Her imagination – abruptly vivid and obscene – supplied all sorts of possibilities. She struggled to keep her voice light and bright, covering the mouthpiece to drown out the noise of the passing traffic.

"Hi, it's me. I'm just wondering how you are."

"Kathy . . . yes, I'm fine.

Wondering why he had used her name, and then

realising that it was his way of alerting Stephanie, she continued, "Where are you?

"I'm in the office."

"Don't stay too long," she said, staring at Stephanie's window.

"Yes, I'll be home soon," he said quickly and rang off before she could say anything else.

No, he wouldn't want her to ask too many questions ... in fact, he probably didn't want her taking up too much of his time. Because he was busy now, busy with the woman he loved. *I love you*. That's what he'd said in the email. *I love you*. She remembered the last time he'd said those three simple words to her. Four days ago. She'd been standing in that house, in that same room, facing Robert and his mistress. She'd asked him out straight and he'd said that he'd loved her. She believed him then.

She didn't now.

She thought that there could be no more tears; surely she was all cried out? But as she sat in the car, clutching the phone in the palm of her hand, she sobbed, heartbroken.

Time ceased to have any real meaning. The world was reduced to the front of the house behind the wrought-iron gates. It snowed again, two brief showers that coated the car in a dusting of white crystals and sent the temperature plummeting, but she didn't feel the chill. She watched, expressionless, as a light went on in the bedroom and a shadow moved behind the curtains.

Then the light went off.

Consequences

And later, much later, she watched a pizza delivery boy on a motorcycle buzz up to the gates, which swung open to admit him, and she had a brief glimpse of Stephanie standing in the doorway, stylish and beautiful in cream and black as she took in the food.

The lights went on in the bedroom again.

So, the mistress had got up and ordered in some food and now she was bringing it back upstairs to her lover.

Kathy could clearly see the shape of someone outlined against the curtains and then, a little while later, the vague shape of a second person moving around the room.

She was tempted to phone again. She was equally tempted to drive up to the door and hammer and scream until they allowed her in, but she wouldn't give them the satisfaction of that type of display.

There was more movement in the bedroom, and then abruptly the hall door opened and her husband appeared. There were clothes – a shirt, ties, shoes – in his hands.

Stiff and sore, frozen through to the bone, Kathy turned the key in the ignition and pulled away as he climbed into his car.

She'd seen enough.

JIMMY MORAN'S FUNERAL

Glasnevin Cemetery

CHAPTER 45

Monday, 30th December

"I thought you spoke very well," Kathy said shortly, as they followed the hearse as it wound its way through the graves in Glasnevin cemetery. They moved slowly, picking their way over the muddy, puddle-spattered ground. A long snaking column of dark-suited men and fashionably-dressed women followed along behind.

"I was just hoping I could get through what I had to say without breaking down," Robert said, ducking his shoulders against the icy wind that whipped across the graves.

"You did." Kathy didn't add that that she found the eulogy almost painfully embarrassing in places.

Robert tilted his head slightly and glanced back over his shoulder. "Looks like most of the entertainment industry in Ireland is here," he said proudly. "I heard someone say that Peter O'Toole had come home for the funeral. Apparently he and Jimmy used to drink together."

"I didn't see him," Kathy said.

She had seen Stephanie Burroughs however.

There had been a single instant when they were driving out of the small irregularly shaped carpark beside the airport church when she'd spotted Stephanie. The woman was sitting in the passenger seat of the latest model Mercedes, alongside a handsome older man Kathy vaguely recognised. She wasn't sure if Stephanie had seen her or not, but she was glad she was there; she was determined to catch up with her today, and the graveyard was as good a place as any.

The weather, beautiful and pristine for the previous week, had finally broken. It had rained during the Mass, a combination of ice and sleet battering the church, tip-tapping off the stained-glass windows, and when the mourners had finally filed out of the church, they found that the ground was littered with tiny pebbles of ice which crunched underfoot and made walking treacherous. As the long winding cortège made its way from the airport church down through Ballymun, flanked by Garda outriders to keep the traffic flowing, it rained again, battering the cars in sheets of icy sleet that the windscreen wipers, even on high speed, had difficulty coping with. Perfect funeral weather.

Only the hearse was allowed into Glasnevin cemetery. The mourners were forced to follow on foot.

Charles Flintoff parked across from the graveyard and

stepped out of the car. He opened the back door and pulled out a midnight-blue umbrella and then moved around to the passenger side to help Stephanie out of the car, always keeping her covered beneath the umbrella. She smiled her thanks and linked him into the cemetery, picking her way along the irregular path, regretting wearing heels now and wishing she'd opted for boots and trousers, rather than heels and a black skirt. She felt vaguely uncomfortable on Flintoff's arm and she knew people were looking, first at him – because everyone knew Charles – and then at her, many of them wondering who she was, and no doubt drawing erroneous conclusions. She was beginning to regret accepting his suggestion that he collect her and drive her to the church and graveyard.

Stephanie had listened to Robert speak in the church. She'd thought he looked exhausted, and guessed he'd had little sleep since she'd thrown him out on Saturday evening. His eulogy had been a little too saccharin for her taste; according to Robert, Jimmy was one of the finest specimens of humanity to walk the earth. She'd caught some of the cynical smiles and even sniggers as Robert had gone on and on about Jimmy's good qualities, and guessed that many of the people crowding the small church knew the real Jimmy Moran.

Mikey Moran, Jimmy's eldest brother, spoke briefly and elegantly about their early years together, and he thanked Robert for everything he had done to organise the funeral. Stephanie remembered craning her neck at that point, wondering where Angela was. She didn't see her in the church and yet she guessed she must be there.

"Neither of them have turned up," Charles murmured, peering at her over the top of his half-frame glasses.

Stephanie looked at him blankly.

"Neither Angela nor Frances," he continued. "Both probably thought the other would be here and didn't want to share the limelight. I understand from a colleague that the only reason Angela turned up to the removal of the remains of Saturday was because she knew that Frances would not be there."

Stephanie nodded. She thought it sad that the two women who had loved Jimmy the most had chosen this particular occasion to abandon him.

Directly ahead of her, moving through the ancient twisted trees, she spotted Kathy walking alongside Robert. Stephanie thought that the woman looked wretched, ashen-faced, her eyes huge and dark in her head. She was bundled up in a three-quarter length black mac and lost beneath an oversize umbrella. Stephanie noted that she didn't seemed too eager to share it with Robert.

Robert Walker was livid.

He was desperately trying to hold his emotions in check. The funeral was bad enough, and having neither Angela nor Frances there was a slap in the teeth to his old friend. But seeing Stephanie turning up on the arm of her boss, that had been the real sickener. She hadn't waited long, had she! Maybe she'd try and claim that the baby was his, he thought vindictively. He shook his head quickly, the sudden movement surprising Kathy.

"What's wrong?"

"Nothing," he mumbled, "everything. Bloody weather." He shook a water-logged shoe. "We're all going to catch pneumonia."

Kathy didn't remind him that she'd told him to bring his overshoes. She knew this part of Glasnevin well; her parents were buried just over there, and scattered about this section were numerous aunts and uncles, cousins, nephews and nieces. When she died, this was where she would be buried; she didn't care where Robert went.

Jimmy Moran was to be buried alongside his mother in the old part of the cemetery, in the shadow of the watchtower at the back of the graveyard. Here the graves were overrun with weeds or lost beneath carpets of tall, withered grass. Many of the gravestones were tilted or listed to one side or the other, while others lay flat along the ground. Some of the graves were still dominated by ornate Celtic crosses, blank-eyed angels or kneeling Madonnas. Irish winters – and summers – had erased the features on much of the statuary, leaving them blank-faced and vaguely frightening, while others were shattered by the elements, time or vandals. Against the seared and brown background, now dotted with filthy piles of melting snow, one rectangular grave had been opened, a grim and uninviting wound in the landscape.

The hearse stopped behind the open grave and when

Robert Walker moved forward to help shoulder the burden, Kathy stood stock still and allowed the crowd to ebb and flow around her until she was almost at the back of the throng. Late-comers hurried up, creating a semi-circle about ten deep around the grave. She didn't want to stand on the edge of that gaping hole and look down. A year and a half ago when she'd stood beside her mother's open grave, she'd felt as if she were being pulled in, and it was only Maureen's strong hand on her shoulder that had kept her upright.

Kathy turned away . . . and spotted Stephanie on the edge of the crowd at the same time that the other woman turned and looked in her direction.

The two women stared at one another, then Kathy began to move through the crowd towards Stephanie, who turned off to the right and started to walk down a narrow muddy path. Kathy stopped and stood by a cross that was missing both arms, though the Sacred Heart was still visible in stone, and waited for the younger woman to catch up with her.

Standing on the edge of the open grave, which was raised a little higher than the rest of the ground, Robert Walker turned in time to see the two women stop and face one another. He felt his stomach twist and for a moment he thought he was going to throw up.

And there was no possible way he could leave what he was doing and get to them.

Kathy Walker spoke first, her voice as icy as the weather.

"I'm glad you're here. I was hoping you would be. Saves me a visit to your house." She shifted the black umbrella to include Stephanie, and the two women huddled together.

Stephanie looked at her, saying nothing.

"I wanted to give you this," Kathy said. She reached into her pocket and passed across a plain brown envelope.

The younger woman looked at it, feeling something solid move and shift in the paper. Holding the envelope in her black-gloved hands, she tore open one end and shook the contents out into the palm of her right hand.

Nestling in the soft black leather was a slightly worn gold wedding ring.

"I don't want it any more," Kathy said, unable to control the tremble in her voice.

"I don't want this!" Stephanie exclaimed, horrified.

"You want Robert," Kathy snapped. "You've got him. And you'll need this to go with him."

"I don't want him," Stephanie protested venomously. "I wouldn't have him if he was the last man in the world!"

Kathy blinked in surprise. If she didn't know better, she would almost be inclined to believe her.

A hundred yards away, Robert was in an agony of indecision.

He wanted – he desperately *needed* – to get to the women, to talk to them, to . . . what? What could he do? What were they talking about? Was Stephanie telling Kathy about the baby? What in God's name was going on?

He saw Kathy hand something over to Stephanie. What was that?

He could feel his heart-rate increase and he was conscious that he was sweating profusely.

"I know he came to you yesterday," Kathy snapped.

"Yes. I asked him to."

Stephanie's answer stopped Kathy cold. She blinked. "You admit it!"

A sudden gust of rain whipped in under the umbrella, and Kathy and Stephanie automatically turned. Now they were facing the funeral, with the rain coming at them from behind. They could both see Robert standing alongside the priest. His face, white and desperate, was turned towards them.

"He can see us," Stephanie remarked. "And we are probably the last two people in the world he wants to get together."

"You were together for most of yesterday afternoon," Kathy continued. "I sat outside. I watched you. I saw the bedroom light go on. I saw food being delivered. I watched my husband drive away with his clothes in his hands."

"That's all true." Stephanie turned to Kathy and the older woman was shocked to see a wry smile on her face. "I demanded to see Robert yesterday. I told him I was pregnant."

Kathy, who believed that she was beyond any more pain, felt this new revelation like a physical blow. She reached for a headstone, convinced that she was going to fall down. Stephanie reached out and caught her arm.

Kathy's lips formed the word, *pregnant*, but she never uttered it.

"He arrived looking wretched and ill. I felt sorry for him, desperately sorry, because I knew how close he was to Jimmy. All we spoke about initially was Jimmy, and I suggested that he have a shower, because I wanted him awake and alert when we discussed the baby."

The temptation was to leave the graveside, push through the crowd, shove his way to the women. But there were photographers present. They would be sure to capture anything out of the ordinary. He'd seen how Stephanie was now holding onto his wife. From the distance, he suddenly noticed for the first time the extraordinary physical similarity between them; they could easily be mistaken for sisters.

What were they talking about?

Stephanie's eyes were firmly fixed on Kathy's face. "He had his shower, and when I went up to talk to him, he had fallen asleep on the bed. I hadn't the heart to wake him." She was still holding onto Kathy's arm, and she squeezed it firmly. "I swear to you, Kathy, I wasn't in bed with him. I didn't sleep with him. I'd just come in off a transatlantic flight."

"So that's why he couldn't get you."

Stephanie nodded. "I went home on Christmas Eve. I came back when I discovered about the pregnancy."

"Pregnant." Kathy licked dry lips, tasting icy rainwater on them. A half-brother or sister for Brendan and Theresa. This wasn't something she would be able to keep from them, and with that disclosure would come the revelation about their father's affair.

The priest's voice droned out across the winter graveyard and in the distance, black and stark against the morning sky, a trio of birds took to the air in an explosion of wings. Stephanie turned to follow their flight. Still watching them, she continued. "I let him sleep. I'd no food in the house, so I ordered in some pizza. He wolfed it down as if he hadn't eaten in days."

"He hadn't," Kathy admitted.

"We finally got to speak about the baby." Stephanie suddenly turned back to Kathy, and her eyes were huge and her face was a mask. "Kathy," she whispered, "he wanted me to have an abortion." She was crying now, rain mingling with the salt tears on her cheeks. "He wanted me to have an abortion." Her breath began to come in great heaving gasps. "He gave me any number of reasons — business reasons, personal reasons, stupid reasons. He offered to pay; suggested that we could have a quick abortion and then take a couple of days' holiday in London — take in the sights, he said — and then return to our lives."

And suddenly Kathy had her arms around Stephanie and was holding her close, while the young woman sobbed.

Consequences

"Kathy, I loved him, loved him with all my heart! He didn't want children. He'd reared his family, he told me. He thought I would just get rid of the child and then life would go on as normal. He was happy to have the affair, but he didn't want to face the consequences. Kathy, I hate him! I hate him."

Seeing Kathy hugging Stephanie was the final straw. Excusing himself, Robert backed away blindly through the crowd, apologising automatically, desperate to get to the two women.

Stephanie still sobbed as Kathy supported her. "I shouted at him, screamed at him. Demanded my key back, flung his clothes at him, and threw him out. I never want to see him again." She drew in a deep shuddering breath. "I thought I knew him. I don't."

"Neither do I," Kathy said very softly. "This isn't the man I married." Still holding onto Stephanie, she raised her head and watched her husband stumble his way through the graves towards them.

Robert came wheezing up. "Kathy . . . Stephanie . . . I . . ." he began, and then his voice trailed away as both women turned to look at him, their expressions identical, a mingling of disgust and contempt.

"You wanted Stephanie to have an abortion!" Kathy practically spat the word onto the ground.

"Now hang on a second . . ." he began to bluster. "Is that what she's telling you?"

"She is. And I believe her, Robert."

"I haven't seen her . . ." he began desperately.

"I followed you on Saturday, Robert." His eyes flashed, but she pressed on, ignoring him. "I saw the letter you sent Stephanie – you said you loved her. You said you would stay away from her, but you lied to me then and you've continued to lie to me. Your every waking moment is a lie. Jimmy Moran didn't phone on Christmas Day either, did he?"

"He did . . ."

"I phoned on Christmas Day," Stephanie said. "Early afternoon Irish time."

"You didn't go in to the office on Christmas Eve night. The alarm company have no record of a call-out," Kathy continued relentlessly. "And Saturday, you weren't going in to the office, you were going to see Stephanie, determined to convince her to have an abortion because it didn't suit you to have a child!"

"OK, I'll admit it. I went to see Stephanie. And yes, I did suggest that she get rid of the baby. I thought it would be what she'd want."

Kathy ignored him. She turned to Stephanie. "I was sure he was in bed with you on Saturday." Stephanie opened her mouth to reply, but Kathy pressed on before she could speak. "I know he wasn't. I know that now. I was going to finish with him then because of that. But now I know the truth."

Robert started to relax.

"And it doesn't change a thing."

Kathy took the wedding ring from Stephanie's hand and tossed it at Robert. He fumbled with it, but it fell

into the dirt at his feet. "We're finished, Robert Walker."
She watched him trying to pick up the delicate gold
band with his gloved fingers. "A couple of days ago, I
swore that next year would be different. I guess I didn't
realise just how different. Don't come home, Robert. I
don't want to see you ever again. You'll be hearing from
my solicitor: I want a divorce."

She turned and walked away, her arm through
Stephanie's. As they wound their way amongst the graves,
they saw a young woman with long dark hair plastered
to her skull hurrying towards the graveside, a bunch of
wilting flowers in her hands.

"Frances," Kathy remarked, "Jimmy's lover." She looked
over her shoulder.

Robert was still where they had left him, staring after
them, completely stunned.

He'd pulled off his gloves and the wedding ring was cold
against his flesh. He kept looking from it to where Kathy
and Stephanie were fast disappearing through the trees.

What had just happened?

Yes, he'd lied to Kathy about visiting Stephanie, but
surely she could understand why? He couldn't exactly
tell her he was visiting his mistress . . . well, ex-mistress.
And how would she have reacted if she'd had known
that Stephanie was calling the house on Christmas Day?

Anyway, he was now finished with Stephanie . . . why,
she'd even arrived on the arm of another man. But like

every scorned woman, she'd had her revenge: she'd turned Kathy against him.

He shook his head and walked away, heading back to the graveside. A divorce? He attempted a laugh, but it stuck in his throat, and came out as a ragged cough. It would all blow over; Kathy would come to her senses. He was sure of it.

"He'll try and come back, you know that?" Stephanie said.

"He'll try, but not today. He'll probably sleep in the office tonight. But I'm sure he'll come home tomorrow for New Year's Eve, or maybe Wednesday. When he does come back, he'll find the locks have been changed. When I discovered that he was having an affair, I gave him his chance. All he had to do was to be honest with me. But he couldn't even do that. We could have started again."

"Maybe . . ."

"You don't sound so sure?"

"There would have been another affair with another woman in a couple of years' time," said Stephanie.

"Probably." Kathy glanced at the younger woman. "We need to talk about the baby," she said.

Stephanie shook her head. "No, we don't," she said. "It was a false alarm. My period arrived this morning." She smiled at the dumbstruck expression on Kathy's face. "Yes, that's exactly how I felt."

"I'm sure you're relieved," Kathy said shakily.

"You have no idea how I felt." She paused and then added, with a poignant smile, "Though, I was actually beginning to come to terms with it," she admitted. "I'd even started to make the plans that pregnant women do."

"You mean those life-changing plans?" Kathy nodded. "Yes, I remember them." She linked her arm though Stephanie's. "So we both begin a new year without a man – the same man," Kathy smiled.

"Interesting times ahead . . . for you especially."

"It'll be tough," Kathy admitted. "I've no illusions about that. But I stood outside the office on Saturday and looked at the sign that read R&K Productions . . . and I've been thinking about the young woman I once was. I'd dreams and aspirations of my own, but I allowed them to be swallowed up with husband, family and home. Half of R&K is mine. I'm thinking I might set up my own independent production company; I know Maureen will come with me and I'm sure we could make it a success. What do you think?"

"I think it's a fabulous idea."

The two women walked on, around by the round tower and out towards the gate.

"Would you think about taking on a partner?" Stephanie asked shyly.

THE END

Direct to your home!

If you enjoyed this book why not visit our website:

www.poolbeg.com

and get another book delivered straight to your home or to a friend's home!

www.poolbeg.com

All orders are despatched within 24 hours.